# BONES
## AND
# NEEDLES

**Also by Keith C. Blackmore**

**Mountain Man**
*Mountain Man*
*Safari*
*Hellifax*
*Well Fed*
*Make Me King*
*Mindless*
*Skull Road*
*Mountain Man Prequel*
*Mountain Man 2nd Prequel: Them Early Days*
*The Hospital: A Mountain Man Story*
*Mountain Man Omnibus: Books 1–3*

**131 Days**
*131 Days*
*House of Pain*
*Spikes and Edges*
*About the Blood*
*To Thunderous Applause*
*131 Days Omnibus: Books 1–3*

**Breeds**
*Breeds*
*Breeds 2*
*Breeds 3*
*Breeds: The Complete Trilogy*

**Isosceles Moon**
*Isosceles Moon*
*Isosceles Moon 2*

*The Bear That Fell from the Stars*
*Bones and Needles*
*Cauldron Gristle*
*Flight of the Cookie Dough Mansion*
*The Majestic 311*
*The Missing Boatman*
*Private Property*
*The Troll Hunter*
*White Sands, Red Steel*

# BONES AND NEEDLES

KEITH C. BLACKMORE

Podium

Published in 2024 by Podium Publishing
www.podiumaudio.com

# Contents


1 The Hospital (A Mountain Man Story) ............................1

2 Private Property ................................35

3 Eat................................165

4 Expansion ................................211

5 The Bear that Fell From the Stars ................................239

6 Ye Olde Fishing Hole ................................331

7 Isosceles Moon ................................351

# BONES
## AND
# NEEDLES

# 1

# The Hospital

(A Mountain Man Story)

The sun was overhead somewhere, blotted out by low storm clouds as depressing as suicide. Underneath this, a single Chevy van pulled off the main road, and approached the looming bulk of the hospital. The Chevy had no windows in its sides, and all of the lights had been smashed out. The rear windows were also shattered, replaced by heavy wooden planks. The van pulled into the parking lot, did a quick u-turn, and backed itself up to the main doors with a huff of gas. There the vehicle idled for a few moments, wary, ready to bolt if anything seemed dangerous. The van was a small freight carrier in the old days, but now it was war on wheels, with enough scratches and dents in its hide to give any carjacker pause. It had a "don't fuck with me" menace about its battered shell, and might have been the inspiration for many a poster in the late 80's.

The engine died and its drone evaporated into stillness. Nothing moved for the longest time, and for all intentional purposes, the vehicle seemed as dead as the surrounding countryside.

The van shook on its chassis, as if caught in a mechanical seizure. Thumps and bangs and the odd curse emanated from within the Chevy's guts, slowly travelling towards the rear. Seconds later, there was a subtle creak just before the doors swung wide. They hung open, draped in shadow.

Two motorcycle boots dropped to the pavement.

He wore black leather, from neck to shin. Leather pants, jacket, and boots. He wore an extra layer of denim jeans underneath the pants, which he had taken from the same shop where he got the jacket and boots. Knee pads and elbow pads protected his joints, while a dark brace covered his neck. Black gloves sheathed his hands, fingerless, to allow a better grip on his shotgun. An aluminum baseball bat was slung across his back, Samurai style, in a crude scabbard next to a backpack. A motorcycle helmet and visor hid his features, and completed the set of armor.

Dressed as he was, it would take a strong bite indeed to puncture the leather.

The second his boot heels hit pavement, his twelve-gauge shotgun came up, its butt tucked firmly against his shoulder and the strap dangling in a loop. He pumped a round into the chamber, the *schlack* as loud as thunder.

Nothing emerged from the hospital.

Nothing charged him from the deserted cars on the nearby parking lots.

His name was Augustus Berry, and he studied the hospital's double doors for seconds, not seeing anything beyond the glass except an empty foyer.

He listened.

Heard nothing. Not a single note.

So he stood there for a few seconds, poised to shoot and retreat, the motorcycle's visor impassive. Gus patted his pockets, feeling the extra shotgun shells there, and then reached over his shoulder and located the bat, ready to grab if needed. Combat knives were sheathed in his both boots, but it was rare he got to use those. He brought them along nevertheless, remembering the old line, *it was better to have and not need, than need and not have.*

He regarded the hospital's main doors. Still nothing moved from the inside, but he doubted the place was empty.

*Game on,* he thought.

Gus shook his head, clearing it, and moved forward, the barrel of the shotgun wavering ever so slightly, like the dark head of a Doberman giving fair warning. If anything came into vision and it wasn't living, Gus would blow its fucking head off with extreme prejudice. Another line from another old movie, but he didn't care. It was truth. And if he discovered anyone alive, he'd exercise caution. People in these desperate days were not to be trusted. He'd heard stories. There were bad people about. Scavengers, like him, but worse.

Boots clicked on concrete as he climbed the steps to the doors. He walked right up to the glass and peered inside. Shadowy interior. He huffed once, not liking the lack of light in the least, and flicked up the motorcycle's visor. His eyes were an alert blue, with lines at the corners. He took another contemplative breath. Of course they were in there, somewhere, just waiting for him. For anyone. If he was smart, he should just about-face and march his leather-clad ass out of there.

But he needed what the hospital potentially offered.

Gus cursed and looked behind, considering the open doors of his van. He studied the empty space of the land, to the tree line beyond. Nothing in sight, but he couldn't be certain it would stay that way. And the hospital was big. Big place like that might stash its medical supplies anywhere. It would take time to find them.

And he was wasting time thinking.

"Shit," he muttered, and pushed at the doors. They wouldn't move. He glanced up and saw the dead motion detector mounted above the frame. There was a push door at the right however and he eased that open with his shoulder, his shotgun ready.

The hall was empty. Light shone through a skylight at the far end of a waiting area. Newspapers, shredded pamphlets, broken glass and tattered bits of clothing cluttered the floor. Bulletin boards hung halfway to the floor on single nails.

Vending machines were broken into and punished. Dark splashes stained the walls, but Gus didn't give them any more attention than necessary. Dried blood was commonplace these dreary days.

It was the fresh stuff he was more concerned about.

The faded stench of something rotten lingered on the air. He proceeded cautiously, drifting close to the right wall, and headed deeper into the gloom of the hospital. His shoulder grazed the wall. Glass tinkled underfoot. He turned the corner to see a larger receptionist's area behind a counter that had been assaulted. It was darker there, the floor smeared with blood, dried in gruesome swirls done by fingers and bare hands. Bloody palm prints painted the walls and covered a photocopier with its lid ripped off. Paper littered one corner like a foul nest and Gus saw bones sprinkled there, dried, old-looking, and gnawed upon.

He moved to the end of the counter, listened, and peered around it like he had seen US Marines do in action movies, side first rather than the top of his head. The corridor ahead was long and devoid of life. A wide blood trail from something being dragged went in that direction and disappeared into darkness.

Gus pulled back. He wouldn't hunt the thing if he could get what he wanted without incident. There were two more corridors in the foyer, leading off to places unknown. There were also two stairways, one going up while the other led to the lower levels. The place was big, too big to explore in a single day, and the medicinal supplies he sought— bandages, splints, and drugs—were not as visible as they were in a pharmacy or supermarket. He'd have to root around a little more. Besides, he'd already tried most drugstores, and those were already looted, their shelves and back rooms picked clean.

The hospital might have its resources taken as well, but he had to make sure.

"Just don't be stupid," he told himself. He had watched a fair amount of horror movies in his time, when the world was merely crazy and not fucking insane with things that bit and chewed living flesh. When he did watch horror flicks, especially in the theatres, he took note of the dumb-as-fuck characters who, as soon as he or she died, the audience cheered.

Dead because of stupid mistakes.

*Don't be stupid.*

That was his code these days, and in reflection, he realized those movies were more like visual survival guides. What to do and what not to do, especially during the apocalypse. Gus learned from every God-awful flick he ever had the misery to sit down and endure. Be prepared. Be protected. Watch your corners. Stay away from dark places—especially at night. Matter of fact, don't ever go out at night if you can help it. And when you're out in the open, stay quiet. Clean your weapons, maintain your ride's engines.

Above all, stay calm, and don't be stupid.

Being stupid got characters dead.

With that in mind, he avoided the corridor with the bloody drag marks. Chances were, whatever was doing the dragging was probably still down there, just waiting for the sound and smell of fresh meat.

Gus regarded the stairways across the way. There was a corridor to the right of these as well, which he'd only just noticed.

Shotgun first, Gus headed towards the corridor. He passed under the skylight, tensed and ready for anything shambling into view. A few windows permitted daylight into the building, so he edged further along. He turned a few corners carefully, and saw a long row of seats, laid out before the open and closed doors of examination rooms. Men and women's washrooms were nearby. Debris covered the whole area, as if a tsunami of garbage had swept through the place.

Gus listened.

Behind him, a strong wind rattled the windows. The hospital remained dead. Or sleeping. *Do the dead sleep? Really sleep?* Gus wondered, shotgun resting his helmet-protected cheek. He shoved the thought aside and proceeded into the waiting area. A third door came into view, just before the washrooms. It had a doorknob, where the others were simply push-opens.

Gus crept to the door, smelling blood on the air, as recognizable as coffee. It wasn't so strong here, but still present. Keeping his weapon level, he reached down and opened the door with a jerk. He went into a firing stance as he pushed his way into the room beyond.

And hit gold.

It was a service room. And, stacked as neatly as bullion in Fort Knox, was the one commodity that Gus would have never guessed would be as valuable as water, gasoline, food, or even ammunition. A luxury that, like all things, was greatly underappreciated back when the world was just crazy.

Toilet paper.

At least forty rolls of ass-cleaning goodness. There was toilet paper to spare in fact, and Gus smiled at the sight. He grabbed a roll and inspected the label. Two-ply. Goddamn. He'd hit the shitter jackpot. If assholes could smile, his was grinning across both cheeks.

He kept the door open and searched for a power switch.

When he found it, he wasn't surprised at the lack of electricity. He propped the door open and searched the rest of the room by the meager light of the hallway. There was an old TIME magazine with an article on Vikings. That went into his backpack, as did a full bottle of bleach and a number of toilet paper rolls. He found a box of latex gloves, opened but three-quarters full, and grabbed those as well. A couple of mops, a broom, and a push-bucket rested against a wall. A large wheeled hamper lay at the very back of the room, partially hidden by the gloom, and it took Gus a moment to realize how fortunate he was to spot it.

With a quick checking outside, he slung his shotgun over his shoulder, and piled the rest of the treasures inside the hamper, making it ready for transport. When the all was packed away, he went to the door and checked the corridor.

Empty.

The wind had picked up outside, sighing impatiently against the glass and making it rattle. But there were no gimps. That's what he called them now. Gimps. It fit.

Gus pulled the hamper out of the supply room with his shotgun laid across a solid pile of Puffy two-ply rolls, his right hand never far from the grip if he needed it. Once clear, he pushed the hamper and cringed at the sound of a squeaky wheel.

*Well, Jesus*, he thought and froze.

He looked about, expecting gimps to come tumbling out of the nearby doorways any second, arms outstretched and moaning their shit, but they didn't.

Seconds went by and Gus realized he was wasting time.

He pushed the hamper through the corridor, back to the outer door without incident, the wheel whistling its tune the whole way, like a high dwarf staggering home to see Snow

White. Gus shoved the hamper through the door with a slight rattle, enough for him to glance around once again.

At the van, loading the goods proved to be no trouble at all. He backed the hamper up to the open doors and started throwing things inside, until the hamper was light enough to lift and jam into the rear. Once everything was in, Gus took a minute to catch his breath. He leaned against the chrome bumper and regarded the dark doors of the hospital.

The toilet paper was unexpected. He wasn't *looking* for toilet paper. But when you were the only game in town, you took what you found, when you found it. Shadows enveloped his hunched form as he considered going back. The van still had plenty of room. If he went back in, he might possibly find more toilet paper, and the medical supplies he was looking for. He only had to look.

What was that Shakespeare line? *A second time into the gash, old buddy.*

*Being greedy?* a voice asked him.

*No, being real. There's still daylight left to do this.*

*Being stupid, now?*

*Fuck off,* Gus projected back, but he would be wary. He remembered the squeaky wheel. Anything could have heard it. Anything could be awake in there and waiting. That thought made him pause again, weighing the risks.

Then he grabbed his shotgun and went back to the hospital.

He was halfway into the first waiting room, in plain sight of the skylight, when he heard it.

The sound wasn't loud, but it was there. A *thump*, dull and clumsy, coming from the stairwell. Gus froze at the heavy note and pointed his shotgun in the direction of stairs. He waited and listened, listened *hard*, willing something to drop again, for the other foot to strike the floor. But it didn't.

Eyes narrowed, Gus closed the distance between him and the stairwell and hugged a corner. He whirled around it, aiming down the stairs, then up. He stretched his neck out over the railing, peering downwards as far as he could see, and saw only the impenetrable black of an empty well. He looked up then, and did the same, then he remembered where he was and spun around on the hall, his finger on the trigger.

Empty. All empty.

His danger sense was perhaps at three now, on a scale of five. Unease spread across his chest and mind, but he wasn't afraid. Gus eased into the open, and cautiously made his way back to the storeroom he plundered. There were no corners to hide around here, but there were doors aplenty. Dark signs mounted above their frames made him squint. *Internal Medicine.* Gus moved to one of the open doorways and glanced inside, shotgun first. The doctor, thankfully, wasn't in, but the room was a mess. The desk was upended, making a low barrier to whoever was coming through. Two flat, smashed LCD screens were on the floor. Fine dust covered discarded books, papers, and other rubbish. Dried blood dappled everything in an arterial spray gone wild. There were no bodies, however. No sleeping gimps.

Gus crept through the room, picking at the desk, and prodding through the wreckage of whatever siege had happened. Fragments of bloody cloth, and he realized it was a doctor's white coat. Ripped from the victim no doubt. Gus hoped the person was dead at the time, and he hoped he wouldn't remember any unpleasant sights yet to be discovered. He suffered during the nights when he was home, trying to sleep. Booze helped when he had it, and drank heavily when he did. It would knock him out and keep the nightmares at bay.

Nightmares that brought their own private movies, with mouths full of rotting teeth.

Gus took a breath and became still, listening for anything beyond the room. He moved to the doorway and glanced about. All clear. He possessed a healthy fear of being snuck up on. It hadn't happened yet, and he meant to keep it that way.

He rooted around the office for a few more seconds, picking up functional pens and a notebook which he stuffed into his backpack. He kicked aside the discarded keyboard lying behind the desk. Computers had no place in the new world. There was a paperback, the one book still on a shelf, detailing vitamins and minerals; what they cured or staved off, and what foods to find them in. It was the only book that wasn't covered in maroon, and seemed like an easy read for him. Posters hung on the walls, clearly outlining digestive tracts, which caused Gus to frown. He didn't want to think of digestive tracts. He didn't need to see them either. That got him moving to the next, the second of four, but there was nothing to be found. In the third office, stashed away behind some files in a desk drawer, was a small bottle of Jack Daniels. Gus's grimace was one of pleasure. He hefted the bottle, practically full, wondering to God above how this treasure was missed, and threw it into his backpack. He moved through the offices with little noise, past examination tables and medicinal items he had no idea how to use or what they were, always careful not to knock things over, scavenging what he could. He found rolls of gauze and bandages and took them all. There was a full bottle of antiseptic, and a box full of alcohol pads, both of which he grabbed.

There was very little else, and the whiskey was the definite prize.

Seconds later he returned to the middle of the waiting area. There were no other rooms to explore in this section, and he thought about the time. He made his way back to the main hallway, and once again studied the long corridor where the blood smears disappeared into the sepulchral gloom. Gus figured that if there was anything of real value, it would probably be down there. Murphy's fucking law.

Then he stopped in his tracks. Just off that dark tunnel was another wing it seemed. He took a few steps and saw, just behind a counter, a wall of what looked to be medical supplies.

"Well, god*damn*," Gus breathed and quickly glanced around. This was turning out to be a very fruity day. He returned to his van and dumped the contents of the backpack into the hamper. Still in shotgun ninja mode, he returned to hospital's interior, wincing at the dead air and the smell of something long gone bad. Gus pushed past it, however, and walked with care towards the hospital drugstore. He suspected there was a gift-shop in here somewhere as well, chock full of items for the sick. He rounded the corner and—

*Thump.*

Gus froze. There it was again, coming from the stairs. He turned in the direction, shotgun poised, and backed towards the counter. At one end was a swing door, waist high, and he edged towards it. The shadows beyond the counter looked clear, so he pushed the door open with his buttocks, only semi-focused on his immediate surroundings

*Something upstairs*, he thought, *but you just stay there, and we'll get along—*

The thumping from above had distracted him, so it was relatively easy for the hand to snake out from just inside the counter and claw into his testicles.

Gus gasped. His leather and denim pants prevented his balls from being totally crushed, but the sudden sickening agony brought him to his knees. His shotgun wavered and fell to the ground. He got one hand on the white wrist of the hand hooked onto him, but before he could summon his strength, what little he had remaining, the fist squeezed again. *Hard.*

"Oh there's a good boy, yes, such a *healthy* boy," a voice trilled.

A sickening weight had attached itself to him, pulling down on his testicular nerves like five hundred pound granite blocks, deep down where his senses buckled and warped and were only concerned with pain. Gone were thoughts of looting. Gone were thoughts of the noise from above. As if submerged under sixty feet of water, Gus slowly bent over at the waist, landing on his elbows. His breath left him. The pain, the pain was crippling. He opened his mouth to puke, forgetting he still had his helmet on. His consciousness retreated but never fully left, as the roaring fire of nausea and pain in his stomach and balls staved off any real release. Gus groaned, lips pulling back from his teeth as if his flesh was being sanded from his skull.

"What's that?" the voice asked sweetly somewhere above him. "What's *that?*" it demanded, squeezing his jewels even further.

Gus collapsed, going fetal, knowing nothing except that paralyzing, gut-contracting agony that did not lessen in the least. Then, right on the cusp of rupture, just as he planted a trembling palm flat against the panel wood near his head, the hand released him.

"I'm sorry," the voice said in a pitying tone. "I didn't introduce myself."

Hands gripped his helmet and pulled it off. Gus didn't care. He was powerless to stop it, his hands cupping his screaming balls. His eyes closed in agony, and he tucked his chin in.

Just before a boot kicked his head back, knocking him out cold.

Blackness, as deep as the cold Atlantic, enveloped him. He came close to surfacing once, as if in a pictureless dream. A thumping roused him, followed by a pounding at the back of his head. Something scrapped at his back. He moved upwards in jerks and heaves. And a voice pierced his barely semi-consciousness.

"*Big* man, big man, coming in here. Didn't know Alice was here, didja? *Didja?* God you weigh a ton. A *ton*. What have you been eating? The natives?" a cackle of icy laughter. "That'd be sumthin. The natives. Dead eat dog eat dead!" another eruption of frightening mirth.

Gus retreated into the depths of his skull, drawing back from his off-line senses, away from the rant, and hiding in the comforting dark.

He drifted, unborn, in a cold place where he could not see, unaware of pretty much everything, except that it was cool and without a sun. His consciousness floated close to waking, close enough that pain flashed through his night like an angry thunderbolts. His eyelids flickered and he moaned. Another cut of agony and his eyes opened. Ceiling. Dark, with stains upon it. He tried moving his arms but they were secured at his sides. Gus's chin touched his bare, hairy chest.

Someone knelt beside him. A woman. With a wild mop of white hair, dressed in the dirty scrubs of a nurse, swishing a scalpel at his shins,

"Hey, fuck off," Gus blurted softly.

The woman jerked her head up as if goosed. Eyes as shiny as marble fixed upon him. The scalpel came up and she hissed like a vampire of old exposed to the sun. She stared at him, transfixed in the dim light, and Gus knew the woman was bug-nuts crazy. He tried lifting his arms again, couldn't, and examined himself to see why. Rubber tubing bound his arms to metal railings. A gurney—he was strapped to a gurney.

He also discovered he was completely naked.

And the mad bitch before him was slicing him up like a piece of Japanese sashimi.

"You crazy bitch!" Gus whined and struggled to free himself. The tubing would not give, and when he cried out a second time, the nurse in the soiled scrubs pounced at his face. She came in close, placing the edge of the scalpel to the curve of his chin, and breathed into his face. Black eyes flickered in their orbital cavities.

Mints. She smelled of mints.

"You shut up!" She fired back, beady eyes blazing. "You shut up right now or I'll gut you here! I'll gut right here, I swear to holy Jesus!"

Gus shut up, grimacing at the cold surgical instrument now poised at his throat.

"That's better," she smiled a horrible grin. Her teeth were yellow, traced with black, and moored in spongy-looking gums. "That's better, you little bastard. Old Alice got ye. Alice got you fine. You can be fresh or you can be dead, doesn't matter to me. The kids'll mind a bit, but not for long, I wager. Not for long. Then I can get back to me flowers on the roof. Heeee! The flowers are in bloom up there. You should see em. But you can't. Youcan'tyoucan'tyou *can't*, HEEE!"

While she babbled, the scalpel drifted upwards, where she punctuated each *can't* by jabbing the surgical tool at his right eye.

Terrified, Gus squeezed his eyelid shut and expected any moment to have two inches of blade lick his cornea.

"That's it, that's it, shhhhh shhhhhh," Alice coddled him. "You be fine. You be quiet. It won't be long now anyway. Shhh."

*Whump.*

The sound made Gus open his eye just a crack.

"You hear that?" Alice asked. "My kids. My little darlings. A mother has to take of her children, you know. Any way she can."

*Whump.Whump.*

Unknown to Gus, his breath quickened. His eyes got wider and flecked from side to side. How long *had* he been out? Long enough for the crazy bitch astride him to tussle him onto a— *Whump! Pa-ta-pa-ta-pa-ta.*

Then the windshield wiper squeal of something being smeared across glass. Gus dared not take his eyes off the woman. She moved in closer, until her eye lashes tickled his. He cringed, smothered in mint.

"Don't you move now," she whispered, "don't you move."

The scalpel's point moved to the base of his neck, down between his man breasts, the steely tip making a line, slowly, over his belly. It paused at his navel, then continued a little more, to his pubic area.

"Don't you move," Alice instructed him. Her fingers did a little dance in his hair down there. "You make a sound now, and I'll cut it off. You hear me? I'll cut it off in the name of Jesus. You hear? Nod if you do."

Gus nodded, and felt his balls go for high ground.

"Now here comes the hard part," she grinned, close enough that, for a moment, he thought she was going to kiss him. She studied his lips for a moment and licked her own. Then her mouth opened slightly and, God was his witness above, she was going to bite his lips off. She was going to fasten on to him and shake her head from side to side until she ripped them from his face.

"Here it comes," she whispered. "Here it comes, no noise now."

Gus had been a big man, not the biggest, and not tall, but fat. He had lost an incredible amount of weight since the world went insane, perhaps ninety kilos or more. Enough that he could presently get into a waist-size of thirty eight. He still had something of a gut which, only a year ago, he would've joked that he had invested a lot of money in it. Excess fat clung to his frame here and there, especially across the upper back, but he figured that, as food became scarcer, his body would burn it off naturally. His double chin remained as well, but his biker's beard effectively concealed it.

Alice gouged that hateful sliver of surgical steel into the fat of his belly, digging it in, and then cutting vigorously across his pubic area in a jagged C-section.

Augustus Berry screamed.

He shrieked loud enough to startled Alice. She reset

herself, screwed up her face, then brightened, and once again gave his already tortured testicles a devastating squeeze and yank. The wind left Gus as if his lungs were punctured, and he whimpered like a dying pup.

"That's what you get," Alice hissed. "I told you not to make any noise and you did so that's what you get. I didn't want to do that."

But her grin said otherwise.

Another *whump* and several more squeegee-like squeals from beyond. Maybe even louder, more frequent. Red-faced and in agony, Gus puffed out his breath but said nothing to his captor. Alice placed her empty hand on the other side of his head. Gus saw she didn't have the scalpel anymore.

Then his features paled.

He looked down at himself and whimpered in horror. The crushing of his nuts diverted his attention away from his pain, but now his own eyes verified what Alice had done to him. She left the scalpel in his belly, at an angle, like a bent over buggy antennae.

There was a hard slap at the other end of the room, and Gus looked past the nurse in an attempt to see. There was something *bad* back there. Something that raised his alert level and made him shiver. He couldn't see anything, nor could he concentrate with the pain he was enduring. His back and neck strained to exhaustion, he plopped back and fell on something cushiony. He turned his head despite his lower body shrieking not to move, and remembered he was tied to a hospital gurney, a *lowered* hospital gurney.

Air hooked the flaps of that deep belly cut.

"I gotcha in tight there, Mister," Alice said and giggled. With a grunt she got to her feet and glanced right. The noise was coming from that direction, but what was making it?

"I saw you drive up from the roof y'see. I saw you but you didn't see me. That's cuz I do this," and a dirt-black bottom of a bare foot was thrust into his face. "And I knew you were down below. Probably coming for medicine or whatever. Just like all the rest. Oh plenty come here. I just let them scrounge around below. Usually they go into the basement and that's that. Only one way down there, and I can close the door and lock it when folks are down there. And oh the *squeals!* It's a metal door but you know something, when someone is scared enough, they put dents in that thing. Not for long though. Never for long."

As Alice rambled, Gus looked to his left. There, on the gurney's padding, was a clump of what look to be a human scalp, complete with a few strands of hair. His stomach went cold. *Who was this woman?*

"But the ones in the basement are greedy," Alice told him. "I have to wait for the stragglers to come along. Someone that I can handle by myself. You were heavy! Too much shit on you. That's why I stripped you bare," she winked, sizing up his prone form, and her voice dropped to a whisper. "Lots of fat on you. Not like the others. The kids like fat."

*Whumpwhumppa-ta-pa-ta-pa-ta!*

Gus's features twisted, wondering what in the hell he'd gotten into? The air traced the edges of his cuts, the cuts that Alice made, and he moaned at the fire in his poor belly.

"You're probably wondering why I cut you so many times?" She asked idly. Then, without warning, she yanked the scalpel out of his belly, getting a hiss out of him, and slashed open his right arm with one flick.

That tungsten jolt of pain caused Gus to buck against his bonds.

"It's because, they smell you see," Alice told him. She

slashed the other white arm, as neatly as opening a fish. "That's why they're making a racket. My babies are hungry. Sooooooooo hungry. Am I bad for doing this? I don't think so. I'm cleaning the world of shitheads like you. What did the babies ever do? Huh? What? Nothing. They just… they just… were here. Not fair. Never fair."

With that, she sat back on her haunches, and stared in the direction of the noise with a sad expression. A big sigh left her and she shrugged, as if confused by it all. The commotion coming from beyond did not confuse Gus. His senses had returned, as did his need to get the hell away from this place. And Alice's children. He suspected now, oh Christ how he suspected, but he didn't want to know. Didn't want to be here to find out. He knew why she was cutting him up, just like deep sea shark fishermen, throwing fish entrails and pig blood over the side of the boat.

*Chum.* The word popped into his mind.

"They can… smell you," Alice confirmed with obvious satisfaction. "Mommy's brought suppers. Mommy's brought suppers!"

She struggled to her feet.

Gus glanced around urgently while testing his bonds. He'd never been in one, but knew by the waiting chairs and the soft pinks and blues, that he was in a waiting area of sorts.

The waiting area in a Maternity ward.

"SUPPERS!" Alice yelled out. "MOMMY'S GOT SUPPERS FOR YOU! ONE BIG FUCKIN ROAST TONIGHT, MY LITTLE SWEETS!"

She stepped away from him. The hand with the scalpel dropped to her side, and she walked away as if she mesmerized.

Gus knew he did not have much time.

He heaved against his bonds again. He yanked upwards and kicked, and the tubing slipped into his wounds. Firecrackers of pain went off and he bucked again, gritting his teeth.

"Hungry aren't you, yes you are, yes you are!" Alice's voice floated somewhere overhead.

The drumming and squeaking of flesh on glass intensified.

Gus relaxed, just for a moment, to catch his wind. He heard Alice at the far end of the room, calling out to her children. Her unholy children that he did *not* want to see. He saw enough of the dead walking around to forever have nightmares where only alcohol would let him sleep and where the alcohol also would summon nightmares. The sounds got louder, a regular screen door holding back a tornado, and Christ almighty above, he could hear them now, he could hear their little whiney vocal chords crying out that yes, *yes*, they were *famished!* They were ready to eat the whole damn thing once dear old Alice let them into the waiting room. They would stampede him then, and he wouldn't be able to do a goddamn thing while their little mouths fastened onto his body and ripped and tore and suckled.

"GO GET HIM!" Alice screeched from beyond.

Upon hearing those words, Gus did something for the very first time. He defecated himself right there and then. He was careful, so very careful about what he did and how he proceeded in town, and by sunny Jesus if he got out of this one he was going to get so fucking shit-faced drunk, it would be a thing of legend, and fuck the dreams, but right now, right this very moment, he could hear and feel the pitter-patter of bare hands and knees as they scurried about the tiled floor, like the charge of newborn sea turtles trying to reach seawater before starving gulls swooped down and snapped them up. He could hear the brazen sound of dead flesh being forced into movement by a will that he didn't understand but *knew* was frightful and unholy. The tiles trembled as this tide rushed towards him, as fast as their little limbs could carry them along and he could hear Alice, that bitch from hell, somewhere back there cackling like a vamp in heat. Just laughing at how her children from the abyss were *growing* as if such a thing was possible! And he heard their *voices*, their little infant *voices*, making the sounds of something so incredibly hungry. *Starving*, the word popped into his head, they were actually *starving* for him.

And they were coming.

That last thought threw Gus into such a fit of pure, adrenalin-injected terror, that he bucked and thrashed and twisted and roared and shook against his bonds and his right arm practically came free with enough force to punch through steel plate. He gawked at the limb, and immediately found the tubing of his left arm and ripped it free within seconds.

Then he sat up.

And his mouth dropped open.

He didn't have a chance.

The door to the chamber where the newborns were incubated or placed just after birth, was dark, dreary, and flung wide open like the red painted steel doors to an abattoir. Alice had made some sort of pulley system to open the sliding doors, with some effort on her part no doubt. But that really didn't interest Gus. What interested him was the oily stream of babies, coated by the slick gloom of the ward. Dead babies, crawling towards him on their hands and knees, their bald heads gleaming in the sparse light like rotten eggs. He couldn't see their features yet, and God help him he had no desire to as he knew he'd have nightmares a plenty from this evil burst of flesh wriggling towards him at best speed. Gus's fingers hooked into claws and instead of untying himself, he tore at the bonds of his lower legs.

Alice shrieked in protest. She saw what he was doing.

Gus didn't care. He was moaning now. The sound of little feet and hands thundered in his ears. Alice was cursing and screaming oaths that would embarrass Satan himself. Gus raked fingers over the tubing and it would not give. It would not release him. *What the* fuck *did they make this shit out of?* He lost several fingernails on his own flesh and the tubing and railing and still he could not free himself and the *babies*, the bloated little corpses of the babies charged him no more than a leg length away and he could smell the dried blood on their little bodies. Gus thrashed and pulled and clawed and one leg came free and Alice was screaming out *you fucker you fucker!* but he got to his feet and with a strength born of an animalistic fear of being eaten *alive* he whipped the gurney about with his free leg into the oncoming tide, just as he could see the first of the little monsters' eager grins. The gurney smashed into them and he pressed its length up against the rush. He reached down and freed his second leg and straightened just in time to see Alice, her face full of diseased gum hatred, stabbing downwards with the scalpel.

The blade passed through the meat of Gus's left forearm and his fingers went funny, like guitar strings snapping, but his right arm was free and he punched. He slammed his fist into the side of the slut-bitch's head with whatever power he could muster and Alice flew away from him, unconscious upon impact as if hit dead-on by a out-of-control Mack diesel truck. Into the rush of dead bodies she went, and the babies immediately crawled over their adopted mother, adoring her with their ghastly affections.

Gus staggered back from the sight, but he still caught a glimpse of the dead newborns in her wild scrub of hair, biting with lipless mouths, gnawing with black gums. Little hands covered her face and she quickly slipped under the grey-black skin of her children.

Naked, trailing shit and blood, Gus ran.


Feet slapping floor tiles, he bolted out into a hallway. He tried to turn, slipped and fell hard on his right side. His elbow smashed into hard tile and the tip of the bone punched through the baggy flesh located there. Baring teeth he got up and looked back at the hallway and the open doorway of the maternity ward. Nothing pursued him yet. Not yet, and he wasn't hanging around for whoever was in the basement, as they sure as fuck had to hear Alice's screams from beyond. Gus looked about. He stood in the crux of an L, with both corridors leading off into the shadows. Without thinking he ran up one hall, over debris covering the floor. It seemed Alice had made the whole section her nest. He ran, feeling the air lift the sliced flaps of his flesh, grimacing against the pain of his many wounds while the relief of escaping star-bursted within his chest. He padded his way down the hall, past dark offices that zipped by, the floor cold to his feet.

A single set of stairs, loomed ahead of him, forcing him to a stop. They only went up.

*Jesus Christ*, Gus thought, clasping the bald crown of his

head. Where was he? He looked around frantically. Was he in the basement already? No, he could remember now, being hauled upwards, by his ankles, with his head smacking against the metal lipped stairs. He wasn't downstairs, he was up.

But how far?

He glanced back the way he came, and without thinking anymore on it, he ran back. Back through the gloom of the corridor, passing the ward and cringing upon hearing the feast, when he turned the corner and went the other way. Down a short hall he raced, past paintings still hanging on the walls, past trolleys and stretchers pushed to one side, and broken—

The glass sliced through the padding of his right foot, stabbing into the flesh between his big toe and the one next to it, and spurting through like a shard of dark crystal. Shrieking, Gus hopped on one foot and collapsed over another gurney. *Glass!* He flipped onto his back and held his foot up to the scant light. One fat sliver embedded in his foot. Gleaming rivulets ran from the wound, over his pallid ankle, and the multitude of slashes inflicted by mad bitch Alice.

Snarling, he tried to grip the glass. The shard was small and the blood made both it and his fingers slippery.

"Piece of *shit!*" Gus winced, sat up, and dug into the space between his toes. Pain sparkled from his foot all the way up his leg and the gurney began to whirl. Gus fought back against the dizziness, heard something as if from a great distance, a shouting of some sort. Then he was digging in again, and again the glass refused to come free. He flopped backwards on the gurney, taking in huge gasps of air and squeezing his eyes shut. There was no time for this. There was no fucking time. Once more he sat up, grabbed his gashed foot and, with all of his remaining might, squeezed until enough of the glass oozed free of his flesh and he could get a hold of it .

He yanked the shard free with a squeal of exhausted agony. He collapsed on the gurney, taking in great deep breaths and staring at a blue-black ceiling, knowing that he'd never been in such a dire situation before this. The blood loss made him giddy, but he forced himself to sit up, placing all his upper body weight upon on his forgotten elbow and *that* reminded him not to fuck around.

He looked back the way he had came and, as if in a dream, a bare head, baby-sized and all in shadows, came around the distant corner. It crawled towards him in a soft, rumbling shuffle of flesh and bone, like a box of oranges or some other fleshy matter spilled across the floor. The sound grew.

Behind the lead baby, obviously the quickest of the bunch, two more crawling forms turned the corner.

Followed by another three.

Then a storm surge.

They charged in a widening wedge. Gus took a breath, blinked, and then got off the stretcher. His gashed foot crackled with pain when it hit the floor. With a sigh, he skip-walked away, one hand slapping the wall, his attention fixed ahead. He shot a look over his shoulder, taking in the close-to-the-ground mass following him, *gaining* on him. Tiny grunts and growls issued from the mass, little sounds of newborn discontent that could only be comforted by the meat on his bones.

A scream stabbed the air, stopping Gus in his tracks like a sword to the chest. He glanced back and there, at the far end of the hall and behind the advancing horde, stood the disheveled form of Alice. Her features were swathed in shadow, but Gus sensed the evil emanating from her person. She stood hunched over like a mythical troll, with one hand low at her sides and fingers flashed wide as if extending talons. The other hand held something.

Gus knew it was the scalpel.

Another scream, one with both lungs behind it, and the inky outline of Alice started after him. She quickly caught up with the last of the infants in the rear and pushed past them. She booted dead toddlers out of her way. The mother presently had no love for her adopted ones.

*Mommy fuckin dearest*, Gus thought as he pulled his carcass around another corner, out of view. He stood in a stairwell. He squinted in the gloom, realizing that it was darker in the hospital just as a third scream lit up his spine and prompted him to turn. Blood continued to dribble from him, and he could smell his own excrement. The tip of his elbow resonated like there was someone right there, tapping the raw bone with a rock hammer.

Then he saw one of his boots, discarded in the stairwell, right on the steps going down.

Gus hopped over and picked up his boot.

And blinked in astonishment.

There, on the next landing down, lay his shotgun.

"What the hell?" Gus muttered and practically slid down the railing to the landing. He scooped up the shotgun and held it close. *Now*, he thought venomously, *now we'll see*. He placed his back against the wall, checked the safety and the breech. There was a shell in there, and he wondered if Alice had even fired the weapon.

There was a growing sound, a swarm of hungry mouths

and dead eyes. Gus didn't have much time. He looked to the level above him and Alice popped into view, a fright of ripped clothing and blood and craziness, her lips drawn back to expose a crunch of teeth. And she spotted him.

Gus fired the shotgun from his hip, blowing out a chunk of the cement frame and sending chips flying. Alice shrieked and withdrew as if yanked from behind. Gus stumbled, off-balance from the blast, and fell sideways. In a split second, he tried to keep a hold of the shotgun while trying to avoid landing on his damaged elbow and foot. With a huff he fell on his chest, his forehead pressed against the gun barrel. The toe of his dropped boot lay just ahead. He collected himself and frantically got into a sitting position.

"You little prick!" came the screech from above. "God *damn* you to hell, you little piece of shit! They bit me! You made them bite me! I'll have your fucking heart for that!"

As a reply, Gus pumped another shell into the chamber.

"Stick your head out, you fucking banshee, and I'll make all it better," he shouted back.

A gasp of pain escaped him then and he looked at the wound in his belly. He prodded it with his left hand, though his fingers were still contrary. Blood seeped from the cut in a thick dew, but he didn't think it was too bad. *Too much fat there*, it occurred to him. *Ha! Fuck the six-pack!* But it still hurt, and the rest of him looked like he was slashed to bloody ribbons. Knife fight wounds, but he had his *boom stick* with him now.

Then he heard the newborns and his defiance shrunk.

They were coming, their infection giving them the strength to motor along the floor. The idea of shooting them repulsed Gus. He couldn't do it. Back when the world was still a world and he watched movies, he had an unspoken rule, *you never hurt the baby*. Not in any flick. Even the producers seemed to know this. It was line that could not be crossed, and he could not cross it now.

With a grunt, Gus got to his feet. He threw the boot down the stairs. Leaning heavily on the railing, he hopped down the steps. Above, Alice swore at her brood. The youngsters were trying to kiss mommy again, it seemed. Focusing on the stairs, he made his way to the landing below, kicked his boot ahead, and descended to the next level. A glimpse of the main floor made his heart flutter. The rest of his gear was strewn about, including his other boot. Just beyond was the bat and backpack.

He gingerly kicked his boot to the rest of his gear. Everything the sly bitch had taken from him, jeans and leather pants included, lay untouched. He hopped to his jacket, pulled it up and looked to his right. There, still where he parked it and gleaming in an evening twilight, was his van, the doors wide open. He dropped the jacket and shifted the shotgun under his left arm, freeing up the right. He checked behind him, looking for Alice, and knew that he was wasting time, knew he was breaking rule number one of *don't be stupid*, but his gear was a part of him, and damn it if he was going to leave it for *her* to wear.

And there she was, flying at him from the dark cave of the stairwell, her marble eyes fixed on his and full of insane hate. She screamed, meaning to terrify him. Her wild hair streamed behind her and the scalpel flashed downwards, aimed for the centered of his bare forehead. Gus got his left arm up and blocked the stab, but her weight was too much. They crashed to the ground and the connection momentarily stunned him. She was breathing frantically, wildly, and on instinct alone his right fist connected with her jaw, snapping it shut and breaking off shards of rotten teeth. Alice screamed, fell back, and Gus felt her scrabbling over him, like some evil crab. Her hand grazed his belly, groping for his thigh and homing in on his balls, fingers scraping them, cupping them…

He punched her, crossing his chest with his right hand. His fingers touched the shotgun barrel and gripped it the same time she touched his nuts again. He whipped the barrel ahead and nailed her square in her temple, dropping her across his thighs. With a flurry of leg kicks, he shrugged her dazed form off as if he were shooing off a huge black spider. One kick took her hard across her jaw. Alice moaned, and Gus did not feel like being merciful. How many others had she taken? How many others had she cut up and served to the newborns?

He got to his knees, got a better grip on the shotgun, and took aim at her skull.

Alice was unaware of him, breathing shallow.

His finger tightened on the trigger. She was dead anyway. The babies had punctured her skin in places, sealing her fate. Once a person was bit, there was no hope for them.

But right now, she was still human, and God above, Gus could not shoot.

Swearing, Gus slammed the shotgun's hardwood butt across her fingers. Bones shattered. He got the rest with a second blow.

Alice only grunted softly.

Gus broke the fingers on her left hand then, knowing full well he was torturing her, but the fury had a hold of him and warped his thinking. He hadn't killed her outright in his mind, as she still had both of her legs. She could jump off a building or something, but he wasn't going to kill her. He wasn't that far gone to take another life. Not yet.

Gus placed the gun on the floor, measured the distance, and slid the weapon towards the main doors with one mighty shove. He threw his backpack, boots, in the same direction. Behind him, Alice stirred. Gus spotted the scalpel. Pursing his lips he kicked it into the darkness, the metal skittering on the tiles.

He looked to see where it went.

There, shuffling into view and passing the drug counter was a gimp. A big one. Materializing from the corridor with the blood streak down the middle of the floor. The thing regarded Gus with an open mouth, its lips torn off. Fragments of gold teeth gleamed and the fragrant stench of dead flesh hit him. The thing shuffled towards Gus and he backed up to the main entrance. He scooped up his leather pants, bat, and shotgun and fumbled with getting it all in his hands, but he stayed aware of the approaching zombie. The dead thing watched him, milky eyes unseeing yet *knowing*.

Then it paused, and sensed the prone form of Alice lying on the floor.

Gus withdrew. He wasn't killing her. She was already dead. This was justice, he told himself. *Justice*.

The gimp moved in on Alice's form, ignoring Gus entirely. There was an easier meal nearby. It dropped to its knees, gathered up one of Alice's arms, and sank those golden teeth into her bare skin. The thing fed slowly, deeply, ripping away flesh as if it were fried chicken.

Gus looked away, but not before he glimpsed blood spurting from the bite wound. He stopped at the glass doors, hearing that awful feeding.

Then Alice screamed.

She screamed and tried beating the thing away, but her

fingers would not work. The thing piled onto her legs, keeping her in place. Her screams became sobs and Alice suddenly arched her back. The thing was too heavy to throw off, but she kicked. She twisted and yowled and even with her wrecked hands, she managed to topple the zombie on her. Alice scrabbled away on her elbows, towards the stairwell. Her cries hitched in her throat, and she no doubt thought she would live, that she could disinfect the bites, that she would survive this…

The first baby she met in the stairwell, the direction she was crawling in, clunked against her forehead with a crack. Alice faltered at the connection.

And then, from the shadows, the rest of the children crawled into sight. The stairs had proved to be a challenge for their little limbs, but they had found their mother all the same. They crept over one another to greet her. Stunned by this tide of dead flesh before her, Alice stalled.

That was all the chance the big zombie behind her needed.

The gimp reached out and grabbed her wild hair. The undead thing yanked her head back and sank its gold speckled maw into the stringy flesh of her neck.

Alice howled, struggled, and pulled the zombie off-balance. They fell together into the mass of her arriving children, with Alice landing on the bottom.

Her children oozed over her person and kept her down.

Gus heard the feeding, the gagging, the gathering shadows spared him the grislier details. He pushed through the entrance and hurried to van, where he threw everything inside. Once done, he pulled himself into the vehicle and slammed the doors shut behind him.

The booty of supplies bumped and annoyed him, but he

moved past it all and hauled himself into the driver's seat. The engine started with a growl. His wounds nagged and he hissed as he put the van in gear. The day was almost done, the clouds hanging low in the sky but Gus wasn't going to turn on the headlights. Lights brought out the gimps.

He drove away from the hospital, hunched over the steering wheel as if he were a man of eighty. Home was a good hour or so away, but he knew how to bypass the city. He would skirt around its rim and ignore the highway's beckoning off-ramps. Not at night. Never at night. It was too dangerous.

Alice and her unholy children lingered on his mind, but not for very long. He drove in silence, struggling to keep his attention on the black lick of road that would take him back, back up his mountain, and finally home.

He drove a kilometer before he pulled over with a curse. Making sure the van was parked, Gus sniffed and got up from the driver's seat. He went into the back of the van where he hoarded the toilet paper.

There, he grabbed a roll, and, grimacing, wiped his ass.

# 2

# Private Property

Ray enjoyed petty crime.

Twenty-seven years old and the system had branded him as a repeat offender. It wasn't like he had aimed for a criminal career. Good Lord, no. It just kinda happened that way. And it sorta interested him. He was kinda, sorta good at it, and it was perhaps the only career choice where practice didn't necessarily equal perfection. He knew the dangers of his work. Knew it was stupid every day he crossed the line. He even tried leaving the trade, swearing it off twice and promising himself to stay out of trouble. He really did. Even got a job with UPS for a while, which, in retrospect, probably wasn't the best choice. The temptation to look inside the very packages entrusted to his care overcame him while behind the wheel of his truck, on a boring, rainy afternoon. It wasn't before long his fingers were clawing into the cargo.

Like Christmas, that day.

The judge disagreed with him, disagreed that Christmas was in July. That day marked another year-long bout of In-and-Out.

His family hadn't abandoned him, but waited for signs of his commitment to rehabilitating himself. To get on the straight and narrow again. Ray knew how narrow that median was, having wire-walked it enough times and stumbled into questionable traffic, sometimes with spectacular results. He missed his mom and dad. Missed his sister. Really missed his sister's kid, little four-year-old Colt, a red-headed dynamo with a gift for reading and building things. Where the little guy had gotten that fiery mop was a point of vocal wonderment, as both his sister and her husband possessed rock-star locks of the blackest pitch. Regardless, Ray missed the little guy. Thought of him like the son he'd probably never get around to having. But sister Dawn and hubby Creed had believed Ray needed his own time-out. A righteous one at that, to get his head in the right place.

A better place.

Ray pinched the bridge of his nose. He thought of himself like a car in dire need of a wheel alignment. Take his hands off the steering wheel and he'd drift off the highway and onto questionable shoulders.

Like this morning.

*Th'fuck am I doing here?* The thought barged into Ray's mind like a cold, unwanted finger, digging away at parts best left alone. He parked his van before a yellow lawn and town house in desperate need of a paint job. Or some siding. Something. Anything to remove the flaky beige coat of shit currently coloring the house.

Ray rolled down a window as if fresh air might smarten him up. He sighed into the cold and, like a drunk sailor, November shoved back. The wind rattled his collar and whipped the leaves into a sloppy spin cycle. He didn't want to be up so early. Really didn't want to be on the go, but the Ball Brothers wanted him to come talk, which meant business. And business meant ripping someone off.

Julian and Joey Pearson—the Ball Brothers—were always searching for an easy steal. The quickest grab-and-bag on items that resulted in the fastest turnaround in street sales with the least amount of confrontation. Confrontation wasn't the Pearsons' style. Confrontation meant having to crack open someone's skull. Joey didn't want that. Your stuff, he wanted. Your blood, not so much.

But he would if he had to, and if he had to, chances were you were dead.

The town house's front door opened and Bernie walked out, stopped on a white step, and dramatically flicked up the woolly collar of his brown leather jacket while inspecting the overcast skies. He wasn't a big man, neither tall nor fat, but he did have a way about him, a vibe of flow, of uninterrupted, take it or leave it. Behind the wheel of his van, Ray quietly marveled at the show, knowing it wasn't all for his benefit. The only thing missing was Bernie cupping a hand to his face to light up a smoke. Wasn't going to happen, however, as the man didn't partake in that particular habit.

Bernie had plenty of other bad habits, however.

Both Bernie and the jacket had seen better days. Ray thought the man said he'd picked it out of a donation bin, along with a few pairs of sneakers and matching jeans. The sneakers Bernie flipped for a few bucks at a pawnshop. The jeans were an ongoing disagreement between the friends. Bernie liked to keep up with the local fashion, as idiotic as it seemed, and currently wore the denim halfway down around his ass with his white boxers on display. Gangster style. Whoever came up with the fashion obviously didn't know any real gangsters, in Ray's opinion, because a real, honest-to-God gangster would not wear their jeans in such a way. A real gangster would probably kick the living squirts out of anyone wearing their jeans like that. Ray could clearly see Bernie's undershorts. The embarrassing exhibition made Ray roll his eyes. It was far too early in the morning for such foolishness.

Unshaved and appearing as if he regularly snorted his

paycheck through his nose, Bernie walked over the leave-speckled front lawn and approached the waiting van, a big cargo model, puke green and sporting an ass that stretched into infinity. Ray once got caught on a patch of black ice on Springwell Road, right on the tail end of a ripening traffic light. His wheels had spun hard enough to conjure up of visions of spiraling supernovas, and when the rubber finally took hold, he shot into traffic and landed precisely in his lane like a guided missile. To this day, Ray remembered that split second of helplessness and total fear.

Bernie reached the door and found it locked. A tired expression followed. "Open the door."

"Not till you pull up yer fuckin jeans," Ray replied calmly.

"Wha'?"

"You heard me. Pull them up. You ain't gettin' aboard looking like you just shit yourself, y'goddamn punk wannabe."

"I paid good money for these things."

"You paid nothing for those jeans."

"I paid in time."

"It took you a *second* to snatch them, if that."

"But they're *worth* money," Bernie pointed out.

"All the more reason to wear them right."

"I am wearing them right."

"You ain't wearing them right. Lookit you. God forbid you gotta run somewhere, and if you do, God forbid I *miss* seein' you run somewhere. Quit wearin' your clothes like you got some sorta disability. Fuckin' physically challenged folks put their clothes on better than you."

Bernie stepped back from the van, clearly unimpressed. "Hey, don't be makin' fun of them folks. They got feelings, too. My cousin's autistic." He rattled the handle. "Open the fuckin' door."

"I'm not openin' the fuckin' door."

"I'll call Julian."

"Julian'll fuckin' agree with me."

"You're bein' an asshat here."

"I'm being an asshat?" Ray shook his head. That was a good one.

Whether it was the cold or the wasting of time, Bernie swore under his breath, the words becoming vapor, as he savagely yanked his jeans up over his hips.

"You tuck them in right, too," Ray told him. "You know I can't see you, but if I open the door and see fuckin' boxers I'll floor it right here and let you pull yourself in."

"They're tucked, all right?"

Ray unlocked the passenger door. Red-cheeked and fuming, Bernie climbed in.

"Marnin' Bern, me old trout."

"Marnin'."

Ray pulled away from the house and concentrated on traffic.

Bernie fastened himself into place. He struggled with the seat belt until he reached inside his jacket's pocket and pulled out a square-edged pistol. Ray looked from the Glock to the traffic, sniffed and shook his head and reached for the radio knob to find some classic rock.

"Jesus Christ," Bernie muttered. "Y'try to be discreet with these things and a goddamn seat belt won't let you."

He placed the gun between his legs and fought to secure the belt, the barrel pointed at his junk. Ray paused in his knob-fondling but ignored this egregious lack of weapon etiquette. That was Bernie. Every year it seemed like Ray had a better chance of shit monkeys flying out of his ass than Bernie making it to his next birthday. Not that he was stupid. Bernie could carjack any vehicle on the planet in less than five seconds. But he did questionable things at the worst possible times.

After his epic battle with the seat belt, a victorious Bernie pulled a second gun barrel out of his other pocket and, holding the Glock below the dashboard, screwed the accessory onto the weapon.

This interested Ray enough to surface from his personal morning fog. "Whatcha got there, Bern?"

"This? Silencer, b'y." Saying the colloquial word for boy as *bye*. "Just got it."

"Where'd you get it?"

"Bought it online. Now I can go for the wicked stealth kills."

Ray smirked. "Since when do you 'stealth kill'?"

"I do. All the time. Just don't talk about 'em is all. I'm a fuckin' ninja, man. Got the certificate and everything."

Ray didn't bother commenting on that. It was too damn early in the morning. The van rumbled to a stop at a red light and he glanced at the overcast sky. "Y'know it don't go pew-pew."

"Wha'?"

"It don't go pew-pew. That's a Hollywood screwup. A misconception. It only marginally lessens the sound of a shot."

"Wha'? Where'd you hear that?"

"Saw a video online."

"*Wha*'? I don't believe that."

"Believe what you like, my son. 'Tis true. Buddy was firing the same make of gun with and without a sound suppressor. Big difference. Pretty loud, too."

That horrified Bernie. "Lord Jumpin' Jesus. What make of silencer was it?"

"He didn't mention."

"Well, maybe he had a Molly Mart version."

"I don't think Molly Mart sells silencers."

"They sell everything else."

"They do," Ray stated as he stepped on the gas. "Freaks buy it, too. Which is probably good enough reason *not* to sell silencers."

That logic struck Bernie hard. "Well, god*damn* it. I was hoping for some quality sniper hits. Deep covert-op shit, y'know? Almost don't want to use the thing now."

Ray gave up on the radio and turned it off. Too much morning chatter. "Y'bought it. Should use it at least once."

"Any dogs around...?"

That annoyed Ray. "Y'ain't shootin' no fuckin' dog or any other animal. Christ, numbnuts. Have a sense of pride in what you do, willya?"

"Should fucking sue the company," Bernie sulked, staring ahead at the thickening traffic.

"Yeah? Who you gonna sue?"

"Dunno. Jesus. Maybe I can return the thing."

"You have a receipt?"

"Well... *fuck!*"

"Thought so."

"D'fuck am I gonna do now?" Bernie wailed.

"Keep the thing," Ray shrugged, eyeing a shiny red Toyota indicating it wanted to get into his lane. Ray waved at the vehicle to do just that. The driver held up a hand in thanks.

A pissed-off Bernie sat and chewed on the inside of his cheek. Ray minded the driving, glancing down at a Honda driving up alongside the car.

"Where'd you buy it again?"

"Online."

"Yeah, where online?"

"Bay Bitches in Bikinis." Bernie cleared his throat. "Dot org."

Ray winced. "I can't believe this. I should be writing all this down. You're a book begging to be written, my son."

The traffic thickened into four dull lanes of colors. Bernie regarded the silenced pistol with an air of poisoned regret before stuffing it into the glove compartment.

"Remind me to get that later," Bernie said.

"You want *me*…. to remind *you*… to get *your* gun out of *my* glove compartment?"

"Yeah. Later on."

"You can't remember that one yourself? It's not a fuckin' pair of mittens you just stashed away in there."

"Just remind me, okay?"

*Fine*, Ray thought with a shake of his head. "You want to stop by Timmy's?"

"Nah," Bernie said, leaning back as if he were anticipating a head-on crash any moment. "Who else is gonna be there, this mornin'?"

Ray checked his side mirror and shrugged.

"Not Wayne," Bernie said.

"Don't know."

"I don't like that guy."

"He's a hothead."

"Man's a fuckin' psycho is what he is," Bernie warned. "A fuckin' rabid animal. You know about that fight he got into over at the Cave the other day? Took on three guys in the washroom. Real mess. Real mess."

Ray nodded. He'd heard about that. "Wasn't that over a girl?"

"That was over him," Bernie stressed. "He was in the washroom havin' a leak like you would, right? And he just happened to be looking to the door when these three guys come in, and the first one locks eyes and says to Wayne, 'How's it goin'?' right? But Wayne thought the guy was hittin' on him."

"Where'd you hear all this?"

"From Coby."

"Coby's full of shit."

"Usually, but he got it straight from Wayne himself. Anyway, conversation started up and Wayne pretty much wrung the unholy dingleberries off all three of them. All by himself. *Three* guys. Big ones, too."

Ray sighed. "He's got a temper."

"That's not even a temper, Ray. Jesus Christ, that's fuckin' unsettling. To go from 'How's it goin'?' to breakin' arms, jaws and legs in six seconds? Yeah, that's what he did. Wayne put all those guys in the hospital. It's a wonder the cops haven't picked him up yet."

"Don't know if Wayne's there." Ray changed lanes and drove onto the outer ring to escape the majority of the morning snarl. Cars zinged by as he looked over his shoulder and eventually merged.

"Just *hope* Wayne's not there," Bernie muttered. "He stares at people, too, y'know. You ever notice that?"

"Yeah."

Bernie rubbed his chin. "Stares at folks like, I dunno, like something weird. Perverted weird. And he can't talk to you without cuttin' you off. I mean, a fuckin' conversation is a dialogue exchangin' opinions and ideas. He doesn't listen to the other guy, just starts talkin' over them. And real loud, too, y'know."

Ray knew. "He won't be talkin' over Joey and Julian."

"No, I s'pose not. But then Wayne's not the brightest. And I hope Jim Fraser ain't there."

"What's wrong with him?"

"Man's a slouch. Too damn sloppy."

This all amused Ray. "Ever see those dentures he's got? He's got uppers and lowers. I remember one time he got so drunk that he took them out and forgot to put them back in. Eddie Kegan goes over to Jimmy's place and he answers the door, looking like shit spray on a wall to begin with, but after five or six seconds, Eddie asks him where his teeth are and Jimmy goes and looks for them. He knocked under his bed and his fuckin' cat had hacked a fur ball over them."

Bernie's features screwed up at that image.

"Eddie said when Jimmy first answered the door and his teeth were out, said his mouth looked like a blown-out asshole."

The two men giggled.

"Is there anyone you can work with?" Ray asked eventually.

"You're okay."

"Thanks. Anyone else?"

"Can't think of anyone right now."

"Uh-huh. Well maybe you'll get your wish this morning."

"Morning," Bernie scoffed. "The hell the Testicle Twins want us out here this early in the morning?"

Ray winced at the name. Julian and Joey Pearson were fifty-something-year-old career criminals. Old hands in questionable trades. The brothers had once been christened "The Testicle Twins" in the St. John's underworld. They were identical, shaved bald, with their lower faces drizzled in about a week-old, arguably fashionable stubble they maintained. As the story went, once upon a time in an urban setting, a guy sitting at an in-house poker game hosted by the brothers sized up the twins in between hands. Perhaps it was the booze talking or some other chemical, but the guy (the tale never identified the offender, exactly) looked at the boys sitting side-by-each and, with a smile on his face no less, remarked that the brothers resembled a pair of unshaven balls. Wrinkles and all.

And thus, the Testicle Twins were born.

Neither Julian nor Joey appreciated the name at the time, as they felt it a slap to not only their appearance, but their intelligence as well, and being referred to as a pair of testicles isn't particularly flattering on any day, chemically enhanced or not. In any case, about a week after the game, the label stuck like dog shit refusing to be scraped off a boot. Everyone started calling Julian and Joey the Testicle Twins. The name continued on, despite the boys' efforts to change it, until one day, or so the story goes, the originator of the offensive name was once again playing a hand at the Pearsons' place. Same smart-ass made the same crack yet a second time, off the cuff with a nod and wink, right in the lads' presence. Up to that point, the two boys had been well and truly pissed off at how quickly the name had circulated in certain circles around town. Word had it that even their own mother asked them about the name at the supper table, which is the ultimate in underworld horror.

Well.

Needless to say, Julian and Joey took exception to the smart-ass's breach of etiquette the second time around and proceeded to punish the source of their torment. "Punish" was a trifle of an understatement as to the physical, emotional, and psychological destruction they wrought upon the guy. It was traumatic, to say the least. Ray had heard details, the same details that quickly changed the Testicle Twins to simply "the Ball Brothers," as in ball *breakers*, which was, oddly enough, more palatable to Julian and Joey.

Ray didn't have to warn Bernie about calling Julian and Joey the Testicle Twins while in their presence. Bernie wasn't stupid. And he knew the story well enough. Everyone did. Even the cops.

"Hey, guess what?" Bernie said. "Went out with Annie on the weekend."

That particular feat impressed Ray. "No way."

"Got another date this Friday."

"Second one already, eh?"

Bernie waved a jazz hand over himself, presenting his figure. "What can I say? She wants it."

Ray said nothing to that.

"I mean, what hot-blooded woman would *not* want it? And she's hot, man. She is hot. Mmm-hm. The hottest one yet. Don't think I can do any better. Perfection. Everywhere. I mean, *every*where. She makes yoga pants look hot, that's how hot she is. She could do commercials for them. I said that to her. And she giggled. When you can talk to a woman about how she looks in yoga pants and she fuckin' giggles, you know you're in good territory. Can't wait for the weekend. Can't wait. Might even get her blouse off this time. Perfect. Did I say that already? She's *perfect*."

Ray sniffed. He'd heard it all before and was already tired of the drone. "She shits, y'know."

That statement visibly mortified Bernie, who stared at Ray's profile for long seconds.

"What did you just say?"

"You heard me. She shits."

"She does not."

"Oh, she does, make no mistake. She plants that perfect ass on a porcelain receptacle every day, spreads those perfect cheeks, and bombs the harbor with daisy killer. Sometimes chunky. Sometimes spray. Maybe even two or three times a day. Just unloads. Probably unloads with violence. Chokes up the sewer lines."

"Oh you take that back."

"Bet she wipes back to front, too."

"Fuck off. Christ, why would you even mention that?"

Ray kept his expression in sleepy neutral and focused on the road.

Ending the conversation.

## 2

The van pulled up to a yellow Victorian with a crumbling stone walkway and a year away from a thorough painting. A pair of Chevy pickups occupied the driveway. One black. One blue. Their hoods pointed to the road. A large four-door Ford that might've been a ghost car at one time and perhaps rescued from a police auction was parked face-first into the driveway, squaring off against the Chevys. The parking ruined Ray's hope of sliding in there. He stopped on the curb.

"Well, Jesus Christ," Bernie moaned. "That's Wayne's shit."

"Huh?"

"The car. That's Wayne Robert's car. Fuckers see that and run for cover."

Ray eyed the vehicle and shrugged. "Well, we're here now. No going back."

"I know, I know. Just… damnit."

Ray got out. Bernie dragged his ass after him, and together they walked up an ancient pathway, scanning for ice. The front door opened before they reached the house and an elderly woman—Julian and Joey's mother—peeked out with all the sweetness of a grandmother whipping up a batch of chocolate chip cookies.

"'Ello, there," she greeted pleasantly in a rogue Irish-English blend with just a touch of French. "Looking for de b'ys, is ya's?"

"We is," Ray answered. Bernie's frown lightened, hands hidden deep in his pockets.

"Go around de side dere, me loves." Mrs. Pearson pointed the way. "Dere's a door on de side, dere. Just go on in. De must be 'avin' a party dis mornin', eh?"

"Thank you very much, Missus Pearson," Ray said.

"Thanks, Missus Pearson," Bernie added.

"Bernie," the older lady said, her smile diminishing a tad. "I'se can see yer drawers. Pull dem jeans up for de Holy Sacred Heart of Mary, my son. No one needs to be seein' ass crack dis early in de marnin'. Not even one as cute as yers."

"Yes, Missus Pearson," Bernie said and did as told. Ray suppressed a smile.

"'Ave a good time, b'ys," Mrs. Pearson said and retreated inside her home.

"Yer some nice," Ray whispered as they went around the corner.

"Lemme alone."

"She likes you."

"Go 'way, now."

"Y'gots de cutest ass crack. Like a hairless peach."

"Fuck off."

The side door to the Ball Brothers' basement apartment swung open and Joey leaned out, squinting. A single gold tooth gleamed in his mouth's left corner, catching the light like a lighthouse glare warding off ships.

"Marnin', b'ys."

"Marnin," Ray said brightly while Bernie muttered his own greetings, still clearly unnerved by Mrs. Pearson sizing up his ass.

Joey Pearson wasn't a tall man, but at one point in time, in the lost days of his lawless youth, he'd been fit. Strong. With a narrow waist that sprouted into a set of meaty swimmer's shoulders. These days, in his mid-fifties, all that muscle had been coated with a thick, armoring slab of lard. He wasn't as sexy as he once was, and his sleek power had been replaced with a menacing ogre's grace.

"You bring that coffee over?" Joey asked, sucking on his teeth.

Ray and Bernie exchanged looks.

"The coffee Julian called you about?" Joey added in a reminding tone, words ending on another loud suckling of his remaining dental capacity.

"No one called us," Ray said.

"Julian called you not twenty minutes ago," Joey said, looking over their heads at the mauzy weather. "I should know 'cause I was there. I put in an order for a large double-double."

Bernie didn't move for fear of drawing fire.

"We were in traffic but no one called us," Ray said, bewildered.

"The fuck you sayin' no one called you? You sayin' Julian didn't call you?"

Ray blinked, wondering if the man had called in alternate dimension, yet doubting his own memory.

"I didn't..." He swung to Bernie, who quickly shrugged in supporting denial.

"You got coffee with ya?"

"No coffee, Joey."

"Jesus, Jesus," the crime boss whispered and inspected his fuzzy slippers. When he lifted his head, he was still sucking his teeth, but smiling.

"Get in here, y'lovely bastards."

Relief flooded Ray. "That was a joke. You were jokin'."

Joey nodded, applied force to an incisor, and kept the door open.

"Christ, you scared the shit outta Ray here," Bernie laughed. "The man was clenchin' so tight I could see the veins in his neck."

Ray took that one, knowing it was revenge for Annie.

"I saw that," Joey beckoned. "Come in quick before the cat gets out. If that furry little shit gets out it'll be all day before it gets back in. And close the door behind ya's."

The two men entered, the air inside the house warm and redolent of baked bread, and followed the older man whose shaven head shone like a stubbly lightbulb. Slurping away on his chops, Joey led them down a flight of steps to a basement apartment, into a well-lit but long living area with a large table covered in empty plates. A comfortable-looking sofa and chairs were positioned before a huge flat-screen hung on the back wall, amidst a huge collection of sports paraphernalia from the local hockey team. Ray wondered how much of it was actually purchased and how much was stolen.

The mirror image of Joey sat at the table's far end, coffee mug clenched, while his other substantial arm was draped over the back of his chair.

"Boys," Julian greeted, chewing.

"Julian," Ray and Bernie greeted.

"Lovely marnin'."

"Lovely, lovely," the men chimed.

Two others sat at the table. To Julian's right was Morgan Ford, a rock concert burnout who resembled someone getting through the week on just a few minutes' sleep. His hair was buzzed on the sides but long on top and tied at the back with an elastic, creating a short tail. The neo-samurai style didn't impress Ray in the least, but at least it wasn't one of those cupcake, petroleum-dipped nipple tips that seemed so rampant amongst the younger crowd. As far as reputation went, Morg was bedrock dependable. Solid. The appointed voice and sometimes hammer of the Balls' will.

Directly across from Morg and with his back to the stairs was the crazy one himself, Wayne Roberts. He gave a questioning scowl when Ray and Bernie entered. After identifying the two additions, he ignored the newcomers and turned his attention back to the table. Ray wasn't too pleased with seeing Wayne Roberts in the Pearson's company. The criminal was bad news, a crooked finger up one's ass, and if Ray wasn't happy with seeing him, he damn well knew Bernie was outright poisoned.

"Y'missed breakfast," Julian rumbled as Joey sat down beside him. Joey and Morg occupied the chairs closest to Julian, leaving two final places to sit. One seat opposite Julian and directly before the two men...and one next to Wayne.

Ray quickly went for the chair at the table's end.

Bernie hesitated for the briefest second, clearly not appreciative in the least of where he had to park himself. Moving as if his shoes were nailed to the floor, Bernie sat next to the mad one himself, who eyed his profile critically.

"We ate already," Ray said, getting comfortable.

"What's that shit about the coffee?" Julian asked his brother. "We could hear ya going on down here."

"Just tormentin' is all."

The twins smirked and, sitting as close as they were, Ray was momentarily taken with the image. Shaven heads, carefully groomed goatees flicked with gray, wrinkly faces. They did resemble a pair of balls, a set of frosty man-pearls. The realization almost made Ray smile, which wouldn't do in the Pearsons' presence, so he bit down hard on the impulse. One brother continued to slurp on his teeth while the other chewed like a sick camel. All the while, Wayne continued to stare at Bernie's profile (who was using every bit of mental fortitude not to look back). All put together, Ray thought he'd stepped into a carnival's sick sideshow without paying admission.

"Well, then, let's get down to it," Julian said, still munching on his last bite. He leaned forward, dabbled at the empty plate with a finger and licked it clean. "Boys, we're getting older now. And we don't have time or energy to get into the one big job anymore. Getting tired of it. Poisoned with it. Looking for the easy stuff now, right? The easy money, and it hit me just the other day. The easiest score of all."

Julian paused and swallowed graphically. Ray thought they'd been eating donuts or something of the like, though he didn't see a box anywhere. Joey, thankfully, had stopped working over his teeth.

"You know what that is?" Julian asked.

"Holding up convenience stores?" Wayne ventured with predatory amusement, still studying the side of Bernie's face.

"Nope."

"Breaking into cars?" Ray offered.

"Close."

"Breaking into trucks?" said Bernie, turning his head only partway so he didn't have to look at Wayne.

"Same thing as cars," Joey frowned, expecting better.

"Breaking into cargo vans?" Ray tried again

"Besides that," Julian rumbled.

"Easier than all that?" Wayne asked, curiosity clearly piqued.

"Holdin' up convenience shops ain't so easy," Morg

clarified in a raspy, storm-sculpted voice that the ladies liked. "Was a time there was only one cashier on at nights and you could go in and demand the cash and smokes and get it. Didn't even need a can of spray or anything, just attitude. Frighten the squirts right outta whoever was on. Not anymore. Now's there's two on at night. And security cameras everywhere."

"And so they should," Julian said. "I wouldn't have a single person at night. Not with the likes of you or him walking around."

The crime boss indicated Wayne.

"Anyway, yes," Joey stated, bringing them all back. "Easier than all that. Minus the shops."

Neither Ray nor Bernie added to the conversation. Breaking into cars was pretty easy in their minds. Couldn't get much easier.

"Cabins, boys. Cabins," Julian informed them.

Lightbulbs flickered to life around the table.

"Cabins are the easiest," Julian continued. "Few years back, brudder and I broke into a beautiful little place down on the Avalon's south shore. Made away with about ten grand worth of stuff. Televisions, video games, furniture, plate sets, power tools, booze—"

"We drank that," Joey corrected.

"Which we drank," Julian agreed without missing a beat. "And a shit ton more I can't remember. Sold it all off downtown. Three hours' work and that was just loading it all into a truck. Hard, but easy. Other things came up, y'see, that kept us from going back and hittin' another one. At the time, you couldn't ask for any better setup. Cabin was on the water and not another living soul in sight. Scoped the place out a month earlier. Owned by a doctor from what I understand. Couldn't get any better."

"Like a surprise box," Joey added.

"Like a surprise box," his brother agreed. "So I got to thinking. Ain't no good to break into a home around town. No way you gonna do anything with that. Too many people around. Too many eyes seeing what you're up to. Too much risk. But out in the country? Way out in the woods? The deep, deep woods where's there not a soul around for miles? A person can loot the place at leisure and haul it all back here over a day or two and sell it downtown in another. A little sweat but no fuss."

"Some cabins are like second homes out the bay," Joey said.

"Like fuckin' castles more like it," Wayne said, warming to the idea.

"Fuckin' castles is right," Julian agreed. "Brudder and I went out to Bonavista Bay a few months back. Right along the water's edge toward Spear's Cove. Lovely little spots. Lovely. We found a dirt road and followed it almost half a klick off the main drag. Led to a closed-off gravel pit. We backtracked and found a second road just off that, nothing more than a wide trail for quads really, but you can get a truck down there. Anyway, we went on and came to a cabin at the very end. Met a feller in there just packing it up and heading back home. Was into pipefitting. We talked to him while sizing up the place and it's ripe. Ripe, says I. Who knows what good things he might have in there? It looks rustic. Two stories. Three or four bedrooms. Probably two washrooms. Made of logs with a little shed in the back. Guaranteed there's a shitload of power tools there. Guaranteed. Anyway, brudder and I been going back to that same place over the last few weeks, watching the cabin turn off, just to see if there was a pattern there. Sure enough, buddy's only in there on the weekends. Goes in on Friday evening and gone Monday morning, with only a rope drawn across that little dirt road leading in. That leaves a huge window of opportunity for us. Huge window."

"No cops around," Joey added. "All the privacy you could want."

"It's perfect," Julian said. "Which is why I called up buddy Ray here with his cargo van. Just a day job. Overnight at the most. Break in, load up the van and haul all the good stuff back here to our place downtown. You know the one."

Ray did.

"Buddy who owns the cabin has good taste," Joey said.

"He does," Julian started again. "Very good taste. And with the square footage alone, we figure it should be worth twenty to twenty-five grand if we get everything in there. And I mean everything. The guy's a drinker. Said his missus was into wine. I daresay there's a thousand bucks in booze alone in there. Anyway, that's the job. We split it all, brudder and I taking a share apiece, of course, since we're organizing. For the amount of work, though, it's a solid deal. Thoughts?"

Ray wasn't keen on moving furniture or any other items back and forth to the van, but he had to admit, it was an attractive job. A few grand at the least for a few hours' work. He nodded.

"I'm in," Bernie said. He was usually game for anything that didn't require guns, knives, or bear spray. Ray guessed he was willing to tolerate Wayne for a day.

"I'll do it," the unstable one said, on cue. Wayne had finally stopped staring at Bernie.

Morg didn't have to say anything. He was a noted

lieutenant for the Pearsons and his very presence at the table meant he was more than up for the job.

"What about if this works, now?" Wayne said. "What about doing a few more cabins around that area?"

Joey leaned toward Julian, and the image of a pair of shorn testicles entered Ray's mind once again. "The place where this particular cabin is located is pretty secluded. Off the grid, y'know? Got them solar panels on the roof for power, even. Fairly remote, which is why we like it. And Bonavista Bay is only three hours out. We don't plan on doing anything more around there, but if it works out, plenty of other places along the shore. On the Avalon and off. Trick is not to focus on one area for too long. We went out that way a few years back. Different area but same deal. Just brudder and I. Made a nice sum of money off the job."

Wayne nodded. Ray could tell that the guy's treacherous mind was considering his own brand of dirty work at a later date. If the Pearsons noticed, they weren't letting on.

"So when do we go?" Bernie asked.

"That's what I likes to see," Julian said to his tooth-sucking twin. "Eagerness to get started."

"Now?" Wayne asked, ready to get to work.

"Tomorrow," Julian said.

3

Tuesday morning was glorious.

Ray, as designated driver, picked up Bernie at his residence.

"I'm not looking forward to this," Bernie grumped as he pulled himself into the van. He wore his work clothes, jeans and a comfortable Molly Mart winter coat and gloves. A stocking cap embroidered with a skull and crossbones pattern kept his head warm.

"Wayne, you mean?" Ray asked as he pulled into traffic.

"Fuckin' Wayne Roberts," Bernie hissed, not pleased at all. "Was awake half the night knowing I'd be working with that psychotic prick this morning. Half the fuckin' night."

Ray heard that. He'd lost a couple of hours himself. "Why do you think he's in this crew?"

"Fuck if I know. Just don't know. I tell you what, though. I got this."

He pulled his prized Glock half out of his pocket.

"That shit snake gives me any trouble, I'll shoot out a fuckin' knee and sing along with whatever comes outta him. Then I'll pop him in that greasy face of his."

Ray winced, not wanting to hear such talk so early.

"Maybe he owes something to the brothers?" Bernie put forth.

"Dunno. Maybe. Can't see Julian or Joey wanting to work too often with the likes of Wayne. He's a small-time shit disturber."

"A fuckin' little dog amongst big dogs."

"He's pretty big," Ray pointed out.

"I meant that figuratively."

"Oh. Well. Maybe that's the reason then. He's a big guy. Strong. Can move the furniture and whatever. And didn't he break a few arms for the Balls?"

"Yeah, he did. I just don't like him." Bernie leaned forward to study the passenger side mirror. "Just don't like him. And I'm not putting up with his shit. Not one goddamn ounce of it. No sir."

"It's only for a day or two."

"Tell that to the folks who died yesterday and woke up in hell."

Ray's eyes narrowed at the analogy.

Twenty minutes later and as mentally ready as they were going to be, they met up with Morg and Wayne at a gas station just outside St. John's. Morg drove a nondescript four-door sedan that induced memory loss at a glance. He got out of the car and sauntered back to the van, splitting wintry smoke trails from various exhausts. He gestured for Ray and Bernie to meet him between the vehicles. By the look of his raccoon eyes, Ray didn't think Morg got much sleep either.

The Pearsons' lieutenant stopped at the van's lowered window.

"Marnin', Morg," the lads chimed wearily from inside.

"Marnin'."

"Thought you had a mustang, Morg," Ray observed.

"I do. This is me work car. Easily forgettable."

"You got that right," Bernie chirped.

"Hey, listen, Wayne's gonna ride with you."

The words scrubbed the cheer from Ray's face. "What?"

"No fuckin' way," Bernie blurted.

"Fuckin' way," Morg said evenly. "Got a splittin'

headache and I can't handle him yappin' in my ear the whole way out. I told him to shut up, but you know what it's like talkin' to that guy. He don't listen. Anyway, he rides with you."

"Morg," Ray eyed the sedan, saw the back of Wayne's head. "We don't like the guy."

"No one likes the guy," Bernie added.

"I don't like the guy either," Morg agreed. "But he rides with you this morning."

Bernie regarded his boots, clearly distressed by the new arrangement.

"Listen," Morg explained, seeking to smooth feathers, "I've told him he's gonna be riding with you guys and I warned him not to flick shit."

"Didn't you just say he doesn't listen?" Bernie asked.

"Don't be a smart-ass, Bern," Morg warned. "Don't be a smart-ass. I wasn't shittin' ya about the headache. Truthfully, feels like an axe got wedged in there. Wayne's too damn big for the sedan anyway. Like jammin' a Saint Bernard into a cupboard."

"Like we give a shit about his comfort level," Bernie fired.

"Look, he's ridin' with you so get used to it."

Morg backed away, his sunken eyes regarding Bernie and Ray with a warning. The lieutenant backed up to his car door and opened it, informed Wayne of the car change. The goon got out of the sedan and made a scene of stretching his arms. *Tall and crazy*, Ray thought. Bernie stood and chewed on the inside of his cheek, clearly unimpressed with the new arrangement.

Morg nodded at the guy and Wayne took his time walking, greeting his new handlers with a smile. Bernie and

Ray didn't return it. Since Morg was the Pearsons' foreman on the job, neither could complain about the ruling.

They went back to the van.

Which was when the fun commenced.

As Bernie reached out to open the passenger door, Wayne shot ahead of him and grabbed the handle. "I'll ride up front."

"That's my seat," Bernie protested and blocked him from opening the door. Wayne stood a full head higher and at least that much thicker across the shoulders than Bernie, but the smaller man didn't back down. He pressed his own shoulder against the door and stared Wayne straight in the eye.

Ray had to give it to Bern. The boy didn't scare easy. He couldn't back down, really, not with an unstable wingnut like Wayne Roberts in his face.

A smiling Wayne yanked the door open, jostling Bern and sending him staggering backwards.

Bern straightened and moved to engage.

Ray took a breath and went in as backup.

"Hey!" Morg bellowed, freezing the three men. "Wayne, I told you not to stir up shit, so get in the back of that fucking van. *Now.*"

"I'm not sitting on the floor the whole way out," Wayne protested, mouth screwed up as if he'd just sampled a shit bar. "Fuck that. Let me have a go."

"That's my seat," Bernie pointed out.

"That's his seat," Ray echoed.

"You'll have it better back in," Bernie said. "There'll be a nice sofa—"

"Any sofa," Wayne interrupted, "in the back of this rig will have shit piled onto it. Fuck that. And fuck you. Why don't you fit that skinny ass of yours somewhere in back? I'm carrying a full load here. A *man's* load."

"You're a fuckin' load, all right."

"Hey," Ray said from Bernie's side. "Wayne, it's my fuckin' van. Bernie's my boy; hence, Bernie rides in the front. You can get in the back or you can go the fuck home."

Victory flashed across Bernie's face.

Wayne absorbed the ruling and regarded Ray before focusing on Bernie, that psychotic gleam surfacing upon his face. "Fine."

Bernie had the sense not to push it.

Ray waved to Morg, signaling that it was all good. The pack leader threw his hands into the air and got into his car. The rest of the lads climbed aboard the van and, in a minute, followed Morg's sedan out to the TCH. Morg was the helmsman, the ranger, leading the van toward the glory that was the cabin. Ray didn't mind Morg. At least with him around, he could sorta control Wayne and report any shittery to the Pearsons. Until then, however, Wayne was right behind Bernie and Ray. Unleashed and unsupervised.

Both men would have felt safer if they could have bound him with duct tape from neck to knees.

"Lovely morning for it," Wayne said from the rear. "Lovely morning. Should be down on George's Street. Y'know, once this is all done with, we should go on down and have a few. Knock back a few shots. That's be all right, I think."

Bernie and Ray slowly exchanged looks. Neither spoke.

"So… Ray," Wayne started, stretching out in the back. "Funny to see you here. I'd heard you left the business. Became all sugary goody and shit. Heard you were going into training for a real career. Long haul driving."

The traffic on Ray's right whizzed by and he read the license plates.

"So how about it?" Wayne asked.

"How about what?"

"You get a real career?"

Ray inhaled and let it out slowly. "Got some training. Still might do something with it."

"Around here?"

"Nah."

"Mainland?"

Ray shook his head and Bernie frowned in the passenger seat. Neither of them wanted to engage in conversation with Wayne Roberts, especially not about future plans.

"Undecided," Ray said.

"Uh-huh. And how about you there, Bernie Cook? This still the life for you? Or you movin' on as well once your buddy does?"

"Thinkin' about it," Bernie said, squinting ahead and scratching at his balls.

"Didn't I hear you got a job with the department of highway? Flagsman?"

Bernie's face darkened in horror. "You got good sources."

"I do. I certainly do, all right. I like to know who I'm working with. So how about it?"

"Didn't get the job. Only had an interview."

"An interview," Wayne chuckled, as if it was hard to believe.

"Yeah, an interview. Even got a job offer."

"Did you now?"

"Yep."

"And you didn't take it?"

"Nope."

Ray glanced over at his friend. He'd heard the story already.

"Long ride here, Bern. Amuse me. Why didn't you take the offer?"

Bernie checked his passenger window, obviously not wanting any part of the man behind him. "The interviewer was a prick. Big guy with a gut on him like he had a fucking turkey stuffed under his shirt. Walked into the office with this swagger and hands in his pockets, jingling the change the whole time he was on his feet. Smilin', too. Smilin' at me with this piggish little smirk, like he knew he had me by the dick thicket. He knew I was on parole. You could just tell. He looked down at me when he started askin' all these questions and such, and I answered every one spot-on. You could see this guy squirmin' and twistin' and not likin' how things are goin' one bit. So, anyway, at the end, he goes, 'Well, when can you start?' I said anytime. He goes, 'How about tomorrow?' So like you would, I said yes, relieved the whole thing was over. But then he goes, 'How do you feel about marnin' prayer?'"

Ray shook his head.

"'Well, says I,'" Bernie reported, "'I don't do marnin' prayers no more, and isn't that against work regulations somewhere?' Well, he doesn't like that. Took the high and mighty road and then he started talking about Jesus and redemption and how he wouldn't work with a criminal who wouldn't accept religion. Even said I should be thankful to even get a job at all. So I told him to fuck off."

Wayne snorted. "You *didn't.*"

"Oh I did. Politely, though."

"Politely," Ray repeated.

"Yeah, I said, 'Please… fuck off.'"

Wayne chortled again in the background, sounding like a dog having its tummy rubbed.

"Bet your parole guy wasn't too happy with that," Ray muttered.

"No. No he wasn't," Bernie admitted. "What the hell, right? I'll find something eventually. Maybe I'll just start shootin' dickheads for hire."

"Shoot folks for hire?" Wayne sniggered, the disbelief thick in his voice. "Pretty little man like you?"

"Bet you say that to a lot of guys," Bernie said.

"Just before I kill 'em," Wayne snarked. "One quick stab. Through the throat."

Ray didn't like where the conversation was going.

And, thankfully, the conversation stalled.

"Just thinkin'," Wayne resumed after a minute. "You ever notice how, like, in movies, the assassins are always pointed out as assassins? Really general, like it's no big thing? Like someone would say, 'There he is, he's a carpet cleaner. Works all over the country.' Just like that. Everybody knows them, too. And course they got this killer reputation."

"Carpet cleaners?" Bernie twisted in his seat.

"Assassins, shithead. Folks who play assassins in flicks and such."

Bernie visibly didn't like the shithead remark, not from the likes of Wayne Roberts. "So?"

"I'm thinking, if you were any good and people knew you were an assassin, you'd probably be arrested eventually. Or killed. Sure as hell wouldn't want too many people to know you were a killer-for-hire."

"In a movie, you mean."

"I mean in real life."

"Who the hell would I be tellin' I was an assassin in real life?"

Ray decided to join the conversation. "You said killer-for-hire, Wayne. There's a difference between hitmen and assassins."

"Yeah? What's that?" Wayne wanted to know. "Enlighten me."

"Assassins only do important people. Hitmen, they'll do the carpet cleaner for a buck."

"Semantics, man," Bernie said.

Ray shrugged. "Don't even know what that word means."

"It means some carpet cleaners can be real assholes," Bernie explained.

Ray cocked an eyebrow. He wasn't exactly sure what that meant either and decided to keep quiet about it.

"I killed this guy once," Wayne started, and Ray knew right then he wasn't going to like the story. "In a bar fight. Big rugby player who looked like he came down off a mountain or something. He was yellin' and screamin' in the club. Drivin' me crazy. Can't hunt the cuties when the likes of that is scarin' them away. When he went into the can to take a leak, I followed him in. Didn't even think about it. Just slammed his head into the mirror and crushed his windpipe. Did it with one karate chop. Just one. Stuffed him in a stall and walked out into the night. Four years ago."

"Karate chop, eh?" Bernie asked, smelling the same bullshit Ray was smelling.

"One," Wayne said.

"You know karate?"

"Just said I did."

"No, you—"

"Just said I did," Wayne's voice overruled Bernie's.

"Where'd this happen?" Ray asked.

"Out west. Calgary."

"Uh-huh."

Silence then, for a few seconds.

"Sounds like you don't believe me, Ray Piper."

"Oh, I believe plenty," Ray said and shot a tired look Bernie's way.

"Fuckin' people up is only part of my résumé. Tell you all about it one day."

*Oh boy*, Ray mouthed. Bernie caught it and smiled.

"Don't either of you bastards doubt me, either," Wayne warned them from the back. "Don't fuckin' doubt me. I've killed people and their dogs for a stick of gum in the past. No one knows 'cause I'm smart about it, see. I don't talk about them all. And no one's ever found the bodies because I'm that good. All across the country and down the states."

Ray and Bernie decided to let that one go, suddenly uneasy with the turn of conversation.

"Nice van y'got here, Ray, me old trout," Wayne said. "Nice one. Perfect size for stealing shit. Even kids. This thing is just the right size for kid pluckin'. Ever do any of that, Ray?"

The very question slackened Ray's face with horror and he glanced over at Bernie, who was squeezing his eyes shut as if in a bad dream.

"Just pluck 'em off the streets or from the strollers. When they're ripe, of course. I got contacts who are looking for that kinda thing. Pays top dollar, too."

A gravelly chuckle then, straight from an open grave.

The words felt like a volley of flaming arrows loosed in Ray's direction, and the wrath bled into his cheeks. He regarded the open highway, lips poised to spit, and thought about the remark for a quick scalding second. With a quick shake of his head, he flicked on his turn signal and pulled the van over to the side of the road.

Behind him, Wayne's brow knotted up in puzzlement.

Morg's sedan continued into the distance before the tail lights flared to life in a decidedly stern look of *The hell you doing?*

The van stopped with a lurch and Ray turned around, his seat squeaking. Bernie leaned in as well.

Wayne's brow crinkled. "Something wro—"

"Shut the fuck up," Ray said, cutting the man off. "Just shut the fuck up. You listen to me, you sick prick. I don't like you. Never did. And after what you just said now, I fucking hate your rancid guts. You don't talk to me about kids. Got that? You don't talk about *any* kids. You remove all thoughts of kids from your shit-filled head. I got a four-year-old nephew, and if I hear you talk about stealing kids again there won't be any jury for you. If I hear of any youngsters disappearing from the city, I'll fuckin' come after you with a baseball bat and a shitload of duct tape. And so help me God, I will fuck you up."

"And I'll help him," Bernie added.

Ray spoke right where Bern stopped. "I don't know why Julian and Joey brought you on this job, but I'm goddamn sure if they heard you talk the way you just did, they'd cut you up into dog chum and drop you in the harbor. Matter of fact, you better be on your best fuckin' behavior for the rest of this trip, and that means not another fucking word. Else I'll be telling them everything. Every-fucking-thing. And you can spend the rest of your short life shitting like a jackrabbit. Scared and on the run."

Threat delivered, Wayne leaned back against the wall of the truck and considered both the men up front. A lazy smile appeared, like a man well fed, but his eyes gleamed in a most unfriendly way.

"Wow. Ray Piper shows his teeth. I'm impressed."

Ray's glare did his talking.

"You got it, chief." Wayne nodded and held up both hands. He mimed zipping up his mouth and then tossed the key.

Ray and Bernie shared a look. Up ahead, Morg pulled over onto the shoulder and waited, no doubt wondering what the holdup was.

Ray sat and fumed at the wheel and Bernie watched him.

"You okay?"

"With that piece of shit sitting behind me?" Ray said aloud, not caring if Wayne heard or not. "No, Bern, I'm not fucking okay."

Morg's car crept toward them in reverse.

"He's gonna wanna know," Bernie said.

"And I'm gonna wanna tell," Ray stated.

Despite being livid about Wayne, Ray put the van into gear and pulled back out into traffic. They shot past Morg behind the wheel, who watched the van pass by with a question on his face. Neither Ray nor Bernie commented.

And Wayne, as instructed, said not another word.

*

After an hour on the road, they pulled over at a gas station and restaurant with a huge wooden moose majestically erected upon a platform. Patrons shuffled toward washrooms while vehicles refilled tanks. Some folks stood outside, marveling at the brightness of the day while sipping coffees.

The atmosphere in the van hadn't relaxed in the least. Neither Ray nor Bernie wanted to talk with the likes of Wayne Roberts for two reasons. The first being the child kidnapper might feel inclined to join in, and the other being Ray and Bernie didn't want him listening in on any conversation they had. Things tended to come out in conversations. As it was, Ray was wondering if threatening the creepy bastard was the right thing to do. Wayne was the type to remember such threats.

*Fuck 'im*, Ray smoldered blackly. He'd bet on his baseball bat against Wayne's imaginary karate chops any day of the week, and twice on Sunday.

Morg rolled to a stop ahead of the van and cracked open his door.

Ray got out. Bernie followed. Wayne remained in the back.

The Pearsons' lieutenant wore a pair of retro '70s sunglasses that hid most of his upper face, but the blunt puzzlement was easy to see. "What happened back there?"

Ray and Bernie joined him in a huddle by the sedan's driver's side.

"You take that fuck head from here on in," Ray seethed, leaning into Morg's unflinching face. "You take him, else I take a bat to his head and leave him in a ditch."

Morg looked from Ray to Bernie and back again. "What'd he do?"

"You know he's a fuckin' kid snatcher?"

That dropped the '70s cool from Morg's face. "What?"

"He's a fuckin' kid snatcher," Ray whispered with suppressed fury. "Said so while I was drivin'. That's the reason I pulled over when I did. Ask Bernie, he'll tell you."

"He said it," Bernie confirmed.

"*What?*" Morg gasped, looking to the van.

"You heard me."

"The fuck is up with that?"

"The fuck are the Ball Brothers doing with that piece of shit?" Bernie wanted to know.

"Look," Morg said, standing with his feet spaced shoulder-width apart and his hands on his hips. "Joey and Julian didn't know about that. They'd put him face-first into a meat grinder if they knew that and guaranteed I'd be the one turning the crank. I mean, what, *how*, did this even come up?"

"In passing conversation," Ray said. "It just bubbled out of him like we were talking about sports or something. Listen. Something's seriously off with that douchebag. I mean seriously off. He rides with you from here on out. I don't want his ball sack stainin' the floor of my van."

Morg thought about the request and nodded. "All right. Send him over. Jesus Christ. He really said that?"

The pair nodded.

"Jesus Christ. That turns my guts."

"I'm poisoned," Ray said. "Poisoned. I was reluctant when I saw the guy. He's got a reputation, y'know. Half the city knows about him."

"We all got reputations," Morg countered as a big rig blasted by on the highway, the wake ruffling the coats of the three men. Morg paused for a moment before leaning in and motioning the others to join him. "Look, Julian figured you'd need him for any dirty work. Roberts got no scruples."

"We know that now," Bernie said.

"I guess we do, but Julian figures every crew needs at least one guy who'll pull the trigger if the need arises. And Wayne has a good rep with the lads. Did a bunch of small jobs without a hitch. So there wasn't any thought when this gig came up. Wayne just got plopped in there."

"Wayne's a goddamn freak," Ray stated.

"I know he's a goddamn freak."

"I don't want him on this job anymore."

"Taxis come through here all the time," Bernie observed. "We could leave him and carry on without."

Morg shook that off. "Wayne would probably hold the place up if we did that. Or worse. Look, I'll take him."

That placated the two men.

"Morg," Ray said, "I'm givin' you a heads-up now. He knows we're talking about him. Knows damn well we hate his guts. If he tries anything, I'll kill him and leave him in the woods for the bears. And that's the best I'll do for the likes of him."

Morg nodded in agreement. "I don't blame ya. Not in the least. All right, let me go take a leak and we'll get back on the road."

Having said their minds, Ray and Bernie watched Morg enter the gas station's convenience store.

"You gettin' anything to eat?" Bernie asked.

"Fuck no."

"Me neither."

"That twisted fuck's unstable." Ray turned his back to the van. Bernie turned with him.

"Job's already gone into the shitter," Bernie said.

"With a plink. You know something? If he tries anything, I meant what I said—I'll put him down. If you lend me your gun, I'll shoot the bastard. Probably shoot him anyway, just on principle. I know me, and I don't think I can let the guy walk away after the job's done."

"I'm thinking of doin' it myself. I got a reason now."

"As if we needed one before."

Bernie glanced at the van. "Hey. Look."

Wayne's head oozed out cautiously from between the pair of seats, looking this way and that, before fixing upon the two men.

He smiled.

4

After two hours on the TCH, the grim caravan of thieves exited the highway and eventually reached Route 235. The men appreciated the wind-scoured visual delights of the Bonavista peninsula. The tension had lessened with Wayne no longer lurking in the rear, and Ray and Bernie almost enjoyed the scenic route as they passed through one small community after another, all built with the water on one side, and sweeping evergreen hills on the other. Harsh rock cuts split the land at times, and signs warning of falling rocks had Bernie hunching down so he might better scan the looming heights.

"Nice down here," he said.

"It is nice," Ray agreed, snatching glances while keeping Morg's sedan in sight. "No trouble seeing why folks build cabins out here. Beautiful country."

"Quiet, too. You could cut loose on the weekends and not have to worry about anyone."

"You could."

The wilderness in between the little towns appeared raw and rugged. Stunted wood grew in thick patches, clinging to edges. Cliffs dropped sharply into surfs that rattled the shore. Up and down the rolling hillside, thick carpets of noble fir thrived, appearing almost impassable.

"See any moose?" Bernie asked.

"Nah."

"Wouldn't mind seein' a moose. Match the wooden one up on the highway."

"I wouldn't mind seein' a bear," Ray said. "Haven't seen

one of those in a long time. When I was a youngster my father would take me up to the dump. You'd see a few going through the garbage. Saw one in the woods, too. Black bears. Young ones."

"Mink in this area, too, I heard."

"I heard that, too," Ray said. "Bet you can see full moons really nice out here."

"You can see full moons in town."

"Yeah, but they're nicer out here."

"I think you need to clean your windows next full moon," Bernie said.

They passed cabins overlooking glorious coves with necklaces of beach rocks, high peaks that allowed a person to gaze across shifting waters, and the odd open scrub with trees grown crooked from the wind's lashing. As they drove along, the road veered away from the water and they passed a few good-sized ponds. The road's wooded shoulders had been shaved clean of trees some ten meters on either side, perhaps done only a year earlier, to improve visibility and to reduce the number of moose collisions, leaving shredded stumps and shards. It made Ray think of punji pits.

Up ahead, Morg's brake lights flared and he slowed to make a turn.

"Here we go," Ray said. "What time is it?"

"One thirteen," Bernie reported.

"And not a soul in sight. This might work out after all. The cabin part, anyway."

"Whaddaya think they're talking about?"

Ray shrugged. "Don't know, don't care. As long as Morg keeps that wingnut on a leash."

"I bet it's something like 'Shaddup' and 'fuck off,' knowin' Morg."

The van skipped upon leaving the pavement and hitting a dirt road that hadn't been groomed in a very long time. Tracks from all-terrain quad bikes left deep stitches up either side of the gravelled lane. Potholes perhaps visible from space pitted the surface, a few containing muddy water. Ray turned hard to the right, then left, cringing when a tire failed to clear the craters.

"Holy Sacred Heart of Mary," Bernie said, bracing himself.

"Good thing we're strapped in."

The van bounced and rattled; one pothole in particular left both men feeling weightless for a split second before impact.

"Holy shit!" Ray squinted into his side mirror, fully expecting to see an entire axel left in their wake.

"My balls," Bernie grimaced and buckled forward in his seat. "Landed on my balls. Oh, sweet merciful Christ our savior above."

"You okay?" Ray asked, glancing over at his buddy.

"Not okay."

Morg wove amongst the treacherous road as well, his rear bumper dipping low enough to kiss gravel.

"Hope you got a spare tire," Bernie groaned, cupping himself and flexing his knees like a set of denim-clad bellows.

"Need more 'n one if this doesn't smooth out soon."

Dense thickets lined the shoulders unchecked, unlike the main road. Long boughs reached out and pawed at the van's sides when the vehicle drifted too close. Trees towered over the underbrush, creating a narrowing lane.

A squirrel popped into the road, its little brown eye

bulging at the sight of the van. Both men yelled as the animal disappeared under the right bumper. The wheel there jumped off a rock. Bernie immediately checked his side mirror.

"We get him?" Ray asked, risking a glance in his own mirror.

"Don't see anything."

"Stupid little bastard. You'd think Morg's car would've scared the little furry nuts right off him."

"They're quick," Bernie said. "Probably darted back into the woods at the last second."

"How far in are we, y'think?" Ray changed the subject while trying his damnedest to avoid the dips.

"Not half a klick."

"Wonderful."

So they rattled along, the bigger rocks crackling underneath the van's tires, some violently pinging off the chassis.

"Gonna take my share to pay for a new set of tires," Ray muttered, eyes glued to the road.

After what seemed like an hour, Morg applied his brakes and stopped just past a wide pathway meant to be a side road. Ray eased his punished van to a stop before the turnoff and stared as Morg and an expressionless Wayne got out. Morg went to his trunk and opened it. He pulled out a crowbar and a screwdriver, which he placed in a coat pocket. He then approached the van's driver side as Ray rolled down the window.

"We go on from here in the van," he said, not looking too impressed. "My car's too low. The fucking road'll chew the bottom off if I go over it."

"This it?" Ray asked. "This the place?"

Morg pointed.

Hanging across the width of the road, truly no wider than a quad, was a rope that could've moored a tugboat to a pier. A slightly slanted sign drooped from the middle of the cord with wording painted onto a short piece of clapboard. One metal post could be seen amongst the trees and faded berry bushes.

"Private Property," Bernie read.

"Rope's up," Morg pointed. "Joey and Julian say the guy's not around when the rope's up, so… we're good. We'll untie it and then string it back up once we're inside."

On cue, Wayne walked up to one post and released the rope's end. The sign sagged to the ground.

"How was your drive, dear?" Bernie asked as he watched Wayne work.

"As expected," Morg reported with a sigh. "He says he was jokin' when he said that."

"Just jokin'," Wayne yelled as he worked.

"Yeah, like shit," Ray said, not caring if the big man heard or not.

"We'll clear this up later," Morg said. "You good with that?"

"Is he good with that?" Ray asked back.

"Fuck what he thinks," the lieutenant said.

Which meant Wayne was in dire straits, indeed. As low as they were in their criminal endeavors, no one had the patience or tolerance to work with an admitted child abductor. Ray knew that, and, suddenly, he realized Wayne might be *realizing* that, which made his head throb with the beginnings of a wicked headache.

"Get aboard, then," Ray said to Morg, and the lieutenant walked around to the van's sliding door. He climbed in and placed the crowbar on the floor before grabbing ahold of Bernie's headrest.

When he was finished, Wayne waved the vehicle ahead.

"Here we go," Ray sighed deeply, wondering how the day would end. He steered the van onto the narrow side road, which seemed more knobby than holey. Boughs slid along the walls, causing Ray to wince.

"Joey and Julian will pay for your paint job," Morg assured him, and went to the rear doors. He opened one and Wayne pulled himself up.

"Lads," he greeted with that frigid crocodile smile.

Neither Ray nor Bernie responded.

"Just sit down and shut up," Morg snapped at Wayne. "Drive on, Ray. And mind the potholes."

"These are not potholes, Morg. They're goddamn canyons."

"Daresay there's a pothole or two out there somewhere."

"How far in is it?" Bernie asked.

"Joey said about two hundred meters or so," Morg replied.

"What?"

"Deep woods," the leader said, wincing as higher branches dragged across the windshield of the rumbling van.

"You won't need to sand the rig down," Bernie said to Ray. "Not for the painting."

"Just hope I keep the walls," Ray said in return as boughs attempted to claw his side mirror from its mooring. Orange needles covered the gravel except in the middle, where the road rose in a hump, molded by thundering quad traffic. The trees hugged the sides, creating a channel that turned every so often.

A second sign appeared, nailed to a tree. Black lettering stood out on a white surface.

*You are trespassing.*

"Too late now," Bernie muttered

A third sign appeared, not ten feet later.

*Turn back now.*

"Someone's got a thing for signs," Ray noted.

"What's with all the fuckin' signs?" Bernie shook his head.

"You should put that up for on the way out."

Bernie brightened, intrigued with the idea.

"Nice country, though, all the same," Morg commented. "I wouldn't mind having a place out in the sticks. Without all the signs."

Ray drew breath to comment when the van's front dropped sharply, slamming him forward until his seat belt locked and halted his momentum. The belt wasn't enough to prevent Ray from biting into his tongue, however. That strip of polyester webbing halted Bernie as well, but Morg suffered the worst. The Pearsons' lieutenant, standing just to the left of Bernie's seat, had launched into the dashboard, where he slammed face-first and crumpled into Ray's legs.

"Jesus Christ," Bernie said and righted himself. "The fuck was that?"

"Don't know," Ray opened the door and spat a bloody gob. "Morg, you okay?"

He fumbled at the fallen man, untangling him from his legs and the gearshift. A red welt rose on the lieutenant's forehead with all the horrific poise of a rising vampire. Three front teeth were sprinkled around the floor, and when Morg groaned, Ray saw where they came from. Morg's mouth resembled that of someone who'd just applied a fearsome shade of rouge around a smashed picket fence.

Wayne had crashed into the back of Bernie's seat, getting away with just rattled nerves.

Ray and Bernie struggled to free their stunned leader, while Wayne stood with his hands on his knees, seemingly unaffected.

"Pull him back, Wayne," Ray blurted, riding out the pain of his tongue. "Make yourself fuckin' useful."

Wayne reluctantly grabbed ahold of Morg's feet and did as told. He hauled him back with more force than needed, pulling until the lieutenant kicked him away.

"Lay off," Morg muttered and prodded at his face. His expression soured at the extent of the damage, while his split lip resembled the cracked flesh of an overripe tomato. The bleeding gash would require several stitches. Morg checked his bloody fingers and tongued the empty grooves where his front teeth used to be. He grimaced.

"You okay, man?" Bernie asked.

"Nah," Morg replied and winced, applying a hand to his mouth. "The fuck was that?"

Ray opened the door and slid out of his seat. His senses returned when his feet hit the ground, brain absorbing what had just happened.

What he saw underneath the front tire surprised him just as badly as the unexpected dive bomb.

A foot-wide trench, covered by a mat of dead leaves and orange needles, had been dug across the road, but that wasn't what shocked Ray. What really shocked him was the makeshift spike strip concealed within the forest detritus. Long nails protruded through the leaves and had impaled the front tires to their steely core. Ray staggered, regained his balance, and gawked at the destruction, his mind numb, until the click of the door brought him back.

"The fuck is this?" Bernie asked from the other side, gesturing with a hand. "The fuck is this?"

"It's a goddamn punji pit, is what it is," Ray whispered.

"Why would anyone do this? Here?"

Ray couldn't answer. As Morg and Wayne got out, Ray backed into a wall of prickly boughs. He turned and saw weathered planks lying beneath their shade, thick and well out of sight.

"Not bad," Wayne said, eying the trap set across the road. "Not bad at all."

"You like that?" Ray asked.

"Gotta admit, it's a great idea. They warned us with the signs."

"You like it so damn much, you can change the tires," Bernie said.

Wayne glared. "Why don't you fuckin' make me?"

"Shut up, both of you," Morg said and bent over, allowing the blood to drip freely from his face. He put one finger to his nose and growled in misery. "Well, shit. Fuckin' nose's broken. Great."

The sight silenced the three men.

"Julian and Joey never said anything about this," Ray said. "Like a prickly moat."

"Well, they never came up here when the rope was across," Morg reasoned. "And when they did, the guy who owned the place probably had those planks put across it. Christ on a stick, I'm bleeding here. You got anything to stop this?"

"In the van? No, sorry."

Morg grunted and squinted against the discomfort.

"Pinch that together," Bernie advised. "Give the blood time to clot. And put your head back."

"Fuck that, it'll run down my throat. Hate the taste of blood."

Bernie left him alone.

"We'll head on to the cabin," Morg said. "They might have something there. Wayne, go get the crowbar and shit. Damn good thing I didn't fuckin' stick myself on the screwdriver."

Wayne left them and Morg stepped over the spike-filled trench, indicating the others should follow.

"Listen," Morg hesitated and pointed at Bernie. "You stay back and see if you can't change one of those tires."

"Me?" Bernie's eyes went wide in protest. "Get that crazy cock-pimple to—"

"Listen," Morg whispered, drooling a bright red froth. "I don't trust Wayne to leave him here alone, got it? I'll need Ray to help watch him while he's with me. You're not the most physical guy."

"So the little guy has to stay back?"

Morg stared, his face pallid, the red kiss of the dashboard swelling to the size of a skin-covered golf ball.

"Shit, Morg," Ray said in a respectful tone. "You need a doctor. Or a bucket of ice. Something."

"That bad?" Morg prodded at his forehead and found the expanding nugget.

"Looks like someone shoved a swollen nut up under your scalp."

"Deadly," Bernie observed.

"Deal with this later," Morg stated. "You stay here. Ray, you come with us. Understand?"

Wayne returned, holding the crowbar at his thigh. The three watched him before Morg held out his hand. Wayne hesitated before handing it over.

"All right," Morg said, passing the crowbar to Ray. "We're heading on up to the cabin. Bern's gonna stay with the truck. You're with us, Wayne."

Wayne shrugged.

"You got a phone?" Morg asked, his eyes squeezing shut as he posed the question. The front of his gray shirt and fall coat were saturated. The man could've been shot in the chest if they didn't know better.

"Yeah," Bernie said.

"Remember this number," and the lieutenant gave it. "Anyone comes along, you got a flat. We'll take care of the van later, after I take care of this."

"We might even luck out," Ray suggested. "Maybe's there's a spare tire in a shed up ahead."

"One that fits the van?" Wayne asked dubiously. "You're a hopeful asswipe, aren'tcha, Piper?"

Ray hefted the crowbar, his expression dangerous.

"You swing that and I'll stick it up your ass," Wayne warned.

"Hey," Morg barked, spraying more blood. "Either one of you cocksuckers give me a hard time and I'll stick this fucking screwdriver into your ear, so shut the fuck up and come on."

Morg got walking. Wayne followed, locking eyes with Ray as he passed, making it clear that their discussion was far from finished.

The two men marched away from the van. Ray held back, however, and faced Bernie. "Gimme your gun," he whispered.

"What?"

"That sonofabitch is gonna try something. I can smell it like dogshit on a boot. Gimme your gun. Just in case he does try something."

Ray stood in front of Bernie, screening his friend as he pulled out the Glock and handed it over.

"You want the silencer?"

Ray shook his head. He glanced over one shoulder at the two departing men and quickly stuffed the weapon down the back of his jeans. "No need for it. Not out here."

"Watch your ass, then."

*Yeah*, Ray's expression said, and he jogged off.

He caught up with Morg and Wayne as they rounded a curve in the road. The three men disappeared behind the forested turn.

Bernie regarded the ruined tires with a sigh.

**5**

The road buckled and flattened, curved and straightened, as if they walked upon a snake's spine. Ray'd done his fair share of hiking during his teen years along the southern Avalon, mostly to escape the wrath and misery of his parents. And the city. In those weekend jaunts to parts unknown, he'd become familiar with several old trails, and developed a keen sense of distance as well as direction. He figured they'd almost walked the length of a soccer pitch, over terrain best suited for a quad or some similar all-terrain vehicle, or a pickup with plenty of clearance underneath. The brush and trees along the road pressed in at the edges and overhead, dense enough that the sun couldn't be seen, but Ray sensed that the trail was slowly, inexplicably turning back on itself, which seemed all weird to him. Several times he paused and looked around, attempting to establish his bearings, breathing in air so clean, so untainted, that to taste it was a gift.

Morg didn't speak much. The Pearsons' lieutenant huffed along, breathing through his mouth. Wayne followed, glancing back at Ray with a bully's annoying smile. Ray believed the man *had* been a crocodile in a past life, one that sunned himself on a sandy bank somewhere, basking in the heat, waiting for an easy meal.

A croc that eventually got shot in the head.

"Where is it?" Ray said, the trail finally confusing him.

"Gettin' tired, Ray?" Wayne asked.

"Fuck off."

Morg didn't answer. His blood dappled the road in wide,

damn-near perfect round inkblots, thick and heavy.

Ray was getting impatient. "Any idea, Morg?"

"There soon," the man grunted, as if wanting no part of the conversation. Ray didn't blame him.

The road eventually came to an end. The end of the tunnel could be seen and just beyond that, the corner of a brown cabin.

"There she is," Morg said and quickened his step. The others followed.

The three men entered a wide, carefully landscaped plot of land. A modern, two-story A-frame sat in the middle of the clearing, surrounded by a yellow mat of short-cut grass. Solar panels gleamed on the roof. Three plush chairs rested upon a deck that stretched the length of the cabin. A white door stood a few steps behind the chairs, while a large picture window granted a clear view of anyone arriving on the property. To the right of the dwelling, a net hammock drooped between two thick wooden posts. Ray wanted to climb aboard that netted slingshot as soon as he laid eyes on the thing. To the cabin's left was a well-used archery range, with a bull's-eye a little bigger than a manhole cover. A stack of old cardboard boxes that might have once contained refrigerators or some other big-ticket appliance was behind the target, to prevent any ill-aimed shafts from going into the woods. A work shed peeked from behind the north end of the house, as well as a brick structure that looked like a fire pit.

It was a beautiful spot for a home, and that's what it was. A second house, hidden in the wild. A secluded castle. Picturesque. Private.

"Not bad," Ray said for them all.

"I wanna move in," Wayne announced.

"Like a little fuckin' oasis," Morg grimaced. "See the hammock?"

"I want one of those," Ray said.

"Take it," Morg said. "String it up in your backyard."

"I live in an apartment."

"String it up in your living room then."

Ray resisted telling the goon to string his balls up in a living room.

"All right," Morg said, his voice nasal-sounding. "Let's get to work here."

"Gimme the crowbar," Wayne said, holding out a hand. "I'll break open the door."

"Aw, don't break any doors," Morg told him. "Leave that. We're stealing from these people, not destroying the place. We'll go around back and pry open a window."

"We're out in the fuckin' countryside here, Morg," Wayne pointed out. "This ain't downtown."

"Look," Morg said, dropping his hand from his bloody face. "With the flat tires, this job just became an overnighter, and I call dibs on the master bedroom. There's also fuckin' black bears around these parts, and we're not going to wreck a door when we can crawl in through a goddamn window. Got it?"

Wayne looked away, clearly not getting it or liking it.

"I got dibs on the second bedroom," Ray said, ignoring Wayne's twitching hand.

"Give him the crowbar," Morg ordered.

Ray relented, smacking the tool into Wayne's palm and hoping it stung.

They crossed the lawn someone had mowed one final time before the snow arrived. The A-frame towered overhead, casting a long, church-like shadow over the men.

Their boots clicked on the deck, and Morg stopped and admired the plush chairs not yet put away for the winter. The front door was a solid wooden slab and appeared capable of withstanding a battering ram, while drawn curtains concealed the interior.

"Take all day to get through that, anyway," Wayne observed, indicating the door. He grasped the brass knob and rattled it. "Window it is, then."

Wayne went around the corner and Morg followed. Ray tagged along, marveling at the cabin's structure. It truly was a castle.

"Shed's back here," Morg pointed, distracted from his injuries and sounding miserable. "Bet there's a key inside."

"Big one, too," Ray noted. "Bet there's three or four grand worth of tools in that thing."

"Definitely an overnight job. Bernie will have to take my car and find a second tire for the van."

Ray stopped beside Morg and together they watched Wayne put his face to a window set in the east wall, cupping his eyes to better see.

"Nice furniture," the big man said. "All quality shit. Flat-screen television. Stainless steel fridge. Lots of open space."

"Get around back," Morg ordered him.

Wayne backed away from the glass and considered both men with an expression that was a little too cool, as if he was thinking about swinging the crowbar. But then he withdrew and sauntered along the wall, running a flat palm against the wood's grain. The thieves turned the corner. The back door was another barrier that seemed better suited for a fortress—flat and featureless and made of metal.

The men stopped and stared at the beast.

"Now that's a door," Wayne deadpanned.

"That's a door," Ray agreed, seeing no knob or latch.

"The hell they get that?" Morg asked. "Off a vault or something?"

Wayne tapped the surface. "Steel."

"Who the hell puts a steel door on a cabin?" Morg wanted to know. "Shouldn't it be like a screen door or something? Let a breeze flow through the place in the summertime?"

"Maybe someone's got some secrets in there?" Wayne cocked an eyebrow. "We all have 'em."

*Some more fucked up than others*, Ray thought.

"What are you waitin' for?" Morg said, pointing at the smaller window nearby. "Get crackin'."

A frown creased Wayne's face before he turned away, just for a second, as if he was growing tired of being ordered around. The crowbar tapped the outer screen and Wayne placed his face against it, gazing in and all around.

"Well?" Morg asked.

"Kitchen sink's right there."

"Can you get in?"

"Oh yeah. Easy. The lock's right at the bottom."

"Get to it, then," Morg said, sounding as if his sinus cavity was on the verge of bursting.

Wayne dug the crowbar into the window's base and worked the tool, eliciting a bullfrog's grunt. He withdrew the bar, adjusted his grip, and stabbed the seam again, sinking the metal deeper. Splinters fell.

Ray glanced at Morg. The man looked paler than usual. "You okay?"

"I'm okay. Just need some painkillers is all. And a place to lie down. Maybe there's a bottle of something good in there."

"Maybe."

"Christ, Wayne," Morg snapped. "You still working on that thing? I thought you were better than this."

"You're in a hurry, are ya?" Wayne asked, not pleased with the critique.

"Yeah, I'm in a fuckin' hurry, in case you haven't noticed."

Wayne pulled back and studied Morg critically. Then, as if reaching a conclusion, he jabbed the crowbar through the screen and glass, puncturing both with a startled tinkle. He ripped away the mesh and raked the crowbar around the frame, sending glass fragments flying. Once complete, Wayne shot Morg an evil grin.

"You're going to patch that up," the lieutenant informed him. "And I mean good. I so much as feel a breeze on my ass later tonight I'll blame you. And lift that thing up."

Smirking, Wayne faced the window and picked at the inside lock. He lifted the broken frame just enough to get two fingers underneath.

"'Fraid you'll cut yourself crawling through?" Wayne asked.

"I'm not crawling through that," Morg muttered and looked to Ray. "You climb through."

"Me?" Ray whined back. "I'll fuck up my back going through that thing."

Morg rolled his eyes. "I can't do it. I'll pass out the moment my feet leave the ground."

"Ah, Morg."

"Don't fuckin' 'ah Morg' me. You squeeze your ass through that window and you open the door and you do it now. Holy shit I'm lightheaded just from the fuckin' conversation here."

Wayne beamed.

"The fuck you smilin' at, asshole?" Morg blasted.

Being called an asshole removed the smile from Wayne's face. He showed the two men his back and shoved the window up all the way. There was a click, a clatter of falling wood, and a flat metal sheet dropped from inside the frame, cleanly slicing Wayne's first two fingers off with a resounding *whump*.

Wayne screamed.

## 6

The big man staggered back from the sealed window, the stumps of his index and ring fingers spurting blood. A new and improved shriek ripped from him as he gripped his ruined hand, eyes threatening to pop from their cavities like cork guns.

"Jesus *Christ*," Morg blurted.

Wayne sunk to one knee and Morg crouched over him, vacillating on exactly how to help.

"Get in the house!" Morg shouted.

The order unfroze Ray. "Huh?"

"Smash out the picture window and get inside! We need something for his hand."

Ray tore his attention away from the dribbling stumps of Wayne's hand to the sealed window that had chomped Wayne's fat fingers off. He scanned the back of the house and, without another thought, snatched up the fallen crowbar. He rushed to the deck out front and stopped. Ray hesitated in front of the picture window, its heavy curtains drawn close, before he wound up with the crowbar. He smashed the glass, blowing shards inward and out in a storm of glitter. Ray doubled his efforts, wondering if a man could bleed to death from having his fingers lopped off. He destroyed the huge pane in seconds, clearing an opening large enough to step through. He shoved the curtains aside. Wide slices of light cut across a living room as he stumbled inside and sidestepped the furniture. Once in, he shot to the kitchen and stopped.

There, right above the sink, was the metallic sheet that

had dropped and chopped Wayne's pudgy meat hooks.

"Ray!" Morg shouted from outside.

Ray broke for the back door and stopped short when he saw the hardware store's display of bolts and locks, one on top of the other, from the bottom right side and straight up to the top. Dumbfounded, he got to work and started at the bottom. Aware of the time, he slapped open one lock after the other, pausing only to finesse a few that required a twist and a flick before sliding. Ray opened them all, counting a dozen all told, and by the time he finished his fingertips stung.

He pulled open the heavy door.

There, on his knees and in a wide slash of red, was Wayne, white-faced and snarling at his diced hand, squeezing the raw stubs of his fingers together while they continued to spritz like baby tomatoes hacked in halves. Morg pushed by Ray. The lieutenant made a frantic search of the kitchen before rushing toward a door and pulling it open. He darted inside and emerged a second later with a white towel. Not two frantic heartbeats later, Morg returned and bound the thick cloth around Wayne's crippling wound.

Wayne hissed at the contact, his face perhaps two shades whiter every ticking second, while sinewy cords threatening to uproot themselves from his neck.

"Hold that," Morg commanded him. "You hold that there. Clamp down on it and get inside."

"What?" Wayne ejected, spraying spit.

Morg didn't repeat himself. He pulled the man to his feet and into the kitchen, leaving red tracks on the floor.

Ray followed like a lost dog.

Morg stopped at the sink, gazing down at the pair of fleshy fingers that had no place being where they were. One finger had rolled into the drain and was stopped by a plastic trap. Despite the horror in the sink and his own wounds, Morg once again took command. He turned to a nearby dining table and yanked a chair free from it.

"Sit down," Morg instructed, pushing Wayne into the chair.

Ray hesitantly took stock of the hairy digits stewing in the sink and snarled with distaste.

"Watch out," Morg warned and pushed him aside again. The leader snatched up the two fingers and strode to the stainless steel refrigerator. He opened the freezer door, spied a full ice tray and packet. He dropped the fingers on the tray and slapped the packet on top, creating a gruesome sandwich even a bear would shy away from.

"All right," Morg said as he slammed the freezer door. "I got your fingers on ice, Wayne. I got 'em on ice. We'll look for a thermal bag and get everything to the car. We'll be on the road in fifteen minutes, be in Bonavista in thirty. Find a hospital and get a doctor."

"He can sew them back on?" Wayne sniffled and hitched, red-eyed and pitiful.

"He can sew them back on," Morg assured him. "You got a good two or three hours at least. Right, Ray?"

Ray blinked as if slapped. "Yeah."

But he wasn't concerned with Wayne anymore. The other windows had snatched his attention. Each one on the ground floor—with the exception of the living room—had a similar sheet of metal positioned above the frame, well out of sight. And truly, who the hell would notice such a thing?

"Holy shit," Ray whispered, inspecting an intricate set of wires and fat wooden pins concealed by thin curtains. He stepped to the nearest trap window to better study the simple mechanics, rigged to drop a flat panel of sharpened metal upon an unwary intruder. The fallen sheet in the kitchen showed the final results.

"Be careful, Ray," Morg warned.

"I'm not doing nothing," he answered, flicking his thumb across the sheet metal's razor edge. "Holy shit."

He could practically shave with the trap.

"You finished?" Morg asked.

Ray turned around. "They're all like this. All of them. Except the picture window."

"Mission's aborted, okay?"

"Huh?"

"Look, Wayne's a piece of shit but he needs a doctor. We're getting out of here."

The first red blots appeared through the towel around Wayne's hand. The sight of those colorful blooms made Ray swallow. His throat clicked. He nodded a second later.

As much as he loathed the guy, he needed medical attention. "Yeah. Okay."

"Check those drawers for a thermal bag or anything we can put his fingers in. And keep them pressed against the ice." Morg approached a closet to the left of the fridge.

"We're leaving?" Wayne asked.

"Soon as we can find something to carry your fingers in," Morg told him and turned the knob on the closet door.

As the door swung open, the three men heard a loud rubber twang, much like the snapping of an archer's bow. A crossbow bolt skewered Morg's left hip, dropping him in an instant. Morg rolled onto his back, grunting short, breathless *eeee, eeee* sounds as if attempting to lift an impossible weight. His hands quivered around the shaft's flights protruding from his hip. A singular vein popped out on his bulging forehead like a fat purple worm, right down the middle of the golf ball-sized welt Morg had sustained earlier.

As Ray stared in fascinated horror, that purple-hued vein actually flexed as if under extreme duress.

"*Ray!*" the Pearsons' lieutenant shrieked.

Morg was no longer concerned with Wayne's fingers.

The cry froze Ray to the spot as he took a moment to process the scene. Then he rushed to Morg's side, wary of the closet. He opened the door with a shy push, spotting the weird contraption that resembled a mash-up of a handheld crossbow and a spear gun. The weapon was empty, having unloaded its single shot into Morg's person.

Ray knelt beside the shaking man and couldn't think. Morg lay on his good side, angling his impaled hip to Ray's face. The arrow wiggled with every motion like one half of an insect's antennae. Morg squirmed violently while blood seeped through the denim of his jeans.

"What do I do?" Ray asked.

"Get a towel. Get a towel. From the bathroom. Over there," Morg blurted in agony, smashed lips drawn back to reveal the full extent of his remaining dental capacity. "*Hurry.*"

Ray rushed to the indicated bathroom, ignored the pleasant design and the glossy, walk-in shower. A collection of towels rested on a shelf and he grabbed all of them, thinking he'd seen movies where guys had bled to death from leg wounds. There was an artery in the leg, he realized, a *big* artery, and if it was punctured, Morg could be dead within a minute.

"Here," Ray said upon returning to Morg's stricken form. "I got the towels."

"Press it, press it around the shaft," he instructed.

Ray did. The white towels, they were *all* white, he realized, quickly turned red.

"Put pressure on it, put pressure on it," Morg gasped.

Ray pressed, drawing a hiss from his companion. Morg stretched out on the hardwood floor and softly yowled until he emptied his lungs.

"Now rip it out," he whispered urgently.

"What?"

"*Rip that cocksucker out.*"

"You could bleed to death."

"Not—*can't* bleed to death," Morg shook his head like a dog fresh out of a pool. "Can't happen. It's not, not in the meat, it's in the fuckin' joint. Right in the ball joint. Spiked in between."

"Should we leave it in there? I mean, isn't that what they say to do?"

"*Jesus,*" Morg swore, and, with a gritty display of will and strength, grabbed the shaft and yanked it out himself.

Except the shaft didn't come free.

Morg's hand slipped off the short arrow and he released a wheezy scream of pure agony. He lay back, panting, delirious from the effort, and attempted to draw his legs up to his stomach. That didn't work either.

Ray grabbed the blood-slicked shaft. He couldn't pull it loose. He placed another towel over what little the protruding bolt offered and couldn't maintain a grip.

"Shed," Morg whispered as his eyes narrowed. "Shhhhh…"

*The shed.* Ray saw that Morg wasn't going to be screaming for the next little while, so he looped a towel around his thigh, hiking it up and around the shaft as close as possible. He made a knot and pulled it tight, hoping that the tourniquet would work for a short time.

Ray stood and rushed outside, leaving Wayne to watch over the unconscious Morg.

Ray snatched the crowbar up from where Wayne had dropped it. A thick padlock greeted him at the shed's door, but he was operating in overdrive. He hammered the lock until it cracked and fell. Remembering the booby-trapped closet, he stepped out of the way of the door and flung it wide.

Nothing fired.

He peeked around the corner and saw nothing rigged to maim or kill. The interior appeared spotless. Dust free. An assortment of hand tools hung from a peg wall. Handsaws, hammers, nails, even a chainsaw. Five-kilogram sacks of limestone were stacked in a corner. Ray spotted a pair of heavy pliers. He grabbed them and ran.

Wayne had a sweaty, decidedly hopeful expression when Ray returned to the kitchen. Morg remained unconscious, all color drained from his cheeks.

"You find anything?" Wayne asked.

Ray ignored him and fastened the pliers onto the bolt's shaft. Morg moaned, squirmed. Ray took hold of the tool in both hands, adjusted his grip, and pulled.

The arrow came free in a bloody burst, but nothing resembling the geyser Ray had expected to see. He grabbed a nearby towel and pressed down on the wound, noting that the puncture was exactly where Morg had called it—right in the joint itself.

"You can tie that off?" Wayne asked, sounding groggy.

"Maybe." Ray left the towel and stretched out his last one. He tied it off in a second makeshift tourniquet and sat back, breathing hard.

"He gonna die?" Wayne asked.

"I dunno. I don't think so. Doesn't seem to be so much blood now."

"It's all over the floor."

And so it was. In his rush to help, Ray had missed how the blood, all warm and syrupy, had pooled around Morg's lower body and his own knees. He inspected his hands. Both looked like he'd just performed surgery.

"Wayne, I gotta go."

"Huh?"

"I gotta get back to Bern. Get him up here. I'll need help carrying Morg to his car. You can't do shit with that hand of yours."

"What?" Wayne said, not processing the information, his features pinched.

"Are you listenin' to me?"

"Yeah, sure."

Ray could see the man wasn't, however. He stood and went to the front door.

"Where you goin'?" Wayne nearly shrieked, his eyes revealing horror.

"Said I'm goin' to get Bern and bring him back here." Ray worked the locks.

"You're leaving us!"

"I'm not leavin' you, y'fuckin' moron, I'm gettin' Bern. Just watch Morg until we get back here."

Wayne rose from the chair and stuck his chin out. "You're fuckin leavin' us both behind, you piece of cowshit. I knew you were a dickless wonder from the very start. Swear to God above I'll—"

Ray didn't have time, didn't need Wayne's rants, and certainly didn't want the mounting pressure, so he punched the man in the gut, doubling Wayne over. He followed up with a punishing left to the head. The bigger man collapsed, dazed and sputtering.

Seeing Wayne doubling up in a sprawl left Ray shaking his head in anger. Striking the bastard down probably wasn't the smartest of moves, but given the situation and Ray's own potentially curt demeanor, it just came natural.

Knowing Wayne, however, payback would come at the worst possible time.

"Christ," Ray muttered and opened the door. *I'll be back*, he thought and ran outside. He sprinted across the front lawn as if he were fresh from a starter's gate in a hundred-meter dash. Once on the road, every footfall kicked up pebbles. Trees sped by and in short time, the adrenaline faded. Ray slowed to a jog, surprised his cardio had failed him so quickly, and chugged onwards. Images of Morg lying on the floor and a pissed-off Wayne Roberts filled his mind. What exactly had happened at the cabin? At least two elaborate traps had been waiting for them inside the weekend retreat. Who knew they were coming? Had they been set up? And if so, why?

Somehow, Ray found the energy to run faster.

The van came into view and he steamed toward it, arms pumping. At a glance, he couldn't see Bernie anywhere.

"Bern!" Ray slowed to a stop and placed a hand on the van's hood. Both tires remained flat. "Bern! Where are ya?"

No answer.

Gasping and not appreciating the dread rising inside his chest, Ray hurried to the van's rear. No Bernie. No Bernie snoozing inside the vehicle, either.

"*Bernie!*" Ray's voice cracked at the height of his scream. The stoic forest crowded in from the edges, barring light and encouraging shadows, a faceless entity that sought to smother the lost man. Ray whirled and scanned the dense thickets, his senses wired, seeing and hearing nothing and no one, verifying Bernie was indeed gone.

*The car.* Morg's car. Back on the road. That's where he'd gone. Bern had obviously needed something. Ray slapped the van's ass and moved on, renewed by his logic. He chugged along like an engine about to explode. His waning strength reduced him to short strides, and even those felt like he was slogging through deep snow. His chest stretched and heaved, his legs were slabs of lead. He reached the rope hanging across the lane and ducked under, grabbing the woven length and rattling the low-hanging sign.

"Bern!"

Morg's car came into view but nothing else.

"The fuck…" Ray coughed, standing at the mouth of the junction. He scanned the dense forest in every direction, then walked to the car and slapped his hands against the glass. Morg's ride was empty, the door unlocked. Ray pulled open the door and had one leg inside when he realized there was no way he could drive the thing around the van. Even worse, Morg still had his keys.

"The hell are you, man?" Ray stood and flapped his arms in frustration. He walked back to the rope, bracing his lower spine with his hands. Bernie might have gone for a leak or a dump, but Ray doubted it. His friend would've responded.

Feeling tendrils of desperation tightening around his vitals, Ray trudged past the sign and headed back to the cabin. The woods felt darker, even though there were still two hours of sunlight left to the afternoon. No sound permeated the dense fir wall, and that played upon Ray's mind. He stopped and listened, hearing only the flatlined drone in his eardrums. Sunlight retreated from the forest heights, escaping the scene as if knowing better, as if knowing it was wise to get to safety before dark. Ray wiped the sweat from his face and forced himself to walk faster along that twisted, dead snake spine of a country back road. He glanced over his shoulder with increasing frequency, recalling childhood ghost stories of haunted woods. Bern was out there somewhere but, for whatever reason, unable to answer. Ray scanned the thickets as he jogged back to the cabin, searching for clues and finding none.

An air of violation hung over the cabin, with its picture window smashed out and the door closed. Wayne must've been feeling the breeze from his own asshole. Ray dragged himself across the lawn, damn near exhausted, and plodded onto the deck. Boots clomped across the carefully fitted planks as he tried the door and found it locked.

Ray pressed his face against the wood. "It's me."

The curtains fluttered and a guarded Wayne peeked from the far side. "You came back."

"'Course I fuckin' came back. I said I would."

"Took you long enough."

"Open the door."

"Thought you bugged out," Wayne said. "You were gone fuckin' thirty minutes almost."

"Open the door or I'll climb in through the fuckin' window."

Wayne shut up and reluctantly did as told. He even closed the door once Ray was inside.

"Where's Bernie?"

"I dunno."

The cabin's interior had dimmed considerably, and Wayne looked even more like shit. His eyes were sunken with charcoal shading the bags underneath, leaving him resembling a person who'd just come off a weeklong chemical bender. He cradled his towel-swaddled hand, the fabric wet and splotched. Wayne looked a little crazy, perhaps from the blood loss and definitely from losing a pair of fingers. Ray very much didn't want to have to deal with him.

"Whaddaya mean you dunno?" Wayne demanded, mouth hanging open and poised to bite.

"He wasn't at the van."

"He's at the car, then."

"He's not there either. I checked."

"You look around?"

"Course I looked around. He's *gone*."

"Well, where the *fuck* is he?" Wayne seethed.

"I said I don't *know*," Ray shouted in return. "Maybe he went for a shit in the bushes and planted his ass crack over a bear trap or something. Or a lynx snapped him one across the ball sack in mid-squat and left him unconscious. He's not out there. Nowhere in fucking sight."

"Hey."

The whisper quieted both men. They turned to see Morg lifting a bloody hand. A set of keys rested upon his palm.

"Get me to my feet," the Pearsons' lieutenant groaned. "Give me an extra shoulder and I'll walk out."

Ray and Wayne exchanged dubious looks. Spread out in a congealed puddle of his own morbid juices, with his earlier facial wounds fully in bloom and his forehead's contusion swollen to epic proportions, Morg looked as if God had heel-stomped him into the dirt like a finished cigarette.

"You sure?" Ray asked.

Grimacing, Morg forced himself to a sitting position.

The very effort probably caused more bleeding.

Ray went to the fallen man and helped Morg stand. The battered leader clutched Ray around his neck and at one point, threatened to choke the last few grains of energy from him.

"All right," Morg groaned. "Wayne. Get your fingers outta the freezer. We walk outta here."

"Don't we need a bag?"

"Wrap them up in a towel with the ice."

"Oh, okay, yeah. Sure, sure." Wayne was all for leaving.

"You okay, man?" Ray asked the battered man hanging off his shoulder.

"Nah. Whole leg's fucked up. Hip is screaming. So's my face."

'Could've been worse."

"Yeah, could've been my pecker, right?"

Ray smiled. "Can you walk for fifteen?"

"I'll limp for thirty," Morg groaned. "As long as we get to a hospital. Don't worry about Bern. He'll show up along the way."

Ray wasn't as confident.

"Got 'em," Wayne said, holding up a dish towel that resembled a checkered picnic bag.

"Get on ahead," Morg ordered as they gathered at the front door. "And don't rush me. All right. Let's boot 'er."

Wayne took hold of the knob and shot a quick, menacing glare in Ray's direction, which he understood without fail. Wayne was going to stay on the team for now, but he and Ray would eventually have words for the earlier cheap shot. Ray had no doubt of that.

The big enforcer pulled the door open.

He stuck his head out and an arrow split the air like a

low-flying jet, sinking into the wooden frame with a loud *whack*, just inches away from Wayne's face. He jumped as if an exceptionally hot poker had been shoved up his ass and fused it shut.

"Jesus *Christ!*" Wayne shouted and slammed the door shut, crashing into the two men behind him and tipping them over. Ray fell with a grunt and took Morg with him.

Another arrow *twacked* into the cabin's clapboard hide, placed near the first shot.

"The fuck was that?" Ray groaned as Wayne's size-twelve boots clattered past his head, sending vibrations through the floor.

"Someone's shootin' at us!" Wayne wailed back.

# 7

Someone *was* shooting at them.

Ray untangled himself from the heap called Morg and pushed himself up, his back against the dining room wall. Wayne hunkered down in a corner of the cabin, below a smaller window.

"I didn't hear a shot," Ray said.

"It was a fuckin' arrow!" Wayne blurted. "A fuckin' arrow nearly took my eye."

Ray gawked at the outburst before focusing upon Morg, who remained in the middle of the floor, on his back and staring at the ceiling.

"You okay?" Ray asked him.

"No."

"Stay down then."

That got a wry frown from the man.

Wayne hoisted himself to the windowsill and peeked out at the distant tree line, breathing into the stylish wood paneling of the cabin's interior.

"See anything?" Ray asked.

Wayne ignored him, eyes flickering left and right. He finally dropped to the floor, cradling his wounded hand and picnic bag of digits. "Can't see anything out there."

"Nothing?"

"There's no one out there. Must be in the trees."

Ray refrained from his initial caustic reply and decided to take a look for himself. He got to his knees and inched his line of vision around the windowsill. A yellow lawn came into view, then the distant road, a dense wall of trees, and nothing else. Ray studied the picture before him and couldn't see anything out of the ordinary.

"He's in the trees," Wayne hissed through clenched teeth, back to the wall and gripping his crippled hand.

"Yeah," Ray said and lowered his head. "Yeah."

"Problem out there?" Morg croaked.

"Some fucktard thinks he's Robin fuckin' Hood."

The weary expulsion of breath summed up what Morg thought about that. "We can't… stay here."

"This is bullshit," Wayne declared and stood. He walked to the door and hesitated before wrenching it open and sticking his head out.

Ray heard the arrow that time, the unmistakable speeding sizzle of a pointed shaft a second before it cracked into the door's frame.

Wayne jerked his head back to safety and slammed the door, bracing it with his back.

"Can't believe this," the goon said. "Someone's shootin' arrows at us."

"Must be the owner," Ray said.

"Don't care who it is, but I'll fuckin' break his spine if I get my hands on him."

"Where's the shots coming from?" Morg asked.

"I didn't see."

"Okay," Morg said, the pain thick in his voice. "This is what you're going to do. Try going outside again, Wayne—"

"Fuckin' Ray can stick his ripe ass out there," Wayne said and stepped away from the door.

There was an anxious gap in the conversation, and Ray realized Morg was waiting for him to respond.

"Yeah, sure. Watch out." Ray stepped by the bigger man and barely brushed shoulders.

Wayne still shoved him back three steps. "Watch where you're fuckin' goin'."

"Hey!" Morg shouted, glaring at the pair. "Knock it off or by Christ you'll never work for the Twins again."

Resembling a hateful ghost, Wayne backed off and Ray let his breath out.

"Ray, when you're ready," Morg struggled, "Stick your face. Out there. And Wayne? You look. See where the shot's comin' from. Got it?"

Nods from both men.

"Then do it."

Determined, Ray gripped the knob and took a mind-clearing breath. He yanked the door open and, as ordered, stuck his face out into the line of fire. The cold air sobered him, questioned the wisdom of his act. A solid barrier of trees stood firm at the lawn's edge. His pulse rate frenzied and his temples throbbed from the sudden pressure. He fixed on one spot, remembering something about how his peripheral vision could pick up movement faster than actively searching for it.

The arrow flew from the forest wall on the right, directly at Ray's profile, and he had a split second before his mind yanked his skull back inside the cabin. The arrow missed his nose by a crusty whisker, smacked into the door, and bounced off, landing with a clatter upon the deck.

Ray slammed the door shut and placed his shoulder against it. A smirking Wayne locked gazes with him, and that instant of scorn, coupled with being shot at, triggered something inside Ray. His anger spiked as it occasionally did at stressful times, lancing through his self-control. He reached around his back and pulled free the Glock, cocked it, and with a very real intent to do damage, pulled the door open. Ray stuck half his body outside and fired five shots at the woods, targeting the area of the archer. Spent casings fell to the deck. The gunshots sounded like howitzers. Wayne crouched, no longing smirking. Morg held his breath, suddenly very much attentive.

Ray stopped shooting and stood there, using the doorway as partial cover, his right arm extended like a killer wand.

No one returned fire.

"That's what I thought, fucker!" Ray shouted at the woods and whipped the door shut.

The men inside were speechless, stunned by the Glock's voice. The way in which Wayne's face fell in surprise was a thing of rare beauty. Ray wished he had a camera.

"Wasn't expectin' this, was ya, cocky?" Ray said, waving the weapon. The snap of metal seemed very loud inside the cabin.

"The fuck you get that?" Wayne asked in wary wonder.

"The fuck *did* you get that?" echoed an equally surprised Morg.

"From Bern. Back at the van."

"That's Bern's gun?" Wayne asked in dismay.

"Bernie," Morg released his breath in an amused hiss.

"He even got a silencer for it," Ray informed them.

Morg chuckled darkly. "Probably thought the thing would go pew-pew."

"You had a gun all this time and didn't think until now to get it out?" Wayne demanded.

"Yeah."

"That's smart, shit-for-brains."

Ray's expression hardened. He assumed a gunslinger's stance toward the larger man and sent him a cold expression of *Don't fuck with me.*

Wayne swallowed, even more uneasy, and drew back just an inch.

"Yeah," Ray said quietly. "Thought so."

Morg groaned as he sat up from the floor. "All right. You see the guy you were shooting at?"

"Saw shit," Ray reported, keeping his eyes on Wayne. "Came from the right. I know where the bastard is. Bet it's one guy, too. If he's still there. Wasn't expecting this."

He held up the gun.

"Wonderful," Morg said softly. "That's good news. Good news."

"I got better news," Ray said, noticing the resentful frown on Wayne's face. "That prick out there didn't bother firing back. That tells me whoever it was is probably running through the woods like a bear with its balls on fire."

"We're good to get outta here?" Wayne brightened.

"I think so."

"Help me up," Morg asked.

Ray looked to Wayne and flicked the gun in the lieutenant's direction.

Wayne hesitated, not impressed with the unexpected shift in power inside the cabin, and reluctantly went to Morg's aid.

"How many shots you got in that thing?" Morg asked. Wayne helped him to stand.

Ray didn't know. Instead he said, "A dozen or so."

"You don't know?"

This clearly perked Wayne's interest.

"Not really, no."

"You gotta check."

"I'll check later," Ray said, daring Wayne to comment with a hard look.

Morg picked upon the untrustworthy vibe. "All right. Later then. You let off four or five shots. Those things carry about fifteen or so, so if it was fully loaded you got ten left."

"All I need to put the fear of God into someone," Ray said, directing it at Wayne. The big man glowered.

"All right, let's be civil here," Morg said. "I'm bleeding too damn much to have you two slapping each other's nut sacks. Let's get…"

The lieutenant stopped talking and took a deep breath. "Blackin' out here."

He fell against Wayne, who caught him and clumsily lowered him to the floor.

Ray's stomach knotted. "You okay, Morg? Morg?"

Morg didn't answer.

Wayne waved a hand over Morg's closing eyes, seeking a reaction of some kind and getting nothing.

"Blood loss," Ray concluded and went to the door. He locked it and took position next to the far corner of the picture window.

"What do we do?" Wayne asked, favoring his hand.

"We can't carry him."

"You could."

"And take my eyes offa you?" Ray smiled. "You'd like that, wouldn't ya?"

"Fuck you."

"No, fuck you. Maybe you should carry him."

In answer, Wayne held up the bloody swaddling around his hand.

Ray didn't force the point. "We wait, then." He pulled back the curtain a crack and studied the far side of the tree line.

Wayne considered his bag of fingers.

Ray didn't like the gears turning over in the freak's head. "Put that back into the freezer."

"Every minute we wait is one lost," Wayne said, not moving.

"Try and wake him up."

Wayne studied Morg's face and, seconds later, slapped it. Twice. The second open palm harder than the first.

"I said wake him, not fuck him up."

"You see anything out there?"

Ray checked. "Nothin'. All clear."

"Oh shit," Wayne said with dawning terror. "The cops. The cops could be on their way. The fucking cops could be on their way *here*."

"Yeah," Ray acknowledged. The asshole had a point. "Makes sense. If someone's shooting pointy sticks at us, chances are they called the cops."

"We gotta go *now*."

"We ain't going anywhere without him," Ray nodded in Morg's direction. "And Bern."

The cogs and gear shafts kept turning over in Wayne's cold machine of a mind. Ray could see the process happening.

"The cops could already have that shitbag," Wayne pointed out. "Think about it. How come he didn't answer you already? Why ain't he here? Or maybe the same person caught him and got him tied up somewhere while calling the cops?"

The thing was, Wayne was making some sense of the situation, but Ray found his attention wavering, flickering to the traps protecting the house.

"We gotta get going, dude."

"Shut up and give me a second to think here."

"Listen," Wayne said, leaning toward him. "I ain't staying here for the cops to show. I got a record long enough that the courts will put me away for a few years this time. I don't wanna *do* a few years in a cage. Morg's got nothing. I bet you got nothing. All you got is that gun, which I bet is illegal. They find you with that and they won't be pleased. All they got on Morg is a B and E and intent to steal. That's all. That's a slap across the ass and no supper, for Christ's sake. He won't be pissed if we boot it. He'd do the same if it was me."

"Guaranteed," Ray agreed, but Wayne had hit a nerve about the gun. Ray's resolve wavered.

"Let's go, then."

Ray looked to Morg, thought about Bernie, and considered the unknown spearchucker in the woods would no doubt be calling in the authorities if they hadn't already. Wayne's proposed course of action had appeal, but the cabin—the traps in the cabin. Why would someone *do* such a thing?

Wayne wouldn't let Ray think the matter through. "I'm goin'."

He went to the door.

Ray pointed the gun at the big man's head. The action halted the Pearsons' enforcer.

"You ain't gonna shoot me," Wayne smiled that greasy smile of his, made even more smug by his pale complexion.

"What day is it? Tuesday?" Ray shrugged. "Can't think of a better way to start the week."

"You shoot and that's discharging a weapon. You ain't gonna kill me. Anything you do will just put you in prison that much longer."

Ray lowered his sights, took aim at Wayne's leg. "Ever wonder how much a blown-out knee hurts? I hear it's pretty bad. Never the same once it's fixed. Your walk's all fucked up."

The enforcer's bluster wavered around the edges. "You... you better not."

"Oh I better not, now? That's it? Well, I just fucking might. You know something, Wayne? Go. Just fuckin' get outta here. 'Cause with you gone I can get some quality thinking done. The place'll sure as shit smell better anyway. So go."

The two men stared off, but Wayne was clearly thinking of doing just that. "You better not shoot me."

"*Go!*" Ray roared, and Wayne opened the door and got halfway out before freezing in place.

Ray was about to shout again but Wayne's wide-eyed profile stopped him. Instead, Ray put his back to the wall, reached for the curtain, and opened it a crack.

He saw the object of Wayne's fixation.

Saw what had become of Bernie.

And realized, with the same cold horror of a sailor lost at sea, floating in a rolling, unstable plane of frigid vastness, just as the first dorsal fin breaks the water, that there was a very good chance that he was not going to make it out alive. That things had become very, very bad, indeed.

Wayne took a step back from the open doorway and Ray didn't blame him in the least. Wayne wasn't upon Ray's mind at all. Nor was the possibility of a police presence, because the police would not have killed Bernie and chopped off his head. The police would not have stuck Bernie's head on a pole and placed it right at the mouth of the cabin's driveway, like a portent to war, a war where no mercy or quarter would be given.

## 8

Ray stared at his dead friend's expression, saw the way the skull listed to one side but still managed to not topple over. Whoever had stuck Bern's head on the pole had stuck it deep, and driven the other end even deeper into the cold earth. The body was nowhere in sight.

At that exact moment in time, Ray knew there would be no police on their way to the cabin. He knew that he and Morg and goddamn Wayne were very much on their own.

The slamming of the cabin door startled Ray and he released the curtain.

Wayne secured whatever locks were available and then put his back to the entrance, searching the cabin's interior for an explanation for what he'd just seen at the edge of the front lawn.

"Oh…" he started but couldn't finish.

Ray knew how he felt.

"I don't think the cops are coming," Wayne whispered.

"I don't think they are either."

"Oh shit."

"Someone wants us dead," Ray said quietly, tapping his thigh with the Glock.

"Why?"

"Well, if it was just you, I'd understand, but Bern never did anything serious to anyone. I mean, not to… not to justify *that*. He only stole *cars*, for Christ's sake."

Wayne chanced a look out the dining room window, shook his head, and jerked the curtains closed, paying heed to the edged finger-chopper mounted above the frame. The light in the cabin dimmed further.

"What do we do?" Wayne asked, worry frosting over his usually bossy tone.

"I'm thinking," Ray answered. It was a long run across the open lawn, then the cover of the trees, all the way to the road. He considered using the table as a shield, but even then it would mean having Wayne carry it, who Ray trusted as much as a rabid dog around a chicken barbecue.

"That's in-fuckin'-sane," Wayne said. "They hacked his head off. That's so fuckin' insane."

*Bern.* Ray inhaled sharply and pinched the bridge of his nose.

"We gotta get outta here," Wayne said.

"Yeah."

"We gotta get outta here *now.*"

"Then go if you're in that much of a hurry."

Wayne relented. "Fuck that," he said and winced over the state of his mutilated hand.

Ray peeked out again, scouring the tree line. "How many you think are out there?"

"I dunno."

"Well then, think. There's at least one. Maybe two?"

"Maybe."

"I think only one guy was shooting arrows at us."

"That's enough."

Ray sighed. Why couldn't it have been Wayne's skull decorating the front lawn? "All right, this is what I'm gonna do. We don't know how many are out there, so we wait for night. Only an hour or so away. We wait and when it's dark, we carry Morg out to his car and get the hell out of here."

Wayne looked at the shadowy lump occupying the center of the floor. "He even alive?"

"I'm alive," Morg whispered weakly.

"Thought you were dead," Wayne grumbled.

"Yeah."

"You know about Bern?" Ray asked.

"A little. He's dead?"

"Yeah." Ray described the sight posted at the edge of the clearing.

"Sorry, Bern," Morg said with sympathy. The recap brought on a moment's silence, then, "All right, I'm for waiting till it's dark."

"We got the gun," Wayne said.

"I got the gun," Ray clarified. "But nothing to shoot at."

"Maybe…" Morg took a deep, weary breath. "Maybe that's why no one's come a'knocking. They know you have a gun. They know."

"So?" Wayne asked.

Morg swallowed, his throat clicking loudly in the cabin. "They might be waitin' for dark, too."

That revelation twisted Ray's stomach, wringing all the heat from his limbs.

"Boys," Morg said, "we're under siege."

Ray fingered the curtain, pulling it back just a sliver, and scanned the front of the cabin.

"Awfully quiet out there."

"They're waiting for us," Wayne suggested. "Waitin' for us to show our heads. Maybe shoot them off."

"Be a real shame," Ray muttered and earned an evil look.

"This is what we're gonna do," Morg said and dragged himself to a wall. He pushed off with one sneaker and his hands, leaving a shiny, wet outline on the floor. He shoved away a magazine stand and propped himself up just below the flat-screen TV. Once done, he took a few seconds to compose himself.

"Wayne, you move that table over to the picture window. Block it so that anyone coming through the curtains will flip over it. Then you take a look around the cabin. See what else is around. If you open any closets, make sure you're standing behind the door. Got it?"

Wayne nodded.

"How's the hand?" Morg asked.

"Stings."

"We might not get to a hospital until later."

That distressed the big man. "What? What do you mean?"

"You heard me."

"What about my fingers?"

"Put them back in the freezer. We'll take them when we leave."

"They'll keep for that long?"

"Sure," Morg said. "Just keep them on ice. And don't forget them. Now get going."

Wayne hesitated, thinking alien thoughts. Then he walked into the kitchen and tenderly placed his makeshift picnic bag into the fridge's freezer. Once done, he flipped the dining room table with a clatter and centered it against the broken picture window.

Ray watched him the whole time.

When Wayne climbed the stairs, Ray and Morg shared a look that spoke volumes about trusting their companion in their current situation.

"What do you want me to do?"

"Keep watch out front," Morg said. "Wayne can check the back when he comes back down."

They could hear the Pearsons' enforcer clomp and bang from one room to the other upstairs, sounding like an elephant trying to squeeze its ass into a closet. Ray looked to the ceiling and shook his head. Morg agreed with a long sigh.

Something slapped the cabin's south wall, the one facing the road, causing Ray to damn-near shit his drawers. He fumbled at the curtains and pulled the edge back a bit, while upstairs Wayne stomped across the ceiling.

An arrow lay on the deck. The missile had bounced off the cabin's hide.

Another slammed into the east wall.

A third punched into the metal sheet that had severed Wayne's fingers, the tinny clang as loud as crashing cymbals.

From there on, a growing, rhythmic storm battered the cabin, pausing only long enough to draw another bead on the structure and loose a fresh arrow. Some of the missiles rebounded off the clapboard, while others stuck firm. One arrow sliced through the picture window curtains with all the dramatic flutter of a magician's cape before twanging off the staircase and falling to the steps.

"Jesus Christ," Ray swore, deep into a crouch and gun raised to his ear. He flinched at every blow.

"Keep your head down," Morg said in between the impacts. "Get your back to a wall."

Ray placed himself in the southwest corner, wedged between the wall and the sofa. Morg remained sitting, head slightly arched back as if offering his throat and appearing oddly at ease.

"You all right, Morg?"

That got a smile from the leader. His marble-black eyes twinkled with cadaverous mirth.

Something heavy bashed against the west wall. The wood shivered hard enough for Ray to feel the vibration straight through his heart. There was another boulder-like slam, followed by another, distracting the men from the minor pops of the arrows. There were no windows in the west wall, and blow after blow thundered through, as if an angry giant had taken to baseball pitching cinder blocks into the clapboard. An incredulous Ray thought someone was trying to smash a hole into the living room. In a vain attempt to reinforce the wall, he splayed a hand across the panel wood and felt it tremble.

Seconds later, the pounding against the west wall ceased. The arrows stopped soon after, like corn tired of popping.

Silence ensued.

But just before all became still, Ray heard a harsh, wheezy laugh, one that quickly faded into nothing, quick enough to make him doubt ever hearing it.

"The fuck was all that?" he wanted to know.

"Shhh," Morg said and listened, the pinpricks of light within his eyes eerie.

Ray did as told, licking his lips. They waited, listening, wondering what might come next. No other attack commenced. No one attempted to breach the cabin. The world outside returned to some semblance of normal.

If you forgot about Bern's head.

"That…" Morg said quietly, "was a message."

"Yeah? What?"

"There's at least three shooters out there now. And one fucked-up drummer. And they're all ready for a fight."

"They can't have many arrows left," Ray noted. "They must've fired off half a forest's worth."

"Sounded like that, didn't it."

"Maybe they're reloading or something?"

They listened, bracing themselves for a second round.

"Anyone creeping up on us?" Morg asked after long moments of nothing.

"You want me to look?"

"Please."

A wry frown hitched up half of Ray's face as he drew back the curtain. The daylight was weaker, the shadows deeper. The once peaceful setting was no longer inviting but increasingly sinister. He widened his field of vision, leaning left and right, scanning the tree line for activity and seeing nothing.

"No?" Morg asked.

"Not a damn thing."

Morg checked the seeping wound on his hip, lifting the towel there before reapplying pressure. "Should've left the arrow in. Listen. Keep an eye on the front lawn. Stay quiet. Maybe we can lure one or two of them out of the bush. Enough for you to get a shot off."

Ray liked that idea.

They waited. Ray counted off the seconds while holding on to the gun like a holy crucifix.

"*What do you assholes want?*" Wayne roared from upstairs, breaking the stillness. "*You want us out of here? We'll walk! No problem! None of us will say a word about Bern. Man was a dick, anyway.*"

Ray turtled his head. Morg dropped his chin and released another weary sigh.

"Well, shit," Ray muttered.

"Get up there and shut him up," Morg said. "Shoot him if you got to."

With one hand on the panel wood banister, Ray took the stairs two at a time. He turned right, looked into a bedroom and saw Wayne with his back to the wall, standing to the left of a window which didn't have a security guillotine fixed above it.

"Wha?" a tensed Wayne asked.

"Get downstairs," Ray ordered, stepping inside the room. He walked to the opposite side of the queen-sized bed. "And shut up."

"Just throwing it out there. You never know, they might go for it."

"No one's goin' for anything, you fuckin' idiot. Get your ass below and don't be shouting out to them."

Wayne didn't move. "I'm gettin' tired of you, little man."

"Yeah? You mean this little man with the gun? 'Cause he's getting tired of you."

Whatever might've been on Wayne's mind didn't come forth; instead, he screwed up his lips as if sucking hard on a lemon's ass and walked out of the room. Ray held the gun at his thigh in case the guy tried anything. He even waited until Wayne was halfway down the steps before following.

"Morg," Wayne greeted at the base of the staircase.

"Wayne."

"Was only tryin' to talk to them."

"Shut the fuck up, Wayne. The plan is to stay quiet and wait," Morg said.

Ray descended and stopped on the landing, eyeing the goon.

"So we hold up till dark, that it?" Wayne asked.

"Yup."

"I don't like it."

"I don't care," Morg said. "Now go check on the back door. Make sure it's all locked. By the way, was there a window in the west wall upstairs?"

"What west wall?" Wayne asked.

Morg pointed.

"Ah, no."

"All right, once you're done with the door, come back here and plant yourself by the dining room window. See if anyone tries to sneak up here. We can't see what happens at the west wall, so we'll have to cover the ones we can see."

"What do you think they'll try?" Ray asked, appreciating Morg more and more.

"I don't know," the Pearsons' lieutenant replied. "But they're up to something. Guaranteed. Someone's way too prepared for all this shit."

"We could make a run for it," Wayne ventured.

"There's three or more shooters out there," Morg pointed out. "And even if you leave me behind, chances are they'd stick you eventually."

"We wouldn't leave you behind," Ray said and meant it.

"I know you wouldn't," Morg directed at him.

A sullen Wayne marched off for the back door. Ray took up position in his corner and drew the curtain back a crack. He figured Morg was right.

Whoever they were, they were up to something.

*

Wayne stopped by the back door and placed his forehead against the surface, drawing a refreshing comfort from the cold. His hand ached dearly, and he didn't like being talked to like a moron, especially not from a little shit like Ray fuck-chops Piper. Little man who thought himself top-dog because he had a gun. A *gun*. If Wayne saw the chance, he'd take that equalizer away and stick it up Ray's ass.

A deep throbbing from his mutilated hand distracted him. Who the hell put traps around their windows? There had to be a law against that shit. Wayne took the pain and again thought of Ray as far back as the morning, when he and Bern both were being pretty brave. There was nothing more aggravating to a man of Wayne's size than a pair of little men yapping at him. He had to admit, fessing up to the kidnapping wasn't the brightest thing he'd ever done. Not around those two. And not around Morg.

Word would get back to the Testicle Twins, no doubt about that.

Morg. The condescending bastard wasn't fooling Wayne. Hanging around the cabin into the night lessened the chances of Wayne's fingers ever being sewn back on. Wayne couldn't see himself attaching his little toes atop the stumps. That shit would just look too weird for the ladies.

With a finger tapping a sliding bolt lock, Wayne made up his mind. It was easy. Get rid of the loose ends, as cliché as it sounded.

He was going to get that gun off Ray first chance he got.

Then he'd put two rounds into the prick's face. He'd put another round into Morg, to ease his suffering but also for bossing Wayne around. With those two gone, things would become a lot easier around the cabin and a shitload less stressful.

Once the baggage was taken care of, Wayne intended to retrieve his severed fingers and get the hell out of this shithole.

# 9

The room darkened as the last sliver of sun departed. A few strands of light retreated across the front lawn like long shards of gold being swallowed up into the woods. Morg's breathing deepened, his mouth gummy. Every time he shifted his tongue, Ray could hear it. A semi-wet, mucus-soaked smacking that picked at his nerves. Wayne was the exact opposite. He stood in the southeast corner, tall and brooding, his white face an eerie beacon atop a column of deepening shadow, a reaper just waiting for the best time to strike.

Ray looked over at the enforcer every so often. Sometimes, Wayne would glance away. Sometimes, he would stare back.

Ray preferred it when he looked away.

"This is so fucked up," Morg whispered, but in that growing, bitter silence, his voice seemed to come across at full volume. "Who are these people? Who…who puts up razor blade choppers in the windows and crossbows in closets?"

"Someone watched too many horror movies," Ray added.

"Or someone is just wingnut crazy," Wayne offered.

*Spoken by a crazy wingnut*, Ray thought and gripped the gun a little tighter.

"They ain't crazy," Morg declared. "Not crazy at all. Someone planned all this shit. Probably more than we'll ever know. They knew what they were doing. Question I wanna ask is why? Why all this?"

"Some people's children," Ray offered, but knew that

wasn't going to satisfy Morg's curiosity.

"That's only part of it. Y'know, I've been breakin' into properties for over ten years. Never went into a place I didn't scope out first. Always had an idea of what I might find inside. Never went in blind. Always tried to be as prepared as possible. But there were a few places that made me think... well... that I should just drop the knife and back away, just get out, because I went somewhere I didn't belong. Somewhere no one in their right mind would want to be, and if you *were* there, chances were you weren't a guest, you were a captive. A fuckin' prisoner. I remember this one place over on the Hill. Looked like an ordinary town house on the outside. Nice curtains, kept up well. Knew the guy who owned it had a dance club down on Duckworth. Wasn't his main residence but he went there at times. Like a ladies' pad, right?"

Morg stopped then and winced, either in pain or at the memory.

"Yeah? And?" Ray asked.

"Sorry. Had a moment."

"You okay?"

"Yeah. Just thirsty is all."

That prompted Wayne to leave his post to search the kitchen.

"Anyway, me and Jimmy Fraser were in the guy's club and overheard he'd gone out to Spaniard's Bay for the weekend. Chance favors the prepared, or some shit like that, so Jim and me finished our beers and hit the road. A little after midnight, we were knifin' into the guy's back door. Clipping chains with the bolt cutters. Easy, right? We found a shitload of stuff from the main floor and upstairs. Computers, televisions, you name it. The big ticket? A hockey card collection probably worth thousands of dollars. You name the player and he had the rookie card. Jim and I actually considered leavin' all the electronics just because the cards were worth it. Anyway, before we left the place Jim was leanin' up against the stairs and a fuckin' section of the wall came away. An honest-to-God secret passage that led out to the other town house. You get what I'm sayin'? That one wasn't so pretty. That one… was freaky."

Morg paused and even Wayne was listening intently.

"Not sure what or who the owner was into, you understand. Might not even belong to him. We had no idea. All we knew was that we'd walked into something… weird."

"What?" Ray asked.

"The place it opened up into was like a mosh pit. An empty mosh pit, but classy. Upscale. The whole level was cleared away and there was a wrought-iron staircase leading up to the second floor. There was a bar set against one wall, like where the livin' room would be, and three months later after we drove by there, I noticed that the windows there weren't clear but—but the stuff beyond the window didn't seem right. Anyway, there was a bar set against that wall with bottles and shit stacked as high as a pipe organ, all a glitter under our flashlights."

"Nothin' weird about that," Wayne said and moved to the kitchen.

"What was weird was the walls. All painted in paint that was reflective, like a black light or something. And there was a stage, with a bed or a massage table on it, and these shackles at the head and base. But what really spooked us out was the basement."

"There was a basement?" Ray asked.

"An open door to a basement."

"How big was this place?"

"That's just it. It was *huge*. And the open door led to a downstairs landing, right. We just stood at the top and looked down. There was light down there. And there were people. We couldn't see them but we could hear them. Chanting, as God is my witness. Chantin' away. Not that I could understand what was being said, but I figure there were a good twenty or so voices. And the air smelled all wrong. Spicy. We were gettin' buzzed just standin' there. And while we were there, a shadow started comin' up the stair from below."

At that point Morg swallowed thickly and his jaw twitched.

"And?" Ray asked.

"It wasn't a person, Ray. It wasn't a person."

"It was a shadow, man. Could've been anything."

"That's what we told ourselves, but you see, there was a good twenty steps to the landing, right? The wall's all concrete with wooden beams acting like pillars. No banister. We waited to see what it was when these long fingers reached around the corner and fastened onto it. Right at the height of the chantin'. Long fingers, like they'd been stretched somehow. With... with black fingernails that looked like talons."

Morg swallowed, the smacking even louder in Ray's ears.

"Anyway," Morg said, "we got out of there before we saw the rest of that thing. Left the door open and ran out the back. It came after us, see, and I can still hear the footfalls coming up from the basement, or whatever that place was."

Morg paused, gathering strength. "We didn't take the hockey cards. Or anything. Left it all there. Jumped a few fences and drove away. Never looked back."

"You didn't take the cards?" Wayne shook his head. "Why the fuck didn't you take the cards? Dude, you probably had a fortune there."

"Yeah," the Pearsons' lieutenant nodded. "Probably. Except I wasn't about to steal anything from a bunch of freaks, you understand? A bar owner, sure. A fuckin' cult? No way. That's a kind of crazy I don't need. You'd have been looking over your shoulder everywhere, twenty-four seven."

"They didn't come after you?" Ray asked.

"Nah. But…" Morg smiled weakly. "There have been times when… when I think I'm being followed. Or there are two or three people hanging around the front of my house at three or four o'clock in the morning, watching my windows. I've moved seven times over the past six years. They've found me every time. Now? I live in an RV. Hook the car up to the back and move everything once a month or until I get that feeling."

"Jesus, Morg," Ray whispered.

"Bullshit," Wayne said gruffly, believing none of it.

But Morg didn't reply.

Wayne shook himself like a great, meaty vulture ruffling its feathers. With a guarded glance in Ray's direction, he went to the fridge.

"Where you goin'?" Ray asked.

"Where does it look like? I'm checkin' out the fridge. See if there's anything to drink."

Ray watched him with suspicious eyes.

Wayne stopped before the stainless steel fridge and pulled it open, the resulting light purifying him. His stern face brightened at the contents and he pulled out a bottle of beer.

"That beer?" Ray asked.

"Yeah."

Morg turned his head.

"Some leftovers in plastic containers, too," Wayne informed them before studying the bottle's label. He tried to twist the cap free, failed, and placed the bottle at an angle at the countertop's edge. One palm swat later, the cap popped free and Wayne drank.

He drank hard, downing the bottle in one breath.

"That's good," he whispered through clenched teeth. "Real good."

"Bring me one," Morg said.

"That okay, warden?" Wayne asked with a saucy air, eying Ray.

"Go ahead," Ray answered. He'd get his own later. Damn if he would ask Wayne to do him a favor.

Wayne placed his empty on the counter and retrieved two more bottles. He opened both, and passed one to Morg.

Then, surprisingly, he extended the other bottle to Ray, a question on his face.

Ray paused, not appreciating the gesture, and considered telling Wayne to fuck off. In the end, he sighed and reached for the bottle.

Only to have Wayne draw it away. "Fuck that," he leered and downed half the drink.

"You're a real gentleman, Wayne," Morg muttered, taking a sip of his own.

"The guy's threatening me with a gun."

"We got bigger problems out there."

"Don't worry about it, Morg," Ray said. "Once a prick, always a prick."

"Big talk," Wayne said and glared. "You're so tough. Just oozin' from every pore."

"Fuck you," Ray shot back, and stole a peek out over the front lawn.

To his surprise, a dark silhouette stood next to Bern's impaled head.

In that instant, Wayne's face hardened, suddenly furious, and he whipped his beer bottle at Ray's face. Ray only sensed the beer flying at his head, a tail of froth spilling from the neck, before the bottle shattered against the wall to his left. Wayne lunged. The big man crossed the floor and caught Ray's wrist before he could point the Glock.

"Gotcha," Wayne smiled and snapped his head forward, clacking his forehead into Ray's face. His nose exploded and reality compressed before being stretched into a wire. He crumpled. Wayne drove a knee into Ray's chest, rammed a second knee into his jaw.

Ray plopped on his ass, both legs kicking out as if made of metal springs.

"Not so tough now, are ya?" Wayne huffed and punched the man trapped in the corner.

Ray glimpsed a meteor of a fist before it crashed into his cheek. A second punch cracked his head into the wall.

Morg was shouting, *Stop it, Wayne! Give it up!* but Wayne wasn't listening. In dazed glimpses, where Ray snuck peeks at his attacker, Wayne actually had a nasty smile on his face.

Three quick lefts battered Ray's face, rattling his head like a trapped bingo ball.

"How about that, my son? Huh?" Wayne punched the man twice more, bouncing his skull about the corner. He loomed over the trapped man and unleashed punishing elbows. The first one split Ray's scalp to the bone. A second elbow opened an even wider cut. Blood blinded Ray.

Wayne grabbed Ray's chin, snarled hatred about having

to use his left hand, and pile-drove the heel of his right into Ray's exposed ear.

"Jesus *Christ*," Wayne howled and drew back, holding his crippled fist and swearing a line of oaths.

Feeling as if he was trapped in a spinning fishbowl, Ray managed to open a rapidly swelling eye. Spite made him smile weakly.

The worst thing he could've done.

"Funny," Wayne whispered and snapped a front kick to Ray's face, the boot heel connecting like an old-fashioned maul. "How's that for funny? Huh? That's fuckin' funny if you ask me. That's fuckin' *hilarious*!"

Ray didn't hear a word.

After a moment, he became aware of being moved, just a little, and puzzled over it. He certainly wasn't going anywhere and wasn't in any condition to drag himself from the corner. As it was, Ray had to admit that Wayne, the sneaky psychopathic cocksmoker that he was, got his timing down just pat. Voices spoke in the heavens somewhere above and Ray believed Morg was one of them. Then a throaty click, like a mighty fissure in the earth's crust opening up, eager to swallow anything thrown down its gullet.

Ray opened his eyes, discovered that it was difficult to do so. Fluid caused him to blink, the picture flickering like a television with connection issues. The room had become darker, but there was light from the open fridge. Not a lot, but enough to discern Morg still sitting against the wall, just beneath the flat-screen, and Wayne poised just to the side of him. Wayne had taken up center stage in the living room

He had Bern's gun and was pointing it at Ray's head.

Ray grimaced and tasted blood, discovered Wayne had

knocked out three lower teeth. He pushed another one free with his tongue, the spring dribbling, and drooled a lower incisor into his hand.

"Don't worry about it," Wayne advised, the gun not five feet away from Ray's face.

Ray didn't. He kept on blinking, though. His eyes were being watery bitches.

"You know what I think about guns?" Wayne asked. "About them being the great equalizer? I think the world's a fuckin' better place without them. Only small shits like yourself invent these things, just to boss around big shits like me. If there were no guns, the world would be a much more manageable place."

"Wayne," Morg started.

"Shut up, Morg," Wayne said, eyes darting to where the lieutenant lay. "Just shut the fuck up and get them car keys out. And for your information, I ain't gonna shoot this little shit, anyway. Figure I'll need the bullets to get out of here. Why waste a bullet when my boots'll do the same job? And I'll enjoy it more, too. You hear that, you little prick? Eh? You're about to get your head kicked in."

Wayne leered, inspecting Ray for a few seconds, before stomping on the man's right hand and breaking four fingers in one blow. Ray cried out, a curt shriek that pitched him forward. Wayne grabbed his hair and kneed him back into the corner in a near-dead clatter of limbs.

"Just like that," Wayne declared, wincing before catching his breath. "You little, little piece of shit. Howzat feel, huh? Bet you're wishin' you had more 'n a couple fingers chopped off, eh?"

"Wayne, you crazy bastard," Morg said from somewhere in the shadows.

Ray held up the flattened mitt that was his hand. He moved his thumb, but his fingers resembled a crooked autumn branch, bereft of leaves.

Wayne kicked at one of Ray's knees, spreading both legs. "Ever see anyone die when their ribs are kicked in, Morg? Kinda freaky. You kick hard enough, you can hear the crack. Then the guy starts twitchin' and gets all spastic and spits blood all over the place. Like a little garden hose."

Morg didn't respond, but Ray heard everything, knew then he'd missed his chance to shoot the bastard standing over him, smiling as if he'd just climbed Everest by hand.

"Pay attention, now," Wayne said and licked his lips as he readied himself to cave in a ribcage. He tucked the gun away behind his back. "Hell, I might even get my leg up far enough to squat on that head of yours, Ray, my little trout. Squat it just like a fat little grub."

Ray swung his head up, feeling its weight for the first time in his life, and waited.

Poised to kick, Wayne's smug expression suddenly dissolved. The big man hesitated and lowered his boot. He took several deep breaths, clutching at his midsection like a gunshot wound, and grunted.

Ray's eyes widened as far as they would go.

A great whine of pain escaped Wayne then, just before he turned his head to the window and barked, spraying dark matter onto the curtain.

"Ray," Morg gasped.

But Ray couldn't take his attention off Wayne, who stumbled back, growling like a sick dog. The big man backed up past the picture window and placed a shoulder against a wall. He tried to straighten himself but his guts knotted in pain and dropped him to the floor.

"Guh," Wayne got out, forehead pressed to the hardwood strips. "Guh. *Guhhhhh.*"

A gush of ink rushed from Wayne's mouth, pooling around his chin. Wayne puked a second time, and Ray could only stare as the Pearsons' enforcer flopped over like a mighty oak that had been buzz-sawed to the core. Wayne kicked spasmodically, twice, before a violent seizure overtook his heavy frame. He looked to Ray, bloodied chops and eyes narrowed to slits...

Just before his head thumped onto the floor.

The entire episode reached its messy climax in less than a minute, and Ray couldn't have been more surprised in his life.

"Ray," Morg tried again, sounding like shit.

"Yeah?" Ray asked and took the throbbing wave of pain, grateful to be alive.

"Don't drink the beer."

That got his attention. "What?"

"Don't. Drink. The buh...."

Ray looked toward the man lying on the floor, his frame jerking with increasing frequency. "Poisoned. Po...Po..."

The bottle rolled away from Morg's side like a scorpion having delivered its lethal dose. Morg spasmed. He stuck a fist at his battered partner in crime and, with a mewl of pain, opened his hand. Car keys dangled from a finger.

The sight stirred Ray to a sitting position, and that's where he stayed until the room stopped spinning. When it slowed enough for him to continue, he crawled on his knees and made best speed to the dying man, halting at intervals when the spiraling floor became too much to bear.

When Ray reached Morg, he gripped the lieutenant's hand with the keys.

And held it tight.

And, unlike Wayne, who'd chugged an entire bottle and a half of whatever tainted concoction was contained therein, Morg took a lot longer to die.

## 10

The squeak of a floorboard brought Ray back, rousing him from a battered daze. He still held on to Morg's hand, the keys pressed between the dead man's cooling flesh and his own. At first, Ray wasn't sure if it was the deck or just some part of his skull caving in under pressure, so he stayed still and listened. The refrigerator door remained ajar, the light allowing Ray to discern his companions' morbid outlines. Morg had been bad. At least Wayne was over in seconds, but the poison took its time to work its foul magic on the Pearsons' lieutenant. Ray held on as long as he could, cursing Wayne for every second of Morg's suffering.

Ray looked around the cabin. There was no clock and no way to tell the time, but he was grateful for the dark. He inspected and prodded himself, feeling the flesh about his eyes as soft and malleable as overripe plums. His nose was squished. Just touching it blasted a lightning strike between his eyes and through his brain. He swallowed and cringed at the slick knob sinking in his throat. His tongue gauged the holes in his gums.

With miserable reflection, Ray scolded himself for not shooting Wayne right after firing those initial shots into the woods.

Someone rattled the front doorknob. Ray lifted his head at the sound.

It was them.

Voices, low and whispery like evil fairies plotting. Ray lay there, knowing he was in no shape for a fight, and spotted the gun jutting out of Wayne's ass crack. Ray only wished he'd had the opportunity to fire the anally parked weapon while the bastard was still breathing. He forced himself to move, reaching with his good left hand, and grabbed the weapon. He slumped on the floor then, sliding his gun out of sight behind his hip.

The curtain shifted and moved at one end, and, like an emerging nightmare, a ghost eased out from behind the fabric. The figure stopped, a dark twinkle of hazy pitch, and didn't move. Ray watched through the narrowed slits of his puffed eyes, knowing he looked as good as dead, and was grateful for it.

The gauzy figure moved from the corner where Wayne had trapped and pummeled Ray's ass to great effect. Ray didn't breathe, didn't move a muscle, for fear of alerting the intruder. He had to correct himself. The guy was probably the owner, or one of the owners, or maybe even a neighbor.

As if he were tiptoeing through a minefield, the ghostly outline crouched and touched Wayne's corpse. Ray's temples thumped, exacerbating the ache of his kicked-in face and skull. The guy wasn't five feet away, prodding at Wayne's neck, and turning his attention to Morg. Ray's heart rate increased, every thud painful, and he made to lift the gun when someone knocked on the door.

The ghost paused in his inspection, his face swathed in shadow, and rose.

Ray's heart ached with the building pressure, his breathing quickened and he struggled to keep it noiseless. The ghost paused, swaying left and right at the hips before stepping to the entrance. A series of clicks cut through the silence and the front door swung open. A second wraith entered the room, this one with a formidable hunter's bow held at the ready.

"All clear?" the new arrival asked.

"Seems to be."

"Jesus, what a mess."

"Yup."

The first ghost moved as the second one stood in the center of the room, the place once occupied by the dining room table.

"Shit did the trick," one said.

"Hope they died squealing, the sonsabitches."

"Goddamn right."

Ray's gun hand, his awkward left, twitched and his brow furrowed. The pair standing before him went quiet as a third ghost entered, all dressed in clothing that seemed strange, patched and mottled. Ray's brain identified the gear as camouflage.

*Hunters?*

"Holy Sacred Heart of Mary," the latest man said. "Cleaned up shop. Craig was right. They got to the beer eventually."

"Just glad it didn't come down to a shoot-out," commented another.

"I'd a fuckin' loved a shoot-out, especially with these pricks."

"You check them all?"

"Except that one there."

"Holy shit, someone put the boots to his face."

"Yeah…"

That one word stretched on forever, and Ray sensed that all was suddenly not as clear as it should have been.

"Heyyy—" the first ghost started as Ray pulled out the gun and shot him through the knee. The figure dropped as if grabbed by the ankles. That single blast in such close confines startled the living shit out of the other two and for a flash, both men were paralyzed.

Ray shot the second wraith through the gut, blasting him backwards where he spattered against the wall. The third ghost disappeared out the front door, much too fast for Ray to alter his aim. He fired two rounds into the door and then a third through the curtains.

"*One's still alive!*" the shout pierced the night. "*One's still alive.*"

The words cut through the dizziness, threatening Ray's senses. He took a deep breath and aimed the gun at the front door while eyeing the window. He listened, catching the receding sound of a man sprinting in full retreat.

"Missed," a groggy Ray whispered in self-reproach and got to his knees. He sucked down a deep lungful of air, liked the cold taste, and was very much grateful the room didn't spin. He stood and shoved the front door shut. Placing his forehead against the wood, he locked the top bolt and left the rest. The two men he'd wounded writhed and rolled on the floor. Both were crying like kids. Ray didn't give a shit about that and, without a lick of remorse, shot the one wounded in the guts, adding a second bullet to the chest. The man crumpled as if deflated.

Ray kept his back to the door, mostly for support, and regarded the first ghost. The camouflaged man pulled his ruined knee up to his chest and stared back with wet eyes. When Ray leveled the gun at the ghost's head, the man actually moaned.

"Shut up," Ray commanded.

The guy shut up—probably shit himself in the process—but Ray cared squat about that.

"Weren't expecting me, were ya?" Ray asked. "Alive, that is."

The wounded prisoner shook his head.

"How many more are there? Of you?"

"Huh?" he blubbered, moist eyes revealed in the fridge's meager light. He wore a mask, one that covered his face from his eyes down, identical to the mottled pattern of his outerwear.

"How many are out there?"

"Uh," the brow crunched in concentration. Ray let him have some time. An unnerving gasp came from the dead man in the dining room, but he didn't do much else.

"Well?" Ray asked.

"About six."

"Minus you two?"

"Huh?"

Ray kicked the man's foot. "You a fuckin' dingbat or somethin'? You say that one more time and I'll shoot you again."

"Yeah," the wounded guy blurted. "Yeah, four of us now."

"Weapons?"

Ray thought the ghost—the *hunter*—before him was about to say *huh* but nipped it at the last second.

"Weapons?" the hunter asked.

"Yeah, weapons, any guns like this one?"

"No, nothing like that."

"Shotguns? More of these?" Ray kicked the fallen bow, recognizing it as one of the fancy Olympic-style compound units.

"Yeah."

"Give me specifics, you bastard, or I'll make you sing."

"Maybe two shotguns. Everyone has bows and knives."

"Everyone, huh?"

"Yeah."

*Four against one.* Ray sighed and didn't like the odds. "Start talkin'."

That got the wounded man blinking. "About what?"

"This place. You. Everything. We just came to rob the place and we walked into a goddamn deathtrap. Who the fuck puts those things on the windows? Puts poisoned beer in the fridge?"

The bullet in his knee must've hurt something bad, as the hunter thumped his head on the floor and squeezed his eyes shut. When he came to, Ray could see the defeat as plain as the blood oozing from his ruined joint.

"We knew you'd be comin'. Someday."

"What? You were waitin' for us?"

"Yeah."

"Why? Who put you up to this?"

The guy exhaled, puffing the thin fabric of his mask. "It was a group decision. A lot of cabins were broken into around this area about four or five years back. Cops couldn't find anyone. After a year they found one guy in a place some thirty klicks from here, and only because the owner found the asshole passed out on his kitchen floor, high on meth. That was after this… animal had shit in the poor guy and his wife's bed, pissed on the beds of his children, wrecked the living room and the kitchen, and smashed every bottle and glass window in the place. I mean, an animal wouldn't have been as destructive. Pure evil, it was. Pics of what that sack of pus did was all over the net. Wasn't in his right mind, the defense said, and you know what that fucker got? For breaking into a man's cabin? For violating that family's privacy and ruining their home away from home, a place they invested time and money in and made memories? Two.

Years. Prick actually winked at the camera outside the courthouse and said he'd be out in about half that. Well, he was right 'cause he got out in eight months. Walking the streets. Same guiltless idiot did the same thing on the west coast a year later. And the cops caught him again. Far as I know, he's serving his time, but who knows when he'll be out again. Probably do the same thing over. You think that's right?"

No, it wasn't right, but since he was cut from the same cloth, Ray kept his mouth shut.

"Well," the hunter continued, anger seeping into his tone despite his pain. "A few of us didn't think it was. Not in the least. Crimes were dealt with a lot faster and lot more decisive years ago. We decided to form a watch, just in case someone got it into their heads to try the same thing around here. Decided to set one cabin up as a mousetrap and wait. The waiting was easy. The watch stayed at the cabin on the weekends. It wasn't a chore, it was fun. It was during the week when no one was around that the place had to be monitored."

"Six guys watch this place during the week?" Ray asked, incredulous. "Jesus, you guys got lives or families, or at least a fuckin' dog?"

"Never six guys here," the hunter whispered. Blood seeped between the fingers laced around his knee. He groaned before elaborating. "Never six. Always two. Come in the morning and leave at suppertime. But always someone watching… always someone…"

The mask muffled a raspy giggle. Ray lifted the gun just to make a point. The hunter quickly quieted.

"You sick bastards were waiting five fuckin' years for us?" Ray asked in dazed disbelief.

"Yeah. Well, not you exactly, but whoever thought they could rip the place off. And it was four years. Took some time to get things set up."

"I bet."

"But we gotcha."

"You got them," Ray pointed out, indicating Wayne and Morg. "Didn't get me."

"Not yet," the man huffed, his eyes taking on a decidedly crazy shine. "But you ain't gettin' away. We got a grave waitin' for you. All of you. One size fits all. No one gets away. You sure as hell ain't gettin' away."

Another evil, wheezy giggle that Ray didn't care for. "You high on something?"

"Only on fuckin' justice, y'piece of dogshit. You picked the wrong fuckin' castle this time."

"Yeah, well, I got you."

The giggle became a full-blown laugh. "We *planned* for this situation, you stupid squirrel-nut bastard. Y'think we were all just sittin' around with our thumbs up each other's bungholes? Just shiftin' every now and again and talkin' shit? Ha! We're fuckin' *committed* to makin' sure you don't trespass on another person's property. You ever have anything stolen or ripped off or a car broken into, then you might know the level of goddamn rage you're dealin' with here. But I'm guessin' you don't have a fuckin' clue. We're honest men, women, defending shit that we *earned*."

Ray had no reply to that. He'd learned long ago there were plenty of speckle-bellied wingnuts and endangered dingbats in life. He wasn't sure which category this breed of vigilante crazy fit into.

"We got them," the hunter whispered with a nod to the corpses of Morg and Wayne. "We'll get you."

"Four guys," Ray repeated and glanced to the window. "You make it sound like an army."

Another bout of laughter, weaker this time, but just as scalding. Ray wasn't prepared for such defiance. Not in a simple cabin job. It was disturbing.

"See, you don't know nothin'," the hunter said. "Not a goddamn thing. Two guys watch the place and if anyone comes along, their job's to hold them in the cabin while they make phone calls. You understandin' things now, dickshit? Huh? Yeah, now the light's comin' on, eh? Fuckin' reinforcements are on the way. Probably five or six more guys arrived since our little chitchat here. Hell, could be as many as twenty. Some of our members live a little farther out than others. Lots of small communities around here. Old ones. Salt of the earth type. Warm and friendly as anyone when needed, to the right folks, but biblical wrath of God vengeance for the bad ones. They're gonna get you and fuckin' hang you from the rafters. Let you dangle on rusty hooks and let you squeal until you run out of breath. And to the world, you'll just up and disappear. Never to be seen or heard from again."

Despite the comfort of the Glock, Ray swallowed and glanced around uneasily. "They'll want you back. I'll bargain my way out with you."

Again the laugh, accentuated by a headshake. "They won't listen. We fuckin' made a pact."

"A pact?"

"A pact, y'moron, a pact. A group vow. An oath to nail your worthless dogshit ass to the nearest wharf by any means necessary. No matter what. It's perfect. No one's gonna come lookin' for you, anyway. You'll just cease to be and we'll have done honest, hard-workin' people a favor. Cops?

Ha! They'd fucking shake our hands if they knew."

Ray couldn't muster an argument to that.

"Shit," the hunter carried on. "I bet the whole gang has gathered out there by now. About forty or fifty. Best bunch of bastards and bitches ever to hunt these woods."

The hunter's eyes blazed. "You're so fucked."

Another bout of rattlesnake merriment.

The cabin room started to spin, and Ray pressed one hip against the doorknob for balance.

"Hey," his captive asked. "Hey, listen. What's your name anyway? Tell me. Maybe they'll just drug you or something before the meat hooks. I doubt it. I mean, you should hear how some fellas talk around campfires when they get on this topic. What they'd do to the brazen-ass bastards who stole something from them. Or broke into their house or cabin. Justice. Of settling scores. I can hear the 'If I had a hold of them' stories now. Wanna hear some?"

"Fuck off."

The wounded man chuckled, truly tickled, the endorphins taking the edge off his knee. "Don't matter. When they get you, you'll tell them your name. You'll tell them everything. Your address, your family, the name of your fuckin' cat. All that important shit. If a piece of dogshit like you *has* important shit, that is. See, whatever you tell them, they're gonna go and fuck it up. I mean, they're gonna punish whatever they find. You hear that? They're gonna go and violate your property. In extreme ways. Very extreme ways. How's that make you feel, you slack-jawed chicken fucker? Huh? Knowin' that when you're dead and gone, some friends of ours are gonna get an extra pound of flesh or two? From folks belongin' to you who had nothin' to do with any of this. That seem right to you? I mean, does it?

Seems pretty fuckin' excessive to me."

Ray decided he'd had enough and pointed the gun at his mouthy prisoner.

The hunter stopped giggling entirely and tensed up. "I ain't afraid to—"

Ray shot him between the eyes.

## 11

Individual pools of blood widened and made contact in the middle of the floor. Ray's face and jaw ached, and for long, lonely seconds misery grabbed hold and squeezed. Time back, he wished for, time back to give it all up, to firm up and make a better effort at staying away from the business. He thought of his family, patient until patience was all gone. Bernie popped into his head then, poor old Bern, chopped up by some righteous savage seeking justice. Bern didn't deserve his head on a post. He never hurt anyone, not knowingly. Neither did Morg, as far as Ray knew. Wayne, well, fuck him. Wayne was the kind of monster who deserved what he got.

Ray slumped against the door, neck deep in despair and wallowing in it, and heard someone moaning. It took him only a moment to realize it was him. His swollen eyes leaked bloody tears and he carefully dabbed a coat sleeve against them.

"Hey!"

The voice tightened Ray's scrotum. He turned to the picture window.

"Hey you! In the cabin! You shoot someone in there?"

The innocuous question reminded Ray of one kid asking another if he had a tuna fish sandwich for lunch.

"Hey! I said did you shoot someone in there?"

Ray regarded the dead hunter on the floor.

"Goddamnit, answer me!"

Ray stuck his gun out the window and fired off a round, in the direction of the tree line. *There's your fuckin' answer*, he fumed, enduring sinuses packed tight with fluid.

"All right, buddy, all right," the voice drifted from the dark. "Don't matter. We'll catch you soon enough. Have a beer in the meantime…"

"Like hell," Ray muttered. He considered his gun and wondered how many rounds were left. Probably not too many. It would be awkward to check with one hand, which got him thinking about escape. It was nighttime and he was supposedly surrounded. He wondered just how much of his captive's story was true regarding the number of people outside. Ray shook Morg's keys and stuffed them into a pocket. He was getting to that car and getting out of this place. He'd report back to Joey and Julian and whatever they decided to do would be fine with him.

As of that moment, Ray was out of the business.

But he knew he just might have to get a little dirty for the next hour or so.

The first thing he did was lean over the guy he belly shot and check him for weapons. He found a short skinning knife with a bone handle and clumsily transferred it and the scabbard to his coat pocket. The other hunter had nothing except his bow, which Ray ignored. The camouflaged coats and head gear were stained with blood, so he left that as well. At one point he stopped and pressed his gun hand to his forehead, steadying himself and taking the dizziness that seemed to radiate from the back of his skull. When the feeling subsided, he went to the fridge and closed the door, completing the darkness within the cabin interior. He felt along the wall, remembering where the back door was, and shortly located it. The locks clicked loudly, and Ray winced with every sound.

Get out the door and hit the tree line. Hit the tree line

and cut through it. Eventually he'd find the road, and then the car. He considered going through the drawers for a flashlight but decided against it. The flashlight would mess up his night vision.

Ray cursed Wayne Roberts for stomping on his right hand. Fuming at the clumsy grip, Ray jabbed the Glock into one armpit and remembered Bernie nipping the same pistol between his knees. That almost got a chuckle.

Taking a breath, Ray did the one thing he hadn't done in a very long time.

He blessed himself.

Then he opened the door and staggered into the night.

Cold November air filled his throat as he pulled the door closed and ran to his right. A full, pearly white moon radiating beauty hung in the night sky, but he didn't stop to appreciate it as he would have liked. Ray sped across the grass, glancing around him, waiting for an arrow's hiss or worse. The forest loomed ahead, and before he could slip into that tangled wall, unseen branches licked at his tenderized face. One straight twig scraped along the skin of his temple, missing his eye by millimeters. Ray flinched and shoved the coarse tendril away. All he needed was to stumble through the woods at night like a drunken moose with an eye poked out. He could barely see as it was.

"Who's on the back?" a voice shouted. "Just saw someone run from the back!"

Ray bolted, crashing through branches, stomping down wiry lengths of frigid foliage. Rough fir boughs pawed at his body. He tripped and crashed, his right hand a floppy paw of searing pain. A grunt escaped him and he rolled onto his back in reflex, seeing how low the moon hung, its face scraped by hairline whips.

"Over there! Over there!"

Bodies waded through the bush. Hurried footfalls chugged toward Ray's position. Amazingly, he still gripped the gun. He pulled the firearm to his cheek, snarling a ruined smile and swearing to put a bullet into whoever tried to stop him. His scalp bled anew, the flow trickling into his left eye. He wiped the blood away with the back of his wrist.

The footsteps grew louder.

Then… nothing.

*The fuck…?* Ray thought and forced himself to be quiet.

A dull shadow passed by not two feet away, hunched over and holding a bow. The phantom moved without so much as a snap or crackle, which perplexed Ray as the ghost vanished into the woods. Ray waited, forced himself to be patient, and waited a little longer.

Another silhouette moved past his position. Another silent bowman.

Then a nearly indistinct third.

The fourth man floated by like a grim reaper. Ray stopped breathing until that one went past, fearful of the axe the figure carried.

Four ghosts. Hunters. And the forest had grown quiet again.

Not daring to move, Ray lay there, hidden in the undergrowth, and counted off the seconds.

Ten.

Twenty.

Thirty.

*Time to move.*

He shifted and froze at the crisp, potato-chip crunch of detritus underneath his body. With desperate effort he stumbled to his knees and plunged forward—onto a beaten path. Ray stopped and, through the white-hot siren of his smashed fingers, squinted in stunned amazement at the trail before him. Though the moonlight was fragmented by overhead boughs, the ground itself was illuminated by two dimly lit lines that looked like the emergency lights down an airplane's narrow aisle. The white lights, like low-powered Christmas strands, revealed hard-packed dirt, swept and carefully maintained. Knee-high hedges rose on either side of the lighting, containing the glow so that it wouldn't be noticed from the cabin clearing. Ray took a hesitant step in the direction of the ghosts and discovered the noise of his walking had been greatly reduced. The lit pathway snaked off through the forest gloom and he followed it, making like a ninja.

He realized his pursuers would be equally stealthy.

The pathway kept straight, and at one point Ray came to a second trail veering off to the right. He followed it for only a few steps before stopping and gawking in wonder.

*Well, holy shit.*

The path ended in a camouflaged wall that hung from the trees. An old chair, its seat dark and worn, faced forward and a narrow slit about eye-level height had been cut in the hunter's veil. The shape of a camera stood poised upon a tripod. A headset and black box appearing all spidery with wires rested on a nearby milk crate. The setup amazed him. Ray listened, heard nothing move, and bent over to peek through the gash.

The cabin stood in the clearing, awash in moonlight, as stark and imposing as a mausoleum.

*Holy shit!* Ray straightened, horrified, and turned around just as a figure stepped into the path.

A ghost. Armed with, of all things, a prong.

There was no time for pleading or bargaining and, at that range, no chance to miss. Ray fired from the hip, the gunshot as loud as a cannon blast, and blew the top off the surprised hunter's head in a grisly puff of chunks. The body landed some two feet back and Ray jumped over it, crashing into the low hedge. Branches stabbed his lower legs and clawed at his face. He fought through, and, though he couldn't hear them, he knew whoever had surrounded the cabin was converging on his location with haste.

Ray ran, the trail's lights flashing by his feet like laser beams.

Something dark rushed toward him.

On impulse, Ray jumped the path and steered right, crashing through the woods and avoiding another fight. Branches slashed at his face. He raised his gun hand to deflect the stinging whips and hooked his foot into a stump.

"He's gone off the path!" a voice shouted behind him.

"Get after him."

"I ain't goin' in there."

A meeting occurred then, but Ray couldn't understand the mutterings as he struggled to rise in the thicket. His right hand felt as if he'd plunged it into a vat of flaming pitch. He lifted the trembling palm and moaned when he noticed his last two fingers had been plied backwards at boneless angles. The sight evaporated the rush of endorphins flooding his system and left him gasping. He squealed, spat, and crossed wrists, his left hand over his right. The fingers had to be straightened, and he either did it now or later.

With a suppressed yelp, he raked one hand over the other as if sharpening a stick. In that searing supernova burst of pain, bones shifted, rolled and were reset in their proper direction. A cold fire seized Ray's hand and blowtorched frayed nerves all the way to his brain. After a second wild squawk, he collapsed in a starry-eyed daze.

"Over here! He's over here!"

The shout reanimated Ray and he gulped down air. They couldn't capture him. He wouldn't allow it. Not if they were going to find his family. Stuffing his suffering hand into an armpit, he rose and stomped onwards through the wilderness, all thoughts of stealth lost. He splashed through a brook, the frigid water soaking his sneakers and dousing his lower legs. Roots tripped him and he tumbled to his knees once again, but managed to catch himself before landing flat on his face. The woods crowded in and reached for him, extending shadowy limbs. Weaponized twigs scratched at his face and eyes. Always the eyes, as if the trees knew a good blinding would deepen his misery. The water numbed his feet and legs and Ray forced himself to keep still in the prickly mesh, to endure the shivering and listen. His pulse hammered along, the beats becoming a muffled klaxon situated right behind his eyes and in his ears.

Underbrush crackled to his right.

Ray didn't dare move, very much aware that the slightest twitch would draw murderous attention.

Another step toward him, cautious and testing, followed by twigs zipping along weatherproofed outerwear.

Ray cringed, every deep breath sawing at the toothless holes in his mouth. His mind screamed at him to *move*, that he'd been found and he should be running at full speed, that he was about *to fucking die.*

The noise stopped, but in its absence other things moved, all around him, farther away, but they were out there. Listening. Creeping. Searching. In Ray's tortured mind, men no longer stalked him. Monsters did. Wicked creatures with wings folded, attracted by blood. They walked on two legs, their heads gray and bald and fixed atop crooked necks and narrow shoulders. Whispers permeated the woods, sinister exchanges no human could possibly utter or understand. Ray heard every snap and crinkle, every malefic murmur, fully tuned into that evil wavelength that putrefied his ears and befouled his brain.

A descending weight squashed the underbrush nearby, much closer than before, and Ray stayed still.

*It's dark. They can't see me. They can't.*

His temples were on the verge of exploding, his blood pressure soaring.

Another step, and Ray felt a presence invading his personal space like noxious gas, but that wasn't what truly disturbed him. What truly disturbed him was the abrupt hole of silence just behind him, as if the hunter himself sensed he was close, very close, and that it only took a moment's patience to locate the rabbit. Just a moment and all would be revealed.

Ray didn't breathe, and in those mile-long seconds, he heard someone take a breath, a very quiet breath. just above the forest's silence.

A breath before someone committed to action.

Fright ripped through Ray and he propelled himself forward as if he'd had a rocket strapped to his ass. The falling axe, swung with all the might of an angry titan, missed his foot by a flesh-splitting sliver and bounced off the frozen earth.

"HE'S OVER HERE!"

The forest burst into action.

The trees whipped Ray as he charged forward, keeping his head low. He glimpsed a faceless specter emerging from the bush ahead. The apparition held a wicked bow and snapped the weapon up to a ready position.

Ray was faster.

He barreled into the meaty ghost, bowling him over with a grunt, and landed on his chest. The hunter released the bow as Ray pounded the Glock's hilt onto a nose as if striking a nail. Ray struggled to rise but the hunter beneath him clutched at his clothing, dragging him back down.

*"Got him! I got the bast—"*

Ray shot him through the face, blasting the man away. He rose and spun in time to see the axe man had arrived, swinging from the shoulder and chopping at a hip. Ray twisted and fell flat on his back. Springy saplings cracked under his weight. The axeman howled as he reset. Ray fired three times. A chest erupted. A shoulder exploded and the axe dropped. The man staggered back and crashed to the ground, boot soles pointed at the heavens.

Ray panted, unbelieving at his luck, and pulled himself up as sounds of pursuit closed in from all quarters, summoned by the recent killing.

He flinched at a shotgun blast. The pellets ripped through the trees like a killer rain, close enough for him to hear. He wondered when the big guns would start shooting. Through the forest gloom, shades materialized.

Ray took aim at the nearest hunter and fired.

*Click.*

That single note frightened him more than the collection of killers on his tail. Ray ran, still holding the gun, the empty weapon raised before him like a lantern. The men hounding him gave chase, shouting at times, shrieking at others. Ray didn't think. All thoughts were focused on finding the road. Find the road and Morg's car.

He increased his pace, pushing himself, the trees flaying him as he plowed through, pinballing off dark pillars that only materialized at the last possible second. His lungs ached. Blood found his eyes and his mouth. A heavy bough slapped the gun from his grasp and he left it, no time to retrieve the weapon. The woods had to clear out soon. He had to have covered a kilometer cross-country, and if there was a road he should be hitting it any second. A baleful moon hung above the landscape, fat and ivory-white and scarred, the pupil of an angry god.

Voices cut the night. Missiles hissed past him. Another gunshot peppered the trees behind him as he turned and beheld the forest wall. Ray screamed and thrust his good hand forward, bursting through the barrier of vegetation like an exhausted missile. He fell, dropping as if going over a cliff, and hit an embankment of solid earth. The impact confused him as cold gravel jammed itself into his ruined mouth. Ray righted himself and clawed out of the ditch, fingers raking pavement.

*The highway.*

He stumbled onto the cold asphalt, triumphant in his discovery, and heard crashing waves on a far-off shore. A starless void lay ahead.

A delirious laugh escaped Ray. Hope spiked. All he needed to do was locate the dirt road and backtrack to Morg's car. He'd drive all fucking night to get back to Julian and Joey and damn well sure those two would plan bloody revenge on whoever owned the—

A rush of motion charged in from his left, drawing Ray's attention. He glanced ahead as a gleaming wall rushed toward him, momentarily befuddling his pain-wracked mind.

Twin moons blinked to life, blinding him, freezing him to the spot.

The car struck Ray while approaching ninety kilometers an hour, killing him upon impact.

# 12

The vehicle rolled over the organic speed bump and pulled off onto the road's shoulder. The engine hummed, elated over its kill, as the driver's door opened and boots clicked on pavement. Beyond the red glow of parking lights, one figure appeared on the highway beside the crushed body. The person nudged the body with a boot. Three other shades detached themselves from the tree line and gathered about the corpse.

The driver waited, hands on his hips. "Well?"

"Jesus, Cory. You flattened his head."

"Pays to be late," Cory declared and pulled a pack of cigarettes from his coat breast pocket. "Didn't even have to waste a shot or anything that time."

One of the men next to the body soccer-kicked the ribs.

"They get some of ours?" Cory asked.

Names were reported, surprising the driver enough that his hand trembled when he finally lit up his smoke.

"Goddamn crook," Cory hissed and took a deep solemn draw. "Well, we planned for that, too. In the off chance. How many of the sick puppies were there?"

"Four of them, altogether," someone said. "Four bastards. A regular gang."

"What do we do?" another asked, the reality of the situation hitting hard.

"Do?" The question seemed stupid to Cory. They'd planned for this very scenario ever since he came up with the idea of using the cabin as a man-sized rat trap. An irresistible chunk of bait to proactively remove the growing criminal element on the island without ever getting tangled in the justice system's inconvenient loopholes that favored the perpetrators.

"The hell you think we're gonna do? Get that piece of shit off the road and bury him with the others. Should be enough limestone in the shed. Y'know something? Dump them all in the one hole and save that shit. I got a five-gallon bucket in the trunk. One of you go on down to the shore and get some water. Wash the blood off the road."

"Then what?" the same guy asked. "Tell you the truth, Cory, these guys seemed organized. Some of their friends might come lookin'."

"Fuck 'em if they do," Cory shrugged. "I *hope* someone comes lookin'. By that time we'll have the cabin all set for another round. And just to be on the safe side, we'll double the lookouts this time. Maybe for a week or three. See who shows up."

The cigarette's end flared red as he took another deep, calming draw. The adrenaline abated as he exhaled vengeful justice.

"Maybe we'll get lucky," he said.

# 3

# Eat

Roses gushed red like berries in August beneath the glass countertop of the bar. People moved out of the corner of his vision, and he was distinctly aware of being eyed by the bartenders, for weal or woe. Music, like comfortable silk, channelled through battle-scarred loudspeakers. He didn't know the words, but found it relaxing anyway, easy to listen to and better than some of the roosters-having-their-nut-sack-shaved-off vocals he'd heard recently. The chair made his ass hurt; as the owners obviously hadn't paid for comfortable furniture, he wondered where all the money was going. Maybe he'd make a suggestion to one of the bartenders before he left. Maybe not. 'Twas but a thought. There was more ice in his drink than booze, a good sign they didn't want him to stay long, or the owner was an extremely cheap shit who didn't care for the customer's satisfaction. There were a lot of cheap bastards about. God only knew. *He* certainly knew.

It was almost time to call it a night. Ricky "the Juggernaut" Mobera sighed and checked his phone. There was a message. Not a moment's rest for the king. Another competition, no doubt, another slew of fierce competitors trying to take his title. Ricky smiled and sipped his Cuba Libre. Good looking, dark-haired, and well-dressed, he was just shy of being an even six feet tall. His ocean-blue silk shirt was opened three buttons from the neck to allow a generous view of his thick chest hair. He possessed a belly, a *paunch* as the folks back home would say, but he didn't think it was detrimental when picking up women. They loved it. The heady scent of some carbonated cologne hung about him, and he tried hard to appear somewhere between *cool* and *bored with everything.*

One of the bartenders, a cute brunette with a pierced nostril, lip, and eyebrow, caught his eye. She ducked under the counter and then straightened, arranging a tray of glasses.

"I like your petals," Ricky said with an evil wink and a nod at the countertop.

She ignored him, finished what she was doing, and went over to chat with some other smiling bar hound.

The Juggernaut kept his expression cool and took another sip of his Cuba Libre. *One chick I won't be seeing naked,* he thought. *Probably a dyke, anyway, with all that metal.*

She whispered in the hound's ear. It didn't bother Ricky in the least. Obviously, she was trying to make him jealous.

"Doesn't work, babe," Ricky said, his teeth clicking against the ice in his drink. "Can't make me jealous. Not the *Jug.*"

They were laughing over there now. It was a good act, Ricky thought, but not the game. Far from it. The *game* was only just beginning. He glanced around, still cool, and decided now would be a good time to see who had called him. The number on the display belonged to Craig Float, his agent. Craig knew not to call him on a Friday night. Ricky, deciding this once to break his own rule, hit *Send* to return the call.

"Ricky!" A deep voice greeted with enthusiasm. "Sorry to call y—"

"'S'up, Craig?" Ricky cut him off. "Bitches are waiting here, y'know?"

"Any luck?" Craig had been married for thirteen years and continuously dropped hints that he was on the cusp of seeking something on the side. Ricky didn't care for the curiosity in his voice, but decided to indulge him.

"Yeah," he replied in a bored voice. "Got two here now. Talking them up. Might get some sandwich action later."

Craig snorted. It was part of his laugh: peals of high-pitched mirth ripped with sinus-clearing snorts. Ricky sometimes wondered if he did cocaine.

"Drive one for me," his agent replied.

"Not even with your dick," Ricky riposted. "So, what is it?"

"Sorry, brotha." Craig wasn't Australian, but he liked calling Ricky *brotha*, as he thought it endearing. It wasn't. It was annoying as hell, and he was about two or three *brothas* away from being told off. "I got work for you."

Ricky scratched nonchalantly at his chin. Across the way, there actually *were* two women wearing sparkly tops with spaghetti strings. He loved spaghetti strings.

"What is it?" Ricky asked again, catching the eye of one, a dyed blonde. He gave her an approving nod.

"It's a private competition," Craig informed him.

"A what?"

"A private competition. Closed audience. Gonna be televised later on."

"This something new?" Ricky asked. The other woman glanced his way and whispered to her friend. He knew he was something to whisper about. "And it better not be anything Japanese, goddamn it."

"What's wrong with the Japanese? They pay good—"

"I'm not playing any fucking warped Japanese game on TV. What's wrong with the Japanese? You remember the show with the sashimi and wasabi? And then they wanted folks to puke it all up again? What kind of sick shit is that? And you ask what's wrong with that?"

"Okay, okay, I got you."

"I'm serious, man, nothing Japanese. Seriously. You say anything Japanese in the next breath, and I'm hanging up. Those guys pissed me off last time."

"It's not Japanese," Craig grated. "It's something else—totally different. And no reversals."

"Better not. I mean, Jesus Christ, I'm a *gurgitator* man. A pro athlete! What goes down stays down, right?"

"Right, I gotcha, I gotcha," Craig soothed.

"Alright then, what is it?" Ricky had caught the eyes of both women now. Both were sick hot. The brunette had a one-zip dress. Ricky *died* for those. Absentmindedly, he ran a single finger through his carpet of chest hair.

"Okay, here's the deal," Craig went on. "We get a thousand just for showing up. All participants get a grand regardless, just for signing on. How about that, brotha?"

That *was* something. "You've got my interest. Continue."

"Twenty contestants."

"Twenty? That's a game."

"It is, it is," Craig agreed excitedly. "Damn straight. Twenty of you, in a closed studio, televised nationally. The exposure will be worth thousands alone. And first prize is… are you ready?"

"Shit, man, you want ready? Just say fucking *go,* and I'll show you ready. What is it?"

"Fifty thousand! Fifty K for the winner! Can you believe it?"

Ricky the Juggernaut was speechless. The figure caught in his throat like a dry chicken bone. First prize at the other main event, the main *money* event, was never any more than half that number.

"Second place is twenty-five Gs, third is fifteen, fourth is ten, for Christ's sake, and it goes on down to a grand for everyone, on top of the grand for showing up!"

"Who are these people?" Ricky asked. This kind of money was unheard of.

"Don't know. But they're bringing in talent from all over, brotha! All over. Even fuckin' Hide is coming in!" Craig said the word as *he day*.

"*Tabihodai* Yamanichii is in it?" The Japanese champ was retired. Apparently, the number was interesting to him, too. "Who else?"

"Already confirmed is Johnny Cloke, Amy Duncan, Marty Crazier, Sick Machine, and, uh…."

"They got Sick Machine?" Ricky felt a pang of disgust. Sid "Sick Machine" Green had been ejected from the last competition for a reversal infraction. While reversals weren't uncommon, Sick Machine had been sitting next to the Juggernaut when he cut loose. It stunk like hell, and Ricky almost yarked himself out of the competition. He had to continue for three more minutes with the pungent smell of vomit surrounding him.

"They got everyone who's anyone, brotha." Craig was way over his *brotha* limit, but he was bringing some very interesting news, so Ricky let it slide. "Everyone."

"Sweet Jesus. Anything else?"

Ricky could hear the grin on the other end of the line. "Yep, two things… there's no time limit."

This caused the Juggernaut to blink. No time limit was unheard of.

"And…. if you break the record, *your* record, the prize money is doubled." Craig paused to let that sink in. "It's scheduled for next month. You game?"

The women across the way were almost forgotten. Ricky was game. "I'm there. Where do I sign?"

Craig supplied the initial signing date, the address, and the day of the competition. There would be a little bit of paperwork to be signed, giving permission for the competition to be recorded and relayed at the sponsor's choosing and waiving rights to distribution fees. There would be another contract for all athletes to be signed on the day of the event, but that would be discussed then and wouldn't be a "big thing." Craig said it was something in a comical light, as the sponsors wanted to have fun with it. And if anyone wasn't comfortable with the arrangements, they were free to go home.

Ricky the Juggernaut hung up with a smile on his face. He felt good. Hell, he felt great. Fifty grand and the possibility of breaking his own record? There was a good chance of that happening. He leaned back and caught the eyes of the ladies across the bar. They smiled back coyly. Feeling saucy, Ricky got up and went over to introduce himself. He placed an elbow on the counter while his other hand stroked his chest hair, as if he were a sensual matador. They were all grins and giggles, very thankful when he ordered another round of drinks. The drinks were served by the pierced bartender who went out of her way not to look at Ricky. That suited him fine. He was on his way to the big time. He could feel it. He was a celebrity, and tonight, he was going to get celebrity-sized sex.

"So what do you do, Ricky?" Angela asked, the brunette in the one-zip dress.

The Juggernaut gave them his sexy look. "I'm an Eater."

The following Monday, Ricky the Juggernaut Mobera and his agent, Craig Float, got out of a Yellow Taxi onto the very busy 34th Avenue of New York. They stood in the middle of two currents of people moving around them and gazed upward. The building they faced was tall, at least forty stories, and covered in a rectangular copper plating that gleamed. Craig dug out his iPad and checked the floor they wanted.

"Issat glass?" Ricky asked in an awed voice.

"Yeah, it's glass. They redid the outside, apparently. Something about solar energy or something."

"This?" Ricky stood back, a rock in the stream of people moving around him.

"Yeah, why?"

"I dunno," Ricky admitted. He didn't know the first thing about solar energy. He rubbed his belly, feeling the silk cloth covering it and giving it a tweak. That was the trouble with silk; he was always feeling himself up. Ricky wore his good clothes today, the same pimp fashion he would wear out on the town. He figured if he was about to be paid a thousand as a signing bonus, he should at least look respectable.

"Okay, the forty-fifth floor," Craig said.

"This thing is that high?"

"What? You get nosebleeds or something?"

Ricky frowned. "You just do your thing is all, and I'll do mine." He didn't like it when Craig got smart with him.

The other man simply grinned and led the way.

Once inside, they were faced with a room-wide partition with entrance and exit checkpoints. Business people were herded into a short tunnel for a full body scan and metal detector sweep. There were a dozen or so guards at these bottlenecks. They wore bulky-looking body armor with full helmets and visors, complete with raised collars, and looked stone-faced about their jobs. Their belts contained one-click holsters holding side-arms of a make Ricky didn't recognize. They also carried tasers hitched on shoulder straps and positioned just under their left nipples. Extendable clubs were visible as well, and as he approached his turn to go through the checkpoint, Ricky also saw sheathed knives. The guards looked constipated and not fun in the least. Monday blues, he thought in mild wonder. But they were certainly prepared. He supposed he should feel secure, but he didn't.

They were motioned to the entry check point in single file, toward a desk and a low partition that looked like black steel plates. A large guard, towering over a computer, stood behind the partition. Three extremely alert-looking security specialists stood behind him.

"Name, please," the security guard behind the PC asked, looking directly into Craig's face from behind a clear visor. Ricky noted that his agent was also taken back by the armor these men wore.

"Uh, yeah, Craig Float and Ricky—" Craig began.

"Your name only, sir," the guard interjected. "If I want his name, I'll ask him. Is that understood, sir?"

Craig blinked at the face behind the visor. "Sorry, I thought we were in New York and not—"

"You are in New York, sir," the guard stated. Ricky wondered if they sprayed the visor material with something to keep it from fogging up. "You are at one, two, one, Thirty-Fourth Avenue, just inside the Warwick Building, at security checkpoint one. Be advised that our conversation is being recorded, and anything you say may later be used in a court of law."

The smile left Craig's face. "Jesus, we just want—"

"Are you refusing to provide proper identification, sir?" the guard challenged. Ricky became aware that a half-dozen other guards had become very attentive and were studying both of them with dangerous interest. Ricky also noted two security cameras focused on his agent.

"Who are—" Craig got out. It was the wrong thing to say.

"Further delay will result in your ejection from the premises, sir. I will ask you one more time, and *one* more time *only*, so think very carefully about what it is you want to say. I hope I've made myself perfectly clear in this regard. What. Is. Your. Name?"

Business-suited people entering and leaving the building slowed to watch. Some, after seeing the disturbance, changed their minds and walked faster for the doors, while others waited like vultures perched on cacti limbs. They could smell trouble. They were in the mood for watching it, too.

Chagrined, Craig shut his mouth. "Craig Float," he said.

"State your business, sir," the guard ordered. Ricky caught a glimpse of his face. The guard wore the same dead expression the players on the *Champions of Poker* showed. No emotion shown. Emotion equalled weakness.

"I have a business appointment with a Mr. Edwards," Craig said, and his head dropped a little. "Forty-fifth floor. At one thirty."

"Please display two pieces of identification, sir."

Craig complied, digging out his wallet and handing over two pieces of plastic.

"Thank you, sir," the mouth said, but the eyes bored into Craig's face with the silent message of *"You don't know how close you came, motherfucker."* The guard snatched the identification cards, did some quick typing on the computer, and handed them back. He did not immediately let go when Craig reached for them. "Upon exiting the building, you will proceed through the checkpoint on my left. If you do not exit at this point, you will be denied entrance on subsequent visits. Furthermore, we will find you and eject you forcefully from the premises. Am I understood, sir?"

"I understand," Craig replied.

"Proceed through the tunnel, stop when you are ordered to stop, and follow the instructions given. Please note that during this time your actions will be closely monitored and non-compliance will result in your person being forcefully ejected from the premises. Do you understand, sir?"

Craig acknowledged that he did. With that, the guard motioned him through. The agent hesitated, bravely chanced a glance at Ricky, then marched ahead as if he were walking the plank. The guards flanking the entrance to the tunnel kept their hands free at their sides. Beyond the partition, Ricky could see black helmets gathering in force. But where was the threat? It was just his dumbass *brotha-*spouting agent. Ricky felt coils of anxiety in his stomach. He watched as Craig moved forward slowly, lifting his arms over his head when told, and turning in whatever direction commanded. They performed an X-ray scan, and Ricky wondered if that was even legal outside of airports. He wasn't brave enough to ask.

What would they have to go through when they were leaving? Before he could ponder further, it was his turn, and the same guard motioned him to step forward.

"Name, please."

The Juggernaut did not fuck around.

They were escorted by a guard across a black marble floor to a series of gold-plated elevators. Ricky thought that the guard would be heading up with them, but he remained behind when he and Craig boarded an elevator with a bright interior with more gold plating, red felt trim, and a polished mirror. They kept quiet until the doors closed, and even then, they waited until the elevator passed the second floor. There was a security camera inside the elevator, but that didn't hinder their conversation.

"What the hell was that?" Ricky blurted. "I thought they were going to kick the living shit outta you."

"I don't know, but you can be certain I'll be discussing it with this Edwards character."

"Seriously, man," Ricky went on. "I would've told that guy to suck on a nut if he went on the way he did. Make an example of him."

Craig only shook his head, his cheeks bright red. "Whatever, it's over. I'm just thinking about the money right now."

"I can see why there's a signing bonus if everyone has to go through that shit down there."

"Yeah. Look, just don't say anything to Mr. Edwards, okay? I'll take care of it."

"You better, or I will," Ricky promised.

"Hey, you can't talk shit unless it's in a bar, and you're on your fourth or fifth Mai Tai, okay? So you let me handle it, alright? You don't say anything. Let me do my job."

Ricky could feel some residual heat from Craig's words. The encounter with the security guards had shaken him up more than he was willing to let show. He decided to keep his mouth shut and let Craig do his thing.

"Cuba Libres," he eventually said around the thirty-second floor.

"What?"

"Not Mai Tais. I drink Cuba Libres. If I can. Mai Tais make me sick."

"*Brotha*, you get this deal, and you can drink whatever the hell you want," Craig responded, visibly brighter. Relief flooded through Ricky. He didn't want his agent playing a bad game with the approaching negotiations. As much as he got on his nerves sometimes, Craig did his job and, the Juggernaut had to admit, he did it well.

The doors opened, and a tall, exceptionally thin man dressed in a black and silver pinstriped suit clicked his heels together and bowed. He smiled hugely and motioned with one hand for them exit the elevator.

"Hello there. So glad you could make it. I'm Mr. MacIntosh." He spoke with an English accent and a hint of something exotic, implying that English was not his first language. He was an older man, perhaps in his late forties, with his hair cut military-style short. As he finished introducing himself, he smiled again, and Ricky could clearly see the molars in the back of his huge mouth.

"You must be Mr. Mobera?" MacIntosh shook his hand.

"You can call me the Juggernaut," Ricky said dramatically, feeling the soft grip. A limp handshake marked a wuss, in his opinion.

"Ah, delightful," MacIntosh replied, grinning even wider. "Always a pleasure to meet people who are in character. And you must be Mr. Float?"

Craig took the extended hand and pumped it twice. "A pleasure, sir."

"Excellent. I hope the dogs below didn't frighten you too much?" MacIntosh inquired.

"Yeah, about that," Ricky said. "What was that all about?"

A frown crossed MacIntosh's clean-cut features. "My apologies, Mr. Juggernaut, but we are in a state of semi-lockdown at the moment. We've had some disturbances recently that necessitated the hiring of an outside security force. Very efficient, but not exceptionally pleasant. I've had complaints about them already, and I can assure you, I will be looking into it personally. Can't have the dogs barking at the guests now, can we?"

He showed his molars again. Ricky smiled back, but he knew it probably didn't look genuine. He felt as if MacIntosh was about to sell him some land in Florida.

"This way, gentlemen, and we can get right down to business." MacIntosh led them down a beautiful hardwood hallway dressed with immaculate paintings of bloody sunsets, some surreal, and others simply breathtaking. "We've been talking to some of your competitors today. One by one. Mr. Edwards prefers a *cara a cara* rapport, if you will. He has built his empire on such intimate relationships. But I must warn you not to shake his hand. He is something of a mysophobe, you understand, and we have no desire to offend you in the least with his eccentricities."

"*Myso* wha?" Craig inquired, saving Ricky's own question.

MacIntosh beamed as if Craig was a grand old chap for asking. "Mysophobe. The noun form of mysophobia, *myso* being Greek for filth, and phobia needs no explanation, I'm certain."

Ricky wanted more of an explanation, but instead he kept his mouth shut and rubbed his silk shirt.

"Mr. Edwards is an older gentleman; his name originally means 'Son of Edward,' but also means 'guardian' or 'to prosper,' as you will soon no doubt experience. If he seems a little slow, please do not be misled or alarmed. He is quite lucid and something of a sport, which is why he's organizing this competition—for the sport. He has a fondness for food and drink himself, you see."

With that, MacIntosh halted before a great set of ornate redwood doors with gold handles in the shape of pawing griffons. Ricky wished he'd brought a screwdriver with him. The gold in one handle alone would probably be worth a year's salary, especially for him.

"Here we are," MacIntosh declared, and rapped upon the mighty doors. He paused, lessening his ferocious grin, and listened.

"Come," answered a voice from within.

The doors opened, and Ricky noted the lack of guards. It appeared there weren't any other people present, either. The entire floor seemed to consist of a single hallway and the one set of doors. Not knowing anything about interior design, he figured it was a statement of some sort, probably one of wealth.

Inside, a sun-filtered gleam washed over them. The copper plates on the outside of the building acted as a screen, reducing the glare to cast the chamber in a sepia light. The room was wide, taken straight from any *James Bond* movie where the mega-corporate villain manipulated world events to his own diabolical ends. The carpet was a deep hue of maroon and luxurious beyond belief. Something pleasantly fragrant lingered in the air, making Ricky think of exotic spices. Four black marble columns took up the four corners of the room, and behind a massive desk of expensive looking wood, sat a silent Mr. Edwards, a shadow with the smoldering, early afternoon sun positioned just above his head.

Three chairs of a baroque nature were placed before the desk, and MacIntosh gestured Ricky and Craig to sit. They did, both men slow in lowering themselves to the maroon cushions.

"Place good enough for you two douche bags?" Mr. Edwards blurted, exposing a set of teeth that gleamed a fierce white. *Dentures*, Ricky thought. They had to be dentures as Edwards, with his bald head covered in mottled age patches and his sallow face, had to be approaching a hundred.

Both Ricky and Craig were struck speechless, causing Edwards to chuckle. "Fear not, lads, I'm not senile. Not yet, anyway," he muttered, and his brow crinkled evilly. Ricky was reminded of a wicked goblin, hunched over and ready to instigate.

"I'm Edwards, as this royal bastard has probably informed you. I know who you are already, and time's something you can't trade on the market, so let's get to it, eh? Let's get to the trim? The nasty, as the youngsters would say today," he growled as if he had a throat full of phlegm. "Oh, first things first, you rapscallions. MacIntosh, the money if you will. And no fucking around," he ended with another rumble. To the speechless in front of him, he winked. "MacIntosh is, without question, my best aide ever. A humorous lad, and at my age, it's good to laugh. I like to laugh. And I like competition. What say you?"

The men were stunned. They were stunned even more when MacIntosh appeared with two monogrammed envelopes displaying the words *The Edwards Corporation*. Craig held onto his as if it were a used tissue, not quite certain of what to make of it.

"Open it up. Go on," Edwards encouraged. MacIntosh moved to stand at his right flank, like some tall, grinning flag pole. "Hurry up, now. C'mon, that's it, that's it. Certainly count it all. Yes, count it. I'd do the same. Yes, yes."

Ricky stared down at the extravagant envelope. It held

ten pristine hundred dollar bills. He glanced at Craig, whose mouth hitched upward into a smile.

"You didn't think I'd give you nothing for your time, did you? Not knowing how much your time was worth to you, well, I took a guess." Edwards fixed them with eyes partially filmed over by cataracts. "I know full well how much my time is worth, youngsters."

"Now then, no bullshit." Edwards looked at one, and then the other. "Which one is the champion?"

Hesitantly, Ricky held up his hand.

"Ah, the Juggernaut," Edwards flashed his too-white smile. "You *are* a devourer, my son. What was your record? Sixty hotdogs in twelve minutes? Un-fucking-believable. Truly monstrous. And with only that plum of a gut to show for it. You," Edwards punctuated with a shaky, liver-splotched hand, "are an Eater of *epic* proportions. Truly, lad. My little contest would mean nothing if you weren't a part. The others are Eaters, too, no doubt, but *you* are the one that will legitimatize the whole event. What's a joust without the king's champion? I ask you." He sank back into his chair, his energy apparently spent.

Neither man had anything to say to that. They sat, wide-eyed, holding the envelopes as if the tall MacIntosh would, at any moment, try and snatch them away.

"Um, Mr. Edwards," Craig began. "My client is prepared to sign whatever documents you have at this time. He's very excited to participate in your event."

"Excellent, excellent," Edwards grumbled, then he rotated his jaw as if he were chewing on something. "Then take it away, MacIntosh."

Startled, both men looked up to the designated man, who folded his fingers together over his midsection. Ricky thought he was about six four or six five, but now he was staring at the length of the man's spidery fingers. He caught himself and directed his attention to MacIntosh's face.

"There's been a change in plans, I'm afraid. We won't have you sign anything until the day of the event, which will take place October thirtieth. We've decided to have a Halloween motif for this competition, all CGI integrated on a green screen. All for fun, you understand. For the kids. We wanted something a little more interesting than bobbing for apples or the like. As such, we thought it would be grand fun to have you all wearing ankle chains in plexiglas cells, where you will be ordered to eat until you win or die. With the order being, hopefully, somewhat dramatic. It's for show, you see," MacIntosh added with a chuckle. "You'll be eating hotdogs, with the bun, and allowed water as per official competition rules. Any competitor will be disqualified in the event of reversals. There will be no time limit, as I've stated to Mr. Float, and the extra money will be awarded to the individual who can eat an additional twenty hotdogs over the record of sixty. I'm sorry, but we reconsidered the rules there. We thought it was too easy to beat the record without the time limit, so an extra twenty was arrived at. And just the Eaters will be allowed onto the premises at the time. No agents, no friends or family. You will all sign confidentiality agreements as well, to not spill the beans, so to speak, until after the broadcast. Are you agreeable?"

The two men exchanged glances.

"We agree," Craig announced.

"Hell," Ricky grinned, "for an extra fifty, I'll shit right there to make room for the extra twenty."

MacIntosh pursed his lips in a grimace, the only time his teeth had disappeared. Edwards barked a laugh and rattled in his chair hard enough that MacIntosh gave him a look of concern.

"I like the Juggernaut's candor, MacIntosh. You could learn something from a guy like this."

"I'm certain I would, Mr. Edwards, sir. Well." MacIntosh faced the pair of men. "That's all for now. Take this." He handed Craig a piece of paper. "It contains everything just said, as well as my own personal number if you have any concerns or questions you might have but forgot to ask. Oh, and the venue will be here, on the forty-sixth floor. Any questions?"

They had none.

"Well, then." MacIntosh exhaled and shrugged. "That's that. By your leave, Mr. Edwards, I'll escort these two gentlemen back to the elevator."

Displaying his own near-perfect smile, Edwards dismissed them with one ancient looking hand. "Best fortunes to you, Juggernaut. I look forward to seeing you in competition."

"You'll be there?" Ricky asked, pleasantly surprised.

"Of course," Edwards exclaimed. "That's why it's closed to audiences. I certainly will be in attendance. I positively adore these contests!"

"Oh," Ricky said, caught unprepared and at a loss for words. "Well, see you then."

Still smiling, Edwards gave a little wave.

With one outstretched arm, MacIntosh led them both from the room, the heavy doors closing on their own once they crossed the threshold. He chatted about past competitions televised on the major networks and relayed that it was there Mr. Edwards learned of the world of competitive eating in the first place.

"He was simply astounded by the sheer willpower you

and your fellow Eaters display during a contest. We often wonder where exactly it all goes."

"In the shitter, usually," Ricky answered, eliciting a short laugh from MacIntosh. Then they were at the elevator, doors already open and waiting.

"Until the day, gentlemen," MacIntosh declared with a flourish of his arm.

Ricky and Craig got on board, and as the door closed, they both saw the twinkle in MacIntosh's eye. It wasn't as friendly as when they had first arrived, but neither man spoke of it to the other.

"Fifty grand," Craig breathed.

Ricky shook his head. "A *hundred* grand."

They began talking of the days to come, all the way down to the first floor.

On the day of the event, the contestants gathered in a dark studio on the forty-sixth floor of the Warwick building. True to MacIntosh's word, there were no episodes with security this time around, and Ricky and the other contestants experienced no difficulty in entering the premises. They gathered in ones and twos and stood in an open seating area, where twenty plexiglas booths, arranged side by side in a horseshoe pattern, greeted them. Ricky wandered over to the booths. A chair and a clear plastic table sat in the middle of each booth. There was a transparent door in the rear with a slot about six inches high and the width of the booth. The feed slot, Ricky assumed. They would be shoving the hotdogs in through that gap. He looked at the floor and noted there were no chains, which made him pause.

"Hey, Ricky!" came a familiar voice.

He turned about to see Johnny "Xtra Large" Cloke

grinning and holding out a fist. Johnny was plum-shaped and was probably the only Eater with a weight problem, not that it slowed him down in the least. At five ten and well over three hundred pounds, Johnny played a lot of football and ate a lot of pizza. He wore blue jeans, baggy around his thighs, and suspenders to hold them up. Johnny sported a dapper-looking moustache and beard, and he appeared happy to see Ricky.

"See anything back there, man?" Johnny asked, as Ricky tapped his outstretched fist with his own.

"Only the furniture. Like a fucking cell, man."

"Yeah, but the money's right!" Johnny smiled. "Already spent the grand on a Samsung fifty-two-inch Plasma TV! *Tron's* gonna look sweet on that!"

Ricky had to agree with that. "So who else is here, Johnny?"

The big man leaned against the side of the cubicle. "Most of the same crew. Sick Machine is over there."

Ricky made a face.

"Yeah, I know," Johnny said. "But the guy's okay otherwise. And his girlfriend's hot, man. Anyway, I get along with him, so I said hi."

"Anyone else?"

"*Tabihodai* will be here soon. Hey, y'know, that bastard lied to us. He said his nickname meant "Big Pervert," but it doesn't. I got a friend who's Japanese and speaks it fluent-like, and he said it meant "all-you-can-eat.""

"Hide," Ricky breathed. Hide had a reputation on the circuit. He loved blondes and chased after skirts just as often as The Juggernaut.

"Yeah, well, I'm gonna ask him about that when I get the chance, man."

"Who else is here?" Ricky looked over Johnny's fleshy shoulder and saw shadowy figures, but he couldn't tell who was who.

"Uhh… Marty's here, Rex, Stella, Dougie, a bunch of new guys. Pete Bert is here, Manny Mojito, Craig Roberts…" Johnny trailed off, appearing thoughtful. He knew who Ricky was waiting for. It was no secret, except maybe to Ricky. "Oh, yeah, Amy's here…"

"Amy Duncan?" Ricky asked, wearing cool, but Johnny saw the little hook the Juggernaut's chin took.

"Yeah, Amy's here, man. Right over there." Ricky winced as Johnny pointed and, on cue, Amy "Cheese On Everything" Duncan looked in their direction.

"Yeah, there she is." Johnny's face lit up. "*Hey, Amy!*"

Ricky grimaced as if swallowing a chicken whole. "Okay, okay man. I'm going to go over and say hi."

"You want me to come with?" Johnny asked, but he knew the answer.

"No, no, I'll do it. I, ah, I…" Ricky stammered. He didn't finish. It was obvious Johnny knew. He had been at the last competition down in Philly. He saw what went on, and what didn't. The Juggernaut stepped around his friend and fellow Eater and made his way over to the young woman, cute, in her late twenties, brunette with her hair tied back in a single glorious pigtail. She had an anime-shaped face, and the thighs of a soccer player. When he had met her in Philly, it was late June, and she had been wearing shorts. The woman had a set of muscular legs that the Juggernaut, Lord help him, wanted to simply nibble on.

He crossed the floor, saying hello to the people he knew. She stood with her back against an invisible wall and watched him make his way over. Her eyes twinkled, and she ran a hand over her dark hair. A little smile played about her lips. Ricky could nibble on those, too. *Best behavior now*, he told himself. *Best behavior, or I'll slam the door on my dingle, I swear to Christ, if I screw this up.*

A wall of flesh stepped in front of him. Ricky looked up and groaned. It was Walt "Jaws of Steel" Bridges.

"Well, hello, Jughead," Walt greeted. The sneer on his face made him look as if a fly hook had caught him in the cheek. "Today we rumble for all the marbles."

Ricky ignored the jab, but he stopped. There was no going around head-shaven Jaws of Steel; the man was almost a pro-football linebacker. He towered a full head over the Juggernaut, pounds heavier and all of it muscle. It was Walt's second championship competition; he had lost the first one by only five dogs. Walt didn't like to lose, and he swore revenge the next time around. Next time had come.

"Today's the day I kill the king, Jug *Head*," Walt smirked. "Double-fisted and haven't eaten since eight this morning. Mmmhmm, I like dogs, too. Whaddaya say there, Ricky? Think you're up for this? Are you down?"

Ricky wasn't scared of the man, far from it, but his focus wasn't on this potential threat to his title. "Yeah, whatever, man. Good luck."

But that didn't sate Jaws of Steel. "What's that? Good luck? Fuck luck, man! *You* were lucky last time. You won't escape this round. You just be ready to eat my ass."

"Luke, I am your father," Ricky quipped.

"What?" Walt pulled back, squinting in confusion. Then he looked over his shoulder and saw Amy. Walt wasn't stupid by far; he knew what was up. A douche bag he could be, but even he wasn't douchy enough to come between a match made in an all-you-can-eat restaurant. "You and me.

Today, man. Then only me," Walt said, and wagged a warning finger at the Juggernaut.

"Fuck you, Walt!" someone yelled from the far side, drawing a Medusa gaze from Jaws of Steel and distracting him long enough for Ricky to slip by. Walt wanted to say something, but decided to let him go. Then his expression morphed into one of pleasure. "Hide! You *bastard!*"

Ricky left the big man and made the last few steps to Amy. She stood with her back against the wall, her hands behind her. She wore jeans and a black t-shirt, and in the gloom Ricky thought she looked just fine.

"Hi, Cheese."

"Hi, Juggernaut. You never called me."

"Yeah, well, I…" Ricky decided to try honesty. "I got nervous. Y'know?"

"The Juggernaut got nervous of little old me?" Amy smiled with her nice teeth, and almost stole his heart right there. Months ago, they had sat next to each other down in Philly and had the opportunity to chat before they ate. In those few moments, something clicked. Ricky knew that he had found someone special in Amy. The vibe was there, full and flowing, and somewhere, somehow, without even asking, "Cheese on Everything" was giving him her cell phone number and telling him to call her after the competition. It was that easy.

And he had fucked it up by not calling.

"Yeah, but…" Ricky said, not sensing any hostility. He was being given a second chance, and he was going to make good on it this time. "You wanna get something to drink? Afterwards?"

"Cuba Libres?"

*She remembered.* "If you want."

"I want. I love `em."

Ricky smiled. This woman was made for him. He was willing to lose the gut for her, and shave his chest, even his ass and junk if she wanted.

"Ladies and gentlemen, shall we begin?"

Even though it had been a month, Ricky could have sworn that MacIntosh was wearing the same clothes as he when they had first met. He was still tall, still stick-thin, and still wearing that big shit-kicker smile that suddenly reminded Ricky of the DC comic villain, The Joker.

"EEYAH!" thundered Jaws of Steel. He smacked both hands together and wet his lips with grand theatrical gusto. "Let's roll, baby! Let's eat!"

"We certainly do appreciate your enthusiasm, Mr. Bridges," MacIntosh said with one eyebrow cocked, as if uncertain how to proceed with the big man. "So, without further delay, I'll get to the point. The cameras will begin rolling upon my signal that all is ready. You may sit in any of the booths that you like, and the judges will lock you in. We had to forgo the chains due to legal issues I won't get into. Regardless, we will still place you into the boxes, and you will proceed to eat as many as necessary for you to be declared the winner. There will be only one victor, so I hope you are hungry enough to survive what is about to happen. There are no time limits. You will eat until you can eat no more."

Semi-lively applause followed this statement.

"Now, before you enter, I'll be introducing you one by one. You will be asked to give an oath, a very serious oath, but all in good fun, I assure you, and asked to sign the document you will find on the table in your booth. Any questions?"

There were none.

Nodding, MacIntosh appeared very pleased with the group of competitive Eaters. He raised his hand, and the room lit up in brilliant green. The Eaters were momentarily surprised by the bright display, but only Johnny "Xtra Large" Cloke commented loud enough for all to hear. "Oh, yeah, baby! That's a green screen! For the special effects!"

"Yes, it is!" MacIntosh pounced, spinning, pointing, and scaring the shit out of Xtra Large. "You are correct. This being the day before Halloween, our digital artists will weave their pixel dust and conceive a medieval castle for our viewers. My friends, you will be eating in a dungeon on television."

There were hoots and shouts of "Cool!" from the Eaters. Ricky thought back to the chains. That would have been cool as well, but not this time around, apparently. He would ask later on about the legal issues that had prevented it, probably fire codes or something like that.

MacIntosh placed a tendril of a finger to his ear and nodded, receiving instructions from an unseen director. Then he straightened and threw his arms wide. "Ladies and gentlemen, it is almost *time*. Allow me, your host for this evening, and overlord of the accompanying judges, to introduce our Eaters. First, from Alberta, Canada, their national champion and the *Mouth* of the North—Danny Pelezki!"

Ricky had never heard of the guy, but a spike-haired Danny ran to a booth while shaking his arms above his head as if he had already won something.

"From Nagoya, Japan, the reigning Japanese champion— Hide, *Tabihodai*, Yamanichii!"

Wearing a white and red headband covered in kanji

characters, a confident looking *All- You-Can-Eat* walked toward a booth with one fist raised.

"Next, from parts unknown, Sid, Sick *Machinnnnne, Green!*"

Hearing his name, Sick Machine strutted onto the stage wearing a t-shirt and stretchable jogging pants. He had a grim look on his plain features, as if he meant to redeem himself on national TV. MacIntosh went straight into introducing the next Eater.

Ricky looked to Amy. "You be good now," he said, and winked.

"I will," Amy replied.

"Amy, *Cheese on Everything,* Duncan!" MacIntosh howled, throwing down his arm as if starting the Indy 500.

She winked back at Ricky and walked to a booth. Taking her time, she spun once, waving at unseen cameras, and smiled. Then she stepped behind the glass.

"Yeah, man!" came the roar, distracting Ricky from Amy's thighs.

"From New York, New York! *Steam*rolling over the local competition…"

"Yeah, man!"

"The Jaws of Steel!" MacIntosh snarled. "Walt…"

"Yeah, man! C'mon!" Walt urged, dancing from foot to foot. Ricky thought he could feel the floor tremble.

"*Bridges!*" MacIntosh howled, seeming on the brink of snapping his vocal cords.

Walt charged the booth, ran up to the one to the right of Amy, and ripped off his T-shirt. He went into a pose down, almost bursting his impressive biceps, then roared "Yeah!" one more time as he whirled on the Eaters behind him. He straightened, puffed out his chest, and rolled his gut, screaming "Yeah! It's mine, baby! All mine!"

MacIntosh seemed amused for all of three seconds, then he continued, introducing the rest: Jonathan "Xtra Large" Cloke, also from New York; Marty "The Hole" Roberts; Rex "TexMex" Hool from San Diego; Craig "Motor Mouth" Roberts from Detroit; Stella "Supersize Me" Tulk; Dougie "Abdominal" Snowman from Baltimore; Manny "The Spanish Canyon" Mojito; Pete "Gar-Gut-Uan" Bert from Omaha; and others that Ricky didn't recognize. He was last, as fitting for a champion.

"And now… *intro*ducing… the current world champion and record holder, the devourer of sixty hotdogs in the regulation time of twelve minutes… from New York, New York, *Ricky*… The Juggernaut… Moooooooooobera!"

*'What did the baby bull say to the papa bull when looking out over the herd?'* Ricky once again played the joke in his head. It was his mantra, his internal battle cry. *'Let's charge down there and fuck a cow, Pa!* To which the papa bull replied, *'Easy, son. Let's* walk *down there… and fuck 'em all.'*

His game face on, the Juggernaut walked to the last remaining booth, two to the right of Amy's. He did not raise his arms. He did not look at the cameras—he didn't know where they were anyway—but he stopped directly in front of the booth of Jaws of Steel.

And popped him the finger.

A furious Walt slammed both hands against the plexiglas, rattling the entire frame, but it didn't shatter. Curses that would be labeled "expletives" and censored by bird tweets or some other cute sound would mask the man's savage rant from the broadcast. Ricky ignored him and slowly, *deliberately* showed him his back before making his way to the final booth.

MacIntosh had to admit, he liked the balls on Ricky the Juggernaut Mobera.

Once in their respective booths, the competitors stood, looking expectantly out at the green chamber. Then, from the back of the room, a wheelchair, pushed by an overweight, hairy belly-bulging, medieval executioner complete with a black mask, rolled into view. Sitting in the chair, his lower half covered by a thick blanket, was an excited-looking Mr. Edwards. He held up a hand, signaling for the pusher to stop at the mouth of the arranged booths. More executioners stepped out from secret places, moving along the booths and locking them from the outside. Ricky saw that there was no way out unless someone let them out. He also noticed the bored holes in the floor, each as thick as his thumb. He moved the wooden chair aside, as did most of the other Eaters, and found a single document waiting to be signed with a feather quill. A two-liter plastic pitcher and cup, both filled with water, had been placed on a corner of the desk. It was all interesting, and he looked forward to seeing what the dungeon would look like when all was done.

Sitting quietly and clenching his hands together, a delighted Edwards gave the nod to MacIntosh. The henchman whirled and walked by each of the contestants' booths. He carried a wireless microphone, wielding it like a sword.

"You will now stand and raise your left hand," MacIntosh ordered. "Only your left hand. Repeat after me: I do solemnly swear…"

As a chorus, they repeated the words.

"To consume all that is placed before me… until my last breath… and Kaltos takes my soul."

The last bit made Ricky raise an eyebrow. He glanced to

his left and, lucky him, Sick Machine was there with Jaws of Steel next to him. Then there was Amy. Sick Machine returned his questioning look. Ricky was glad he wasn't the only one who thought the oath strange.

"Now, sign your documents on the designated line." MacIntosh intoned.

They complied, and Ricky noted that the ink was a dark berry red. When he finished, he brought the quill in for closer inspection. He smiled. *Blood. Fake blood. They're really going all out here.*

When they looked up from signing their names, all were startled. MacIntosh was no longer dressed in a business suit. The stick-man now wore a flowing robe marked with arcane symbols along its length. His microphone had been replaced with a staff topped by a glowing crystal. From somewhere overhead, Ricky heard the collective gasp of the Eaters. That was a cool special effect.

"All done? Excellent! I'll take them now." He walked, robes swishing, past each booth. As he did, the contracts disappeared from the tables or grips of the Eaters, much to their amazement. Finished, he stepped back to the sitting Mr. Edwards. The tall man dropped to a knee and offered the materialized documents to his employer. Edwards took them in both hands, and the contracts disintegrated in a flash of flame.

Another impressed gasp rose from the onlookers. The effects in this production were *killer.*

Then, the executioners, grim and ponderous, appeared at both ends with full trays of hot dogs. They delivered the food to each of the Eaters by slipping the trays through the slots. They gave each Eater two large trays, placed side by side. Ricky did a quick count. There were fifty total. The first wave. *You are all going in mah belly!*

"Well then, that's all done," MacIntosh said pleasantly, looking at an eager Edwards.

"Certainly is," Edwards commented. "Now, let's get these gluttons moving."

Nodding, MacIntosh turned back to the competitors. His toothy grin suddenly turned savage. "It's *time*, everyone! It's time to see who can eat the most. Who will live, and who will perish? And who will walk about with the *ultimate* prize? Are you ready?"

They answered that they were. Ricky was looking at the first dog to be consumed. *Fuck 'em all*, he thought over and over, *fuck 'em all.* He felt a shot of adrenalin and the need to just *go*, as he did at the start of every competition, but this time, it was more. He was *on fire.*

"Then… *Eat!*" MacIntosh shrieked.

The booths erupted in a flurry of hands and jaws and energy. Ricky grabbed the first wiener and wolfed it down while simultaneously dunking a bun into the cup. A second later, that followed. Then he grabbed the next wiener and devoured it in three bites. He chewed, swallowed the meat in one large lump, and shoved down the bun. He inhaled the food as quickly as an industrial vacuum cleaner. He scarfed number three down just as quickly, dunking the bun in the water and sucking it down in a second. He began bouncing, which he sometimes did as part of his technique, and felt his stomach beginning to expand. Not much, as three hotdogs in the gut was a teardrop compared to what he could potentially put in there. With the bonus money on the table, he was prepared to test his limits to the extreme.

Next to him, Sick Machine ate at a similar pace, wolfing down numbers four and five, complete with waterlogged buns, and getting into his own rhythm. Sick Machine bent over the tray of dogs and, with eyes closed, resembled a huge meditating contraption, sucking in hot dogs from the base and sipping water every fifth bite.

Just beyond, Jaws of Steel engulfed his fifth and sixth wieners, holding two at a time and munching away at both until gone, where he would then tackle the buns. Each bite he took made him appear as a great white shark, powerful and terribly efficient. Food fragments collected on his cheeks, and Walt palm-wiped and lapped them up with a bestial roar.

Edwards watched the Eaters from his wheelchair. If any of them paused to look in his direction, they would have seen his teeth become pointier, as if filed, and his lips thinner, so that even as he closed his mouth, his jaws were still visible. His eyes dilated until they were utterly black. "Eat, you fuckers, *eat*," he snapped loudly, ogling them eagerly.

MacIntosh stepped back and watched impassively. He leaned on his staff at times, dividing an equal amount of attention amongst all of them. Exhilarated, he didn't want to miss anything. The suspense built, and he knew, he *knew*, that things would become even *more* interesting as the competition progressed.

Ripping into his tenth dog, Ricky belched and drank some water. He reminded himself that there was no time limit, so he only had to pace himself. He could do that easily, he thought. Speed was not needed, but compacting every bite and allowing his stomach to expand for comfort was critical. He glanced at the bent-over form of Sick Machine, so low that Ricky thought the man was snorting the food instead of eating. He glimpsed the profile of Jaws of Steel and saw water splash as he took a violent sip. Walt was ripping it up, but to what end? It perplexed Ricky as he chewed onward, grabbing number eleven. Didn't the stupid jock get the memo about no time limit?

Then Amy straightened, doing her little *pom-pom* routine, as she called it. She moved her hips and bopped up and down, but there was control in her method, unlike the sheer gorging of Jaws of Steel. She took a little sip of water from the cup and picked up the next dog in a smooth, unrushed way. She was doing it right. *That's my girl*, Ricky thought. Funniest places where you meet *the one*.

To his left, Dougie Abdominal Snowman straightened and both hands went to his throat. His face went crimson and he roared. He gulped, took a ragged breath, and bawled again, drawing the attention of several executioners. Dougie bent over and rammed a fist on his table, making the hotdogs bounce. He hit his chest several times in succession. Then he came up again, shook himself, and took a deep breath. He tore back into the meat as the particle that had momentarily choked him dislodged and went down the right pipe.

Eating dog number sixteen, Ricky paid the man scant attention. Choking sometimes happened, but if it was too bad, there were paramedics to rush in and give aid. Abdominal had recovered and dived back into the competition. Munching away, Ricky glanced around the room again, and it occurred to him that there were no medical professionals in the wings, which was odd. All main events had a waiting ambulance and supporting staff nearby in case of mishap; perhaps he just couldn't see them. He took in number eighteen, deciding that the paramedics must be present, but out of sight. He couldn't believe that such a well-funded event would fail to have first responders on hand in case of emergency.

He felt the first notable stretch of his gut, just between a brief breath and dog number twenty. He had devoured a sizeable chunk of the hotdogs in front of him, and he wondered briefly if the executioners were keeping an eye on things. They would have to bring more food before he ran out. Almost as soon as the thought hit him, he saw a group of them move into position at either end. As the Eaters finished their first trays of twenty-five, they were removed and another was slipped in. The event had just passed its first marker without any incidents, other than Dougie's choking episode. By the time the executioners got to him in the center, he had finished the first twenty-five and gulped down number twenty-seven. Taking a needed sip of water, the Juggernaut plowed onward. He felt great. He felt the urge to devour *everything* before him. In his mind, the money was his.

He felt eyes on him and glanced to his right. Jaws of Steel fixed him with a hateful gaze, as he shoved numbers twenty-nine and thirty into his face with feral abandon. Particles flew from his mouth and covered his lower chin. Snarling, Ricky matched him. He didn't shove wieners into his mouth two at a time, but he kept a steady flow of meat going into his maw. They stood like this for long seconds, going into a minute, consuming hotdog after hotdog like ravenous wolves. He didn't know how many Walt had downed, but Ricky guessed he had just inhaled number thirty-four. He wiped his mouth with his fingers, flicked them clean, bounced on the balls of his feet, and scooped up the next.

Overhead, MacIntosh's voice, projected from powerful speakers, cut through the back glare of the green screens.

"Throughout the ages, gluttony has been a sin, a sin of selfish overindulgence of food and drink. Never in all of my existence, have I, have *we*, witnessed the unabashed celebration of this terrible, terrible sin until this century, where competitions are organized at the behest of corporations, and the throngs stand by with eager and glazed eyes."

*Jesus*, Ricky thought, *he's laying it on thick*. The Juggernaut was eating faster now, feeling the swell of his stomach and knowing that he had plenty of room remaining. He had downed number forty, and the tray before him was thinning out.

"So we, my partner and I, decided to make examples of the gluttonous vermin on stage this night. The exalted ones of the day, praised only for their ability to mindlessly consume, when so many cannot feed at all. When so many who hunger look upon their glorified antics, and wish for but one *bite* of that which the gluttonous so feverishly devour. At first, we thought merely to transport them to some desolate place, where worms, maggots, and other earth-ridden filth would be the only sustenance present. Where *Famine* rules with an emaciated fist and squeezes out suffering as a sun laying waste to exposed flesh. Where they would realize *true* hunger as punishment for their sin, and be humbled and weep because of it. But then Famine had a much *better* idea, and conspired with *Gluttony*, manifested in flesh, to fabricate this contest of will, strength of jaw… and *death*."

Still eating, Ricky looked up and saw MacIntosh, arms flung wide as if in worship, rambling off what sounded like a sermon. In the back of his mind, part of him wanted to stop eating and ask what was going on, but the greater part merely kept him chewing. He hoped Macintosh would shut up soon. He was becoming as big a drag as some celebrities who spoke out against his sport.

Then it happened.

Ahead of him, in the last cell on the right, was one of the new people that Ricky didn't know, one of the guys from a few regional competitions who felt he had a chance to run with the big Eaters. He stood, wobbled on his feet, and puffed out his cheeks. Ricky knew, whilst downing his forty-second hotdog, that the guy was about to do a reversal. He was about to throw up. Big time. He watched as the man grabbed both of his knees and opened his mouth to vomit, to roar forth a torrent of undigested food and stomach acid. His face turned red with the force the sphincter to his gut was under, but instead of releasing a river, nothing came up.

Again the guy heaved, bent over at the waist. He heaved until water flowed from his blood-rimmed eyes, and his head shook with the fury of unspeakable pent-up pressure... but he produced nothing.

MacIntosh stopped preaching, captivated by the Eater's struggle. Edwards followed his gaze and clapped his hands together in evil mirth, his head bouncing up and down like a happy chimp.

The man did not throw up. Instead, he gasped for breath in between powerful dry heaves, a painful wracking of his entire body, akin perhaps to a childbirth where the newborn refuses to enter the world.

"Eat!" MacIntosh swooped in and jabbed his staff at the stricken Eater. "I command you to eat! Goddamn you!"

Grimacing, food mashed against his teeth, and under a power no longer his own, the Eater reached down, picked up another hotdog, and did just that.

"Excellent!" MacIntosh squealed, and pulled back a step. "I knew you could do it! I know *all* of you can do it!"

Ricky looked down at the food before him and knew he should feel something at what had just happened. He reached for hotdog number forty-seven. He felt the growing sandbag in his gut, but chewed on. He couldn't slow down, not with Jaws of Steel competing.

Then, somewhere to his left, Marty, The Hole Crazier reached his limit. He swayed on his feet, much like the new Eater had done, and gasped for breath. Unlike the new guy, whose upper esophageal sphincter had simply refused to release the build-up in pressure, Marty opened his mouth, and a second later he sprayed a red torrent onto the food, plexiglas, and table before him. All of the Eaters heard his volcanic roar, and those next to him saw him vomit with such force that, when Marty tried to check himself, it sprayed out of both nostrils instead. Vomitus, like dark coffee grounds, pooled around the man's ankles, and Marty The Hole continued heaving, holding onto his knees for support.

*"That wasn't supposed to happen!"* Edwards shouted in his phlegmy voice, pointing a hand at the finished Marty.

MacIntosh's face became a thing of red fury. He marched over to the cell of Marty The Hole Crazier and held up his staff. With an audible *snick,* a long tapered blade sprung from its head, and MacIntosh jammed it through the slot of the cell and skewered Marty through the middle.

"Holy shit!" Sick Machine exclaimed, a mashed pulp of meat falling from his lips unchecked. Ricky slowed his eating, but didn't stop; neither did the remaining nineteen Eaters. As soon as the food fell from Sick Machine's mouth and onto the floor, Sid stooped, no longer in control of his body, picked it up, and popped it back in. His eyes bulged at what he had done. He tried to stop, *willed* himself to stop, but found he could not.

"Someone obviously didn't say their oath as they should have," MacIntosh grunted, his grin savage. He kept stabbing the crumpled form within the cell until Marty The Hole died in a pool of his own blood and stomach acid.

The Eaters, now fully aware that they were *unable* to stop eating, kept right on munching while trying desperately to control their ravenous bodies.

Ricky *tried* to stop again. He willed his arms to stop feeding food to his mouth and fought to keep his jaws shut, but he was powerless. In fact, to his horror, the Juggernaut picked up speed. He gobbled number fifty-one, cognizant that he barely chewed the thing. He slurped water, dunked a bun, and sucked it in with a building, frightening energy.

"The game's afoot, MacIntosh!" Edwards howled in unholy glee.

The Eater who had tried to vomit was in trouble once more. He could no longer swallow effectively, and each bite of food backed up into his throat so that, every time he opened his mouth, pulped food dribbled and fell out.

The vulture that was MacIntosh drew near and inspected the man with evil interest. The tall man shook his head without sympathy. "No more?" he asked. "Mercy?"

The man behind the plexiglas cried out and turned away. He clawed at the smooth surface of the cell, but couldn't free himself from the trap. MacIntosh stood and watched for a moment. Then, he summoned the executioners, and the Eaters discovered their true purpose.

The executioners opened the Eater's cell and manhandled him out of it. Six of them held him to the floor and stretched out his limbs. Another big man dressed in black medieval garb stepped up and kicked the Eater repeatedly in the stomach. The intestinal tract ruptured from the internal stress, and he died with his tongue protruding obscenely from between his lips.

The remaining Eaters continued cramming food into their mouths. In between gasps for breath, they screamed. Stella Supersize Coker shrieked, choked, and collapsed against the door of her cell.

MacIntosh appeared at her cell in an instant. "Eat!" MacIntosh bellowed. "*Eat!*"

Stella could not eat, however, as a huge chunk of hotdog had clogged her airway, choking the life from her. As darkness clouded the edges of her vision, the skeletal figure called MacIntosh stood gleaming before her. Her last instinctive urge was *still* to take a bite…

*No time limit*. Ricky almost cackled. Of course there was no time limit. These boys weren't bullshitting when they said it was to the death, or perish, as they put it. And he had sucked it up as a figure of speech. Now, he was sucking up number fifty-five and loving it. His gut expanded, and he jumped about to help it along. Still trying to stop, but laughing in between bites, Ricky snarled. He truly was the *Juggernaut*. Nothing could stop him!

There was a grunt to his left, and he turned to see Dougie Abdominal Snowman fall backward and tumble over his chair. He landed on his back with hotdog guts smeared about his chops.

He was number four.

And the eating became that much more intense.

Eaters who could never have eaten as much as they were currently consuming surpassed their own personal bests, but with explosive results. When they ate and filled themselves beyond capacity, food still being accepted into their stomachs but not permitted to leave, the musculature stretched to its maximum until bleeding began. For some sorcerous reason, they could not expel the food from their stomachs or their bowels. Eaters danced or jerked spasmodically in their cells from the internal pressure. Abdominal pain, sparkling bright and stabbing, caused some of them to collapse to the floor while their arms kept right on feeding them like an elephant's trunk. In some, the stomach ruptured, and death was instantaneous. Johnny Xtra Large Cloke's own stomach, stretched and then stretched even more, burst internally and dropped him dead as quickly as a sniper round between the eyes. Pete 'Gar-Gut-Uan' Bert ate until streams of sweat and tears ran down his flushed features before his eyes rolled up, and he collapsed onto the table, then rolled off onto the floor. Other Eaters, the newer ones, died just as quickly, leaving the true elite. Craig 'Motor Mouth' Roberts could no longer put food into his mouth. When they came for him, his entire stomach cavity felt as if he had consumed a sack of needles instead of meat. The executioners splayed him across the cold floor and kicked him to death.

But the Juggernaut ate on.

*Seventy* hotdogs. He grinned madly. It was a personal best. Still dunking and chewing, he went to work on seventy-one as Rex' TexMex' Hool, in a pitiful display of agony, was dragged from his cell and had his belly stomped until something burst. Danny 'The Mouth of the North' collapsed and MacIntosh impaled him again and again with his spear-staff through the cell's slot. Danny must have fallen beyond the reach of the weapon because MacIntosh, screaming profanities and frothing at the mouth, went to the back of the dying man's cell, yanked open the door, and stood over the man to continue his stabbing.

The Juggernaut paid no heed.

He looked to his right, his vision swimming as if hotdog pulp had invaded his sinus cavity, and spied the four who remained. There they were, all in a row, the best of the best and still chewing. No longer bouncing, Ricky met the sorry-looking eyes of Jaws of Steel. The fight had gone out of him, yet he continued to consume, slower now, but consuming nonetheless.

Suddenly, Walt reared up and fell backwards. When the executioners came to his cell and unlocked his door, the once pro-footballer rose to his feet, not nearly as done in as they originally thought. With a roar, he punched one executioner and dropped him to the floor. Another executioner produced what looked to be a taser, but Jaws of Steel yanked it away, twisted it around, and jammed into the guy's testicles. The masked man stiffened as the current ripped through his body, then he collapsed to the ground. Working his way to Ricky's cell, Walt turned to another attacker and blocked a thrust meant for his painfully swollen stomach. Walt threw an uppercut into the guy's jaw. He connected and threw the killer backward.

Walt placed a hand on the first clasp of Ricky's cell, and the Juggernaut, still chewing, moved to spring free, but a solid steel-toed boot crunched into Jaws of Steel's side, popping the man's tongue out. The connection froze the half-naked man in his tracks, and he sunk to his knees. Moments later, the black-masked killers danced on his body. Ricky turned his back to them only to see Sick Machine stabbed through the middle by a grinning MacIntosh. Even through the plexiglas, Ricky could hear the meaty, perforating sounds of each puncture.

Number seventy-four. His guts begged him to stop, but he couldn't halt the motions. His limbs refused to do anything else. He was the last, or so he thought for a brief moment before he glanced around and saw Amy, still eating, just as full as he was, and suffering every bit as much. They were the last. His breath hitched in fear and distress, and hotdog bun particles flew from his lips. He could see her sweating profile and how horribly distended her midsection had become. He wanted to shout out to her, but Edwards's high pitched maniacal laugh was the only sound he could hear. *Amy*, he thought, and for a brief moment in time, they weren't in the cells anymore. They were in a bar, clinking Cuba Libres, and eyeing each other over their glasses. She was giggling at his bad jokes, and he was adoring her.

Halfway through hotdog number seventy-five, Ricky felt the dagger-like pain in his innards, piercing and deep; his world spun. He saw only the flash of a green wall. He distantly felt an impact as Amy was yanked away from him.

Then... blackness.

"We have a *winner!*" MacIntosh announced, belting out the final word at the top of his lungs. No sooner had the words been spoken than the horrible compulsion to keep shoveling food into her mouth ceased, replaced with an almost overpowering urge to scream from the pressure of her abdominal cavity. Sweating and aching, Amy "Cheese on Everything" Duncan dropped to her knees and did something she had never done in her professional eating career.

She threw up.

Exhausted and in pain, her jaws and midsection tortured

beyond anything she'd ever felt before, she emptied the contents of her stomach. She did not care where she puked, only that she voided. Somewhere in time, she drew a breath, and looked up with red-rimmed eyes. The green walls were bright, and across from her, she saw the unmoving train wrecks representing the other Eaters. She saw Ricky Mobera lying on his back with eyes glazed over and staring at a ceiling he would never see.

Amy began to cry, and after a while, she felt hands lifting her to her feet.

"Congratulations, Ms. Duncan," MacIntosh said, smiling gently. "You've beaten the field here today. Quite the feat."

Too tired to respond, Amy wiped her mouth and glared at the stick man. Somewhere nearby, she could hear the squeaking of wheels.

"Here you are." MacIntosh handed her a cloth bag. "Fifty thousand dollars. As promised."

She didn't take it, making no effort to lift either arm.

"I understand," MacIntosh consoled. "The contest was physically draining. Mentally as well, I imagine." He lifted a string strap attached to the bag and carefully placed it over her head until it hung around her neck

The squeaky wheels were closer now.

"But you are triumphant. And for that, the grand prize of *life* is yours. I am sorry to inform you that you did not manage to win the bonus, but I'm certain that isn't too upsetting. Not after all of this. We have all the footage we need. A podcast will sweep the net tomorrow, in all of its delicious glory, right up to the exciting finale. Uncensored. Uncut."

Amy's jaw clenched, and she had the sudden urge to fight, to soccer-kick the smug bastard right in the balls. She didn't; she was too exhausted.

"One last thing, MacIntosh," the rumbly voice of Edwards said. Amy turned her head and spied the little man, or whatever he was, hunched over and smirking. Beside him were two muscular executioners. Producing a remote, Edwards turned on the overhead lights to reveal the full size of the studio, along with a balcony section. The overhead lights reflected off a plexiglas partition, and Amy's mouth dropped open in horror. Behind the soundproof barrier were seats for about a hundred people. Naked writhing bodies missing arms and legs filled half of them. Amy saw their faces, full of shock and agony, their mouths stuffed with ball gags, and her knees felt ready to give away.

"Ah, yesss," Edwards growled, not content in just allowing Amy to simply *see*. "A formality and nothing more. I just wanted you to meet *who* you were eating…"

# 4

# Expansion

The power went out at 9:23 AM.

The abrupt end to Professor Billsbury's PowerPoint presentation on Erwin Rommel and his Afrika Korps' armored drive into the Egyptian El Alamein brought on a muttering of soft expletives.

"Cheap piece of—sorry," the grey-haired professor caught himself before he cursed in front of a university classroom of about forty-five students. The lights in the classroom were off to "provide a better theatrical experience," in Billsbury's words. He paused at the podium when he noticed his laptop was dead.

"Oh, what the hell is going on?" he whined loudly, drawing both smiles and puzzled expressions from his watching students. It was a little early in the season to be affected by a winter storm, and the video failure meant the return to a lecture only the Army reservists in attendance would find interesting. Billsbury fiddled with his laptop for a moment. With a sigh that could be heard at the back of the class, he shrugged and turned to switch on the overhead lights. A student sitting close to the door got up before he took two steps.

"Oh, thank you, Brad," Billsbury said.

"No trouble, Professor," the twenty-year-old replied. Brad flicked the switches, frowned, and flicked again.

"Would someone open the drapes back there?" Billsbury asked. Two students rose to comply, and sunlight soon brightened the back of the class. The layout of the room didn't allow the natural light to reach the front of the class. Students buzzed as they attempted to revive their notebooks and laptops from sleep modes only to find their batteries had failed. A few discovered their cell phones were also dead.

Brad looked at his watch. The digital face was vacant.

"Now this is… is weird," Billsbury muttered in a puzzled tone. He fished his cell phone out of his blue jacket, tried to switch it on, and frowned at the lack of life. He stepped back to the podium while he tried in vain to grasp the concept of electronics and power sources failing simultaneously. The power in the room going off he could understand, but what could affect the batteries of portable devices like cell phones and laptops? The professor rubbed his chin, feeling the stubble there.

"Anyone here an engineer?" he asked, peering at his class over the rims of his black-framed glasses. He got feeble laughter.

"What's that?" Brad asked guardedly.

"What?" Billsbury turned his attention on the young man dressed in fall clothing—jeans, sweater, and a light jacket which he hadn't bothered to remove for class. Brad kept his hair cropped in a short military style that reminded Billsbury of a brick. Brick top. The name sounded familiar. Brad stood as if in the middle of a huge plane of thin ice, having just felt the first crack. His arms were spread out at his sides, as if for balance, and his eyes focused on the carpeted floor of the classroom. "Feel that?"

Billsbury stopped thinking and stood still.

The floor was trembling. Softly.

"An earthquake?" another student asked. He was a big man with a varsity sweater displaying the university's *A.*

"In Nova Scotia?" someone scoffed.

"In *Wolfville?*" another stressed.

"They can happen anywhere," a young woman declared, then darted beneath her desk. Billsbury didn't think that the university desks would save anyone if a quake was big enough to collapse the cement ceilings overhead. If it *was* a quake. Strangely, the room kept shaking. And it was slowly, but most certainly, getting stronger.

"Not a quake, man," Varsity *A* stated. His hair was shaved to the skull, and his eyes were wide with fear, fear that grew with the intensity of the shaking room.

Billsbury did the only thing he could think of. "Everyone, please exit through the back of the class. Don't bother with your things, just get—"

His words were cut off by someone bolting from his back seat and through the door in a flash. If the door hadn't been there, Billsbury imagined the escaping man would have left his outline in the wall just like a Saturday morning cartoon. The woman who had taken shelter under her desk bolted from her cover and made an *L* toward the emergency exit. Like a bottle of something loud and bubbly draining out of a sink, people bobbed and weaved their way outside, their speculations popping the air. Billsbury watched his students go and hoped to Christ it wasn't a terrorist attack. That was all he needed on hump Wednesday. He was the last one to reach the door, and he noted that his was the only laptop left behind. This would be one for the Arts Faculty weekly beer fest at the pub if it was all some sort of elaborate examination scare. And his goddamn computer had better be in the exact place he left it after all was said and done.

Billsbury emerged from the Beveridge Arts Centre into the parking lot and breathed deeply of October air fragrant with the smell of burning leaves. The ground was covered with patches of yellow, orange, and brown, and bare trees stood before the houses along the nearby road. Students milled about, looking up at the arts building with expressions of fear. Some made jokes. Billsbury heard one varsity voice shriek, "*Yeah, baby!*" but didn't get the reference. He gazed up at the red brick expanse of the centre and wondered again what was happening. The earth still shook. Visions of a Japanese airport being swept under a tsunami played through his head. He'd seen footage of the terrible earthquake and the devastation it had wrought only months ago. Nova Scotia wasn't in an active quake zone as far as he knew, but he also knew that quakes could happen anywhere. And the quake that had destroyed billions worth of property and claimed the lives of thousands in Japan had lasted for an unbelievable five minutes.

Billsbury figured this tremor had just passed that time limit.

Students got in and out of cars with some shaking their heads, some wearing expressions of fear, and one or two swearing loud enough to be heard.

"What do you think's happening, Professor?" a young woman asked. She was one of his students, but for a moment he couldn't remember her name. Then it came to him—Selena Burlington. He shook his head and shrugged. He had no idea. His attention was then taken by his colleague, a big Brit named Elders, who was taking huge strides in his direction with his own body of students in tow. Bald on top with a wild fringe of hair ringing his gleaming head, he was a tall man in his sixties with a huge sweater-covered gut. He wore seventies-style black-rimmed glasses. Knowing Elders, it was probably the same pair he had worn as a student, and he was simply lucky enough, and old enough, that the style had come around again, placing him at the height of fashion. The big lecturer got on Billsbury's nerves, and he was grateful that he stopped well away to look up at the arts center.

"Step away now, step away," he called to his students, flicking his hands in the air as if he was about to magically produce something. Elders struck a pose then, hands on his hips, as if to say, "If anything is going to happen, let it rip." *He* was ready.

"Stand back a little further," Billsbury instructed Selena and the others gathered around. "Just in—"

The tremors intensified. Women shrieked. Men shouted, "*Whoa!*" The vibrations became stronger, hard enough that Billsbury could feel it in his teeth fillings. People braced themselves with broader, closer to the ground, stances.

"What the hell is going on?" Billsbury asked.

Emergency sirens blared in the distance, coming from further down the bay. People across the street came out onto their front porches and looked about in wonder. A male student wearing an Acadia blue leather coat yelled, "*Quiet!*" Amazingly, he got it.

Then they heard it—a low rumble coming from the Bay of Fundy coastline. Anxious to see the source of the sound, everyone turned in the direction of Main Street.

Suddenly, people began screaming and running up the side road, away from Main Street. Some of the students needed no further encouragement. They turned and ran for higher ground. The arts center was located at the base of hill, and students bolted up the steep incline. Billsbury stood firm, his attention divided between the mass coming at him and the students taking flight to higher levels. Over the noise he heard something else, like a low rush of leaves almost, becoming deeper in tone and gathering momentum. It sounded huge, and immensely powerful. Darkness was visible in the distance between the houses and the other buildings built closer to the mudflats, but it was growing.

Feeling the first grip of panic in his lower extremities, Billsbury began to back up. He kept his eyes on the low line of buildings perhaps two hundred meters away. Then his jaw dropped. The students had been correct in running. Swirling across the flat plains, just behind the shop fronts populating Main Street, came the dark surge of ocean water.

People escaping Main Street passed him. Billsbury turned to jog, heading up the hill in the middle of a paved road, which quickly filled with people seeking higher ground. Their expressions were all about self-preservation. A dog shot by. Billsbury looked over his shoulder, and fear exploded in his heart. *Tsunami!* his mind shrieked. *It's a fucking tsunami!*

*"Run, David!"* Elders shouted at him while back pedaling up the hill and looking back. *"Run!"*

Fear propelled the crowds higher. More people came out of the houses along the road on the left and from the Student Union Building on the right; all of them stopped and stared. The elevation was about two hundred meters above sea level, and exhaustion started to slow most of the runners.

Billsbury stopped running just across from the Student Union Building. His chest heaving, he turned about to see what was happening. The first few shops on Main Street were consumed by a wave that stretched across his field of vision and beyond. The wave, a good thirty meters high, swallowed more single- and two-story structures without pausing and slammed into a Catholic church. The church's steeple bent and disappeared into the surge. Cars, trucks, and debris could be seen bobbing along the crest of the wave, and the whole front slammed into the rear of the arts center like a whale inhaling a shrimp. Water broke across the roof of the fourth floor, and came toward the hill. The monster wave consumed the lower houses and rushed up the lower half of the hill's face, splashing down as if it were a living thing just shot from behind.

Below where Billsbury stood, a few stragglers just past the waterline ran back with arms outstretched to reach those who had been slapped off their feet by the monster wave. The water thrust weakly against the rise of the land, its energy seemingly spent, but didn't recede. He saw Elders moving off, reaching out to people. Billsbury didn't help those struggling in the surf. Fear had gripped him anew in his limbs and torso. He began moving higher on the hill, gawking at the Bay of Fundy.

Rising like a child's building block once submerged, a dark box shape crept up from the ocean's depths. It was an incredible sight, and sobering when compared to the mere splash of water before it, heralding the thing's approach. Billsbury estimated the approaching block to be more than fifteen stories, much taller than the Beveridge Arts Centre. He didn't know how wide it was, but from his vantage, he could see the far right corner and believed it to be at least a kilometer in length or more, as it went beyond sight to his left.

The thing was *gargantuan*. And it grew as it got closer.

What really got Billsbury moving, however, was the glimpse of its twin, emerging from the right of the first and pushing east. The block approaching the hillside filled his vision. Around him, townspeople and students climbed the hill as their cries of terror pierced the air. Billsbury could see others just standing and watching, but that wasn't for him. He headed further up, toward the soccer pitches on the top, panting and feeling as if his chest might explode. He had just sprinted up a hill in five minutes he would usually drive up in thirty seconds. When he could run no further, he turned again to see where the behemoth block was.

The sight paralyzed him.

He was only a third of the way up the hillside, but the thing charging the coastline was much larger than he had first thought. Its purplish blue bulk, perhaps a little under two kilometers wide, was still higher than where he now stood. The thing blotted out its twin and, as Billsbury watched, the land began to shake harder. A steady thrumming arose, causing him to crouch and eventually sit while others stumbled by, some of which stopped and stared at the monstrous construct coming inland.

Then it hit land.

A shriek of metal on rock accompanied a sound of churning on a scale that Billsbury could not imagine. He watched as the water receded, slapping up in a frothy surge against the base of the wall, where glimpses of a strip of blackness and flashing steel could be seen.

"Professor Billsbury, we better get out of here," a voice said. He turned his head and stared at a face he thought he knew.

"Professor?"

"Yes?"

"We have to get moving. Now, sir." The young man from his class hooked a hand under Billsbury's arm.

"They're coming," Billsbury said. "Whatever they are." He was pulled to his feet. More screams could be heard halfway across the campus.

"Yes, sir, I know," the young man responded. He was athletic, barely breathing hard, and almost half a head taller than Billsbury. "But we can't stay, sir."

"Alright," Billsbury said. "But I can't run anymore."

"That's okay. We'll walk the rest of the way and save our gas for when we need it."

"Alright."

They got moving again. Billsbury kept looking over his shoulder at the approaching purplish blue titan. The sounds were getting louder. The ground thrummed underneath them, and he doubted they could have run anyway with the earth shaking so.

"Look there," the young man stated. Billsbury saw that his companion meant Crowell Tower, a thirteen-floor student residence to their right, standing tall and surrounded by the soccer fields. Scores of people stood in front of the structure watching the thing coming in from the bay.

A thunderous grumbling began, then a crunching and splintering sound, punctuated by the snare of metal on metal.

"What the hell?" his student exclaimed, and stopped to turn around. Billsbury did the same. He was along for the ride and knew it. He was witnessing something historical in the making. Elders would know it, too, and he wished that he could see the man's reaction.

The block had come inland, moving over the lower mudflats like a huge iron, pressing all before it. Billsbury couldn't see exactly what was happening to the low buildings and houses at the waterside. A transformer-like hum disrupted by wooden *pops* permeated the air.

"I think that thing is steamrolling the houses down by the water," Billsbury's companion said.

"I think you're right," the professor responded. It came along at a steady speed, already reaching the first line of houses and shops along Main Street. The structures went under the block with a pop as they disappeared. Billsbury saw that the black stripe he noted earlier was in fact a wide slot. Water sloshed inwards, as did debris, and vanished from sight. The thing towered, and that dark space at its base was stories high, perhaps even as high as the arts centre, the very building it now approached.

Billsbury's breath caught in his throat. From the shadows of the slot, a bank of gigantic auger-like cylinders extended, each one ending in a point with the metal glinting in the morning sun. Along the base of the block, these massive tusks stretched ahead, like the claws of a languid cat. But that wasn't the scary part.

They all began to spin.

"Oh, Jesus," Billsbury muttered.

The leviathan's teeth were massive augers, and as it flowed over the land, it bit into the rear of the brick and cement building. Shrieks of metal scratched the air, and a plume of dust went up. The rear of the arts center shook as if in a seizure before being drawn into that terrible mouth. A Catholic church, to the right of the center and erected perhaps a few meters back, stood firm in the face of the monster's advance. A wooden cross held high atop the church's steeple seemed to defy the hellish block, but then the row of augers bit into the brick and mortar, two-hundred-year-old foundation and ripped it down in a cloud of dust. Water sloshed, and for a moment, the base of the attacking block seemed to throw off steam as it moved forward, crushing everything.

Billsbury then heard the eruption of human screams. It seemed he wasn't the only one watching.

"My God," he said, turning.

"Yeah," the young man said. "Let's get the hell out of here."

They ran at Billsbury's best speed further up the hill, past the university grounds, past houses and student-rented apartment buildings, past trees and piles of leaves piled up for burning. The ground continued to shake and roll, and several times they found themselves floundering for balance. Other people, stretched out as a line across the landscape, fled as well. Some, refusing to leave the machines, tried to start their cars, while others moved on mountain bicycles. Behind them, the block continued chewing up the concrete and steel buildings of the university, as well as anything in between. The nearby library, another five-level construction, was consumed, as was the University Hall. Some people, stragglers, for whatever reason, stood in the path of the advancing line and disappeared in the rolling dust and debris clouds. In the racket of destruction, their coughing, choking screams were swallowed as easily as the structures the block rolled over.

The hum intensified, and Billsbury and his companion turned around. They were perhaps another hundred meters from the top of the hill and a four-lane highway that cut across the land. Behind them, the crushing of the campus and town continued. They stopped only for minutes to catch their breath. Billsbury glanced back the way they had come and saw billowing dust clouds rising above the valley floor. They started moving once more. They soon reached the highway, which had fragmented lines of dead vehicles stretching in both directions.

"Where now?" the young man asked, panting.

Panting even harder, Billsbury looked up and down the highway, noting that there were other people gathering along its grey length. Beyond the highway, the hill flowed into a small valley dotted with copses of trees and old fashioned houses. He used to drive back there sometimes in his Honda Civic. It seemed that there would not be any driving happening in the near future.

"North Mountain," Billsbury said, and pointed. "I know a place there. A cave with fresh water. I'm going there, and you're welcome to come along."

"Sounds good."

They crossed the road, the land shaking less on the other side, and proceeded at a brisk walk. Billsbury knew that the fellow at his side was in better shape, and he was grateful that the student stayed with him.

"You don't have to wait for me," he threw out.

"Professor, I got nowhere else to go," he returned. "I'm from Ontario, and somehow, I don't think anything is flying today. Nothing from Earth anyway."

"What did you say?"

"Nothing from Earth," he repeated. "C'mon. Those things back there aren't Chinese or Russian. Looks like Stephen Hawking was right. Someone heard our signal in space, and they aren't friendly."

"What's your name?" Billsbury asked.

"Art Cope, sir."

"Well, Art, you've said it right there," Billsbury confirmed. "We've just been—"

The ground shivered violently, as if stabbed to its core. Both men fumbled about, trying to keep their balance in the quake. It didn't ease in the least.

"North Mountain?" Art yelled.

Billsbury nodded. "Probably the only safe place to be right now."

"How do you figure that, Professor?"

Billsbury didn't answer right away. "I don't know. I just

have a feeling. Has to be better than here, though!"

Art didn't respond. His gaze went across the valley, the scattered rooftops, and up the other side to the tree-covered North Mountain. Billsbury followed his gaze. It was going to be a long, harsh run-walk, he knew, but he was also motivated by the shaking of the ground.

"Do you hear that?" Art half-shouted.

Billsbury did. The closing sounds of metal gnawing on metal and wood. He looked back, but there was nothing over the hilltop. He had another feeling that it wasn't going to stay that way for long.

"This way," he roared and ran, summoning strength he didn't know he possessed. They ran in a straight line for several meters, then burst out onto a paved road leading further down into the valley. From where they stood, they could see people coming out onto the front lawns of the houses ahead and then onto the road.

Billsbury's feet were killing him; the hard soles of his shoes weren't the best thing to be running in. His strength drained as they got to the bottom of the valley. Drawing closer, they could see the expressions of awe and terror on the onlookers' faces. Once again, Billsbury and Art stopped and turned about.

The snapping and crinkling noise was growing, even over the thump of blood in Billsbury's ears. If he had been scared before, he was now paralyzed with terror.

The block had reached the top of the hill. The star-metal augers punched through the raised highway, sending gravel, chunks of pavement, and even boulders flying. Debris cascaded down the side of the valley, and the alien block, impossibly high, blotted out the sky as its girth plowed through.

Seeing the block for the first time, the people standing near the historian and his student stepped back. Children were scooped up by fathers and mothers as they ran for their houses while others scattered from the approaching monster.

"Run!" a terrified Art yelled as he blasted past several people, leaving the professor behind. Billsbury ran after him, his own panic lending him energy he never thought possible. He tried to catch the younger man, but soon fell behind. He saw Art sprint across the valley floor, and then he quickly lost sight of him. The professor ran past a couple of houses and over a short cement bridge spanning a river. He stumbled in places, glancing back every few seconds. There were a few people following him, their faces full of fright.

"This way!" he shouted, feeling his voice crack hoarsely.

A sepia-colored wave of dust billowed and fell down into the valley. The people, some seniors in their seventies, ran as fast as they could before the dust clouds smothered them. Billsbury could hear their violent coughing even as he began climbing the paved road up the side of North Mountain. The people behind him helped each other along, and Billsbury even allowed a farmer-type individual to grab his arm and haul him along.

Behind them, the block crossed over the ridge of the hill, not even pausing to take in the depth of the valley.

When Billsbury stumbled and fell, a woman helped the farmer scoop him up, and they hooked his arms around their necks. They were younger and stronger and didn't let go even when his feet started to drag. The air tasted gritty and harsh, while the sounds of pursuit thundered in their ears.

Up the face of North Mountain they went, following the road on its long north-easterly curve. Their small pack strung out along the asphalt, trying to get as much distance as possible between them and the block. They were unaccustomed to running up such a steep slope, and each stride sapped their strength a little more, until not even fear was enough to energize them. They covered their mouths with their shirts and sweaters, but the grit went into their eyes as well. Less than halfway up North Mountain, Billsbury and the remaining few, sucking in lungfuls of dust-soaked air, began to stumble and slow down.

The block came down the side of the valley at a slow but steady speed. It reached the bottom and rolled over the houses without slowing. It filled the valley to the left and right like a terrible combine, then paused for a moment as it faced the mountain before it.

Through the dust clouds, a huge dark wall reared up, skyscraper high, and the terror that shot through the people struggling to the top of the mountain knew no bounds.

"Oh, Jesus, Jesus!" the farmer squealed, then he bolted. Billsbury felt him and the woman holding his arms let go as their fear got the best of them. He followed, stumbling, bending over low—almost on all fours—as he threaded his way upward. He looked back once or twice and, through the billowing clouds, saw the gloomy outline of the block high above him. The humming could still be heard, but the grinding had stopped. The earth continued to shake, however.

They continued until they were above the dust cloud, but still not above the block. The survivors clambered over a steep, rocky incline a third of the way up North Mountain. He caught up with the folks who had once held his arms, but didn't blame them. He led the few remaining to the cave he had talked about, where they found shelter. Looking back the way they had come, the block filled the valley completely, and the humming and vibrations from its bulk continued.

Sitting at the mouth of the cave with the others, all terrified but too exhausted to do anything but watch, Billsbury looked down across the block's flat top and wondered why its back end wasn't sticking into the air. The valley wasn't wide enough to fit the block completely, and he knew that its rear should be propped up by the opposite incline. Yet, the block seemed perfectly flat. In the escalating gloom of dust clouds that turned the sun into a polluted-looking ball, a thought occurred to him. Could the thing actually morph itself to fit the contours of the valley topography in such as way that the top was always flat?

"What are you thinking about?" the woman next to him asked. She was one of the pair that had helped him earlier.

Billsbury regarded her haggard face for a moment. She was in her forties, with a shock of black hair tied in a frayed bun. "I'm thinking about that thing down there."

"Where it came from? I can tell you that," she responded.

"No, I can guess that myself," Billsbury replied. "But it's waiting for something."

"You work at the university?"

"Yes."

"What's your name?"

"David Billsbury."

"I'm Judy Walsh. And that one's my husband, Roger." An exhausted-looking Roger held up his hand in greeting.

"I'm Selena," a younger woman spoke up.

Billsbury nodded at the three of them. He recognized Selena from his class and was comforted that there was at least one person he knew. "Where are the others?"

"Kept on running." Roger grunted. He was dressed in jeans and a sweat-soaked t-shirt. "They're in better shape than me. I couldn't go another step."

"There's nothing over that way, anyway," Selena informed them. "Just some old houses spaced out, but no towns. The road even turns to dirt after a while. It's all country. I tried telling them, but they just kept right on going."

"While we wait here." Roger shook his head. "There's nowhere for the thing to go anyway. Can't get up the mountain. Too steep."

"I'm not so sure of that," Billsbury said. "I was in class when the power went out. We went outside, and that thing came up from the Bay of Fundy. Then it proceeded to mash the town and university and creep up the hill,"

"He's right," Selena confirmed. His companions became silent, thinking.

"Why did the power go off, do you think?" Judy asked quietly in the deepening dark.

"Strategy," Roger informed her. "Phase one, knock out communications and power. That's how most invasions go."

Billsbury agreed. He looked out of the cave and studied the dark shape below. He placed a hand to the rocky floor and felt the vibrations, mild, but present.

"But why did it stop?" Judy asked. "It's got us. It can get us whenever it wants. We've got no place to run. Look how big it is! I mean, it's *three* fucking mountains placed side by side! We can't go around it! We can't—"

Moved by her rising voice, Roger reached over and pulled her closer, quieting her with an embrace. He was unshaven, with a salt and pepper chin, and looked to

Billsbury with expectation. But the history professor just turned his attention back to the thing resting in the valley.

"What is it, David?" Selena asked. She was slim and had long blonde hair. Billsbury looked her and wished he had a better answer, but he was a world history buff. So he gave it to her straight.

"It's Blitzkrieg," he said quietly. "A lightening strike against us, and I'm sure the U.S. as well. Maybe even the world over."

"Why?" Roger asked. "The water? Natural resources? Hell, I watch *V*. Maybe they want us for food. "

"Maybe." Billsbury couldn't rule out anything. "Maybe. We've got a lot going for us here. There's a lot we're blessed with. And now…" he trailed off. *Now, we're being fucked over for it all*, he thought.

"Probably just come here to save the world," Selena said. "We've been destroying it for so long now. The U.N. just released a report saying that the ozone layer is thinner than ever."

"There are all those icebergs floating down," Judy whispered.

"And we drink and piss and shit into our drinking water," Roger added. "Wash our cars, water the lawns."

"Car exhaust polluting the air," Judy added.

"Car exhaust nothing," Billsbury said. "You know how much exhaust comes from one jet liner flying overhead? And there are something like seventy thousand flights a day, all over the world. You never hear about any of that."

"Underwater oil plumes, radiation, and plastic filling up the ocean," Selena went on. "The more I think about it, the more we deserve whatever it is we have coming."

Roger fixed her with a quizzical look. "You sound like a tree fucker to me."

"That's tree lover. An environmentalist, to be exact."

"That's what I said, a tree fucker."

"Great," Selena said with a shake of her head. "Three people to be holed up with, and one of them's a redneck."

"Hey," Roger warned quietly. "You watch your mouth there, honey, or I—"

"You'll what, *honey?* Throw me out there? Well, fuck you." With that, Selena got up, dusted herself off, and started to leave.

"Hey, where you going?" Roger disengaged himself from his wife and stood up. He reached out and grabbed the younger woman's shoulder. It wasn't a smart move. Selena gripped his hand and twisted it. Roger was suddenly held at arm's length, his arm straightened and plied into a joint lock. Selena twisted his hand further and bent the man over.

He grunted in pain. "Let me go, little *bitch!*"

"Let him go!" Judy shrieked, jumping to her feet. She rushed Selena with her hands hooked into claws. Selena released Roger, sidestepped her newest attacker, and inserted an arm underneath Judy's. With little effort, she hip-threw Judy three feet to land on her back with a rattle of rocks.

"Fucking little bitch!" Roger punched Selena, rocking her head back and knocking her on her ass. He had recovered fast, and he moved to kick her in the stomach while she was down.

Billsbury got in the way. "Wait a minute," he said, but Roger pistoned a hard right into the historian's soft belly, dropping him to his knees and leaving him gasping.

"Fuck you, too," Roger said, pointing a finger. "I'll kick the shit outta anyone I want or haveta. And right now, I'm in char—"

Selena's right foot snapped out and up, crushing Roger's testicles to his pelvis. With a breathless huff, he went down, clutching at his broken balls and bouncing his forehead off a rock. Blood spewed from a gash in his forehead, but Roger lay on his side, his knees curled into his chest.

"Redneck *fuck*," Selena breathed. "Of all the people to be holed up with at the end of the world." She punctuated her last word with another kick to Roger's face. She stood back for a moment, then turned to a moaning Judy. "You try anything more, bitch, and I'll break something of yours and then his."

Billsbury felt hands on his back. "You okay there?" Selena asked.

He nodded.

"Okay. Listen." She glanced away from the helpless forms of Roger and Judy. "I'm heading out. Can't stay here with the likes of these two. I'm going to head further inland, away from all of this. You coming?"

Red-eyed and grimacing, Billsbury got to a sitting position. "I'm in no shape to run anywhere. I… there's water back there that's safe to drink, and I might be able to hold on here for a while. My… my wife lives in Kentville. I can't go too far from her. I think you should stay, but—"

"Stay here?" Selena's mouth got ugly. "I can't stay here with Ma and Pa Kettle. Fuck 'em. I'll end up killing them if I do."

"You can't just leave."

Selena looked at him with hard eyes. "I can do anything I goddamn please, David. Civilization as we know it has just crumbled. In record time, I might add. I think you better come with me. You're going to be in here with a couple of hicks, and that one," she pointed to a prone Roger still bleeding on the rocky floor, "is trouble. And *she's* trouble cuz she's with him. Both were pretty quick to get physical."

Billsbury blinked. "But you swung first."

Selena's face hardened, and she drew back from Billsbury. She looked outside, sizing up the day and thinking.

"Where's that water?" she finally asked.

Billsbury pointed. Selena went to the back of the cave to drink, leaving him to watch over the still forms of Judy and Roger. Judy was moving weakly, but the flat landing on the rocks had beaten the breath from her. Billsbury listened to her sucking air in little gasps, then tuned her out to listen to the continuous drone of the thing in the valley.

Moments later Selena walked by.

"Are you going now?"

She paused in the mouth of the cave and met Billsbury's eyes. There was something in them, pity and disgust rolled into one. He didn't know this young woman, but he realized his mistake now, taking her for a follower. Selena was no follower.

"Good luck," she said, and left.

He listened to her padding away, her sneakers slapping the mountainous terrain and making some rocks roll, and then there was only the droning hum. Part of him wanted to leave with her, but he had his wife to think about and moving through the wilderness in dress shoes wasn't something he wanted to do. *Stupid*, he thought, referring to everything. He took a deep breath, coughed on dust, and smelled the earthy scent surrounding him.

The ground started to shake once more. He looked ahead and thought he saw something incredible. After a moment, he knew that this would be his grave, and there was little else to do except sit and wait.

"Where'd she go?" Judy asked, getting to her elbows about fifteen minutes later and looking about in alarm.

Billsbury didn't bother answering.

Judy got unsteadily to her feet and made her way to her husband. She sat down beside him and placed his head on her thighs. The movement brought Roger back to consciousness.

"Where… is she?" he wanted to know.

Looking out over the valley, Billsbury shook his head. Stupid questions again.

"Hey, you! Dickhead!" Roger sat up and grimaced, holding his bruised testicles with one hand. He pushed his wife away and slap-wiped his forehead. "I'm talking to you!"

The mountain began to shake violently, enough that earth and rocks from overhead fell in clumps. Pebbles fell on Billsbury's head and shoulders, but he didn't move. There was no point.

"We've gotta get outta here, Roger!"

"You got it!" Roger pulled Judy to her feet, both of them swaying from the vibrations. Then, the tremors increased threefold, and they were both flung screaming to the ground. Billsbury wished they would just be quiet. He moved a little further out of the cave, fearful of being caught in a collapsing tunnel and suffocating to death. The alternative wasn't particularly attractive either.

Roger and Judy made their way to the mouth of the cave as well. They looked below, and both began howling. Roger screamed at him to come with them, but Billsbury ignored him. There was no escape. They were simply too terrified to realize it.

A second later, they fled. Far below, the purplish blue alien block, the one that had chased them from the coast, moved up the valley to the east, covering everything with its vast bulk. It moved out of the way to allow a larger, heavier industrial earth shaker that Billsbury watched with ever-widening eyes. The machine had gleaming augers, much like its veering companion's, but bigger. Billsbury now knew that the first block was only a surface scourer, designed to crumple and level buildings. The beast now biting into the rocky base, the same monster machine that he had watched burst through the dark dust cloud earlier, was made for bigger jobs, like leveling hills and mountains. It would cut the mountain from the face of the earth like a razor removing stubble. Even now, as the teeth in his head shook, and he tasted the dust and dirt storm being flung into the air, he knew there was no escape.

Then he was falling, rolling down on top of a rockslide toward the bank of flashing star-metal. Billsbury shielded his eyes as best as he could as he was pelted with rocks and, for a split second, he looked up and to the right. His mouth hung open. He only caught a glimpse, but enough to realize that they, as an intelligent species, were not alone in the galaxy. *We're ants*, he thought for a second, and then he was sucked from the mountainside by a powerful wind and drawn down into chewing metal.

The figure the doomed Billsbury had spotted high above the machines it employed stopped in its tracks. The male, covered in a purple and silver environmental suit, looked down at the drones working at clearing and leveling the planet's surface. It sighed behind the huge faceplate of its helmet. The alien then examined the instrument readings of a pad displaying the energy levels of its drones. Already, the *Gvol* model was running low on energy. Cursing, he bent over and ran three fingers over the top of the drone heading east. A liquid display appeared, and an internal diagnostic was performed. The alien's fears were confirmed. There was a leak somewhere in the drone's mechanical guts. He swore, cursing the amount he had spent on used equipment. He straightened and watched as the heavier drone to his left chewed its way into the mound before it. He was more than happy with the *Tojpa's* performance. Thank the Makers that he had transported enough of them to this place.

He checked his information pad then looked upward to the star-filled heavens. He would scour this geothermic mudball in about five galactic hours, then bring up the *Lerqers*, which would begin digging on a global scale. Later, he would drain the annoying bodies of water. Although, he had to admit, the deep sea trenches had been helpful for gathering and hiding his equipment in preparation for initiating the surfacing phase of construction.

With a sigh, he glanced to his left then right, inspecting the progress of the multiple drones cutting their way inland along the coastline. Able to see well over the horizon of the little planet, he looked behind and saw his foreman standing tall in the middle of what had once been known as the Atlantic. The foreman waved, acknowledging that the drones were well into the land mass on his side. Everything was on schedule thus far, barring any other mechanical failures.

Five G-hours to clean the planet; another seven to dig and install the necessary tanks and piping needed; eight to pave everything; nine to construct the lots; perhaps ten to erect the buildings; and no more than fifteen to complete the wiring and other little things necessary before flipping on the power switch.

At that time, an estimated forty-five G's later, the newest

franchise of the Super Nova Mini-Stop Vax Shop would be up and running. The alien smiled. This minute ball of mud situated just off a vector ramp was ideal to set up a little take-out business specializing in deep-nuked *Suhg*. One of his daughters would manage the outlet while he went on to find another suitable planetoid, perhaps one of the pretty silver ones, in the next galaxy over…

And start surveying all over again.

# 5

# The Bear that Fell From the Stars

1

The servant led Haruki Miyazaki through an opulent garden. *Green is good for the eyes*, it was often said, and Miyazaki's traveling brown and white robes were in stark contrast to the soft foliage surrounding him. He held before him a medium sized box, carefully wrapped in fine silk from his own shop, containing the finest *sake* he could buy. A path of white stones slipped through a carpet of short grass, and huge, white and red blossoms in carefully sculpted beds greeted him on both sides. Surrounding it all, a collage of *sugi* trees, almost too beautiful to behold, towered above and dappled the earth with showers of shadow and light. The air was moist with the summer's heat and hot to breathe. It felt as thick and intoxicating as a Zen Buddhist's incense. Birds sang somewhere high above, giving music to the scene, and Miyazaki felt sadness in his heart.

How could a monster create such beauty?

He buried the thought by memorizing every detail of the lush grounds. The servant, a short woman with her head bowed, moved with little steps. She was perhaps in her forties, and not unattractive in her brown kimono and her dark hair tied in a bun. Miyazaki found it easier to distract himself with thoughts of her than the surrounding forest. He dared not speak to the woman for fear she was of greater value than she appeared to her master. Or worse. It was whispered that demons inhabited the gardens of the Maker in plain sight, and Miyazaki was superstitious enough to believe it. Even in a place of such serene calmness and beauty, he was only half certain of leaving without his throat cut and his flesh boiled from his bones.

They continued on without speaking, his sandals clipping off the white stones, while the woman glided across without a sound. The silk merchant suspected she was much more than she seemed, and dropped back a cautious step.

Then, the scent of water.

A pond of green and light and as unblemished as fine silver became visible to Miyazaki. The trees thinned out and a shoreline of dry stones came into sight. The silk merchant marveled at the beauty of this secret body of water, and how well the tall *sugi* trees hid it from the world.

Ahead of him, the servant stopped and gestured with an arm.

Miyazaki stopped in his tracks. A short distance away, in the shade of an old *sakura* tree laden with green, was the Maker.

He sat cross-legged on a raised platform of *sugi* wood, staring out across the pond, watching dragonflies soar in patterns. The Maker had the air of an emperor, and his tanned features were as set and grooved as the flesh of the forest surrounding him.

The servant glanced at Miyazaki, and they met gazes. He realized he had stopped walking.

"*Gomen nasai*," he blurted out respectfully, just in case the woman *was* a demon in disguise. He hurried towards the edge of the lake, and the man known as the Maker.

"*Konichiwa*," Miyazaki greeted with a deep bow and introduced himself. As he did, he offered the carefully wrapped box he had carried for days.

"*Konichiwa*," returned the Maker, and also bowed, but not as deep. He nodded his acceptance and approval of the gift before him, and a smile played about his dark eyes. "Please sit," he offered in formal Japanese, and gestured to the spot across from him.

Miyazaki knelt, noting that he could see the pond easily if he looked to his left. He dared not, however, not unless the Maker did so first.

"Thank you most kindly," Miyazaki replied, bowing again.

"Something to drink?" the Maker asked.

"You are too kind," the silk merchant replied with another bow.

"You have come a long way to see me," the Maker said, his voice surprisingly soft for a face so stern looking. Dark hair, streaked with silver, was tied in a neat bun at the back of his skull. He raised a hand to his servant, whisking her away.

"I have a problem in my land."

The Maker's eyes settled on Miyazaki, mildly piqued.

"Forgive my rash words," Miyazaki quickly apologized with yet another bow. "It is not often I'm in the presence of someone of your importance. And reputation."

The Maker did not reply.

Miyazaki feared he was a dead man. He became aware of the thunderous harmony of a thousand unseen cicadas, and he dared not move. If he did, Miyazaki knew there would be one less silk merchant in the land. And one more story to add to the legend of his host sitting across from him.

However, the Maker's chin dipped ever so slightly, and the relief Miyazaki felt was barely concealed.

"Very well," the Maker said. "What is your concern then?"

The woman servant brought a serving tray with a long neck bottle of *sake* upon it, and two drinking glasses made of ornate wood. She set the tray down and began to pour.

Miyazaki took a breath. "There is a very large stone within… my garden. It has been there for years, and I've had to build around it."

The Maker looked to the dragonflies.

"For years, this stone has given me pain," "Miyazaki continued. "I've tried removing it, with the strongest men I could find, but none have been able to take away its bulk. That is when it was suggested to me that I should seek out a gardener. One whose skill is spoken highly of in certain circles. One whose name is dwarfed in reputation to yours, of course, Master of Flowers and Trees. Thus, I am here this day, after a very long journey."

"I have many gardeners beneath me," the Maker rumbled, and banished the servant with a curt flick of his chin.

"I have need of perhaps three," Miyazaki said.

The Maker's eyes regarded him with a warning. "One of my gardeners is worth ten of any other."

*Oh shit.* Miyazaki paled. His throat bobbed and his mouth hung open. The fear he felt for his slight robbed him of his voice. When he found it, he blurted out his apologies and bowed until his nose touched the wood he knelt upon.

The Maker waited until the silk merchant had finished. "You speak with a brash tongue, man of silk. I am no simple customer here. And you are not in your shop."

Another flurry of apologies from the silk merchant, and the Maker allowed them to continue until he grew weary of them. "What do you call this stone?"

"Takai Mamoru."

"And where does it reside?"

"Kamakura. In a small town near there."

The Maker mulled this over. "He is a well known official in the Kamakura Shogunate."

Miyazaki's nose continued to touch the fragrant wood and any moment he believed he would greet the darkness of death. Above him, he heard only birds and cicadas.

"In my garden there is a bear," the Maker said. "A particularly skilled bear. I have taught this bear all manner of tricks since it was a cub. I have taught him how to hide not only in the forests, but the cities as well. How to fish, and to hunt. I am reluctant to offer you this bear, as he is worth much. For him, I will require ten times the amount. Agreed?"

"*Hai!*" wailed Miyazaki, praying for his own life.

Without a word, the Maker reached for one of the *sake* filled cups. He grunted and gestured for the silk merchant to do the same. Miyazaki quickly complied.

The Maker lifted the rice liquor in the air. The man before him wasn't worth it, but it was his custom to seal the transaction with a drink. Another of his minions would discuss further details with this worm, and collect the fee from him. There was no worry that the silk worm would betray the clan or their dealings. Whole lines of families had been erased from time for such folly in the past, and the Maker's clan remained. He would inform Kuma this day of his newest mission. He would tell his bear that not only was the official to be killed, but so was any other that got in his way, be they man, woman, child, or beast. When the news of the deaths reached the public, both they and this silk merchant would know that the reputation of the Maker's clan was justified. And to be feared.

With that thought, the Maker sipped.

**2**

In another part of the *sugi* forest, in a low building with no walls, the sound of flesh striking stone met the Maker's ears. He stood at one corner of the building, behind one of six thick columns of *sugi* wood holding up a clay tiled roof. He had removed his sandals and walked barefoot to the training hall, the song of the cicadas masking his approach. He left the silk worm, as he now thought of the merchant, to his servants.

The Maker thought about Jimmu *Kuma* Kazaka for a moment. He was perhaps the most skilled of all his ninja, second only to the Maker himself. Sending *Kuma*—the Bear—to kill the official would be a task worth much honor to the clan's name, and coin for its coffers. He inched around the wooden pillar, and saw his minion practicing at a stone brazier. The Maker did not reveal the embers of content he felt warming his breast.

The Bear thrust his hands into the depths of the wide receptacle, and a clatter of beach rocks could be easily heard. The Maker frowned. His disciple was getting sloppy. He eased out from behind the wood, his hands slipping underneath his robs for a hidden blade. It was time for the master to teach his student something about—

The Bear spun and hurled a rock at the Maker. The speed of the attack caught the older man by surprise, but the *sensei* still dodged the blow, sinking and rising smoothly, like a hurried sun. He did not draw the knife from beneath his robes. There was no need.

Recognizing who he had just attacked, the Bear sunk to

the *tatami* mats of the training hall, placed his forehead against the straw, and let loose a stream of apologies.

The Maker stood over his student, allowing him to apologize. There was no wrong in letting him do such. It would keep the younger man humble. The Maker looked to the stones in the brazier. He saw beach rocks, rounded and heavy, and felt approval. The Bear continued to toughen his paws. And his claws.

"Enough," the Maker commanded his student, invoking silence.

The Bear kept his head lowered. "Upon your command, I shall kill myself for what I have just done."

The Maker's face remained expressionless. "That is not my wish."

"What is your wish, *Sensei*? May this dog of a servant do your bidding."

The Maker stood directly over his student, his toes inches away from the back of the Bear's head. He had thick hair, shaggy, just like the animal he was named after, but that was where the similarity ended. Jimmu *Kuma* Kazaka was not a big man, and the more the Maker thought about it, he should have had the nickname of *cat* instead.. He was strong as well, deceptively so, and on several occasions the other ninja noted just how strong the Bear *was* in training. Kazaka also possessed the frightening appetite of a bear for blood.

And the Maker suddenly wanted a demonstration.

"Stand," he commanded, and the Bear did so.

The sensei looked about and saw a set of *hashi* lying across a wooden bowl. He bent at the knees, and picked up the chopsticks.

The Bear watched him.

The Maker looked to one end of the training hall, where

straw had been fashioned in the shape of a man and stood on two legs of wood.

"Show me something," he ordered.

And tossed both chopsticks at the Bear.

*Fast*, so incredibly fast, the wooden utensils were plucked out of the air, *one-two*, and fired at the straw man twenty paces away. The first chopstick punctured the straw man's left eye, or where the eye would have been, imbedding half its length with an audible *whock*! The second missile, a split-second behind the first, took the straw man in the forehead and punched the head from its shoulders.

The Maker studied the 'kill' for a moment. He could ask no better from anyone. He, himself, could do no better.

"I have a task for you," the Maker said, hiding the sudden sun-burst of pride he felt for the ninja standing before him.

# 3

In the early morning light, Kenjo Otake watched the hunched over woodcutter wobble his way up the empty street. The way he was staggering, it was easy for Kenjo to see that the man was drunk. It was too early for such foolishness, the *izakaya* owner thought, but then he realized, if the woodcutter hadn't actually stopped drinking from the night before, then he was merely continuing with his merriment. Kenjo shook his head. He was young once, and had drunk enough sake in his time, and enjoyed enough women to last him the rest of his days. Now he was married, the father of two children, and owned a popular business. Even better, his food was gaining popularity in the land. Drunken nights were far behind him. Still, a little smile spread across his face as he watched the man sway on his feet and remembered times gone by.

The woodcutter had appeared a week earlier, dressed in the same poor clothes, and made semi-regular rounds throughout the village, selling the wood he had cut down and split the day before. Kenjo had no opinion of him, but noted how the children would make fun of him, tease him about his smell, and the hump of his back. Kenjo would bark at the children if he saw them do such a thing. He had no patience for such rude behavior, no matter what a man's station was in life.

The woodcutter came closer. He was without his cart, and had a glazed look to him. Yes, Kenjo thought, he was drunk out of his skull.

"Good … morning, sir," the woodcutter slurred with a

bow that almost tipped him over.

Kenjo stood on the front step to his izakaya, between red paper lanterns that hung just to the left and right of his opened doorway, and nodded. "Good morning. Are you in good health?"

The woodcutter smiled and displayed well kept teeth. "I am. I am indeed. A beautiful morning."

Kenjo looked to the skies. They were overcast with grey lumpy clouds. It wasn't his idea of a good morning, but since the rainy season was upon them all, any dry morning was one to be appreciated. Then, he thought about where the woodcutter spent his nights, and deduced it was probably out in the forest or the hills somewhere. For him, a dry day, and night, were probably enough to remain drunk about.

"Are you still drinking?" Kenjo asked politely with a smile.

"I am finished," the woodcutter smiled back and produced an empty jug. It was the cheap kind, but still potent. The poor man stepped closer, and the pungent smell of unwashed flesh and alcohol assaulted Kenjo's senses. The children, it seemed, had reason to tease.

"I am," the woodcutter repeated, hunched over. He looked up at Kenjo. "For today I must earn more coin. There's a storm coming. I can smell it."

Kenjo nodded. "I think you've supplied the people here with plenty of firewood this season."

"People will…" the man paused, and his cheeks puffed out ominously. He caught himself, and for a brief moment, Kenjo feared the woodcutter would vomit right in front of his izakaya. "People will… always need wood."

Kenjo released his breath and glanced around. He had no trouble talking with the poor man, but he did not want to be embarrassed by him emptying his stomach right in front of his business, especially a food and drink business.

"My apologies," the woodcutter said, "I will… I will not be trouble… to you this morning, kind sir."

"That would be most good of you," Kenjo remarked.

"I'm afraid to ask however, kind sir, if you… have any need of firewood this day."

"Not this day."

"Tomorrow then."

"Nor tomorrow. No."

"I see," the woodcutter's swayed on his ankles, and then steadied himself with noticeable effort. "Perhaps I will ask the others then."

"You might have better luck," Kenjo agreed. "But come back next week. I'll have need of wood then."

This brightened the woodcutter's drunken features. He was not an unhandsome man, Kenjo saw, simply hairy and dirty and born with a hump. He felt a moment's pity for him.

"What about the house on the hill?" the woodcutter asked and suppressed a belch.

"The manor?" Kenjo smiled. "You may ask, but I think Takai-san would have his servants cut his wood for him."

"He has servants?" the woodcutter asked in disbelief.

"He does. Guards too."

"Guards?"

Kenjo nodded.

"Phah," the woodcutter said and spittle flew, causing Kenjo to retreat a step. "I'm not afraid of any…gourds."

"Guards," Kenjo corrected him. "And perhaps you should be."

The woodcutter grimaced. "I can fight them all right now."

"He has perhaps twenty or thirty."

"Oh," the woodcutter said. "That many? Perhaps—"
more suppressed gas—"I won't fight them today."

"Very wise of you."

"You would not think… think it of me, would you?"

Kenjo shook his head. He would not.

"Well, then," the woodcutter began. "I feel…" a great
sigh left him. "I feel sleepy. And hungry. Would you happen
to have any… any scraps to eat, kind sir? From last night?"

Kenjo paused for a moment. He looked about the street.
It was still early enough that there was no one else about.
"Wait here," he said and went inside.

When Kenjo returned, he had a small wooden bucket full
of half eaten chicken bones and untouched cooked beef
cubes. Food for the dogs, but in this case, it would be
breakfast for the man before him. There was some uneaten
white rice lumped in there as well. All of it was enough for
three meals perhaps. He had nothing against this man, and
one act of kindness, on a grey morning on the eve of the
rainy season, might bring good fortune to him later on.

"Here," Kenjo said as he offered the bucket.

The woodcutter took it, examined the contents, and
grinned. "Thank you, kind sir. I shall bring you wood when
I am able."

"It is no matter," Kenjo said, waving his hand.

"It is… a matter to me," the woodcutter declared. With
that, the man bowed deeply. "I remember such things."

"I'm sure you do," Kenjo said, waving him off.

The woodcutter smiled and again Kenjo noted how
white the man's teeth were. He may smell like a shithouse,
but he had good teeth.

"I will return, another time," the woodcutter announced

as he walked backwards up the street, bowing in Kenjo's direction and holding onto the wooden bucket. He stumbled and fell on his backside, yanking a gasp out of Kenjo, but he did not upset the food. Still grinning, the woodcutter got to his feet, popped a half eaten chicken leg into his mouth, and continued walking.

Kenjo noted that he was headed in the direction of Takai-san's manor on the hill. He shook his head. He hoped the guards there would leave the poor dog alone. It was no good to make light of those less fortunate, not in his mind. With that last thought, he went about the washing of his izakaya's front.

The approaching typhoon brought rain crashing down upon the earth, and powerful winds that leaned on dark fences of trees. The people of the town stayed inside, hoping that the might of the storm would miss them, or if it did hit, it would pass over quickly. They peeked out from behind storm shutters at the darkening sky. Sheets of rain rattled roofs and wooden walkways, pelted walls and drove peasants to whatever shelter lay nearby. As the night moved on and the intensity of the storm grew, there were few that would venture outside in such terrible conditions. Parents put their children to bed, hoping that their sleep would be uninterrupted, and stayed up as long as they could before dozing off.

Kazaka watched as the roads quickly filled with water, and dark streams began to run. The winds became louder and stronger, and it seemed that the typhoon was going to hit the town. The streets were deserted, and looking up, the only visible light in the night sky belonged to the lanterns of the Takai residence. It was not a castle, perhaps the lord of the manor did not fancy himself important enough to have such defenses, but he did possess a modest number of guardsmen, befitting a well-respected man serving the Kamakura Shogunate. Exactly what Takai did for the Shogunate did not concern Kazaka. The man could be an angel, for all the Bear cared.

He was still going to die this night.

For the last two weeks, Kazaka had lived in the hills nearby the town, gathering information on his prey. During the day, the Bear appeared as a hunched over woodcutter, peddling kindling for the townspeople's fires, speaking in the informal tones of the uneducated. Kazaka had pissed and poured *sake* over his grubby clothes for days, knowing full well people, and especially guards, would have very little to do with him smelling of urine and alcohol. Except the izakaya owner, and for that, the Bear wished good fortune would find the man. The other townspeople, however, berated him, the children mocked him, but they were all fooled by his disguise. He spent a little money on food and drink, using *sake* as medicine to get other town drunks talking. Mamoru Takai, the official Kazaka had to kill, was an honorable man it seemed, and well thought of by the people living below his hill. He helped the poor amongst them. He shared his food and water in hard times, and protected them all from bandits with his small force of soldiers. During the festivals of the summer, he would purchase fireworks and set them off over the nearby river, for all to see. Mamoru Takai seemed a decent and respected soul. It seemed to Kazaka that he rarely had the opportunity to kill someone truly deserving death.

At night, the Bear would venture forth as a shadow. He watched the town's guards, always in pairs, walk in a half daze as they completed their rounds. Several times, the guards walked right by Kazaka, and they did not know it. Such guards deserved to die for their carelessness. Twice, he made make his way to the walls of the Takai residence, not to enter but merely to study the defenses. He walked the road leading up to the guarded walls. He tried selling his wood there, dragging a small cart of it behind him. The guards searched him and his cart, and cursed him to be on his way. In truth, Kazaka knew all he needed to know about his target and his soldiers. It was only a question of when to kill the man.

He waited only a week for the storm to arrive.

On the evening of the typhoon, under a sky filled with clouds as dark as a dead man's entrails, Kazaka did away with the woodcutter's disguise. The storm was just beginning. He gazed out at the falling rain, and breathed in its pureness. He loved the rain, and loved watching it fall. There was nothing more beautiful in this world, nothing more cleansing. Or so he often thought.

Perched on the side of a hill, overlooking the town but well out of sight from those below, Kazaka sat cross-legged in the ragged little shelter that had been his home for two weeks. He was naked, and breathed deeply of the thick incense he always burned just before he changed into his shadowy form. He prayed for himself, for the honor of his Maker, and for the successful completion of the mission given unto him. Kazaka was not a deeply spiritual man on the surface, but even he admitted that, when one had to kill a person, a little prayer probably wouldn't hurt. It took less than an hour to prepare himself, spiritually and mentally.

Then he tended to more earthly affairs.

He donned his *shinobi shōzoku*, the black garb of a ninja,

and his hood and mask. He gathered his tools: a *ninjato*, made from the broken katana of a dead samurai, and coated with the smoke and ash of his fire to help hide the gleam of the short sword's razor edge. He sheathed the blade in a long scabbard, the tip of which could be removed to access blinding powder if needed. At his waist, nine star-shaped *shuriken* were stowed, along with a *kusari fundo*, a piece of rope ending in weighted balls. On his forearms, three *bo-shurikens* were sheathed, the long iron darts almost the length of a chopstick. He slipped two more of these around each ankle. He hung a blowgun off his back, complete with five poison darts that could drop a man in seconds. A short, thin dagger went between his buttocks.

Thus armed, Kazaka waited for the storm to intensify.

# 4

"*Kuso*," one of the guardsmen swore as the downpour grew stronger, soaking the clothes of both men to the skin. They were at the foot of the road leading up the hill to the home of Takai, standing with spears and sheathed swords. They watched the town, and because of this, Kazaka decided to let them live. There would be two more at the gate above, and the Bear did not want to draw any unnecessary attention to missing men. Not yet anyway. Under drenching darkness, the Bear slipped by them. With the wind screaming and the rain hissing, bypassing the sentries was not a difficult thing. The Bear would kill them without any hesitation if he were detected. The Maker had instructed him to kill as many as he could, and he would do just that once the initial target was dealt with. *Kill as many as you can, even the children*, the Maker had said. While Kazaka did not like the idea of slaying children, he would do just that in his master's name. But Takai would be the first.

In almost total blackness, Kazaka moved through the wet undergrowth towards the top of the hill. The rain saturated him to the bone, but he ignored it. Death was visiting the residence of Mamoru Takai on this night of storms, and did not fear nature's wrath. He drew closer to the outer wall, keeping low and not taking any chances at being detected. Water ran off his masked head and into his eyes. His robes were heavy with rain, and he realized that he would leave a trail once he was inside the house. In the end, he decided it could not be helped.

There were two guards posted at the gateway, looking

like clay statues standing before the storm. Kazaka ignored them. He moved along the wall, staying hidden in the bushes. There was a cleared pathway surrounding the residence, about five paces wide. Kazaka knew it was a defensive measure to prevent someone from doing what he was about to do, but under the ferocity of the typhoon, there were no lanterns lit, and all was in darkness. He wanted to climb the wall further away from the gate. He got moving.

And paused. Kazaka looked up, on instinct alone, and spotted a glowing light through the trees to his left. It was not bright, but through the waving of the trees he saw it. Guards, he thought at first, but then realized something strange about the illumination.

It was moving.

"*Hora!*" a voice said just ahead on the pathway. The Bear froze. There were two sentries, just turning the corner of the wall, shadows against the paleness of the stone. One was gesturing at the light.

"Look," the man said again, pointing. The other guard moved forward cautiously to the edge of the pathway, a hand on the hilt of his katana.

"What is it?" the first man asked.

"Very strange," the other said. They stopped a step off the path.

They were but five paces in front of the unmoving Bear. His hand crept with infinite patience until he gripped the ninjato's hilt. If the guards spotted him, he would rush and kill them both. He slowly lowered himself further into the bushes.

"It's moving this way!" one of the men exclaimed over the roar of the typhoon.

The Bear stayed low to the earth. He felt warm rain

against his back. More dripped into his eyes and he blinked it away, not daring to move even under the cover of the brush.

"It's a devil," a voice said, but his voice sounded different, as if succumbing to sleep.

"A… devil…" Kazaka heard the other say.

Through the wet undergrowth, the Bear looked up and saw both men standing, illuminated as if by dull moonlight. He could not see their features, but there was something wrong in their stance. They were too relaxed.

Then, the light reached Kazaka, and he again became as still as stone. Over the roar of the typhoon, a new sound perked his ears, like the singing of a single cicada, except perhaps not as harsh. The light grew about him, and the Bear knew he had been discovered. *Unfortunate*, was his only thought. He would make them pay.

Kazaka looked up, his hand on the hilt of his blade, the strange sound louder in his ears.

The light dropped down directly before his eyes.

And he knew no more.

# 5

From where he stood in the shadows, the Aush watched as steam and disinfectants sprayed three bodies as they were manipulated through the air on legless platforms. Their limbs were splayed out, and held in place by invisible barriers of a construct from another place in the cosmos. Their bodies, chemically treated to prevent organ deterioration and muscular atrophy, as well as to ward off desiccation, had been kept in stasis for centuries. Alive, and in a state of unending torpor; without dreams, in theory, although it had already been proven on previous expeditions that flushing and completely erasing the primitive memories of the bipeds was difficult to accomplish. Through transparent tubes the bodies floated, one following the other, still wearing their primitive garments and bits of metal protection. Past checkpoints of computer banks they flowed, as lights twinkled, readings were taken, and analysis conducted. Otherworld magnetic resonance images were recorded, providing imagery as precise as autopsies, storing the results in databanks. They were paused at one station, and, in midair, each was slowly, as if in a dream, rolled over onto its back. Thin biomechanical cords, ending in a sea urchin's array of formidable looking needles, were poised over each specimen's body at regular intervals. On cue, they punctured both cloth and flesh to deliver chemicals and compounds necessary for tissue revival, and to suck out spent gel-based desiccants. The parietal sections of their craniums were drilled into and fluids injected. Each specimen displayed no feeling of the invasive procedures. Occasionally blood would appear from damaged tissue, but only for the second it took for an octopus-like instrument to appear and cauterize the tear or puncture.

Each man slept.

They were guided into a laboratory of shadows and star-pricks of lights. In a row, they were halted and their platforms inclined to almost upright position. The lead specimen was closest to an array of otherworld surgical devices on a seemingly fixed metal table. Phantoms moved around them, passing through light at irregular intervals, and giving only glimpses of their physical shape. Checks on equipment to be used were performed, and the air filled with the smell of preservatives. It would soon be filled with more.

The Aush continued watching as a smaller figure, an Aqjm, crossed his field of vision. A long willowy arm, with flesh the color of snow, reached out towards a bank of instruments. Spidery fingers fanned over a small control interface. A green display formed in the air, bearing alien characters and numerals. The scientist's thoughts activated tabs, and leafed through lists of readings taken from the once dormant organisms. Huge compound eyes, almond shaped and black, took in the three bodies coming from the remaining circuit checkpoints. A lipless mouth, a gash really, arched upwards in a satisfied smile. It was naked, as were most of its kind, having long forsaken decorations for their outwardly asexual frames. When working on alien species, however, the scientists—in this case the *anatomists*—chose to wear a non-staining, bio-degradable material that coated and shielded them from any possible unsavory humanoid fluids. A small metal instrument, much like a fork missing the inner tines, was picked up and activated. A green beam snapped to life between the two prongs, and the anatomist moved to the first subject. With a thought, biomechanical arms dropped from the inky heights of the ceiling, and began peeling away the specimen's outer garments.

All the while, the Aush watched from the shadows. He did not care about two of the subjects taken out of stasis, but the third one, the one in black, intrigued him. He had existed in the cosmos for centuries, and had made several trips to this particular world, protecting his brothers and sisters as they pursued research and objectives of little interest to him. They had traveled together for too long, it seemed to him, and they carried themselves with a growing air of self worth, much more than they actually were. What was worse, they had little time for the Aush, beyond protection. They were not the ones who would conquer the worlds in this particular solar system. They were the ones who would sample and study and ultimately catalogue whatever life remained after the invasion.

And yet, they looked *down* on him.

Little did they know he conducted his own studies. He made note of the warrior castes of the worlds he visited. He examined their primitive weapons and armor. He had already examined the man in black's curious assortment of edged and throwing weapons, laid out on a carefully sterilized platform. The *sword*, which he knew the name of, was shorter than a regular *katana*, yet the scabbard was for a much longer blade. He assumed it was for a reason, but could not deduce what. Primitive weapons of the planet were of great interest to him, only outdone by the manner in which these *men* used them.

And this man in black piqued his curiosity.

*—What are you looking at?* one of the anatomists mentally projected with the feeling that he didn't expect to

understand the warrior's reply.

    —*That one.* the Aush projected back.

    —*What about him?*

    —*He interests me. Might I have him?*

The anatomist, the leader of his particular team, frowned. —*What for? So that you may perhaps remove his skin simply to gauge how long the subject would take to expire? This is a study of **anatomy**, **physiology** and **biochemistry**. Not… playthings.*

The Aush's mouth was a tight line. He did not appreciate the emotional discharge surging from the little anatomist's mental projection. Other scientists flocked around the projector, almost identical in appearance, lending their support. Though his face did not reveal it, the loathing the Aush felt for his fellow travelers rose to dangerous levels.

    —*I'm not even exactly certain why their weapons or how they use them is of any interest to you, anyway,* projected the anatomist. His compound eyes locked gazes with the black visor of the Aush. —*Yes, we know of your little study sessions, and we find it amusing that the soldier wishes to play the intellectual. You didn't think we knew? Predictable. Your sort is only suitable for one thing, and that one thing is never an issue during research expeditions. In fact, once we exit this galaxy and return to our own, I shall forward the motion to bar all military Kajst from further projects. Your presence simply is not necessary. Really. Does a full grown biped need protection from… ants?*

The Aush contained himself.

    —*Thoughts?* The anatomist prodded the challenge, allowing a discharge of abhorrence to escape.

The Kajst Aush kept his thoughts to himself.

    —*Nothing?* the little Aqjm needled again.

    —*I think,* the Aush projected carefully, —*that for ones so intellectually gifted as yourselves, you can be, at times, quite… obtuse.*

The offence rippled through all the researchers. The tension rose and was palpable.

*—Leave us*, the Lead Anatomist commanded. *—If we have need of any squashing, you can be certain we'll summon you and your warriors*, mighty *Aush*.

The Kajst Aush did not leave immediately, knowing full well that pausing for effect would needle these arrogant little Aqjm. Before the head scientist could project further argument on the matter, the Aush walked towards the table of archaic weapons. He studied them for a moment, before deciding on a sword and scabbard belonging to one of the *hu*-mans. The Aush took the sword without any projection, and left the research lab. As he exited, two other green armored Kajst—his personal soldiers and all of what was assigned to the expedition—fell into step behind.

The three Annihilator Kajsts made their way to the command bridge, two levels up.

Projecting a very unflattering expletive in the direction of the departed Kajst, the Lead Anatomist focused his energies on the task before him. As soon as the Annihilators were gone, the researchers went about their studies. *—Preparations are complete*, one of them projected with a discharge of excitement. The Lead motioned for the individual to step back. Excitement was not something to open up a specimen with. A steady appendage was required.

The Lead Anatomist motioned to the other, who dutifully handed over the surgical beam, the green band of light snapping with energy as he did so.

*—Pay attention, all of you*, the Lead commanded. *—These subjects were placed in stasis specifically to test the elasticity and durability of their vital organs, musculature, and… skin, over hundreds of cycles. I will now proceed with the surface scouring. Pay*

*attention, and have the servos at the ready. These* men *contain a surprising amount of fluid which, for the validity of this procedure, has been thawed. It goes everywhere once they are opened.*

Adjusting his surgical device, the green laser extended outwards and widened. The beam crackled once more, became stable, and finally turned blue. Holding it between long white fingers, the Lead Anatomist placed one hand against the bare chest of the still unconscious Japanese guardsman. With a practiced skill, the Aqjm brought the blue beam parallel with the man's flesh.

He then made his first incision.

**6**

The screaming woke the Bear.

He discovered he could not move his head, nor any of his limbs. From the corner of his eye, he could see figures standing about an upright man. At least, he believed it to be a man. Kazaka could not see his lower body, but he could see his outstretched arms. The shadows to his right moved again, rippling with motion. There were many of them. There was light…

Jimmu *Kuma* Kazaka finally knew terror.

A guardsman, one of the pair Kazaka had watched, was being worked upon by a multitude of short, white devils with bulbous heads. Though he could not see clearly, he could hear the man's tortured howls as they administered tools on his flesh. Kazaka saw white limbs rise and fall on the guardsman's person. Blood geysered in a black sheet, and he caught whiff of it, coppery and strong. Another shriek from the man, riding out the very last gush of wind in his lungs. He heard the curt intake of breath again, and another howl scorched the shadows. *What were they doing to him? The devils! No warrior deserved to be held and tortured in such a manner!*

*"Nandaro!"* Kazaka roared.

*"Kuso!"* swore the other guardsman, also to his right.

"Eh!" Kazaka yelled. "You're alive?"

"Hai! Who are you?" the guardsman demanded.

But Kazaka didn't have time to answer, for as soon as he cried out, a multitude of heads looked in his direction. He could see them in his peripheral vision, just out of focus. Then one detached itself from the masses and rushed the

Bear where he hung in place. Like a quick moving spider, the creature came up close to him, and he felt his stomach turn to ice. The thing had eyes like those of a fly, yet they were shaped like oversized eggs. The face came in close to his chest, lipless mouth parted, silent, ready to bite. Kazaka breathed deeply, struggling to control his terror and his trembling chest. The other guardsman kept his tongue, terrified that he would attract the devil's attention.

The creature stared and stared at Kazaka, for what seemed a very long time.

The screams from the third guardsman began to die away.

There was movement to the right, and the group of devils stepped back in a single tide as the platform holding the screaming man upright lowered itself to their height. They then crowded in.

The white devil before Kazaka turned its head towards the examination platform, and for a moment, the Bear knew that this one was more interested in what was happening over there. It looked back to the trapped ninja once again, before flitting away to join its brethren at the edge of Kazaka's vision.

"Oh no," moaned the other guardsman. "Oh Lords of Heaven and Earth, no…"

Kazaka heard the noise. He'd heard it many times before on the fisherman's wharf, where men removed the guts and ripped the spines from their catch.

The guardsman screamed once again, a short yelp punctuated by a series of grunts and moans. The smell of shit sprayed the air, and still the man grunted in the most pitiful manner. Then, the sounds of cracking bones. Another grunt of pain, weaker still. More sounds, wet and organic, of tissue being sliced and stretched.

Kazaka glimpsed one of the blood spattered devils, his arms dark up past his elbows, stepping away from the table, and stretching out something very long and rubbery from the guardsman's body. More grunts of agony from the victim. The man was, unfortunately, very strong.

"Oh Lords of Heaven and Earth…" the other guardsman moaned. None of the white devils paid him any heed, they were so enraptured with what was happening on the platform. "They are… they are *peeling* him like an apple."

"What can you see?" Kazaka demanded.

"Oh Lords… Oh Lords…"

"*What?*"

As if not possessing the breath any longer, the barest grunts could be heard from the guardsman on the table.

"Oh Lords…" the other man moaned.

"Can you move?" Kazaka whispered harshly.

"We are in hell…" came the wail.

"*Can you move?*"

"We…" the guardsman stated as if in a nightmare. "We are in *hell.*"

Kazaka gave up speaking to the man. His mind was gone.

He listened to the devils' work. Sometimes he heard them, in his head, say something that was not quite words, but a long and deep note, not unlike the song of the cicadas. But he did not know what it meant.

The guardsman on the table became quiet after long moments. The white devils continued working on the corpse. Wet sounds, splashing at times, dripping at others, made Kazaka cringe. He tested his limbs again. They were impossible to move and yet, he could see nothing holding him. *Magic,* he thought. The blackest magic had seized him.

"Lords of Heaven and Earth, Lords of Heaven and Earth—" said the remaining guardsman.

Kazaka's eyes flicked to the right again.

Like an embankment of evil, the white devils surrounded the guardsman. Their arms ended in things that glowed blue in the shadows.

"LORDS OF HEAVAGGGHHH!" came the shriek. The guardsman had learned plenty from his companion. He screamed and screamed, and screamed again. He kept right on screaming even as he was lowered in amongst that mass of white heads and long arms.

Then, much to Kazaka's fright and dismay, the man *truly* began to sing.

## 7

From the command bridge, the Aush watched the last few moments of the evisceration and then segmentation of the first specimen on a circular monitor. He directed the bio-eye past the bloody mess on the platform, moving it over the frenzied work being conducted on the second specimen, whose screams were so loud, the Aush mentally switched off the bio-eye's audio. The meat could be noisy at times, and the Aush wondered why the Aqjm had not sedated their experiments to begin with. Probably some secondary purpose that only the scientists knew of.

The Aush straightened and fumed.

His flanking Kajst, the only two on this particular mission, knew their commander's body language when they saw it. The Kajst was pissed.

The commanding Kajst steered the bio-eye towards the man in black. He was next to experience the unmedicated administrations of the Aqjm. Helpless evisceration. The Aush scoffed again. And the Aqjm called *him* barbaric. Not them however. Their studies were much too important to be called anything but valuable. This was not his mission. He was not a protector, he was an Annihilator. He did not like being talked down to by an arrogant Aqjm. To think that the Aqjm believed he and his two Kajsts were not needed on such a mission. *Any* expedition that involved the Aqjm needed protection. They were naïve in everything beyond their bagging and tagging and segmenting. If the Kajst didn't accompany the pompous intellectuals, anything could happen to them. *Any manner of accident.* And then the Kajst would have to *correct* things.

He thought long and hard then, even as the bio-eye drifted to the left of the man in black, and revealed the extent of the operation being performed on the second specimen. They had already cut into the abdominal cavity and were delighting in exploring the internal organs. They were like newly born young. The Aqjm were perhaps the most annoying of the four sexes. These *hu*-mans had only two, typical of a species ranked low on the evolutionary grade, and so boring in more pleasurable matters of the flesh. The Aqjm routinely banished the Aush from the science bay during their work and denied him any and all access to their records. It all infuriated him.

But now, he saw an opportunity.

*Any manner of accident… could happen.* He thought.

The Aush took control of the bio-eye once more and veered to the platform where the man in black's weapons were, those oddly interesting weapons that he had not once seen in all of his missions to this particular planet. He had observed whole armies of *hu*-mans clash in the past. He had studied their battle tactics and strategies, which were interesting and often entertaining in a two dimensional way. He watched them from the use of stones and clubs, to the *sword*, to the more recent invention of the projectile *gun* and *missile*. But not these weapons. Not these. Some of these weapons, like the knife extracted from the creature's buttocks, reeked of secrecy, of infiltration.

The Aush made his decision right then. The two green armored Kajst behind him would support any story he later concocted, their loyalty to him was never in question. And it had been a long time since he had seen any activity of a more interesting sort.

The Aqjm were still playing with the second man's innards.

The Aush felt a rush of excitement as he positioned the bio-eye higher up in the shadows, where it could observe events unnoticed. What was it the *Ro*-mans would declare at the beginning of their captive gladiatorial tournaments? The Aush remembered.

*Let the games begin.*

With as close to a smile the Kajst were capable of, the Aush faced a control panel, located the science bay, thought-touched the necessary coded sequence, and powered down the invisible shackles of the man in black.

# 8

Sounds Kazaka knew would haunt him for the remainder of his days filled the starlit chamber. Again he tested his bonds. He tried to see what held him, but as far as he could determine, *nothing* restrained him. No ropes or chains bound his arms. *Sorcery!* His jaw clenched at the unfairness of it all. He was in hell, and he would be feasted upon next by the mass of maggot-white ghouls gathered at the edge of his vision. More sounds of tissue being cut, of bone being sawed, and the stench of disembowelment. The guardsman still moaned, much to the horror of the Bear. Kazaka felt a twinge of deep pity for the man, it was not the way a warrior should die. It was not the way *he* should die.

Baring his teeth and arching his back, the Bear heaved against his invisible bonds for seconds... then collapsed.

*You must never surrender*, the Maker's voice reached him. *You must never surrender, even if defeat is certain. A ninja is to the night what the sun is to the sky. Take your own life before admitting defeat, and in the next, your powers will be even greater. But you must do* everything *before that.*

Kazaka drew breath once more and again pushed against his invisible shackles. His eyes focused on his right fist, willing it to break free of whatever had chained it. He pushed until his limbs ached and his mind began to scream on its own.

And still he remained frozen.

*Lords of Heaven*—he began and stopped. Beyond his right fist, one of the devils stepped away, a dark ribbon of gut held high in unholy celebration. The guardsman was quiet now.

*Everything.* He must do everything. Kazaka's mind raced. He did not have much time. His eyes went to the dark ceiling and saw nothing that could help him. He could not even move his head, how could he do anything in such a trap? Rage began to build within his chest, fueled generously by the fear of the monsters nearby; for when they finally finished with the guardsman, it would be the Bear's turn to be embraced by those long, white arms. Sweat moistened his mask and *shinobi shōzoku.* It could not end like this. It *must* not end like this. There had to be a way!

Then he was falling.

The freefall caught Kazaka by surprise only for a moment, then his training and reflexes took over. He landed on the balls of his feet, and rolled over, coming up on one knee with his hands hooked and ready before him. The abrupt freedom was savored only for a split second. He needed to arm himself.

The Lords were obviously smiling: the table of weapons was in plain sight before him.

# 9

One of the white devils turned at the noise. The creature's head snapped up when it saw that the last subject was gone. Almost immediately, the others directed their attention to the empty platform. Lipless mouths dropped open in confusion. Compound eyes searched the chamber for the missing biped. Several of the Aqjm saw the man in black at the same time. Some of them gestured with arms that were red with blood.

The Bear stepped away from the table to face them, crouching.

Sounds began to fill his head; the sounds of angry cicadas. The devils faced him, their mouths open as if to scream. One of the creatures moved towards the freed man.

And Kazaka unleashed his shurikens.

# 10

The angle of the bio-eye caught just enough light to see stars rip into their targets. The first Aqjm died with one embedded in its oversized eye. The others charged the *hu*-man in a desperate attempt to seize him. There were perhaps seven or nine of them.

The bio-eye caught it all and the Aush rushed to activate the audio.

Faster than he could process the scene, the *hu*-man's arm rose and fell. Stars flew from his hand and cut into the advancing mass of Aqjm. The scientists fell bleeding, their black life-fluid spilling from their bodies in alarming arterial sprays. One Aqjm staggered to his knees when a silver star cut into his unprotected chest, shredding the delicate organ matter within. Another's head snapped back, a star buried in its forehead. Another whirled about when a weapon half-severed its thin arm at the shoulder, and fell flat when a second stabbed him deep at the back of his thin skull. One Aqjm slipped away from the stalled mass, and tried to flank the *hu*-man.

But the man in black saw him.

Two stars killed the Aqjm. The first one shattered his cheek, the second gashed open his neck.

The man dropped back. A blast of smoke appeared in the center of the room amongst the survivors.

The living Aqjm hesitated. It was perhaps the only time they might have had to escape, for the *hu*-man attacked them a second later. Through the haze, the tail of a silver comet cut the head from one of the scientists, its neck bursting life-fluid in an inky gout. Another had its arm hacked off.

The Aush noted, with a master's approval of a weapon well used, that the *hu*-man was using its sword to great effect.

Screams burst through the audio of the bio-eye. When was the last time the Aush heard an Aqjm actually *use* its vocal chords? He suppressed a dark chuckle.

One Aqjm fled the massacre, and the Aush guessed who it was. The bio-eye recorded the Lead Anatomist fleeing the chamber, and sealing it behind him. The *hu*-man paid this no mind. It was too busy killing.

Then the Aush watched the man as he retrieved his throwing stars. There was still much to see.

With a silent command, the Kajst Aush accessed the examination chamber's door and re-opened it. He commanded his two Kajst inside the bridge. A second after that, he sealed the blast doors leading to the compartment, initiating and following starcraft protocol in the eventuality of a bio-threat, contamination, or decompression. Bright symbols reflected in the black visor of the Aush while he turned his attention to the still fleeing Lead Anatomist. The Kajst activated more bio-eyes, and switched to split-visuals so he could simultaneously monitor the *hu*-man's activity.

*Now*, he thought to the Lead Anatomist, *let us see if you have need of... squashing.*

# 11

The door opened with a hiss. Kazaka froze, his hand filled with the guardsman's longer katana. He listened, hearing only the weak groan of one of the nearby devils, one of the few that hadn't died immediately from the shurikens. The Bear waited, and realized that no attackers were coming. He moved, catlike, through the smoke and gloom and located the creature. It had been disemboweled with one slash from the sword. Those large black eyes regarded the ninja, blinked, and the devil resignedly rolled its head to one side.

The Bear lopped its head off with one chop.

Kicking the head away, Kazaka decided that the creatures were frail things. He did not believe them to be gods. Gods would not have their heads taken by mere mortals. Devils, possibly. In any case, he was pleased that they had died. He glanced at the two tables where the guardsman lay. Both men had been savaged in such ways not even the ninja knew were possible. It was one thing to kill, but to take the men apart a piece at a time, while they still lived, filled the Bear with loathing. There was no honor here. There was only a curiosity about death.

Kazaka flicked the gore from his length of steel. It was a good sword. Well kept, and very sharp. He looked about the dark room, noting how the lights above were like stars. Perhaps they were. He knew he was in a place of black magic, and that he would have to use all his skill to escape. The devils had their chance to kill him, but they were too slow, too complacent in thinking he was helpless. Woe upon them. The Bear was free. Worse, he had his weapons, and was very much inclined to use them. He gathered up his ninjato and blowgun. Kazaka wanted to be away from this place, and moved without a sound towards the open door. He kept to the shadows, and peered out. The corridor beyond was poorly lit and empty.

Kazaka eased into the corridor, sword poised to kill.

## 12

*Boom boom boom* the sounds reverberated as the Lead Anatomist slammed his fist against the metal doors of the sealed bridge. Several members of the science research team stood behind him with their compound eyes wide and staring. Some looked back in the direction of the gravity wells, one on opposite sides of the starcraft, which connected all four levels of the craft. Some wondered where the rest of the team were. Others expected the black garbed monster to appear around a corner and attack them at any moment.

—*Open this door at once!* projected the Lead Anatomist. —*We've been breached by a hostile organism!*

But the doors did not open.

—*Why won't they acknowledge?* One of the Aqjm asked. —*Are they not receiving you?*

—*Silence!* commanded the Lead. He had no time to spare on mere botanists.

—*But why won't they open?* persisted another.

—*What's happened below?* demanded a small pedologist, maintaining his dignity.

—*A specimen escaped,* replied a geophysicist. Others, drawn to the ruckus, gathered about the door.

—*There were deaths,* said one.

—*No!* came a collective gasp.

—*Open this door at once!* the Lead Anatomist projected over them all, silencing them. —*I know you are in there!*

In the surface of the metal, a dot of light appeared. The dot expanded into a screen filled with the dour expression

280

of the Kajst Aush. His black visor rippled as the image stabilized itself.

*—Aush! Open this door at once.*

But the Aush did not reply. Instead, his visor filled the view screen as he drew closer, studying the gathered scientists outside of the bridge.

*—I see there are still a few of you left*, the Aush noted. *— Excellent.*

*—Why are you doing this?* the Lead demanded. *—Explain yourself!*

*—I think*, the projection came slowly, *—that you are better using your time arming yourselves. There is a hostile organism on board… and it is proving itself extremely capable at killing.*

The Lead Anatomist paused in his fury. How did the Kajst know the organism was effective in killing? And how did the specimen free itself in the first place? In his panic, these were questions that he had not considered. Until now.

*—You released it! You purposely freed it! Only you could have done such a thing! Are you completely unstable?*

The shock of the accusation silenced the remaining scientists. Here and there, compound eyes stared at the combat specialist's image.

The light screen flickered. *—It's coming*, the Aush projected, and severed communications.

# 13

The Bear exited the laboratory and made his way down a metal corridor ringed with dull lighting. It was dark, and utterly perfect conditions for the ninja. He moved along, his *tabi* footwear making not a sound. The metal was warm to the touch and there was so *much* of it. What manner of Maker could construct such a castle? It must have taken years.

Just ahead was a doorway. Kazaka hugged the edge and slowly peeked around it. It was empty of the white devils. He did not recognize the laboratory for what it was. He did not understand the computer banks, the specimen tubes, or the machines pulsing with eerie internal lights, as if lightning was trapped within. He saw naked bodies of men and women, in various stages of experiments, too horrific for him to comprehend. Dead. All dead. There were heads missing their eyes, torsos without limbs but with long tubes, like those of leeches, attached to where limbs should be. There was a head on a black box just beyond the doorway. It was the head of a man whose flesh was dark. Kazaka had never seen the like before.

The head's eyes opened. It groaned and spoke to him.

The Bear almost screamed. The head talked in a tongue he did not understand. He backed away. It was too horrible. Fright exploded in his chest and lower legs, and Kazaka stepped back out of the doorway and placed his back against the bulkhead. The head continued to cry out. Its cries became a moan.

Breathing deeply, Kazaka ran past the opening, towards the end of the corridor, where there was a shallow cave made of metal. A low hum reached the Bear's ears. He edged towards the opening, trying to ignore the head still shouting madness. He cocked his head to look, and saw that it went up and down in inky darkness, illuminated by tiny stars. But there were no stairs. Kazaka stepped into the cave, thinking to climb his way up. The walls of the cave were not smooth, but knobbed. Climbing would be easy.

His feet left the ground.

The Bear shrieked in spite of himself. Upwards he flew, far too quickly for his liking, swimming in the air until he came to the opening of the next level. He grabbed the edges of the portal and pulled himself in. He almost collapsed with relief and pushed himself against the nearest wall. He took a moment to compose himself and take in his surroundings.

There was a wall before him, as well as a long corridor ahead and to his right. Also to his right was a dark wall full of holes coated in what looked to be clear ice. Kazaka brought his sword to guard and made his way to the wall without a sound, staying within the gloom of the halls. He came to the first panel of ice and peered in. It was a living quarters of some kind, that much he knew, dully lit in pink and purple with devices and shapes unknown to him. Strange pictures adorned not only the walls, but the ceiling as well. He could see nothing comfortable about the domicile, but it reeked of foulness. As he peered in, his head bumped the ice. The Bear jerked back. It was warm to the touch. He tapped it with the hilt of his blade, testing its strength before placing a hand on its surface. *Warmth.* Kazaka's eyes opened wide behind his black mask. He touched the surface again, marveling at the smoothness of it.

Drawing back, the Bear took in the rest of the wall. There were several of these strange quarters, if they were indeed the devils' dwellings. Did the devils sleep? Would they sleep if he hid until night? He thought about it. Was there even a day or night in hell? He decided not.

He stepped along the wall, passing the other domiciles, until he came to a new passageway hidden by shadows. He glanced down the new corridor and saw nothing. Darkness ruled here, that much was obvious to him. Ninja bathed in shadow, and were silence manifested in flesh. There were many things unknown to Kazaka, but he was not a stupid man. The white devils lived in strange places. They ripped people apart and left speaking heads, but what was important above all else, was they bled and died easily enough.

The Bear glanced around. There were plenty of places to hide. The ceiling was low and bulging with thick black ropes.

Hell. He was in hell.

Underneath his mask, a grim smile spread.

But it was a *ninja's* hell.


The Lead Botanist stood before a bank of computer poles and studied the numerals and characters floating in the air before her. With a thought, she brought up another series of images, and studied them with great interest. There was a problem with the depth of the soil in the chamber, and the root systems of the towering *sugi* trees could go no further in the space that was afforded them. The Lead glanced up, taking in the towering heights of the trees, their foliage blocking out the starlight. She wasn't quite certain what to do with the situation. The growing trees were an experiment spanning centuries, and they were brought aboard the starcraft when they were mere saplings. No one knew that the plant-life would flourish so well in space. It was an Earth forest in the heavens, and many had doubted her team's ability to make it thrive. But thrive it had, to this point, where it could grow no further. It just went to prove what the Lead Botanist and her team of dedicated scientists were capable of.

She studied the dark height of the trees and breathed in the gift of the purest oxygen she had ever tasted. It was wonderful, the rush more satisfying than any of the stimulants found on their world. A few more years perhaps, and they would transplant these magnificent giants to their homeworld, and begin the phase of introducing new flora into their environment. The Lead Botanist looked down, and took in the vast domed chamber about her. She took a step away from the floating images of data and the problems they presented, and walked to the edge of the platform she stood upon. Here, from the observatory in the center of the dome, meters above a nutrient-rich earth floor covered in humus, she gazed at her creation. The dome was filled with thick foliage not only from the trees, but the vegetation allowed to grow and flourish underneath it like a thick, breathing blanket. Here and there, she spied her team members moving through the forest, conducting their research and recording their findings. The plant life rose up to their waists in some places, giving the illusion of the Aqjms wading through a deluge of woodland green.

She kept on watching and gradually became aware of a tapping coming from the entranceway to the dome, the only entry and exit portal in the entire chamber. It persisted for a short time, an irregular metallic sound, and then stopped, only to resume again. Curiosity, an Aqjm's greatest weakness, prodded her to project a command to an Aqjm closest to the portal.

*—Investigate the source of that,* she instructed.

And a tall, white botanist, as willowy as the bushes surrounding it, moved towards the source of the sound.

Hidden amongst the mess of strange ropes in the ceiling, Kazaka watched as the white devil stepped through the circular doorway. The creature was a tall, frail looking thing with an oversized head. It was a good thing he took into consideration the size of their heads, for he could not make a noose big enough to fit one. He waited until the devil took another step, further away from the portal and into the shadows of the corridor. It was no doubt looking for the source of the noise. Without a sound, the Bear shifted and tensed his legs where he had hooked them through the ceiling ropes, and lowered his upper body, upside-down, just above and behind the white devil's bulbous head. Holding his breath, he tossed the length of rope, his *kusari fundo*, over his target's neck and yanked with all his strength. The devil half turned when it was jerked off its feet, upwards into the air. There was short, audible snap of bone breaking, a brief dance, and then nothing. Dead, as easy as that. Kazaka snarled behind his face mask as he held the creature up for moments longer. Then he crunched his abdomen, curling himself back up into the shadows of the ceiling, and like a predator of the night, hauled the carcass of his prey up with him.

The Bear stowed the body away and then dropped to the metallic floor with barely a sound. He eased himself to the edge of the portal, peered in, and his mouth dropped open. It was a forest, a grand timberland almost as beautiful as that of the Maker's. Kazaka wondered how such a grand woodland could exist in hell? He decided it did not matter.

He could see the devils moving through the shadows of the forest, as white as maggots on dead meat. The light was strange in this place, twilight or such, as if the sun had just sunk below a range of mountains and darkness had not yet claimed the land.

As a breath of wind parting willows, Kazaka slipped into the forest in Hell. He dropped into a crouch, and moved in a zigzag pattern, pressing forward. The Bear held the guardsman's katana flat against his back, like a scorpion ready to strike. He moved as a fish would through water, barely disturbing the vegetation surrounding him. Shadows were the cauls of death, and friend to the ninja. It was not long before he came upon his next two victims.

The pedologist straightened and felt unease, though he did not know why. He glanced about the trunks of the mighty trees and finally looked up. There was something wrong, and he could sense it. He could discern a terrible concentration in the air, a menace, just barely noticeable, but present. It grew closer, and when the soil scientist paused to better understand exactly what it was, he could sense it hesitate. His compound eyes took in the form of his companion, not far away and stooping amongst the underbrush, no doubt studying some species of flora.

The pedologist stood in confusion, thinking of how to proceed, when something zipped through the air and sunk into the hollow of his cheek. His long fingers came up in reflex, touching the thing embedded in his flesh. A burning sensation spread outwards, lighting up his senses, and he realized with horror that a foreign and toxic compound of some sort had invaded his body. He tried turning to his companion and project a warning, but then he was falling, and the ground swallowed him whole.

The other pedologist nearby heard the sound of something crashing and turned to see his fellow soil sampler gone. He projected a question, and received no reply. Puzzled, he stepped forward to the location where the scientist once stood, the underbrush crunching beneath his white feet. He projected again and thought, for a moment, he received the barest flicker of pain. Then something entangled his legs and he was falling. He blurted out a thought of surprise just as the humus covered ground raced up to his face. He landed on his hands and elbows, face down.

There was a solid connection to the back of his neck. His vision bounced, went awry, and for the briefest of moments, before everything went eternally black, he saw his white torso, headless, spraying streams of black life fluid.

The Lead Botanist turned in the direction of the shocked mental outburst coming from her left. She went to the edge of the platform and called out with her mind. All but three of her science team reported back, and she could sense their collective consciousness converging on the point where the distress thought rang out.

—*Is something wrong?* one of the team asked her, but she did not answer. Instead she gave the command to proceed to the area where they heard the cry originate.

—*With caution*, she informed them all with a wary afterthought.

Kazaka pressed his dark form up against a tree, and watched three of the white devils coming through the brush towards him. As they came forward, he slunk further back, around the massive trunk, easing out of their sight. When they had gone by, he waited for a moment before bringing up his blowgun. He had four darts remaining, all coated with the Maker's poison. Kazaka noted that a previous victim taken down with the dart had an interesting reaction to the poison. It ate away at their flesh as it rendered them senseless. Fortunate for the Bear.

He loaded the gun and brought it to his lips. Two darts stuck out from between his fingers, ready to be loaded. Three targets. He would not have much time, but then he realized, neither would his prey. With that thought, he huffed into the blowgun.

*—There's some*—was the final thought the Lead Botanist received from an Aqjm in what was now thought of as the danger zone. It was weak, dying, and filled with a sensation of burning. Then silence.

She would take no further chances, and ordered all remaining Aqjm to stay away from the dangerous area in the forest. She then quickly stepped to a communication stalk, the tall reed-like device was almost indistinguishable from the computer poles except for its triangular head. With a thought-tap, she called security.

There was no response.

Puzzlement filled the Lead's face and before she could do anything more, a scream of pain erupted from the forest behind her. She whipped about, scanning the undergrowth for signs of anything wrong. Here and there, she saw her fellow scientists, standing in the vegetation waist deep and looking in her direction, where she stood on the central platform. They were all frozen to the spot, uncertain as to how to proceed.

Then she sensed it, as clear as the oxygen she breathed. Fear rose in the thoughts of her companions. It riveted them to their places. She projected a thought of comfort while simultaneously hailing security once again.

—*Aush?* She called out once more with her mind. —*Kajst?*

Silence.

Then another outburst of pain.

The Lead Botanist whirled about, just in time to see a single Aqjm amongst the trees disappearing from sight, yanked into the underbrush by something below. There was a quick, high-pitched squeal in the Lead's mind, then a stillness that made her lower extremities quiver with fear. Something was out there killing Aqjm. She darted back to the communication stalk and once more hailed the Aush and his Kajst. Again nothing. Behind her, the few remaining Aqjm fled through the forest, their frantic cries for help scrambling her thought patterns. She forced them out, and again called for the Aush.

She looked over her shoulder and caught a glimpse of something black floating through the shadows of the upper regions of the trees. It moved and paused in the air, moved and paused, coming closer to the platform.

More screams.

*A bio-eye?* She thought over the death cry of yet another Aqjm. Below it, a scientist was running madly through the brush, heading directly for the platform. The Lead saw him dart between two trees and make a line towards her. Both of his arms were above his head, waving to catch her attention. Her growing sense of dread chilled her core.

—*What is it?* she screamed at her approaching team member.

The Aqjm staggered, as if struck from behind, but there was nothing following it. It crashed and disappeared into the undergrowth. There was a ripple in the sea of green, as if something was feeding just below the surface, then it subsided. High above the area and just beyond, the bio-eye hung in the air and watched.

Terror, the likes she had never experienced ever in her centuries old existence, seized her mind and she shrieked a single thought into the communication's stalk. —*AUSH!*

She called and called, unawares of the silence descending upon the forest in the heavens, unaware of the slow approach of the bio-eye, heading in her direction. —*AUSH!*

The Lead Botanist glanced over her shoulder and saw the surveillance device bearing down on the platform and could not, for the very existence of her being, understand why security was not responding to her situation. She screamed again and again into the stalk, and realized at one point that she was even using her vocal cords.

The Lead Botanist glanced behind again, heedless of the stillness surrounding her.

There, suspended in the air just beyond the edge of the platform, was the floating bio-eye, studying her with its dark lens.

Terrified, the Lead abandoned the useless stalk and ran to the platform's edge. The bio-eye was right there. The Aush was manipulating it. *Only* the Aush could control it. She frantically waved her arms at the device and sent out frantic projections for aid.

The bio-eye hung in the air and stared.

—*AUSH!* she screamed out with both her mind and mouth.

It was then something grabbed her ankles, brought her

crashing down to the unyielding metal of the platform, and yanked her dazed form to the forest floor below, into the shadows smelling of earth.

## 14

The blast door to the bridge opened all of two seconds, and only wide enough for a plaz-case to be shoved through a crack. Stricken with terror, the scientists did not think to go underneath the door. It was perhaps not wise. The manner in which the Aush was acting, he might have closed it on one of them.

The Lead Anatomist grabbed the plaz-case and opened it. His smooth features frowned. The case was full of weapons. Worse, it was full of archaic weapons. His frown deepening, he pulled out a long shafted mace. Even with both arms, he could barely hold the weapon up. The others mulled around and looked into the case, a mixture of puzzlement and growing horror filling their heads.

*—What is this?*

*—Is the Aush truly unstable?*

*—What does he expect us to do?*

The Lead Anatomist knew what it was the Aush expected them to do. He spotted the floating bio-eye above, and wished he had the chance to prod the Aush with one of his surgical lasers under conditions of his choosing.

*—He expects us to die*, the Lead informed the Aqjm standing about. *—The Kajst assigned to this mission has betrayed us.*

*—Why?* some of the scientists wailed, still not understanding.

*—Because*, the Lead Anatomist declared, *—the Aush is, simply put, a jealous, unprofessional…* and a foul stream of expletives erupted from the head scientist, aimed directly at the floating bio-eye.

*—And he intends for this alien to kill us all*, the Lead finished.

His projection stunned the scientists into dejected silence.

*—But the Aush has made three mistakes,* the Lead Anatomist stated.

*—What?* asked a geophysicist, her hands holding the pale hollows where a human's fleshy cheeks would have been, her features full of fright.

The Lead Anatomist did not reply right away. He knew he was correct in his thinking, and he struck a defiant pose for the bio-eye. He did not show the fear he knew the Aush wanted to see. He refused to. There was more to him than just research and eviscerations.

*—He has armed us,* the Lead replied, locking a vengeful gaze upon the bio-eye, knowing the military Kajst received him. *—He has also forgotten that we are specialists in our chosen fields. We are the intellectuals of this mission. He is simply the brute force, and in locking us out, he's proven his thinking is inferior. And—*he paused for dramatic effect—*he has left us access to the remainder of the ship. He has not locked us out. He has locked himself in. We have control of the rest of the ship. Most importantly, the* engines *of the ship. Engineer!*

*—Lead Anatomist,* the Aqjm instantly reported back, nowhere near as terrified as the others.

*—Take us to Engineering. The rest of you… choose your weapons.* Already a plan formulated within the Lead Anatomist's head, and it was a simple one. He would take the remainder of the research team into the bowels of the star craft. With the engineer, they would not bother opening the door to the bridge. A direct confrontation with the Aush was predictably futile. While there were escape pods on this deck, no doubt locked out, the majority of them, however, were below. And the Aush knew that the engineer could effectively override the lock codes from his station, cripple the ship's engines

and perhaps even program them to self destruct while they made their escape to the nearest science station in orbit behind the Earth's moon.

—*What are we going to do?* asked the chronobiologist, hefting a short spear.

The Lead Anatomist made a face. —*We are going to get out of here.*

—*But there are others…*

—*If they are not here by now, I suspect them to be dead.* With that, he walked towards the gravity well. The engineer marched right behind him, a spear in his fists. The rest of the bewildered scientists followed, struggling with the weight of their ancient weapons. They made their way to the gravity well, and the Lead Anatomist peered into its depths. The man in black was down there. Its primitive mind was no doubt struggling with its predicament. Probably curled up in a corner somewhere, with its senses lost. The Lead scoffed at the image.

He stepped into the gravity well. The others followed, eleven of them in total, all clutching their weapons from the ages.

The Lead Anatomist projected the level he desired, and the well lowered him and the others to where the engines and storage vats were located, four levels down.

—*Can you disable the well from here?* he asked the engineer.

—*Most certainly.* The engineer's long fingers accessed a hidden panel to the right of the gravity well's opening. Lights glowed and died as a series of codes were entered. A low buzzing became audible, then abruptly ceased.

The engineer turned back to the other Aqjm. —*Done. Now the other.*

As a group, they marched towards the second gravity well, on the far side of the ship.

15

The Aush watched them leave the command level and instructed the bio-eye to follow. A glow of hatred began to burn for the Lead Anatomist. If the *hu*-man could kill that particular Aqjm, then all would be well within the universe. The scientist was clever, however, and the Aush reminded himself that, as much as he loathed the little Aqjm, he must not underestimate him. Not now, when his plans to kill the entire team were underway. The Aush considered the Lead Anatomist's plan. It wasn't a bad one, but there were escape pods on the bridge as well. If the game got out of hand, the Aush would initiate the destruct sequence of the ship, and he and his pair of Kajst would evacuate. The disabling of the gravity well might be a problem however. Not for the Kajst, but for the *hu*-man.

He thought about his Kajst. They were engineered for battle, and not above killing one of their own species if necessary. He might have to send one or both of his soldiers after the Aqjm, though he did not want to. He wanted the *hu*-man to further demonstrate what it could do. It would also make it easier for the Aush to lie if the creature killed them. He switched to the bio-eye monitoring the man in black. It was difficult to see him in the shadows of the forest, camouflaged as he was. The creature had killed the entire science team in the botanical dome, the Lead Botanist being the last, almost too quickly for the Aush. And the *hu*-man moved without a sound. The Aush approved. Upon command, the bio-eye switched to a thermal sensor, and the shadow warrior's glowing image filled the Aush's view screen.

What was even better, the *hu*-man was making its way out of the dome, back towards the same gravity well the Aqjm had used moments before. It reached the well at the same time the Aqjm below finished disabling the transport device. It paused at the threshold, like an animal sensing blood. It peeked in and studied the walls. Then it considered the ceiling behind it, and began unwinding a length of rope from its midsection, the same rope it had used to strangle an Aqjm earlier. The creature tied it to an overhead protrusion, and gave it a tug. It threw the rest of the rope into the well. Then the *hu*-man disappeared, downwards.

The Aush was pleased. Resourceful. He wondered how many other surprises this shadow warrior possessed. The bio-eye followed the creature into the well, keeping back a respectable distance, and observing its progress.

The man in black climbed back down to the lower levels.

It had the scent of the Aqjm.

# 16

They made their way across the ship, clustered together like a group of frightened young. The Lead Anatomist held his mace before him like a huge crucifix of war, his little mouth twisted in a snarl. He wanted the *hu*-man to show itself. They hadn't been prepared when it attacked them the first time. They were ready now. Though they were not engineered for combat, the Aqjm were far from helpless and were more than capable of using the ancient weapons the Aush had supplied. The Lead Anatomist thought about the weapons. The Aqjm wished he possessed a plasma bolt or even a white-matter inhibitor. This business with the hostile specimen would be finished quickly if he did.

—*Where is the creature?* one Aqjm asked, looking everywhere as the group moved up the corridor.

—*Let it come*, one of two entomologists declared. She was armed with a short sword and wielding it as if she were a Kajst, swishing it from side to side.

—*If we went back to our labs, we could access the cast-cloud canisters*, suggested the second entomologist. —*It would render the hu-man helpless.*

—*We are deactivating the wells*, the engineer added. —*That is the first priority.*

The Lead Anatomist halted the group at a junction. To their right was a long corridor leading to the engines and escape pods. There was no need for all of them to proceed, and he wanted to be free of the ship as soon as possible. He looked to the Aqjm behind him. —*Who else knows how to disable the gravity well?*

A biotech raised his mace. *—I can, if given instructions.*

*—We'll save time if we split the group up*, projected the Lead.

*—I believe that is a strategically poor decision*, the pedologist informed them.

*—What do I care about what you think?* the Lead Anatomist snapped. *—You are far removed from your field of study. Who are you, one who studies soil samples, to think you know anything about strategy? I have not been in any armed conflicts, but compared to all my years of existence and research, you should remain still.*

The pedologist did not dispute this, and lowered his eyes.

*—I'll give instructions for the gravity well*, the engineer broke in, saving the pedologist from further mental lashings.

*—Do it then*, the Lead Anatomist ordered, and the engineer complied. The Lead glowered at the pedologist. He wanted to strike the soil-sampler for such impudence, and in front of the others. Who did he think he was?

*—You four continue on to the well and deactivate it as quickly as possible.* The Lead commanded, singling out the sulking pedologist, and three others. *—The rest will follow me.*

They obeyed without further question or protest. The smaller group broke away, heading towards the gravity well. The Lead marched down the dimly lit passageway, towards the ship's engine, intent on sabotaging the starcraft. The Aush's betrayal of the Aqjm enraged him. Too many good personnel had perished in the laboratory. He wanted to avenge them in spectacular fashion.

They reached the chamber doors after a time, and the engineer thought-activated entry. Heavy metal doors slid open without a sound, and the Lead Anatomist looked to the two entomologists.

*—Stand guard here and listen*, he commanded. *—Alert us if you sense anything. When the others get here, enter. We'll have the pods ready.*

*—If the specimen shows itself*—began the male entomologist.

*—We'll kill it,* stated the female.

*—Not without me, you won't,* the Lead Anatomist vowed, rage fuelling his vengeful thoughts.

With that, the leading Aqjm, along with the engineer with his spear, the two botanists armed with knives, and the chronobiologist who also carried a spear, filed past the two appointed guardians. Once inside the star lights of the chamber self activated, illuminating the room.

The heavy door closed.

Time passed. The entomologists regarded each other.

*—I hope the bug comes this way,* the male projected, grasping his short sword.

*—As do I,* added the female.

*—The anatomists made a serious error this time.*

*—I agree.*

*—If only we were in the laboratory when it happened…*

*—There would have been a different outcome,* the female stated.

She suddenly jumped in her tracks, as if startled. The male gave her a puzzled look. Then he saw the dart, sticking out of the side of her head. The female opened her mouth to scream, but a star ripped into her chest, knocking her from her feet. Her sword clattered to the floor. The male spun about, and a shuriken took him in the eye, whipping it to the side in a supernova of pain. He was falling when the third shuriken hissed over his head and clattered off the metal door.

Not quite dead, the female opened her mouth. The agony in her neck robbed her of coherent thought as well as command of her limbs. She could still see however, and to her horror, a dark shadow flittered up the corridor, like one of the huge species of hunting spiders they regularly captured and studied from the planet below. A single fang could be seen. Then the thing was standing over her.

And the fang stabbed downwards.

## 17

—*What was that?* an Aqjm projected with alarm. He leveled his spear at the closed door.

The others faced the sealed entryway. There was no other sound.

—*What do you think we should do?* a botanist asked.

The chagrin in the Lead Anatomist's single projection was unmistakable. —*Open the door and kill it!*

From where he stood over his panel, the engineer looked uncertainly at their leader. —*The escape pods are accessible now.*

—*Open the door!* the lead Aqjm shrieked in their heads, overriding the engineer.

They readied their weapons. The Lead Anatomist brought up his mace, the botanists gripped their knives, and the chronobiologist stood braced with his short spear. The engineer held his own spear at hip level with both hands. He reached out with his mind to activate the door. It opened. The Aqjm tensed.

There, in an ocean of black life fluid, lay the two dead entomogists.

The chronobiologist looked to the Lead. —*What is this cre—*

A star bit into his brow, whipping his head backwards.

The man in black surged into the room. His sword swept up in a brutal flash, cutting the engineer from crotch to spear. As the engineer staggered back, a brave botanist lunged with his knife. The sword parried the knife to the outside and a hard hand-heel cracked into the scientist's face, smashing cheek bone. The other botanist actually shrieked, a high childlike sound, and stabbed for the man's chest. The man in black jumped away from the thrust. He held the sword before him at low guard. Black eyes met the compound eyes of the botanist and the scientist felt a stab a fear.

The *hu*-man blurred forward, its sword dazzling in a series of cuts and stabs. The botanist jerked backwards, grossly outmatched. He jabbed with his knife in reflex. The man's whirling sword took the smaller blade away from the botanist at the wrist. Black fluid splashed and a scream left the Aqjm's mouth. Two long lines in the botanist's chest were slashed open and bled ink. The scientist felt the strength leave his legs. He dropped to his knees, still holding his gushing wrist.

The man in black spun about, his blade snapping out and stabbing the second botanist through the chest. The Aqjm with the broken face barely screamed before the sword was yanked out and stabbed into his flesh again. It punctured him a third time, the steel twisting to the left and then upwards and out, spraying black fluid in a thick arc. The botanist tripped and fell over the form of the engineer, landing flat on his back. The *hu*-man stabbed the Aqjm through the face.

Turning back, the man in black pounced on the other, still kneeling botanist, and chopped an arm off. The scientist crumpled to the black floor, its features crunched in agony. The *hu*-man gutted him, going in through the back.

Its mouth hanging open, the still breathing chronobiologist looked up, holding its terrible wound and wanting to desperately pull the weapon out of its head. Life fluid half-blinded him and he tried to stem the flow with his other hand. The pose struck looked pitiful in the dim light.

The man in black hunched over, his dark blade held to one side. There was no mercy in his eyes.

The chronobiologist tried to scream again, but a sword perforated his throat in one meaty punch.

## 18

From the bridge, the Aush watched the butchery from the angles of two bio-eyes. The speed of the *hu*-man's attack was astounding, the ferocity without mercy. *As it might be,* the Aush thought to himself, remembering the experiments performed on the other captured *hu*-mans. There was never a question about the concept of revenge in the creatures. The Aush expected no less from the animal. But the manner, the techniques the creature employed to eliminate the Aqjm were fascinating. The beast was as precise with its weapons as one of the anatomists with its surgical instruments. The Aush held his own sword, flexing it, holding it the same way the *hu*-man did.

Then he watched the creature kill the last Aqjm—the chronobiologist—and tense up. The Aush found himself shaking his head. It knew something was amiss.

Without a word, the creature bounded up the passageway, in the same direction the Lead Anatomist was fleeing. The Aush sent the two bio-eyes off to monitor the hunt, and satisfaction coursed through his person. He knew that particular Aqjm was utterly pompous and arrogant. He could now label the scientist a fool and a coward. *Don't need Kajst on research expeditions?* The Aush wished he could torment his adversary with the recorded events in the engine room and laboratory, just to crush the superiority complex the scientist possessed and consistently displayed.

He doubted he would get the chance. The primitive was too skilled for the Aqjm. But before he had died, the engineer had successfully bypassed the emergency crafts' locks.

The Aush turned to one of the Kajst standing behind him. *—Go to the escape pods. Kill anything trying to access them.* The Kajst obeyed.

The Aush continued to watch the screens, following the chase as it developed, and practicing the various chops, slashes, and stabs as demonstrated by the *hu*-man. His eidetic reflexes had recorded every movement, every attack the creature made. In seconds, he programmed his augmented reflexes to act as if he had years of training. It was in every Kajst's engineering to quickly assimilate how a weapon functioned. He continued to practice the movements until he felt more than comfortable in his execution.

In the minute it took, the Aush mastered the way of the sword.

# 19

*—WAIT!* came the projection of sheer terror.

The remaining Aqjm turned to see the Lead Anatomist running towards them, still carrying his mace. The biotech stopped entering codes. His attempts to disable the gravity well had failed, and it earned him the mental lashings of his edgy companions.

*—Have you deactivated it?* the Lead Anatomist blurted out.

*—No, I have not,* the engineer began. *—There was—*

*—FLEE!* the Lead projected in terror and jumped into the gravity well. He immediately began to rise. Not needing any further encouragement, the four Aqjm followed him. Upwards, they rushed.

Mere moments later, and braver now that he saw the well in use, Kazaka jumped into the device, meaning to end the hunt the moment he reached the top.

# 20

The engineer was not dead.

But he hurt so much, he knew he was close. It only took a glance down to see how badly the *hu*-man had damaged him. The creature's weapon was so embarrassingly primitive and yet, it had taken the life from the Aqjm in an instant. Or at least put him on the painful path to death. Grimacing, the engineer looked down at his lower body and wished he had not. The weapon had cut him deeply down there, and he did not think he could move his legs. Purple viscera seeped through a long, fish-gill slash, and seeing his own guts spilled onto the floor filled the engineer with an almost overwhelming sense of futility. He was dying. He had only moments remaining.

He attempted to move one of his legs, drenched in the black life fluid of the dead surrounding him. There was a deep, pain-sparkling *tug* from inside his abdominal cavity, and a little grunt of breath escaped him. *Fine*, the engineer thought through the dark matter of his mind, he was the star craft's engineer. He knew all of the tricks.

He inhaled and concentrated, projecting a mental command to a nearby console's interface. Lights responded. The interface detached itself from the console, and floated towards him. Slowly, it came so very slowly. His vision blackened and returned, and he knew that he had little time. He didn't want to expire in such a manner, in such a faraway place, but it was going to happen. Despair set in.

Then the floating interface was before him, pulsating with luminous life.

The engineer reached up. It was too high for him and his arms were too heavy. He commanded the device to come closer. When it rested on his chest, his spidery fingers did a slow dance across its glowing surface, initiating forbidden codes that only he was aware of.

He did not have much time.

But neither did his killer.

## 21

The Lead Anatomist did not wait for the others. He reached the top level, and bolted from the gravity well as if escaping the pull of a black hole. He rushed to the first of three sealed hatches leading to the escape pods. His hand swept over an entry interface, turning it from purple to gold. The hatch hissed opened, and the interior of the pod illuminated with dull silver light. There were three pods located on the top of the starcraft, but one would suffice.

—*Wait!* pleaded the pedologist as he and the last three members of the science personnel left the gravity well.

The Lead whirled upon them. —*There are two other pods here,* he threw back at the emerging foursome. —*Take one of those. I have no time to waste on you.*

—*Where are the others?* the geophysicist asked.

—*Where do you think? Think for once in your miserable existence! They are all dead! The hostile executed them. Waste no further thought on the matter and get to the pods if you wish to sur*—the Lead Anatomist stopped projecting and stared. The others did the same.

There, emerging from the mouth of the corridor leading to the bridge, stood a fully armed and battle-armored Kajst. It leveled its plasma weapon at the Lead Anatomist, its dark visor fearsome in the dim light.

—*What are you doing, you imbecile?* The Lead bellowed. —*I am the Lead of this expedition. You obey* me, *not the Aush. That idiotic Kajst has become irrevocably unstable. Who do you think you are, to aim at my evolved person. Do you know how* superior *I am to your kind? Lower it! I command you to*—

For an intelligent being, the Kajst thought the Lead Anatomist was being incredibly stupid. He fired. The plasma weapon blazed in the confinement of the upper level. The sound of rattling chains and the repeating muzzle flash, like an exploding star, cut the air. A single destructive line of light lashed out and cut the still projecting Lead Anatomist in half, flinging the two pieces inside the readied escape pod. The plasma bursts continued, and a small explosion erupted from the opened pod.

The Kajst ceased firing.

The silence was almost as frightening as the weapon discharge. Sparks and fires snapped and crackled from the ruined pod, filling the corridor with smoke. The Kajst stepped forward, weapon readied and seeking new targets. Knowing that the end was near, the biotech and the physicist threw down their weapons and began pleading for their lives.

*Located*, the Kajst thought.

The roar of plasma burst the silence, punching huge chunks out of the two willowy scientists and heaving their carcasses backwards. A firm advocate of overkill, the Kajst continued firing, blasting the burning body parts towards the gravity well. Plasma ripped into metal bulkheads, leaving deep melting craters and the smell of burning chemical compounds.

In the dragon's belch of continued weapon's discharge, and under the cover of increasing smoke, the geophysicist grabbed the long arm of the pedologist and dragged him to the remaining pods. Her hand swiped the entry interface, turning it from purple to gold. The hatchway opened, sucking smoke inwards.

The Kajst stopped firing.

The two Aqjm fled inside the pod. Flinging the stunned pedologist to the deck, the geophysicist turned back and promptly sealed the pod's hatch behind them. Through the grey smoke and light, she could see the green figure of the Kajst. The soldier was facing the gravity well, its helmet and visor searching for something. Then its armored form turned towards the closed portal.

*—Initiate the launch!* the geophysicist commanded the pedologist.

*—I don't know how!* wailed the soil sampler.

The Kajst aimed the plasma weapon at the closed hatch. Though a small view portal, it seemed as if the weapon was directed right at the geophysicist's face.

Then something rose up behind the soldier. It grabbed the Kajst's armored head, and twisted it to the side. Without a sound, the soldier dropped to the smoke filled floor. Standing in its stead, was the man in black.

The geophysicist almost cried out with relief. The *hu*-man regarded them, watching them through the smoke, and walked towards the sealed hatch.

*—I found it!* projected the pedologist from behind her. *— Initiating launch now. You should strap in.*

The *hu*-man stepped up to the view portal. Its black eyes met the compound gaze of the geophysicist. Fear coursed through her again.

But then the pod's engines lifted the Aqjm up and away.

# 22

Kazaka placed a hand on the surface of the closed doorway. He did not know how the magic worked. All he could do was watch as the creature that stared at him from within was lifted upwards. The metal thing they were in moved towards the ceiling, and did not stop. It slipped through the permeable bulkhead, like a raindrop entering the sea. Then it was gone.

*Sorcery*, the Bear thought as he peered upwards, searching the smoke filled ceiling for a passage that was not there. Nearby and behind him, fires burned from the impressive weapon of the warrior whose neck he'd snapped. The Bear thought that was a close thing. He tried stabbing the warrior with his sword, but his steel would not penetrate the warrior's armor. It was a good thing the samurai did not have such protection.

Something made him tense. He could feel the approach of another on the air.

Holding his sword, Kazaka disappeared into the smoke.

## 23

Never in a thousand cycles of this solar system's sun did the Aush think that a *hu*-man could kill a Kajst. The bio-eyes recorded the death so that he could replay it as many times as he pleased. The smoke. A combination of the smoke and the carelessness of the firing Kajst resulted in its death. There was no remorse for the soldier. Soldiers died all the time. The Aush half turned to the remaining Kajst.

*–Kill it.*

The Kajst left, determined to do just that.

The Aush watched on separate view screens as the escape pod pulled away from the starcraft. They were spared one death only to be delivered into a more spectacular one. The Kajst watched it for a short time. There was no rush here. The pod was well within range. With a thought, the Aush activated the starcraft's outer weaponry. A targeting display converged on the fleeing pod.

The Aush diverted his attention to the two bio eyes floating around beyond the bridge. The Kajst he had just dispatched entered *the neck*, the long walkway connecting the rest of the starcraft with the bridge. He looked back to the pod flying towards distant stars.

And gave the mental command to fire.

## 24

A microsecond before the Aush's command was processed by the starcraft's weapons systems, the engineer, with his last gasp, entered the final code.

In his dying state, he had rushed things, and had made mistakes. Instead of all of the engines self-destructing, only one exploded. Mercifully, it was the one closest to him. A violent rush of force and flame consumed the engineer. The blast ripped through a bulkhead...

And rocked the starcraft.

The canon fired just as the explosion tipped the orbit of the ship. Bolts of plasma lanced out and grazed the escaping pod. It was far from being a direct hit, but it was enough to send the smaller ship into a tail spin, and send it earthwards.

Inside, the pedologist and the geophysicist held on for dear life. They spiraled in momentary weightlessness until gravity was restored. The other systems remained offline or damaged, and the pedologist looked at the instrument panel with eyes full of despair. The shock of being fired upon was just settling in.

*—They'll pick us out of the atmosphere with the next blast!* he screamed in the geophysicist's mind. She forced him out and clambered to the controls. She understood that the pods were programmed to fly themselves, but as far as she could tell, the blast from the mother ship had crippled it. Alarming symbols flashed in gold across view screens. She thought-tapped an interface, and a monitor displayed the image of their mother ship hanging in space. Fire flared briefly in the vacuum of space, and she remembered the engineer and felt a moment's sadness.

He did it.

# 26

The Aush lost balance and his arms flew out to grab onto something. Moments later a second explosion jolted the ship. The starcraft stabilized itself, and the Aush jumped to the weapon's control. He commanded the plasma batteries to fire upon the wounded escape pod, but the system would not respond. The Aush initiated a weapons' check, but movement from one of the bio-eye's view screens caught his attention, and stunned him into disbelief.

Kazaka ran across the mouth of the corridor, a black shadow against a fog bank, disappearing behind a corner.

Detecting movement, the approaching Kajst thought fired his weapon. Plasma roared, the blast splitting smoke. The Kajst continued walking along *the neck*, and fired straight ahead. His weapon repeatedly tore holes into the bulkheads, crippling the remaining escape pods. An explosion blew particles of metal outwards, and again the air filled with the heat of flame and the smell of unknown compounds melting.

The Kajst ceased firing. He stopped walking.

Kazaka jumped out from behind the corner. Shuriken flew from his hands, finding and ricocheting off the Kajst's emerald green armor. The Kajst paused, analyzing the attack. The primitive was throwing its *stars* at him, and half a smile hitched up the soldier's face.

Kazaka leaned out again and another storm of shuriken and bo-shuriken flew into the Kajst. They bounced off the armor with loud *whucks* and *pings*. One struck the Kajst in the head, actually snapping his helmet back, and momentarily distorting its visual display. It corrected itself in a second and the Kajst began to advance again, leveling its plasma weapon at the mouth of the corridor.

The *hu*-man appeared again, poised with its sword.

The Kajst fired.

And blew himself apart.

The green armor was too thick for the Bear's *shuriken* to penetrate, that much was clear. So, Kazaka switched targets. He threw all of his star *shuriken* at the approaching emerald colored devil. Then he saw the muzzle of the weapon pointed at him. In a second, a quick *one-two*, the Bear threw one *bo-shuriken* at the face of the devil, knocking his head back.

The second *bo-shuriken* went down the weapon's throat.

Then, in an act of uncertainty and chance, the Bear stepped out in full view of the warrior before him. He would end this with his sword. He stared down the creature in front of him, just as the weapon it carried exploded.

The force of the blast and the flame that gouted forward drove Kazaka backwards. Fragments of hot metal sliced and sizzled through the air, slashing through his black garb and cutting him in several places. He fell to the deck, and grimaced against the burn and bite of his wounds. When the roar lessened, he looked about. He got to his knees, and pushed himself up with the guardsman's sword.

In the corridor, the green devil was on its back.

Kazaka walked towards it, patting down the little glowing places in his garb before they could erupt into full flame. Behind his mask, his eyes narrowed. The devil before him was unmoving, and looking upwards. The front of its armor had been shredded, and parts of its exposed flesh had holes in it that went all the way through and glowed at the edges. Even the helm had been blown off, ripping one eye from its socket and destroying half of its face. The creature's other eye flicked towards Kazaka and stared at him, like that of a dying fish.

The Bear dropped to a knee. This devil was white underneath the green armor.

There was no resistance as Kazaka put the tip of his sword to the devil's throat.

And stabbed.

He withdrew the blade and stood. He looked up, and his breath caught in his throat. What he thought of as starlight before, was exactly that. The corridor he was in did not have any walls, just the floor he stood upon. Kazaka's eyes went wide as he took in the star-filled heaven in all of its infinite glory. Stars, so many stars, winked and twinkled at him, and the beauty was so striking, he did not do anything. He gazed at the heavens, and looked downwards. There, he saw a huge star, awash in white and blue. He was amongst the gods, truly, and a sense of wonder enveloped him. Until this moment in time, he did not believe there was anything more beautiful than falling rain, or a rising sun. He stepped forward, and reached out with a hand to touch the heavens, but found he could not. The air before him stopped his fingers. The barrier was hard, warm to the touch, and invisible. It did not bother Kazaka so much, for if the magic revealed to him such wonders, how could it be evil?

Then he heard a sound. He looked towards the end of the corridor.

There, stood another green devil.

# 29

The Aush pointed his plasma weapon at the man in black. Another explosion rocked the starcraft. The blasts had crippled the ship, and repairing it was beyond the commanding Kajst's abilities. There was no hope. There was perhaps time enough to locate an escape pod and flee, but the Aush had been held back by the *hu*-man defeating and finally killing his remaining Kajst.

Now, the Aush faced the creature alone. There was not much time, but he did not care. He had seen enough, but before he evacuated, he would gut this primitive taken from an insignificant rock in the blackness of space. He would gut him with a sword. He would show him that, to kill two Kajsts, two fully armored and armed Kajsts, was an incredible fluke.

With one fist, it tapped its armored chest. "*Aush,*" he introduced himself to the *hu*-man, wanting the man to know his rank. The Kajst then dropped his weapon to the deck.

Overhead, a comet split the cosmos.

The Aush reached up, and unlocked the clasps that held his armor in place. He let it drop to the floor with a clatter. He removed the emerald armor protecting his arms and legs. He threw down his helm, but he covered his compound eyes with his black visor. He would kill the creature with it on. Then he brought up the sword, and slipped into a near perfect fighting stance.

The Bear watched it all from where he stood amongst the stars. A white devil faced him, but this one was different from the ones he killed earlier. This one was more man-shaped, heavier and stronger looking. And it knew how to wield a blade. Kazaka slipped into his own fighting stance, and pointed the tip of the guardsman's sword at the devil before him.

"Come then," Kazaka spoke in clear Japanese. "And we will dance underneath the stars."

The Aush had no idea what the *hu*-man said to it, but he advanced.

The Bear did the same.

And somewhere, just beyond the middle of the walkway, amongst the blazing heavens, they met.

30

Kazaka attacked first, lunging with the katana and aiming for the devil's midsection. The creature parried outwards, knocking the sword aside and thrust with its own blade. Kazaka ducked under this, dropping like a stone, and cut for bare legs. The devil leaped, spun in the air, and slashed out at nothing, for the Bear was already moving back to avoid just such an attempt.

They faced one another again from behind their guards.

The Bear moved forward, slashing and thrusting in a series of attacks he had studied since he was a boy.

The Aush moved back, analyzing, studying, and finally parrying when his opponent's sword came too close. He counter-attacked, smashing his blade forward, whirling it for a head, then arms, then the torso of the man in black. Incredibly, the *hu*-man either stopped his sword with his own, or got out of the way entirely.

And countered.

Kazaka's sword came down from overhead, seeking to split the creature's skull and the black stripe covering its eyes. The devil got out of the way. They traded blows then, attacking and countering at an ever increasing speed, the sound of steel on steel rising above the low rumble of flames and destruction from another part of the starcraft. Then the devil pressed forward, stabbing for the Bear's legs. Each thrust was turned aside by Kazaka's katana, but each new attack from the creature was faster than before, and was noticeably stronger. Behind his black mask, the Bear grimaced. *Magic.*

323

Kazaka lashed out, attempting to drive the devil back, but it slipped inside his guard and slashed upwards, splitting cloth and skin and driving him back. He retreated a few steps, holding his katana at arm's length, and gazed down at himself. His black robes had been cut from the bottom to his chest. Blood seeped into cloth and Kazaka could feel the sting of where the steel parted his flesh.

The Bear attacked again, thrusting low, then high, and cutting loose with a series of expert cuts and stabs. A samurai would have perished under the skilled onslaught.

The Aush deflected them all.

On the last rush, a diagonal slash seeking to inflict a similar wound to that done by the devil, Kazaka found himself too close to the creature, who promptly cut off Kazaka's right ear. The cloth covering his face fell away while the ringing of the wound caused Kazaka to retreat. He knew he'd been hurt badly.

The white devil would not allow him.

The Aush rushed in and slashed low, cutting across a knee of the *hu*-man and dropping him to the deck with a resounding *thud*. The Aush stabbed downwards, but somehow the man beneath him dodged out of the way. Worse, the man in black slashed outwards, causing the Aush to jump back to avoid having his lower legs removed. Then the *hu*-man was back on his feet. The nimbleness of the creature was to be applauded, but the Aush had finished his analysis of the *hu*-man before him. The attacks initiated by the man were somewhat predictable, and not at all difficult to deflect once he understood the methodology behind the offensive. It was only a matter of increasing the Aush's already augmented speed and strength. He had enjoyed using the primitive weapon up to this point, but he now decided that he was wasting time.

Kazaka dropped back, his last three shuriken flying at the white devil.

The Aush deflected them all as he advanced. The last missile weapon, a long spike, was slapped out of the air with a growing impatience. Such trickery was beneath him. He closed with the *hu*-man, backing him up against the plaz-wall. It was time to end the study session.

The Aush unleashed a series of slashes, cuts, and lunges. For a moment, his opponent actually stood in front of him and absorbed the brunt of the attack. But then one slash got inside the *hu*-man's guard, splitting him from chin to crotch. Blood splashed onto the deck. Another cut opened up a long gash on the inside of the man's arm, and he dropped the sword. A final chop took his leg half off, just below his good knee, and he crashed to the floor. The Aush loomed over the fallen man and raised his blade two-handed, intending to thrust downwards and kill the bug at its feet.

Kazaka's hand snaked out. It clamped down on the bare white flesh of the Aush's inner thigh. His stone-tough fingers rolled up, clenching loose flesh and compressing into a fist, and the Bear then demonstrated the *shako-ken*.

Or shark bite.

The Bear's hand ripped a chunk of skin off the devil's body as if it were wet paper. Blackness burst onto the floor. The Aush's head snapped back in shock and agony and the claws of the Bear fastened onto and ripped out another chunk on the same leg. The Aush came crashing down. The Bear clambered up over the fallen devil, pulling out huge fleshy lumps of white tissue from the alien underneath him, while its black blood geysered. A chunk from his inner groin, a sizeable amount of skin covering the creature's obliques, a handful from the chest. Black life fluid fountained and pooled on the deck. Then the Bear placed a bloodied hand on the devil's throat, and pulled himself close…

When the Aush stabbed him through the guts.

Kazaka felt the steel enter him, twist, and stay. He reached down and gripped the Aush's wrist, snapping it with one motion. The Bear then let the throat go and ripped the visor from the Aush's face. He pulled forth his *ninjato*, which had yet to taste the devil's black blood, and nailed it through the creature's exposed chest.

In agony, the Aush blinked. His strength left him in a rush. He could only stare at his killer's face closing with his own.

The Bear gazed into the devil's eyes. He placed his hand back over his prey's throat, and bared teeth lined in red.

"*Ninja*," came the word.

With his remaining strength, the Bear gripped his enemy's soft flesh… and ripped.

Kazaka threw away the meat in his fist. White devil. Black blood. They *still* died like a man. The floor beneath him rocked and bucked, like a horse being trained to take a saddle for the first time. He rolled onto his side, and inched towards the nearby wall. He no longer cared if it was magic or not, Kazaka placed his back against it, and propped himself up. He inspected his person, and saw the guardsman's sword that would soon rob him of his breath. Kazaka felt the buzz of his other wounds, but he smiled in spite of it all.

He was still in better shape than the *baka-yaro* at his feet.

Something exploded again, and the floor began to thrum with a frightful energy. Like an approaching typhoon, Kazaka thought dreamily, and blinked. He looked above the bloody corpse at his feet, and once more, for the last time, took in the heavens above.

Another explosion. Greater this time.

Kazaka did not care. The feeling left him, seeping out like water slowly emptying from a vessel. He gripped the hilt of the blade in his guts. When he finally crossed over, he wanted something in his hand to swing at the gods. Just in case.

And there, high above the Earth that birthed him, as the invisible walls of the starcraft failed and a great sucking wind flung him out into the star-filled void, Jimmu *Kuma* Kazaka felt, for the briefest of time, what it was like to fly.

# 31

On a screen, the geophysicist and the pedologist watched in silence as multiple explosions shook and ultimately destroyed the starship they had inhabited for centuries. The interior of the pod had gone from being a gold light to that of universal red. Alarm klaxons warned them repeatedly that things were not well, for all the good it did them. Neither of them knew the first thing about even maneuvering a pod, let alone repairing one. Trailing smoke and the occasional chunk of debris, the escape pod fell planetward.

The two Aqjm strapped themselves into their seats and regarded each other.

—*We're falling towards the planet,* the pedologist commented, eyeing a panel full of screaming navigational instruments.

—*Yes,* the geophysicist agreed, and felt the burst of panic within her breast.

—*I'm sorry,* the pedologist said.

—*Why?*

—*For not being able to help more.* The sadness in the pedologist's projection caused the geophysicist to look up.

Then, with whatever resolve she had remaining, she hid her own fear and doubt. —*Do not worry. We'll will survive.*

—*Really?*

—*Yes.*

The pedologist smiled at her then, and for a moment, the geophysicist wondered if he actually believed her. In the end, she supposed it did not matter.

*—We'll be fine*, she repeated, and looked upwards, towards the stars, for what she knew in her heart to be the last time.

The little pod skimmed the surface of earth atmosphere, enduring terrible heat and lighting up as bright as a comet. It trailed smoke at times, and pieces of debris kept falling from it. Lower and lower it flew, across one of the planet's huge oceans. It burned a trail across the night, flying lower still, until it came to its final resting place in a blaze of light.

Near a small settlement in New Mexico...

Called Roswell.

# 6

# Ye Olde Fishing Hole

The sun had not yet risen over the surrounding trees and hills, and the surface of the lake was flat and sinister, like a sightless eye gouged into the earth. A mist, ghostly cotton with all the time in the world, drifted over the water. Somewhere, a solitary loon cried out, spearing the stillness and giving the picture sound. Nothing moved on the water. Nothing flew in the air above it, not even insects.

Bumping and huffing its way toward the water's edge, the four-by-four pickup earned its keep on the uneven ground with its headlights bright like the eyes of an angel of war. It was a bruised beast of a machine, scratched, dented, and in sore need of body work, but still capable of doing whatever needed being done. The driver would sooner let the beast die in a pasture than remove its face to allow replacements. Every wound on the truck was a story, every metallic dimple, a grin.

The driver took his time, knowing there was plenty of it, and that no one else would be at the edge of the lake. Not this morning. No one came here to fish anymore, no one but him... and family.

The vehicle bounced toward the waterline grunting and spitting exhaust, until at last the driver was satisfied with where he was. The truck stopped. The headlights died. Two doors opened with cranky yawns. A pair of dark figures exited the beast. One stretched and looked about at the distant hills; the other, taller figure, studied the lake. He was older, with a swimmer's build. He lit a cigarette, inhaled smoke and lake air, and stood still, thinking.

"It's big," said the non-smoker.

The smoking man didn't answer.

"Dad?" the other asked, turning in his direction.

"Hmm?"

"Want me to get the shit out?"

"Don't swear."

A pause. "Want me to get the *stuff* out?"

"Wait a minute," the father said, and drew another puff on his smoke, the end glowing in the morning calm. He exhaled a cloud, taking in the peace of the lake. The son looked as well. It was a *big* lake. In the predawn light, a dark line of trees marked a distant shore perhaps two kilometers away, but its edges were hidden in deep curving coves and trees. It might have been two klicks across at its widest, but it was closer to fourteen kilometers around on foot. If one was crazy enough to walk it.

The father had no such intentions of walking anywhere, which was why he had brought the truck.

He gazed across the surface of the early morning serenity. It was a beautiful lake. Picturesque. Unspoiled. Peaceful. God above only knew how deep it was in the middle. A chill enveloped the elder Durham, and he took another comforting draw on his smoke.

"Josh," the man said. "Get the gear down."

Metal squealed on metal, the sound carrying across the lake's expanse, and the boy's father cringed from the noise. Burt Durham glared at his son, sending a message louder than his vocal chords could produce. Embarrassed, Josh tried to do better. There was a lot of gear to unload: plastic boxes containing tools and tackle, regular fish hooks and swivels, or what Josh called *spinners*, extra spools of braided fishing line, bait, and an ornate box the length of Josh's forearm. Once all of the plastic boxes were on the mossy ground, the boy, as his father still thought of him despite his seventeen years, carefully pulled out a heavy wood and metal fisherman's fighting chair. It was the kind a person would see on big game boats, except the elder Durham had modified the chair for inshore, big lake fishing.

Burt eyed the single pier made from logs years ago, its formidable girth protruding into the lake by about thirty meters. It was a pier for the sea, but here it was, marring the dark obsidian glass of the lake's face like a deep, rotting stitch.

Durham took another drag on his cigarette. The treetops were glowing faintly from the approaching sun. He turned and doused the smoke on the hood of his truck. If he could, he would smoke again later. He had two cigars in his right breast pocket, and God as his witness, he intended to smoke them with his boy when all was done.

"Don't worry about taking it all," Durham said. He looked toward the treetops where a line of red had yet to appear. "We still got time."

"Okay."

"Take it out to the edge of the pier. Leave the nail gun to me."

"Okay."

"Get to it then."

Burt watched his boy struggle with his arms full of fishing gear, both traditional and strange. He had bought the best he could afford. Even the big game rod was ultra-strong and cutting edge. Durham didn't think he was violating any of the rules by buying and bringing it. Knowing it was time to get busy, he made his way to the back of the truck.

Durham hauled on his fisherman's vest and zipped it up. Nylon gloves followed, lightweight on the back of the hand, but with the palm fitted with coarse non-slipping material Durham called the fisherman's sandpaper. He picked up the three spears for gaffing, the blades made from whale bone and engraved with glyphs, and balanced them under his right arm. Next, he picked up the nail gun.

With a determined sigh, Durham made his way to the pier. He heard his boy walk over it first, clomping along its length, and then he strode purposefully toward its end. Each hollow sounding *clump* marked his passage in the morning gloom.

The water remained dark and still. Anything could be watching them from underneath, Durham thought, and they wouldn't know until the last second. The idea made him set his jaw. He walked onto the wharf. Support beams rose up on both sides like uneven teeth, and shield-sized cobwebs, almost invisible, hung between them. Bulbous spiders of a species unknown tensed as the elder Durham passed, but they stayed within the centers of their designs.

Burt reached the end of the pier where his boy had set up the chair and placed the fishing line next to it in a neat spool. He put down his gear and readied the nail gun. It was a cordless, powder-actuated model, using gas pressure to punch a nail through concrete, if necessary, and held a clip of a dozen two-inch nails. With professional ease, he lined up the metal brackets running off the chair's legs, brackets that had three bored holes in each, and fired the gun. The *punk punk punk* carried across the lake, making Josh cringe. Burt remained calm as he fastened the chair into place. He tried shaking it. It refused to move. That was good. He reached into one of boxes and brought up a thick leather belt with a quick one-pull release buckle, the kind a person would see on airplanes and draped it over the back of the chair.

Burt dropped the empty gun and readied his fishing rod, placing the butt into the gimballed mount attached to the front of the chair. It was the same setup one would see on the rear of a big game fishing boat. He hoped it would be enough. His father, thirty years earlier, had used the fishing equipment of the day… and had lost.

Burt Durham did not intend to lose.

He studied the surface of the water, still as bedrock and dark as oil. Josh finished spooling the fishing line and removed the hook from the ornate box. Like the spears, it was cut from whale bone, with arcane symbols scratched into its foot-long length. Josh tied on the hook in silence. Then, he baited it with a headless, bloody chicken, skewering the animal through its asshole.

"Done," he announced.

Burt didn't seem to hear. Jaw set, he watched the surface of the lake. The glow above the tree-line seemed brighter. He snapped his fingers, and Josh handed him a Tupperware jar. Burt examined its contents, studied the rod before him, and noted the approaching dawn.

It was game time.

"Get back to the truck," Burt told his son. "Don't come near until it's done, you hear?"

Josh nodded. He knew the legend.

His father looked at him then with hard dark eyes, paused for a moment as if to say something, but nodded instead, prompting his son to leave. Old fashioned to the core, even in this day, the elder Durham had never professed affection for his son, letting his actions speak for him instead.

A mixture of fear and excitement building within him, Josh ran. Burt watched him go. When his son was clear, he got to work.

He unscrewed the top of the Tupperware container filled

with chicken blood. It wasn't the cow's blood that his father had used in his attempt, but it would do. Blood was blood. Burt didn't think that the beast would be too picky in this age. Its followers were nonexistent now, and no one, as far as Burt knew, even realized the lake was here, what it contained, or what it promised to do if a person could defeat the thing that lived within its depths.

*Grant wishes*, his father told him when he was a boy. *Grant a person* anything *they desired.*

Burt Durham was not a greedy man, but the bank had driven him to this. Money. It was all about money. Money was what he needed, what he wanted to wish for.

Grimacing, Burt flung the contents of the container out over the water, spreading it like a fan. Blood dappled the surface. *Gravy for the monster*, he thought. He tossed the empty Tupperware behind him, where it clattered on the wharf. He only had a few moments now, and he had to be quick.

He reached down and gathered up the bone hook and chicken. Taking a breath, Burt swung the thing over his head as if he were about to lasso a bull. He heaved the hook as far out as he could, seeing the feathers flutter in flight, waiting for the splash. The bone hook barged through the air a good forty feet or so and dropped to the surface of the water. It disappeared without a sound. Not a splash. Not even a goddamn ripple.

Burt set his jaw. The time was right. Red dawn lit the treetops like fire, but the day hadn't yet broken into sight. He clambered into the chair, fastened himself in with the belt, and grabbed his rod. He only had a short time to hook and land the thing. He only had until the sun showed its face. If he didn't hook it by then…

It would be another year.

Burt began reeling in the line, pulling it from the lake's depths. The whalebone was heavy. He kept his eyes on the water where the line disappeared in the darkness. He leaned back in his chair and kept a steady tension on the line. There was no sound except that of his own breathing, and the whine of the reel.

Forty feet out. It had been a good throw, but it was a big, deep lake. If sharks could smell blood for kilometers under the water, then how far could *it* smell? Burt didn't know. He figured he had pulled the hook in about ten feet so far.

From where he stood in front of the pickup, Josh watched, his mouth open but breath held. *Old gods*, his father had told him they would be hunting for this morning. *The forgotten kind.* Josh thought his old man was half in the bag, but he was too damned serious about the whole thing to be completely dismissed. And it *was* his dad. Josh had no choice but to follow orders. His family was old fashioned, lived in a small town, and valued simpler times, while hesitantly embracing the digital century. When his dad had said he was going to do something and the boy would help, Josh didn't have a voice in the matter. Besides, he thought the world of his old man.

Through the gauze hanging off the lake, Burt could see the line stretching into the predawn, but he couldn't see where it broke the surface. The reel continued to click and whirl.

At thirty feet out, there was a ripple in the water's surface. It was a big flutter made by something just underneath swimming along in silence.

Burt tensed. It hadn't taken long at all.

Something pulled on the line. It was a strong tug, and

Burt had an idea that the chicken might have just lost a wing. Or a leg. There was resistance, but not enough yet. The thing merely tasted. Burt continued to reel.

Twenty-five feet out, and Burt could just see where the heavy line disappeared into the lake's depths. Nothing else was visible.

Another tug. The hook felt as if it had caught on something, but it continued toward the elder Durham. Nervous energy built in Burt's chest and limbs. He strained to see. There was another flutter on the surface, weaker than before, but just behind the hook, moving toward the shore.

Twenty feet. Any moment now. Burt could sense it.

The line snapped taunt as the thing in the lake finally took the bait. The air *whirred* as the line flew off the reel toward deeper waters. Burt held onto the pole with both hands and set his jaw. It had accepted the challenge. Time for the fight.

It was out forty feet almost immediately. Burt lurched forward in his chair, feeling the leather belt go tight across his gut. *Fifty feet.* He choked the rod between his hands and set his feet against the logs protruding from the wharf. *Fifty-five.* He took one last breath and looked to the still visible stars far above. *Sixty feet.*

"Help me," Burt Durham prayed.

He snapped his rod back, hooking the thing beneath the water, and worked the reel for everything he was worth. He lurched forward. The rod immediately bowed as if it had jigged a car. That didn't surprise him. The creature was big back in the day of his father, and Burt suspected it had grown, but the line and rod he used were ultra-strong, damn near unbreakable. He had nailed his perch to the wharf and secured himself in tight with the belt. The whalebone had a few extra glyphs, as many as he could carve into it, to further weaken the thing. He figured he could hook a great white shark with his equipment.

He cranked the reel and felt the solid pull of the line as the hook jabbed itself further into flesh. The thing banked to the right, turning Burt in that direction. He let it go slack for moment, giving the creature some line to swim with, before digging in his legs again and pulling back with all of his might. He arched his back, feeling the direction change, feeling the thing go *deep*. It pulled hard on the line, the hardest any fish, any *thing*, ever pulled, and Burt reminded himself that this wasn't just any fish. It was a *god* that he had hooked.

The line was tight enough to garrotte a world, and Burt held on, grimacing at its strength. He was strong too, however, and he wagered whatever was on the other end of the line realized it.

Burt leaned forward in his chair, and the line went slack. He let the beast take the hook for a good thirty seconds before digging his feet in again, working the reel hard to draw in the line. He pulled with all his might. *Fifty-five feet*, he thought.

On the water, there was barely a ripple to be seen.

He lunged forward again, letting the god run with the line. Out on the dark of the lake, partially obscured by mist, he glimpsed something big breaching the surface. Burt reeled in another five feet of line before digging in again and pulling against the force underneath the water. It fought back and pulled him forward, slowly stretching the elder Durham out in his chair and toward the edge.

Burt had fished all his life, had landed all sorts of beasts, and he knew how to tire them out. He knew how to hunt. The hook bled and weakened it. The line wouldn't break. There was no escape for the thing; it just hadn't realized it yet.

Burt would make it understand.

Forty-five. The line went slack and for seconds, Burt thought the thing had done the impossible and snapped it. Then he saw the wake.

Heading straight for the wharf and cutting the water like the invisible fin of a shark was a V-shape of something enormous.

*Holy shit*, Burt thought. It was as big as a whale. Times *had* changed. He felt his balls draw up and fear shot into his legs; part of his brain wanted him to jerk on the release of his belt and bolt to higher ground. However, Burt Durham was made of sterner stuff, as was his father before him.

He let go of the rod and grabbed a bone-tipped spear. The belt held him firm in the chair, but he would throw the thing if he got the shot.

The wake charged towards the shoreline. Thirty-five feet. Thirty. Burt tensed. There was no way he could miss it.

The thing cut though the water without a sound, the V stretching out and disappearing behind it. It charged the wharf on a collision course.

Twenty-five feet. In the predawn light, Burt thought he could see something below the surface of the water. Then he realized the sun hadn't moved since he had hooked the god. His eyes darted toward the treetops basking in fiery red.

*Cool*, he thought. Then the water smoothed out. The thing had dived.

Burt dropped his spear with a clatter and grabbed the line. He reeled with whatever strength and speed he possessed, the air buzzing with the sound. He inhaled deeply, and the wilderness air cleared his senses.

Standing in front of the truck, Josh also wondered when the sun was going to rise, but then his attention was stolen by the fight on the wharf.

The line banked hard to the left, pulling Burt with it. His belt went tight against his stomach, forcing out his breath. For a moment, he thought the leather actually touched his backbone. He dug in his feet and pulled, feeling the line stretch. He bared teeth. The rod bent like the craw of a hook, and the force increased. *Strong*, Burt thought. *The thing was strong!* It pulled his ass up off the seat, and his vision began to blacken. He felt the strength in his arms ebb. It was as if the beast was pulling the shoreline into the water, and the rod was the connector. The pressure increased and doubled again, and Burt's limbs, hands, and body trembled in the terrible the tug of war. Beads of sweat popped out of his flesh.

Then the line went slack.

Burt flew backward into his seat, the belt holding him in place. The leather actually felt loose. Could the thing have actually stretched it? He didn't dwell on it. He set to reeling as fast as he could with whatever strength he had remaining. He felt the heavy burn in his shoulders, arms, and legs. It had tired him out faster than he had expected. And the fight had only just begun.

The thing bolted away, parallel with the uneven shoreline. Burt let it go, not bothering to fight it. He needed a moment to collect his strength. It swam deep, not marring the water's surface, but Burt knew he had a train at the end of his line.

When he figured it was seventy feet away, he dug in and hauled backward. He imagined the thing in mid-swim, jerking to a stop underneath the dark water, like a dog on a long leash being yanked off balance. Burt pulled harder, feeling the strength of the creature lessen. He reeled and reeled, leaning out each time he gave up some slack in the line, letting the thing tire itself out in the lake's depths. He yanked particularly hard the fourth time, envisioning the hook halfway in its gullet and ripping a foot-long painful rent in whatever ancient flesh it wore. He took back twenty feet the god had taken from him.

But then the beast regained its strength. It tore off to the right, arcing Burt's rod back toward the deep center of the lake, as if charging out to sea. Once again, Burt hung on for life, letting the thing swim for whatever it was worth, letting it exhaust itself. He let it get eighty feet out before he yanked the hook again with a silent but agonizing *ah-ah ahhhhh* an adult may admonish a petulant child. The fight made Burt smile. He started to enjoy the duel between mortal and god. He felt his strength return in a surge, knowing the momentum was on his side. He was going to *land* this thing. He was going to have his wish.

Twenty minutes later, it was a different story. Burt's clothes were saturated with sweat. His limbs and swimmer's shoulders ached with a fire he had not felt in a very, very long time. He longed for a drink of water. He wanted to cry out to his son to bring him something, but it was against the rules of the wharf. Only one could remain on it when battling the leviathan below. Only one. His own father had told him as much.

Burt knew he was near exhaustion, but the god was nowhere near the shore. It felt as fresh as it had in the beginning. There were ferocious pulls from the creature, and in those times, Burt simply let it run until it tired itself out, and then he took back what the god had gained. But it had happened over and over again, just on the brink of what Burt and his ever-watching son, still watching from the truck, hoped was the endgame. The whale bone was supposed to weaken it. *Perhaps it had,* his mind whispered. A chill encapsulated the elder Durham at that thought.

The sun still hadn't risen.

At the thirty-five minute mark, fear seeped into Burt Durham's lower legs like unwanted arctic water rising. It proceeded up his thighs and cupped his testicles, pure and creeping. Burt Durham realized what was happening. His eyes went wide, and his face screwed up in a grimace.

For the first time since he had cast his line into the lake, as if magically injected into his brain, Burt Durham became cognizant that he might not be the hunter here…

Quite the opposite, in fact.

How many followers did it have in this time? How many followers willing to offer it… *sacrifices?*

The frightening pull of the line jerked both the rod and Burt's mind back to reality. The belt around his stomach dug deeper until tears were squeezed from his eyes. The force beneath the water pulled him toward it. Worse still, he heard the yawn of the nails keeping the chair in place. He wasn't the only one weakening.

Then the line went slack again. With a gasp, Burt reeled for all he was worth. He dragged in the weight at the end of the line. He could feel the lack of resistance. Had he won? A sense of victory surged through him then. The thing was his. The *god* was his! He had it!

Visions of wealth blurred through his mind—a wish for riches in exchange for the god's freedom. The banks could go screw themselves. His rich brother who ignored his pleas for financial help could go screw himself. The neighbors who would excuse themselves when Burt started speaking about his debts could especially go screw themselves. Friends like that made leeches infinitely more attractive.

"You got it, Dad, you got it!" Josh cried.

Burt smiled briefly, still struggling with the line. He was exhausted and thought briefly of tri-athletes at the end of a race. He set his jaw and gasped for breath. He summoned his strength and felt only the ache of spent muscles. Then it struck him.

The thing was coming up from the bottom. And it was coming fast.

The surface of the lake formed another V. It approached Burt on the wharf, gathering speed.

That last thought struck Burt as strange. *Speed.* The beast should be exhausted by now, as exhausted as Burt, at least.

The grand feeling of victory gushed out of elder Durham then. He almost released the rod in fright.

The god was just below the surface of the water, and a mighty surge broke its indifference, reminding Burt of old Saturday movies where a line of cavalry charged an enemy's position. Except in this instance, there was only Burt.

The god's back split the surface. Blacker than the water itself, it glistened in the predawn light.

It was huge.

Fear claimed Burt. Despite all the equipment he had brought, despite all the wards and enchantments placed upon his tools, he realized that times had *indeed* changed, and he had to escape.

Four black orbs the size of bowling balls sighted and fixed on the mortal as its mass drew closer to the wharf.

Burt released the rod. It rattled in the gimballed mount.

He clawed at the quick release of the belt.

The god's flat head rose out of the water. It was the width of the mighty V itself. There was an even greater darkness splitting open below it. Huge teeth, like short sabers, glistened as water flowed in between them.

The belt flew open.

"Dad, *run!*" Burt heard from his son so very far behind him.

He lurched out of the chair and bolted for the shoreline.

A dark rumble stormed across the lake, a sound full of deep water and even blacker mirth.

Burt ran toward his son. He did not look back. He focused on forcing his legs to move as fast as they could with whatever drops of energy he had remaining. Josh stood in front of the pickup urging him to *run faster.* Wind blew past Burt's head, and he heard thunderous laughter behind him. He was almost at the end of the wharf. Josh waved his hands over his head.

A few more steps…

Josh screamed. "Run, Dad, Run! For the love of Jesus, *Run!*"

Multiple cords lashed about Burt's legs, stomach, chest, and neck, lifting him up off the wharf in a crushing embrace. He felt everything explode in pain as if a mighty display of fireworks had let loose beneath his skin. For the briefest of moments, he wondered why he wasn't moving any further. And why wasn't Josh heading for the truck?

None of it mattered anymore.

Burt was yanked backward, and the scene before him flew away. He glimpsed the sky turning blood red. A splash exploded in his ears.

His son's watery screams receded.

Then, an everlasting chill chewed and chewed on his flesh.

The old road leading to the lake was overgrown. The trees on the sides stretched across and locked limbs, as if to bar anyone from proceeding. The October sun hadn't set beyond the surrounding forest and hills, yet the remaining light was gloomy. Four strong headlights lit the wall of trees. The engine growled and pressed forward. There was a snort of gas and smoke, and Josh released the brake pedal and manipulated the gears. Seconds later, the barrier of trees broke against the mass of steel making its way inward.

Josh had waited fifteen years for this evening. He had spent that time growing and becoming strong. He had educated himself, collected a university degree in the occult, pagan gods, and world mysticism. He had gathered the bone and other ingredients needed for hooks and tools, learned the glyphs of power that would weaken the monster in the lake and scratched them upon the bone.

Josh had stayed single over those long years, not needing companionship in the least. He reserved his lust for vengeance.

He took his foot off the decelerator, and the Caterpillar D1N bulldozer shredded the forest wall before him. He manipulated the joysticks, steering and raising the machine's S-U blade, pushing the trees away in a chorus of earthly squeals and groans. He set his jaw. They were casualties of war.

He made two trips in two days. The first was to make the road. The second was to haul in his equipment and prepare.

Money. It was all about money the first time he and his

father had come here. A year after his father's disappearance, Josh and his mother won the lottery for thirty-six million. It was almost as if something had foreseen the future, knew what Josh intended, and tried to dissuade him.

Or maybe his father got his wish after all, only a year later.

The bulldozer made its way to the lake's edge, and Josh got the machine in position, facing away from the water, blade up. He got out of the machine and walked down to the water's edge, ignoring the massive hydraulic winch with three hundred meters of steel cable attached, cable which he would eventually run from the dozer to the heavy harpoon gun he had bolted to the edge of the wharf like some fearsome navy ship battery. A harpoon, tipped with a cruel-looking hook and barb cut from whalebone, crowned the weapon and pointed at the sky.

Josh stood at the end of the wharf. A *phump*-gun loaded with projectile canisters filled with liters of cow blood stood at attention beside his right knee. At the push of a button, Josh could fill the lake with blood. He would chum it into a thick stew just before dawn, at the time when the magic was at its strongest, and the doorway between a god's world and this one opened.

He lit a cigarette, a habit he had gotten from his Dad so long ago. He studied the still surface of the lake and sensed hesitancy in the air.

It wasn't his.

There would be no choice when the time came. Blood was the creature's weakness, and Josh had brought plenty of it.

The younger Durham looked down at the symbols of warding he had drawn with chalk into the wood's surface—

further preparation for the coming fight. Then he gazed at the darkness of the water below. Josh had dreamed and planned and prepared for this moment ever since that morning when he had witnessed his father running toward him, trying desperately to get off the wharf. He had watched the multiple tentacles whip out and wrap around his father's figure, making his father's eyes swell in surprise and pain. He had seen his father yanked back into a mouth rising up from the lake behind him, a mouth filled with teeth the length of knives.

And then…

Josh sighed. He didn't need to remember. He had fifteen years of nightmares.

But things had changed. It was his time now.

And by God above, Josh would have his wish.

# 7

# Isosceles Moon

# 1

Techno music hammered out a taiko drum set hell-bent on demolishing walls. People thrashed upon the dance floor as if electrified, and every beat fried their brains just a little more. Hands rose skyward in worship, resembling a bouncing carpet of fleshy spiders. Strobe lights whipped the crowds with bright beams, stop-go flashes, and glowing green waves of some Aurora Borealis funk.

And in the middle of it all, Molly danced.

Molly danced alone, and Molly danced hard.

She swung her hips, slid her hands along her ribs, and tongued her teeth. She was high on life, fueled by a collective energy, and loving the midnight hour.

Some dance-floor perv grabbed her hips and started rubbing his crotch against her behind. Molly didn't like that, didn't appreciate being floor-spooned by an uninvited cock in the box. She slapped his hands away and danced an escape, getting bodies between her and the groper. The DJ's ball-capped head bounced along with the insane rhythm of keyboards and pre-programed music, punching the air while he tweaked his control board of mix and tricks.

Molly thundered right along with the music's manic pulse and danced closer to the stage. She reached up and lifted her shoulder-length hair, holding her temples and letting her blond locks fall where they might. She worked her figure, all five-two of it, and made every curve sing, knocking out a code only a select few would decipher. Men ogled her while dancing with their current partners. Some of the women did, too. Molly ignored them all.

Molly wanted something special that night. She wanted a trophy.

She wanted the DJ.

The trick was… getting noticed in that stormy ocean of torsos.

Some chick crawled up on stage and approached the DJ from the side. Molly's heart sank as he slipped a hand around his visitor's waist and together they danced into the seamless mix of the next tune.

Molly geared down, lowered her hands, and pouted.

*Well. Shit.*

But she recognized the next song as one of her favourites, and her mood spiked, the opening keys ramping up her spine. *Who needs a DJ boy, anyway?* Not her. She was in the prime of her life, had a good-paying job, and thought of herself as sexy. Enough men had come on to her to prove it.

The DJ hadn't noticed her.

His loss.

Molly danced—danced as she'd never danced before, working out feelings of rejection with an afterburner desire to be noticed. She scorched all three emotions as a cloud of perfume and cologne enveloped her, pheromones for the fire. She moved daringly, a little flirty and perhaps a tad dirty.

Enough to attract *her* attention.

A wall of bodies parted, and a woman approached, athletic, with shoulder-length hair the color of night and west-coast curves and crevices dangerous enough to stop traffic and derail trains—a spicy angel who focused on Molly with an intensity that made her knees weak. Molly slowed, gathering her strength while studying the newcomer to the dance floor. The woman wore a spaghetti-string top, displaying generous cleavage and a bare midriff. She didn't have a six-pack, not even a four, but her belly was flat and hard, and Molly wanted it.

Molly wasn't gay.

Not even a little.

However, she found the woman attractive—oddly yet insanely attractive. Her very presence tempted and strummed vibes Molly had never thought existed within her. The spicy angel's eyes, black in the club, barely blinked as she studied Molly in turn. She reached for Molly and placed a hand on her shoulder, and the contact nearly made her melt. A hand caressed Molly's neck, pausing there while the stranger's shoulders moved like a curtain moved by a sultry breeze. Molly gasped, just a little, and locked eyes. The woman's lips were full on the bottom, thin on top—a face like a brazen heart. A surge of sexual tension coursed through Molly's frame, and she reached for a partially exposed hip. The woman's lips parted at the tentative contact, showing fair teeth.

Before Molly knew what was happening, the woman's hands were around her neck.

They closed, chests grazing, skin perking, the pressure dizzying. They danced, breathing hot cinnamon into each other's face, alternating between soulful stares and lustful body inspections. Her new partner leaned forward and sampled Molly's perfume, breathing deeply. The woman smiled in approval, and Molly's knees trembled once again. Fingers ran sensuously through Molly's hair, teasing it as she herself had done only moments before.

Molly turned her back to her newfound companion, in sync with the beat, and gasped when her new dance partner pressed soft breasts into her shoulder blades. Palms traced

Molly's bare arms. The crowd swished away like bad smoke while Molly watched the hands exploring her, rising and falling, dangerously skirting the outer swell of her breasts. Tingles erupted from the contact.

"I like you," the woman whispered into Molly's ear.

And that was weird.

Weird because those three little words got through the techno blitz shaking the club's walls.

Molly turned around in her partner's arms, discovering they were the same height. "I like you, too."

A dangerous energy crackled between them as Molly lost herself in her angel's eyes. Soft parts brushed and pushed against soft parts.

Molly leaned into her partner's ear, nearly breathless from her perfume. "What's your name?"

"Calithea."

*Jesus Christ.* Even her *name* was sexy.

Molly hooked a strand of her hair behind an ear. "I'm—"

"Molly," Calithea said without a smile. "Hi."

"Hi. Um…" Molly cocked her head. "How'd you know my name?"

"Good guess."

That would do.

"Can you guess what I'm thinking now?" Calithea asked, her breath warm.

Molly dared a smile and bit her lower lip.

*

Just after three o'clock, a damn-near-pristine Toyota Celica parked and gleamed under a flickering light in an underground parking garage, which was filled to capacity. The doors opened, and Calithea exited the driver's side.

Molly bopped out from the other, jumping at the chill in the air. They smiled at each other. Calithea hooked a finger and beckoned Molly to the stairwell.

"We have to take the stairs?" Molly moaned as Calithea smiled and grasped her hand. Molly glimpsed that a section of the underground garage had had its floor removed in what appeared to be a deep excavation. Calithea pulled Molly through the stairwell's door, up two flights and out an exit, where a single security guard sat behind a desk.

The guard stared outward, through a clear glass wall, at the empty lane beyond. A smell of old clothing permeated the air, as if he'd just taken his uniform out of winter storage without bothering to wash it.

Calithea walked Molly to an elevator and pushed a button.

Molly hummed under her breath, moved to the memory of the nightclub's music, and watched the numbers descend. She sized up Calithea's short skirt and lower back. One quick tug of the skirt's hem, *voila*, she'd have butt crack.

Molly glanced over at the guard.

She looked back at Calithea's skirt.

Then, her brow knotting up in a thought, Molly peered more closely at the guard, sensing something not quite right.

*Ding.*

Molly jumped, tightening Calithea's grip on her hand.

The elevator doors slid open.

"Something the matter?" Calithea asked, her tongue moving just behind parted lips.

Molly had already kissed her on the dance floor, probably causing fights between multiple couples. She wanted to kiss her again.

"No," Molly whispered but then gave it up. "Well, yeah.

That guard. Is he like, all right, or…?"

Calithea leaned over so she could see. She shook her lovely head. "Nope."

"No?"

"He's high."

"High?" Molly covered her laugh with a small hand.

"Again."

"*Again?*"

"That's Leonard," she said, leaning into Molly's ear. "He's a little perverted. And strange. And perverted. Did I say perverted? But I like him. You know why?"

Molly didn't dare move, enjoying the hot breath. "Why?"

"Because he knows the best pizza places in town." Calithea drew away with a girlish smile. Molly *tsked* and rolled her eyes.

The elevator doors began to close.

Calithea stuck out her hand to stop them. "That. And he's got a huge thing in his pants."

Molly's mouth hung open. "You're so bad."

Calithea grinned and pulled her aboard the dark box.

"What floor you on?" Molly asked, resting her chin on her companion's shoulder. She rubbed a hand across her companion's bare midriff, fingers rising and brushing against underboob. The caress widened Calithea's smile.

"Heaven," she whispered.

The doors closed.

And the world never saw Molly again.

## 2

The bar's countertop was a long, wet slick of midnight, and one had to wonder if anyone had ever tried to belly slide down that glossy surface. Tube lights marked the bar's runway edges while Japanese Kanji glowed in a black light, decorating the walls with mysterious wisdom. The only people who hung out in the bar that early were the truly dedicated drinkers. And the bartenders who served them.

The clock flickered to 1:01 p.m. A single, casual-looking gentleman sat at the far end of the countertop's black highway. He hunched over a drink, appearing to scry secret messages within the mai tai's depths. He wasn't really scrying. He was trying to forget. The dark helped a little. So did the alcohol. Neither was helping enough.

The bartender, decked out in black jeans and shirt and damn near invisible at points in that shady establishment, divided his attention between his sole customer and a *National Geographic*, held just beneath the countertop, near the glow of a reading light.

The drinker pinched the mai tai's straw and sucked for several seconds. The final slurp sounded like a whirlpool attempting to swallow a city block.

"Another?" the bartender asked, duty bound.

The guy shook his head, a battle-weary sway that spoke of one too many punches. Or too many drinks. His hair was white, colored like snow and cut short for low maintenance. A thick padlock of a goatee flourished around his mouth and chin. Where the moustache resembled spiked frosting, the beard was combed black. The bartender thought it was a weird combo. The guy didn't make the look work in the least. It was more like an adventurous someone who'd mixed the right amount of wrong chemicals found underneath the kitchen sink, and the resulting explosion had forever fucked up his hair. And face. The solitary customer had a unibrow resembling a dead caterpillar stretched across his forehead, thick enough to make one think it might've been glued on. Wide-spaced eyes seemed perfectly round, one perhaps even a tad lazy.

All those particular features might have been a residual effect of the exploding kitchen chemicals.

*Funny looking* came to mind, which made the bartender think of movies.

"Yeah, I'll have another," the guy said, changing his mind while scratching at a wide nose that might've been busted in two or three different places. "Give me… a Long Island ice tea. A real one. None of that premixed shite either. That tastes like piss strained through a pair of dirty tights."

"One LIT coming right up."

The bartender stopped reading about Pluto and worked his magic. A real Long Island. A real Long Island contained four shots of various weed killers. And a lemon-lime slice. A real Long Island knocked most people on their noisy monkey asses. The bartender, whose name was Ricky, hoped that guy wasn't a noisy monkey-ass type, which meant rowdy when booze was added. Ricky hated babysitting that early in the day, and he sure as hell hoped the dude wasn't planning on getting sick. Not in his just-cleaned public washroom.

"You ready for this?" Ricky asked the strange customer.

"Yeah."

"Gonna slide it on down, okay?"

"Why can't you just pass it over?"

"I can pass it over, too. Some folks like seeing a drink slide their way. Just a bartender trick."

"Not much of a trick," the guy said and ran a hand over the counter's surface. "Pretty smooth, though. Wish my ass was this smooth. Okay, slide it over. God bless."

Ricky placed the drink down, squinted one eye shut, and pushed. The Long Island zipped along that star-bright surface as if guided by a phantom hand, stopping in front of the guy.

"Right on the money." The customer chortled, pleased with the placing.

"Practiced shot."

"Any part of the bar?"

"Any part. I kill at shuffleboard."

The weirdo inspected the drink, sampled it, and shivered. "Yep. That'll fuckin' twist a squirrel's tail right there."

Which didn't make sense to Ricky, but he let it go. He turned back to his magazine.

"Whatcha' readin' over there?" Weirdo asked.

Ricky wasn't certain he wanted to say. "*National Geographic.*"

"Oh yeah? Read those all the time. Anything good?"

"The issue with the Pluto pics NASA got. Pretty amazing stuff."

"Pluto." Weirdo nodded. "Never been. Don't think I'll ever go."

"No, I don't think I'll go either," Ricky said with a smile. "But I like the pics. That little satellite rig is heading for the Kuiper Belt right after Pluto. Making for the outer fringe of the galaxy."

Weirdo slurped his Long Island and shivered again. "You know Russia has roughly the same surface area as Pluto?"

"I… did not."

Weirdo pointed a finger at him and gave a nod of *it's true*. "You know what else I was thinking just now?"

Ricky shook his head.

"I was thinking. If English actors can get away with playing Russians by speaking English with Russian accents… you think Russian actors get away with playing Americans by speaking Russian with an American accent?"

That stopped Ricky, and he held his hips while processing. "That's… an interesting thought."

"Most people don't think about that," the weirdo said and sucked on the straw. "Sweet Jesus, this is good. I make them at home but never like this. Must be a different recipe or something."

"I can do a Singapore sling, too. All them umbrella drinks."

"You must be popular with the ladies."

"I'm a bartender, man," Ricky said, as if that explained everything.

"Hey, you know it rains diamonds on Saturn?" Weirdo asked.

"I did not."

"On Jupiter too."

"Really."

"Oh yeah. 'Sall basic principles of chemistry. It hasn't been totally proven just yet, but… I like to think it does. Just picture it. Fuckin' *diamonds*, man."

Ricky nodded, feigning interest.

"Blows the shitty chunks outta Pluto though, don't it?" Weirdo considered his drink. "This is damn fine. I should fill a thermos with this shit. Or one of those super-sized coffee cups, the ones folks gotta carry with both hands. I mean, it's a bucket is what it is."

Ricky nodded again.

"I mean, I like coffee and all, don't get me wrong, but a whole *bucket?* Cause that's what it is. A fuckin' bucket. And the scary thing is—you know what the scary thing is? People go back for *refills!* Don't that beat the shit outta your dog?"

The dog reference put Ricky off.

"I can appreciate a person wanting to be awake," Weirdo continued. "Who doesn't like a morning mug of mud? Get awake. Get wired. Get zippy. But there's a difference between *that* and seeing the fuckin' *auras* offa people."

"You don't get out much, do you?"

"I get out plenty," Weirdo muttered and hung his head. "I'm here, for example."

"In the afternoon."

"It's ten p.m. somewhere."

"Yeah, well, there's probably more people in those places, too."

"I stay away from crowds. Especially dense ones. Never liked the herd mentality. Very dangerous. Dirty, too. You work here. You must know how fucking filthy people can be."

Ricky folded his arms and studied the guy, believing a safe distance was probably wise and in order. "What's your name?"

"Me?"

"Yeah."

"Ah… I'd rather not say," Weirdo looked at his drink.

"You'd rather not."

"No. Names are very important pieces of information. You shouldn't give them out lightly. Unless you know exactly who you are talking to. Guard them. Like your social-insurance number. And e-mail. And phone numbers."

"All right. No names. Guess I can't ask you about your job, then."

"Ah, sure," Weirdo said. "I don't mind that. Haveta talk about something, right? You know about people who find things?"

"Like detectives?"

"Yeah, like them."

Ricky brightened. "You're a detective?"

"Oh fuck no. Not at all."

"All right, I'll go over here if you want to be a prick about it."

"What?" Weirdo exclaimed, surprised. "No—sorry. Listen, sometimes I just fire away without thinking. It's cost me a girlfriend or two. Really. No, what I meant was, you got your people who find things, right? Like detectives. Well, I'm the opposite. I hide things. Professionally. As a home-security specialist."

"You hide things."

"All the time."

"Like what? Money?"

"Yeah, I do that a lot," Weirdo nodded. "Cash, wills, jewelry, pills. Small stuff, mostly."

Ricky frowned. "What did you just say?"

"About huh? What now?"

"You said something about hiding pills?"

"No, I didn't."

"You did."

"Nope."

Ricky shook his head. "Whatever."

"Now you're gettin' it," Weirdo said, pleased. "So, yeah. If you have something you want hidden, you give me a call, and we can work something out."

"So you'd come over to my house?"

"Yeah. If that's where you want your stuff hidden, sure. Or your car."

"My car?"

"Or plane. Whatever."

"You're something else." Ricky smirked.

Weirdo nodded as if he'd heard that a lot and scratched his head.

"So how's business for a professional... hider?"

"I prefer the term *concealer*," Weirdo corrected and took a casual blast from the straw. The sip widened his eyes. "Whoa, that's pure goodness. Business is ebb and flow. Weal or woe. Feast or famine. Constipation or ass squirts. These days, well, it's constipation. Not much going on."

"You advertise?" Ricky asked.

"No."

"Got a business card?"

"No."

"Well, how do you get work?"

"Referrals, mostly. I like those best. No nonsense, and folks pay pretty quickly."

"Huh." Ricky nodded. "And business is hurting these days?"

"Yep."

"Maybe you should think about becoming a finder. Or a detective. Investigator. Private investigator, I mean."

That got Weirdo's attention.

"I mean," Ricky carried on, "if you can conceal things, wouldn't that make you an expert at *finding* things? By default?"

"That's not a bad idea. Ye-e-eah. Thanks."

"You're welcome. Maybe it'll work out for you."

Weirdo thought for a moment. "You know something? The luckiest people in the world are the ones… the ones who know from their earliest age what they're meant to do—what they were placed on this planet for. The ones who recognize what their talents are and develop them and apply them to their work. They're the lucky ones. Just goddamn lucky."

"Or you could be born with money."

"Yeah, but how often does that happen?"

"Not very."

"'Xactly. My point. I'm always jealous of people who know what they're good at from an early age. The shipbuilders. The pro athletes. The musicians."

"Sounds like you're good at your work."

Weirdo appeared to sulk just a little. "Yeah."

Just then, Weirdo leaned back with a start and reached into a pocket. He pulled out a flip phone, opened it, and sighed at the number. He downed the last of his drink straight from the glass, wrist-wiped his beard, and nodded at Ricky.

"Thanks for chattin'," Weirdo said. "Gotta go. Work."

Ricky went back to reading.

*

The weirdo, whose given name was Isosceles though most people just called him Ice, stepped out into the cloudy Halifax day and grimaced. The two drinks were going to make driving risky, but he decided to chance it. Drinking and driving would provide pretty much the only excitement to his miserable day, and he wasn't looking forward to any of it.

*A concealer. Fuck. Did I really say that?* Ice winced at the conversation as a hot shot of self-reproach boiled him from the inside out. He had no idea why he'd said those things, and it would take a shrink to get to the root of it. No wonder he was single. Bullshit should flow smooth and cool and not bob to the surface in frozen chunks. Ice wasn't stupid, but he occasionally had star-bright flashes of stupidity. Sometimes, those flare-ups were jaw-droppingly spectacular, like driving to work under the influence and fabricating stories about his job. There was a disconnect there, he knew—probably a defensive mechanism to shut out the daily shit he had to go through, a reflexive effort to mystify the painfully mundane.

Again, he considered visiting a shrink to get to the root of it, but that was just being dramatic. He knew what his problem was.

Ernie had called him. Ernie wasn't a bad guy, but Ice just didn't know how long he could continue cleaning out the landlord's apartments. The previous day's episode still haunted him, threatening to bring on dry heaves. The apartment had reeked as if the place had been infested with people who refused to use toilet paper, who would simply rub their asses across the carpet until clean. Ice didn't take long to locate the odor's source: perhaps two months of soiled diapers shoved under the sink. That was in addition to the shit streaks on the walls, potato-chip trails throughout all five rooms, and a toilet that had been clogged with pieces of dead fish and shitty crap wrap. All these were the latest volley in the silent war between pissed-off tenants and pissed-off landlords, and ultimately, he was the victim.

He got to clean the battlefield for minimum wage.

# 3

Johnny Marvel drove through Burnside just after six on an evening that should've been on display in an art gallery. Purple paintbrush slashes crossed a canvas of gold, blotted with clouds resembling permed mullets. Or brains. Cottony brains, complete with tapered spinal tails. Or something like that. Johnny didn't care. He'd just finished a wicked day of door-to-door cold calling and was on his way home.

His drive through the industrial park had been all impulse, mainly because of the evening's brilliance and because Johnny had killed it that day. *Killed it.* He must've knocked on forty or fifty doors and gotten a positive vibe from at least eighty percent of the people he'd talked to. A lot of them were pissed off with New Screen's slow monthly price increases in their cable, Internet, and wireless package, and Johnny didn't blame them. No subscriber wanted to be yanked by their dingleberries every seven months or so. A lot of the cable companies did that to their base clientele after signing them, some sooner than others. They would get them with a discounted product and then turn the screws.

That was half the reason Johnny felt so damn good about working for the upstart NowThisIsNow brand sweeping through eastern Canada. It had it all: a five-year fixed price of seventy-five dollars for the same package New Screen was selling for over two hundred smackers a month. At a hundred-twenty-five-dollar difference, viewers got a bunch of speciality channels and top-tier movie networks that other cable companies charged extra for, and from day one of signing.

NowThisIsNow wasn't just a cable company. It was a battle cry. Johnny had spent several minutes hearing horror stories and patiently fielding questions from his potential new customers.

*"Yes, that's right, ma'am. No increases in your cable for five years. Cancel at any time. We don't require you to sign anything."*

Ultimately, it was the price that hooked most people. NowThisIsNow would make its profits from the sheer volume of subscribers, and Johnny had only started on Halifax-Dartmouth. The whole town was ripe for change. He tried not to think of his percentages, but he knew he had the mother lode within his grasp. There were only three other sales reps in the area, and the product was second to none. NowThisIsNow was projected to rule the east coast in a year and then move west.

And Johnny Marvel would be in the spearhead to take Montreal.

He was feeling so good about the day and the future that he forgot about the time and decided to hit a few more apartment complexes if he could find them.

Barely ten seconds later, a twenty-story-plus pillar of dollar signs filled his windshield, a dark obelisk stamped against the spun gold of the evening. Johnny bet that tall bastard was positively infested with potential subscribers. He'd slap big money on it. He reduced speed and got his newly leased Honda Civic off the highway. The building grew, and as far as he could tell, there weren't any lights on in any of the windows above. He pulled into a guest parking lot and eyed the ramp leading into the underground garage.

He switched off the engine and punched up his GPS. *9968 Burnside.*

When the screen displayed nothing, he slapped the unit. A

quick peek out his window confirmed that, yes, the tower was indeed there: a tall-ass condominium built to the heavens. Johnny hated using his paper maps, but he got them out. They were old, and as a result, as far as he could tell, nothing was supposed to be there. That, at least, cleared up a little of the mystery. The building was new, built sometime after the publication of his paper maps, and his GPS was screwed up.

Drumming his hands on the steering wheel, Johnny debated what to do and decided he'd stopped, so what the hell. He grabbed his stack of "Sorry We Missed You" doorknob cards with his business number on them and his folder of promotional guides detailing the bundled goodness NowThisIsNow had to offer. Johnny scanned his nostrils for nose goblins in the rearview mirror and snarled to inspect his teeth—all good. He flicked his brown hair, drizzling his forehead just right, and popped in a breath mint. He sniffed at an armpit and gave it a thumbs-up.

Johnny was good to go.

He popped out of the car like a spring breaking free of a sofa cushion, got his bearings, and speed walked to the glass doors of the main entrance. The ground-floor windows looked dark, perhaps because of drawn curtains, but that didn't disturb Johnny in the least. He was getting into a groove. In the zone. He wasn't selling a product, he was saving people money by introducing a *life choice*, by God.

"Now this is now, baby," Johnny whispered, his enthusiasm percolating as he pushed into the main lobby. A solitary guard sat behind a large desk and gave him the stink eye. Two pairs of elevators were just behind him, as well as a wall of mailboxes.

*Security guard. A good sign.* If the condo villagers could afford on-site security, then they had scads of cash. Getting past the guard, however, might be a challenge.

"Hey, how you doing?" Johnny asked, teeth and demeanor all set to high beams. "I'm Johnathan Marvel, sales representative for the NowThisIsNow cable company and all you're ever going to need in a bundle. I was in the area and noticed this building wasn't on my GPS, so I thought I'd stop by and ask for permission to go on up, floor to floor, and let every person in the building know about the amazing savings NowThisIsNow has to offer."

While he talked, Johnny gradually became aware of the building's air. He could taste it, thick, musty, and dry. Swallowing dust bunnies whole would probably afford more moisture than breathing in that air. Johnny squinted at the guard, wondering if a good portion of the stink he was getting wasn't in fact emanating from the rent-a-cop.

"I don't think folks in this building will go for it," the man rasped, his voice as dusty and congested as a pipe choked with tumbleweeds.

"I understand that, sir," John said, heartened that the guy talked at all. If they talked, they could listen. "But let me ask you this: you have cable at home?"

The guard thought about it. "Used to."

"Stopped because it was getting too expensive?" Johnny asked with a genuine frown.

"No."

"Working too much?"

"Yeah. Work."

"You have a cell phone?"

The guard shook his head and slowly blinked. He looked about fifty-six, unshaven but not grossly prickly with stubble. The way he closed his eyes made Johnny think he was on his last breath.

"You must've pulled a night shift last night," Johnny said sympathetically.

A deep sigh then. "Yeah. A couple of them. Seems like forever. I'm shitbagged."

That startled Johnny just a little. He didn't get such frank security guards too often.

"Well, I won't trouble you much longer, sir. I can see that you're busy."

And in that space of time, in that gap in the conversation, Johnny noticed just how quiet things were inside the building. And it wasn't just inside. He couldn't hear anything above or outside the apartment. Someone had spent serious coin to get such quality soundproofing.

Johnny knew it—could smell it. This place had money.

But the guard gave him no wiggle room whatsoever.

"Could I at least drop off these cards? Maybe have the person who sorts the mail stick one into each mailbox?"

The guard appeared to mull it over. Johnny had only seen the guy blink once, and when the eyelids rose, he wondered if they lubricated the man's eyes or simply reapplied a coat of glue.

"I'll haveta call up," the guard eventually said. "Usually, outside visitors are brought in with a resident. You're alone, so I better call up. See if it's okay."

Johnny nodded. Sounded like a good idea to him. He stepped away from the desk and allowed the guard to make that call. Johnny noted the grime covering the countertop's black surface not immediately within the guard's reach, as distinct as the wiper arc on a windshield. The urge to turn around got him, and he complied, fixing on a blue-and-green garbage bin near the door, a big one encouraging folks to recycle.

The corner of a pizza box stuck out of the bin's mouth, a huge party-sized deal with the explosive "Billy Joe Bob's Pizza" logo on the cardboard.

"Well," the guard said, hanging up, "the owner said it was fine."

"He did?" Johnny said, back in the zone. "Wonderful."

"*She* said to head on up."

"That's great." Johnny said without missing a beat. "Thank you so much for making the call. Here's my card— just in case you decide to get a bundle in the future. We're the cheapest around and provide the same level of—"

"Nah," the guard cut him off, just like that.

"Ah, well, thanks all the same. You made my night. Can I…" Johnny pointed to the elevators.

"Go ahead. Head on up to the twenty-first floor. Guess you'll be seeing everyone, so just pick a door."

"Sounds great. Just great. Thanks again." Johnny speed walked to the elevator and jammed a thumb on the call button.

Far above, something lurched to life and descended.

Johnny looked back at the guard. The man stared outside, looking for nonexistent traffic, his graying hair meticulously combed. And while Johnny watched, a spider the size of his thumbnail scurried from behind the guard's ear and down his collar. Johnny stopped breathing. The sight had to have been a trick of the light. Had to have been. A chill slipped over his person, icy enough for him to jump at the elevator's *bing*. If the guard heard, he didn't bother turning around.

"Thanks again," Johnny said in a weak voice, clearly shaken, as he placed one foot across the threshold. The floor wobbled ever so slightly as he entered.

The guard didn't move, raising neither a hand nor his voice.

*Weird.* Johnny selected the floor number.

The elevator doors closed upon his horrified expression.

# 4

Stu Sweeney sized up the high-rise condo as if it were a metal sliver that had stabbed him underneath a fingernail. The trail for missing Molly Williams ended here. After two months of police investigations that had led nowhere, Molly's family decided to hire their own bloodhound. Sweeney came recommended. He wasn't police, but he had studied and trained under some very knowledgeable people who had been police. He'd also solved enough cases to keep himself working the past dozen years. Molly's case was the kind of work he preferred, not the surveillance of cheating husbands or wives. He liked finding people, thought it a noble undertaking, especially the ones who had seemingly vanished without a trace, like Molly.

Her disappearance was a strange one. In conversations with the Halifax-based constabulary, Sweeney had learned that no one could find a damn thing on her. The whole trail just up and vanished like a baby's fart in a thunderstorm, and conversations with the lead officers conducting the investigations earned him stern warnings about minding his own business. Trouble was, as far as Sweeney was concerned, he couldn't see any indicators to suggest the investigation was ongoing. His contacts reported that the officers on the case were actually, *mysteriously*, repressing the search, like a bad memory pushed way to the back of one's mind and forgotten. Or like a filing cabinet left in a basement and covered with blankets. The case was there, listed, but with no staff assigned to it and nothing being done.

Which was really weird.

Sweeney had discovered his own leads within a period of three days. He'd found out from her family that Molly enjoyed clubbing, and with a photo in hand, he hit up five popular night spots. He struck gold with the last nightclub. His missing lady had visited there and had left with a young woman. Neither woman had been seen since, and no one knew where either person lived.

So much for lead investigators.

To Sweeney, Molly's trail had been as obvious as shit in a sugar dish. Over the past three weeks, from Thursday to Saturday, he'd staked out the nightclub where Molly had last been seen by bartenders and bouncers, searching for the young woman who had escorted Molly from the club the night she'd disappeared.

Then, the night before, he'd spotted the suspect.

The sight had left him breathless. The woman who had supposedly whisked his missing person away wasn't only a looker, she was a cardiac arrest in a miniskirt. Sexuality crackled off her, a nearly violent charge of expectation on the brink of explosion. The reactions left in her wake were immediate and understandable. She'd parted the masses of midnight revelers like a naked celebrity, turning heads of men and women alike. There was no losing her as the crowd either got out of her way or outright gawked.

From the club's second floor, Sweeney had watched her, tracked her slipping through the packs of people. Even Sweeney's own heart of forty-eight years quickened, and his trouser rocket stirred. Given the number of attractive women around him and the miles on his unit, it was a wonder she even aroused him at all, especially at such a distance, but she did. Sweeney caught himself staring, wishing that he was twenty years younger—or, even better, that she had a thing for older guys.

One other thing Sweeney had noticed, however. As desirable as she was, not a single guy hit on her. That observation struck the private investigator as more than weird. It was unnatural. A woman like that should've been outright hounded on the floor, but for some incomprehensible reason, no one pursued her. No one even got in her way, as if an invisible bubble of some mysterious force surrounded her, demanding attention yet repelling all suitors.

Sweeney had watched how Sexy Time—his nickname for his suspect—selected a tall bull of a guy who might've played hockey or football. Sweeney's jaw set with an odd combination of lust, envy, and bewilderment when she stopped to talk with the man for a few seconds. After only those few seconds, anyone on the floor could see the jock was hers. She used nothing more than a look, really, but nothing more was needed. Sexy Time could've had anyone she wanted, yet she chose him.

The couple had danced for a good hour or so, and sometime after the midnight hour, they retired to the woman's car, a vintage Toyota Celica. The private investigator had given chase, tailing the Celica through the night, two cars back. She eventually led him to the apartment tower on the other side of the industrial park, where the sporty coupe disappeared into an underground parking lot.

There was only one road leading into the apartment building, so he had parked on the gravel shoulder about a hundred meters back and pulled out his smartphone. Sweeney didn't want to think about the sex that lucky bastard was no doubt experiencing, so he went online and researched the building to pass the time and keep his mind busy.

*9968 Burnside.* There were old articles dating nine years back, outlining that the tower had been abandoned shortly after completion, as the base had been improperly built. The land was sinking on the one side, creating a lean to the north. The units, consisting of over a hundred studios, two-bedrooms, and three-bedrooms, had been only partially filled before building inspectors condemned the structure and forced everyone to move. The Atticus Y Corporation, who'd overseen the development, had lost millions in misjudging not only the site but the condominium market for the area as well.

The reading was interesting, and it only added to the overall surrealism surrounding the missing-persons case—surreal because, through the wee hours of predawn, Sweeney noticed lights snapping on and off upon various floors, as if they were all on a preset timer of some sort. When the sun had risen, he could no longer see any activity within the building at all. No one drove up to the parking lot, and no one left the underground garage, which seemed about right for a condemned building, at least in Sweeney's mind. He hadn't even moved from his old F150 since stopping on the shoulder, having stayed there until a pink dawn crept over the trees and hills, though he did crack a window at regular intervals for mind-clearing shots of fresh air.

Sweeney wondered why she had gone in there. He wondered why were there such weird lights in a supposedly deserted building. And he wondered why hadn't she come back out.

The passing of minutes did nothing to ease his puzzling.

Nor did the passing of hours, well into the afternoon.

Sweeney glanced at the dash clock—ten minutes after two. As far as he could tell, the building was deserted. He leaned back, generating a leathery creak somewhere beneath both cheeks. The waistband of his shorts bunched up at the baseline and drove him batty, so he took a few seconds to straighten things out. He got out of his truck, stretched, and studied the steel-and-concrete behemoth under the young afternoon sun. Nothing moved on the ground floor, and nothing was happening on the levels above that. No windows were being opened nor people drawing back curtains—no nothing, not even visitations by seagulls or any other birds. Sweeney rubbed his head as traffic entered and vacated the city. Not one vehicle had turned into 9968 Burnside all night or morning.

Sexy Time's Celica was the sole exception.

After a few minutes of stretching his legs, Sweeney hauled himself back aboard the truck, adjusted his balls through the material of his pants, and settled in for another bout of surveillance.

When the clock neared four thirty, he started up his ride, thinking that shit was just too weird. No one was leaving or entering the place at all, and why should they? The building had been condemned. He pulled into traffic and drove onto the building's lot. He parked in a visitor space and got out. Dirt coated the ground-floor windows, yet behind the grime and dust, the figure of a security guard sitting at the lobby's front desk could be discerned. A chill whipped up Sweeney's backbone like a mad flourish over piano keys. The sentinel behind the desk didn't move, didn't react to Sweeney's arrival. The figure was so still, in fact, that for a moment, Sweeney wondered if he was looking at a statue rather than a person.

With the sun slipping from the evening sky, Sweeney shrugged and walked to the double doors. He stopped when they failed to automatically open.

The guard behind the desk—Sweeney could see it was a rent-a-cop—sat and stared as if he'd taken a massive snort off a bottle of furniture glue. Sweeney opened a door with a push and heard it close behind him with a hydraulic huff. The urge to sneeze took him almost immediately.

Dust, thick and unpleasant, layered his face and eyes, making him wish for a mask and goggles.

"You need this place cleaned and aired out," he said, loud enough for the guard to hear, but the guy didn't bat an eye.

Sweeney approached the man. For a rental, he looked to be about in his fifties and crusty. Hard. As if he'd been on a three-day bender of epic alcoholic proportions. A silver, unshaven mesh of hair grew in unhealthy patches under the guy's chin, while his hair could've used a mower.

"Excuse me?" the rental rasped.

Sweeney drew in a few shallow breaths, loathing every one. "You guys have livestock in here? Maybe a goat? Or ever open a window?"

"No animals. Haven't opened a window today. Too cold outside." The rental took his time answering, as if he was preoccupied with something else.

Sweeney figured the guy hadn't opened a window in a very long time. The place really did smell like a goat had taken a dump in a corner somewhere. Part of him was reluctant to even look around, for fear of seeing that goat.

He stopped at the desk and stared down at the seated man with a soft scrutiny. "You okay?"

The guard nodded with all the serenity of a monk contemplating existence. "Just fine. Why?"

"You don't look so good."

"Oh."

Sweeney stooped and studied the rental's sunken eyes—no dilation but filmy, glassy, like dusty marble. "What company you work with?"

"Me?"

"Yeah, you."

"Oh, ah." The guard's forehead crinkled with thought, and a shaking hand rose to latch onto his chin. "I'm private. Hired direct by the owner here. I get a discount off my rent."

"Really?" Sweeney said. "That's not a bad deal."

"Not at all."

"How much you make an hour?"

"Minimum."

"Not much," Sweeney said. "You have the name of your employer?"

"Yes. It's Mrs. C. Lehr."

"Lehr?"

The rental nodded.

"Maybe she's hiring?"

"All the time," the rental answered without a trace of emotion. The guy wasn't even looking at Sweeney.

"She live here?"

"Top floor."

"She home now?"

"Sure."

"I see. You see anyone entering the building in the last twenty-four hours?"

"Only Mrs. Lehr."

"Mrs. Lehr?" That was interesting.

"Yes."

"Same Mrs. Lehr that hired you?"

"Yes."

"She have a guest?"

The guard blinked, and his brow creased in thought. "I think she did. A young man."

The guy was cooperative, to say the least. "She leave since then?"

"No."

"Did he leave?"

"I don't think so."

Sweeney debated how far he should push his luck and decided to go for it. "Possible for me to see her now, maybe?"

"Well…" The pause felt almost terminal. "Usually, I need a resident to escort visitors past this point. But since you're applying for a job, I don't see the harm. Head on up. I'll ring her while you ride the elevator. Take the A lift. It's the twenty-first floor."

Twenty-first. Just like that. Sweeney thought the structure had looked higher on the outside. He peered over the guard at the interior of the building, where two short halls housed a pair of elevators.

"How many people live here?" Sweeney asked.

"Lots." The guard smiled, revealing yellowed dental work every bit as aged as his eyes. Sweeney wondered if that simple movement of facial muscles caused any pain.

"Lots," Sweeney repeated.

The guard nodded and tucked the smile away.

"Great. Well, thanks. Oh, one more thing."

"Sure," the guard said as if he'd returned from a dream.

"Your employer, Mrs. Lehr—she's in her twenties? Black hair, very attractive?"

"That's Mrs. C.," the guard confirmed.

"Mrs. C. Lehr. And she owns the building?"

"Yes."

"That's Mrs. C.?"

"Yes."

"She's a lot younger than I expected."

"She takes care of herself," the guard said in that dreamy voice.

"She does," Sweeney agreed. "She does that. The A elevator, you said?"

The rental nodded. "The light's off, though. Be a little dark on the way up."

"What about the others?"

"Out of service."

"Folks can't be too happy with that."

The rental shook his head.

"Thanks," Sweeney said, wondering about that as he headed past the desk. "See you a little later, then."

The guard didn't answer, and when Sweeney finally faced the A elevator, he glanced back. The rental was as hard to look at as the air was to breathe, with his head somewhat slouched forward, staring toward the front doors. Sweeney watched him while digging out his cell phone. He thumbed in the number of the Halifax constabulary and made contact with an Officer Jones.

"How can I help?" the voice inquired professionally.

"Yeah, well, first," Sweeney said, keeping an eye on the front desk, "this is Stu Sweeney. I was talking to an Officer Bartlett about a missing-person case. Concerning a missing Molly Williams?"

"Ah yes, just hold for a moment."

Sweeney didn't want to hold, and he was about to say as much just as he was placed on hold. The rental continued to face forward, ignoring him, as if he was already a memory. That set Sweeney's senses off.

"This is Bartlett," a smoker's voice suddenly announced in Sweeney's ear.

"Bartlett, this is Stu Sweeney."

"I remember you. Looking for a young lady."

"Still am. And guess where I am now?"

"I don't know."

"I'm standing in a building that was supposed to be condemned yet has power, tenants, and even a front-door guard who looks like he just escaped from an industrial vacuum bag."

"You are?" Bartlett sounded doubtful.

"Yeah," Sweeney said just as the soft *ding* of the opening elevator distracted him. The doors parted to reveal blackness. *Jesus.* Sweeney peered inside. The thing was an upright coffin.

"Sweeney?"

"Uh, yeah, so anyway, I'm at 9968 Burnside if you want to send a cruiser by, check on things a little more. Frankly, I'm even less impressed with your investigation."

"That so?"

"Yeah, I tracked a sweet little thing to this address who might very well be connected to the Molly Williams case."

"Uh huh. At 9968 Burnside, you say?"

"I say. I'm in the building now, about to go on up to the top floor and talk to a Mrs. C. Lehr."

"All right."

That perplexed Sweeney. "You're okay with me doing this?"

"You're already there," Bartlett said. "Suit yourself."

That blew Sweeney away. "You're okay with it?"

"Sure."

"I mentioned the possible link to the missing-person case and that the building was condemned. You heard all that, right?"

"I did."

This was too easy, in Sweeney's mind. "You gonna send over that cruiser?"

"Sure."

"Thanks. Like… now?"

"You got it."

The casualness of the remark put Sweeney on edge. "You're on board with this, Bartlett?"

After a distinct pause, Bartlett said, "My guys will be there in a bit."

*Click.*

Sweeney pulled the phone away from his ear and studied it, replaying the entire conversation and thinking it damn strange. The elevator doors started to close, but he stuck a foot in there, causing the doors to retreat. He studied the interior. *Well, so much for the police.* He vacillated, wondering if Bartlett would send a cruiser and why he might not. In the end, Sweeney shrugged mentally, figuring he might as well go on up and talk to the lady—sniff around. If anything happened, the cops knew where he was and were probably on the way, which was entirely different from the vibe he'd received from them from the very beginning of the case.

Danger bells jingled merrily in Sweeney's skull. Still, he was there. He regarded the elevator and decided to ask Mrs. Lehr about work after all, to make casual contact at the very least. He couldn't really do much more without crossing police lines anyway.

So he stepped aboard, waving his cell phone's flashlight

around, and spotted a slew of Sorry We Missed You doorknob cards heaped into a back corner. Sweeney sighed. The housekeeping in the place was as bad as the security.

*Twenty-first floor.* He thumbed the appropriate button, and the doors slid shut. With a soft lurch, the elevator lifted him away.

Sweeney thought about the rental cop below and went over their conversation while numbered lights lit up as he rose higher. The guy was either stoned or in shock. And seeing how the place had as much life as a dead man's prick, Sweeney believed there was a good chance the guy was high on something. Or he was just a freak. Lots of those around.

The elevator passed the tenth floor, and Sweeney swept his light around the interior, revealing rich wood paneling and brass trim. The mirror in the ceiling had been shattered, leaving only a flat slab of metal. *Savages.* One of Sweeney's fondest pleasures was meeting assholes who got off on destroying public property and making a citizen's arrest, then beating the hell out of them if they took a swing at him. Even though the building was supposedly shut down, it still bothered him to see the ceiling smashed.

The thirteenth went by.

The elevator floor consisted of an oval patch of red carpet—oval because flyers, assorted mail, and door cards covered the rest in a deep litter. The door cards in particular caught Sweeney's attention.

The sixteenth-floor light illuminated and darkened.

The cards displayed a sales rep's phone number in a big font. "Johnny" was right over them, along with some artsy decoration of black champagne bubbles. Damn things resembled the asshide of a dead Dalmatian.

The seventeenth floor sailed on past.

Black dots. They drew the investigator in, prompting him to inspect them a little more closely. The pattern wasn't uniform with the other door cards. In fact, some dappled the edges and rendered them wrinkly, as if they'd absorbed far too much water. Sweeney's forehead crinkled.

The eighteenth floor dropped away as a gear cranked softly somewhere above the ceiling of the elevator. Sweeney focused his cell-phone light at the pattern dappling the cards. He'd been in his share of fights, even crime scenes, and had witnessed a respectable amount of blood, and damned if those ink spots didn't remind him of a spatter pattern. He stooped and shifted through more floor debris, flipping over a few more cards.

The elevator slowed to a stop.

Ruined paper lay underneath the top coating of cards in congealed clumps, soaked and dried with what he suspected was blood. Sweeney's ears popped. His eyes narrowed, and his heart thumped as if demanding him to wake up. An unexpected coldness overcame his whole person, a sixth-sense chill that he'd experienced only a couple of times before, when he'd wandered into a couple of dangerous situations as he should've been paying better attention to the little bells ringing in his brain.

And he wasn't going to ignore it at that moment.

The elevator *ding*ed, and the doors opened. Sweeney whirled around as he rose—his cell phone held high, like a torch warding off the night—and flash-glimpsed a man's pallid face as he lunged through the widening portal. His mouth was stretched impossibly wide and needled with teeth from a nightmare.

Sweeney didn't have time to scream.

# 5

At 4:27 p.m., Ice closed the door of his sedan, stepped back from the car, and sighed at the flattening front-right tire. That was going to be a problem. He stood there, on the wide sidewalk before Larry's Pizza, and shook his head while releasing a second frustrated sigh. *Another expense.* Isosceles didn't have the cash for a new tire just yet. He'd been saving for a new computer. With rent, daily living expenses, and a rust bucket of a clunker car that occasionally dropped important parts on the highway, he wasn't making any great strides in gaining personal financial freedom, and the lottery wasn't paying out as it used to in the old days. That was an old joke his mom would tell at times, and the memory brought a short-lived smile to his face.

Resolving to deal with the tire later, Ice walked into pizza heaven, pushing his way through an aromatic wall of culinary mastery. Larry's was a historical landmark in downtown Halifax, a must-visit destination on anyone's travel itinerary. Larry didn't just have skill, he performed magic. Larry could probably throw a dead fish onto a pizza, and customers would rave at the amazing taste. After a day of cleaning out vacated apartments, Ice actually looked forward to his evening job. Driving around the city and delivering pizzas and donairs didn't bother him in the least. Some of the customers were dicks, and late-night Fridays had the highest percentage for cases of dickery, but Ice had worked out an early schedule with Larry so that he was off at midnight, thus avoiding most of the drunks.

Larry was the man, and Ice appreciated the leeway in the shifts.

David, however, was a dick—though a dapper dick, as he always dressed as though he were a suit salesman instead of a pie driver. As Ice crossed the pizza place's threshold, David—Ice had been warned about calling him "Dave" and to not ever call him "Davey"—eyed him with visible contempt.

"David," Ice greeted perfunctorily.

"You got car trouble out there?" the man asked, forgoing the usual welcoming ritual.

Ice stood between a pair of white tables and walls covered with posters of pizzas and subs and donairs. "Yeah. Got a flat."

"You can't drive?"

"Drove here."

"Just answer the question, numb nuts."

Ice resisted rolling his eyes. "I can drive. I got a portable air pump that plugs into the car. It'll take care of it."

"You need to get that fixed."

"I know."

"Like now."

"Well, it'll be like, tomorrow."

David aimed his best attempt at an evil eye, intended to intimidate, which in reality left him looking retarded. The guy's carefully thinned moustache and beard, artistically mown to distinguish his facial hair from the more commonplace mops of the Halifax peasantry, shifted from left to right as he sampled one corner of his cheek and then the other.

"I'm telling Larry about this," he finally fired off. "Getting tired of all this preferential treatment you're getting. The short shifts. Getting away from Friday nights. It's not right."

"Yeah." Ice sighed, knowing Dave would indeed talk to Larry. "Anything to go?"

"Yeah. Right there. First catch of the evening. All yours."

Three insulated carrying cases for delivery pizza lined the red countertop. One looked less bulky than the others, which was the one David indicated Ice to take. Isosceles went to the box and checked the receipt stuck to the cover. "This is over in Hubley."

"Yeah," David said without interest.

"That's a twenty-minute drive."

"I know."

"It's outside the zone."

"*Just* outside the zone," David corrected, lowering his head so that his eyes became even more condescending when he gazed out from underneath his furry, freshly plucked Cro-Magnon brow.

At times, Ice wondered if the man actually mowed that space.

Ice protested with a glare at the other pizza bags. "Where are those headed?"

"I'm taking those."

*You fucker,* Ice thought blackly, knowing those orders were no doubt all in a nice, tight line across the city.

"Yeah." David smiled in snide victory. "You might get the comfy shifts, but you don't get the money shots."

"Fine."

"Get moving," David added, striking a lecturing, managerial pose. "By the time you get back here, there'll be plenty more."

Ice doubted that, but he got moving.

First off, he tended to the flat tire, spending ten minutes inflating it. Larry had a business car, a little white compact, but David drove that one, so Ice didn't even bother asking about it. Once the tire was inflated, he grabbed the food and got on the road. Thursday-evening traffic wasn't so bad heading over to Hubley, a small town just outside Halifax. Ice made the delivery and received a five-dollar tip for his gas tank and a genuine thank-you for driving all the way over there. Isosceles appreciated the little things. They kept him grounded.

He returned to Larry's Pizza in record time, without attracting the attention of Halifax's finest, and picked up another suppertime order. David had already left with the bulk of the deliveries, no doubt all conveniently lined up so he could save time and energy and maximize his tips. Pushing the guy from his mind, Ice got back into his car and motored on over to a downtown office building right on the harbor front. Getting there in record time earned him another fiver in his hand.

When he got back to Larry's, David was there—taking one of two pizza bags from Ice's pickup section of the counter.

"Hey man, that one's mine," Ice said in a weary voice.

David glanced over his shoulder without a drip of guilt. "First come, first serve, and all that noise."

"Bet you say that to your girlfriend a lot."

That darkened David's complexion. "Say that again. I dare you."

"Or it's probably self-serve with you."

In the kitchen, cooks Nigel and Roger stopped spinning and rolling pizza dough, looking like a couple of white puppets waiting for the punches.

"I think you best grab that"—David glared and indicated the remaining thermal bag—"and get on the road. Else Larry and I have a talk."

"Y'know something, I think Larry and I will have a talk," Ice responded, his bullshit gauge flirting dangerously with the red line. "I'm getting tired of your bitching."

David glanced around the interior of the pizza place, checking to see if any customers were waiting.

"You heard me," Ice said since he'd already scoped the place. "And before you mouth off to Larry about grabbing my orders, just know I have the boys in the kitchen to back me up."

On cue, Nigel and Roger immediately went back to work.

*You ball-less bastards.* Ice seethed, tight-lipped with heat rushing to his cheeks. No Christmas whiskey shots for those two.

"You can bet he'll hear about this." David smirked.

"I don't doubt it."

David left with Ice's order.

Ice considered the remaining delivery. He checked the receipt and saw it was for the other side of Burnside.

"Well… dammit," he muttered and peered into the kitchen.

Nigel and Roger flinched like a couple of surprised cats and got back to work.

"Yeah," Ice muttered and gathered up the thermal bag. "Thought so."

# 6

The dark obelisk of the high-rise building stamped itself against a dimming October sky, spreading red wings of the deepest hue. Ice parked his car and leaned over his steering wheel, taking in the monolithic girth of the structure, and wondered why the hell the almost-a-skyscraper's lights were off.

"What the hell…?" Ice muttered, straining to see. The address on the pizza bag said the twentieth floor. He glanced back at the building before checking the address a second time—then a third. He finally lowered his head in defeat. *The elevator had better be working.* He willed it to be. There was no way he was walking up twenty floors in a dark stairwell to deliver a goddamn pizza. Simply no way.

Ice kicked the car door open then got out, stretched, and kicked the door closed. He winced at the dark heights before him and the dreadful climb he just knew was in his immediate future. Oh, how he hoped to God the elevator was working. It would take him half the night to hike all the way to the top, not that he expected to reach the midway mark. He predicted his heart exploding with shotgun force somewhere around the seventh.

"Oh, Jesus Christ. What the hell is this? What the hell is *this?*" he asked in the nearly deserted parking lot. His car didn't answer him—not that he expected it to, not after having kicked it twice. This had to be a joke. *David's* joke. There was no phone number on the receipt, which was weird. Nigel had screwed up on that part, only Nigel *never* screwed up on that part. Had to be David. And those bastard cooks, Roger and Nigel, had clearly known something was stinking up the kitchen and chosen not to say a word. Ice intended to have a stern talk with both of them. David he'd simply knee in the balls.

Ice arched his back, heard things pop, and studied the tall building. If there was a power issue, he'd leave the damn pizza at the front desk or something. No way he'd walk those stairs. No way. They'd find his corpse on a landing somewhere.

Sighing, Isosceles extracted the pizza bag, took a long, forlorn look at the city lights behind him, and then got walking, muttering curses all the way. City had its lights. Building didn't have its. He thought he saw pricks of lights near the very top, like distant candles, which was weird.

Maybe it was a newfound green-energy thing.

*Goddamn green-energy thing.*

A Ford pickup was parked not three empty spaces away from him, looking very much alone and oddly out of place. No other visitors seemed to be visiting, but the ramp for the underground garage was wide open. The pavement sloped downward and veered to the left, so if there was a grate somewhere below that closed the route off, he wouldn't have seen it anyway.

"Meat lover's special," Ice muttered with venom and dragged his ass toward the building's entrance.

A thin light illuminated the lobby, as faint as a ribbon of flame, and Ice thought that weird as well. The doors didn't open automatically, so he pushed his way through, back first, to protect the food. A gust of night air whooshed past him, but it wasn't enough to dispel the deep-rooted smell of dust, neglect, and body odor. Ice stopped just inside and caught his breath for dear life, squinting at the security guard seated behind the desk.

The guard didn't look the greatest, in Ice's mind, which was a pleasant way to say he thought the man looked like shit. Gray haired and sallow cheeked, the guard didn't move, and the shoulders of the guy's uniform appeared liberally sprinkled with dandruff. He looked old, but there was something not right about that. If Ice hadn't known better, he would've sworn the guy had that disease that prematurely aged people by years.

"Hey," Isosceles greeted.

The man's eyes didn't flick over to Ice—they kinda rolled, like a pair of matching boulders being pushed from behind. Once they were in place, the guard stared as if he were at the end of a very long chemically induced stupor.

"Uh, sorry, uh, I got this." Ice lifted the pizza. "For upstairs. The twentieth floor. Apartment—"

"Four."

Isosceles didn't have to check the receipt. "The guy orders pizza a lot, does he?"

The guard didn't blink. In fact, there was no reaction at all. Ice thought if this were a scene in a horror flick, the guard would open his mouth and release a stream of flies or some other winged pestilence. Seconds passed, stretching into an uncomfortable silence.

"Uhhh, yeah," Ice said. "Well, anyway, okay for me to head up?"

"Sure," the guard replied, sounding out of wind. "Take the A elevator."

*Oh, thank fuck.* Isosceles sighed mentally.

The very instant he thought the last word, a spider eased into sight. The eight-legged shiver tiptoed out from the fissure between the guard's neck and his uniform's collar— a black one, the size of a peanut, front legs tensed as if sensing it had been detected. Ice stopped and watched, waiting for the guard's reaction, disbelieving that the guy couldn't feel those legs upon his skin.

The old-timer continued his brain-fried stare, oblivious of the arachnid at his throat.

"You, ah…" Ice's voice fluttered as he attempted to broach the subject, "have a, uh…"

He wiggled a finger at the guard's throat.

"What?" the man asked in a voice as rusty as the flakes coating his shoulders.

"Don't freak out or anything." Ice didn't believe freaking out was within the guard's physical ability. "You have a spider there. On your neck."

"Oh."

*Took that rather well*, Isosceles thought. "Yeah, right…" He touched his own throat for reference.

But the guard didn't bother with doing anything, let alone remove the spider.

"Well." Ice gave up. He had no intention of messing around with crazy, so he marched past the front desk. When he reached the elevator doors, he glanced back and saw the guard hunched over, his entire frame leaning toward the main entrance.

*Freaky.* Ice shook his head. He pushed a button and waited for the elevator to descend. A single overhead light provided the only illumination for the area, draping the walls and hall in heavy shadow. Ice bounced on the balls of his feet, casting fleeting checks toward the guard.

The elevator arrived with a worrisome mechanical rumble and opened, revealing a lightless interior. Isosceles stepped inside without a second thought, kicking up some papers littering the floor as he did so. That put a sour look on his face. If that were his place, he'd make damn sure he'd keep the elevator clean. Ritzy places like that needed to be kept clean. Air filters did too since something was seriously broken in that department. The whole place reminded him of a carpet that had absorbed way too much sweat. Someone needed to crack a window every now and again.

Ice thumbed his number, and the doors closed, leaving him with only the meager light of the control panel. Numbers ascended as the elevator rose, and he counted off the floors. The place had twenty-five. *Big place. Probably really nice apartments as well.* He shifted the pizza bag from one arm to the other, sniffed, and kicked back some papers that had rested against his left foot.

Ice closed his eyes and relaxed, enjoying the elevator ride for what it was worth. In ten minutes, he would be on his way back to Larry's. Ice didn't think he'd want to live in such a place. A zombie for a front-desk guy and punks smashing out the elevator lights signaled big problems. And if the management let their elevator get that cruddy, then he didn't want to see the basement. Wouldn't surprise him if the place had rats.

Fourteenth floor—the number brightened and winked off. Fifteenth floor.

Ice thought about the person who'd placed the order. He remembered one time when David apparently had made a delivery and a hot chick in a microbikini answered the door. The same chick had tipped him ten bucks and given a generous show of her underboobs. Or so said suave Dave. That story so reeked of horseshit even farmers would gag.

Seventeenth floor.

For Ice, however, after three years of various delivery jobs, Larry's being the most recent, plenty of babes had answered the door—although none of them were dressed in skimpy attire. However, there was that one time a woman answered her door in pajamas and a tight pink T-shirt that read Loveboat. Ice remembered her fondly.

The elevator stopped with a lurch on the eighteenth floor, yanking him from his distracted state. He shuffled to the left, placing his back to the wall as he freed up a hand to thumb the twentieth-floor button again. Nothing happened for long, annoying moments. Ice huffed, shaking his head. Then the elevator door opened and a blur charged in, slapping the pizza bag away with a violent clap and spattering the meat lover's special against the far wall.

Ice screamed. The thing wasn't a hot chick—wasn't even a person. In the sparse light of the button lights, a gruesome apparition had plunged through the doors and stopped just inside the threshold, unable to proceed any farther because of its wings—bat wings.

"Holy—" Ice tried to say.

Red eyes as bright as back-lit rubies fixed upon Ice's face. A mouth stretched open like the jaws of a yawning tiger, except much faster and with many more teeth. The beast shifted and swung a handful of knives at Ice, who darted below the swinging limb and lunged for the door. Wet, dangling matter slapped his face as he dove underneath a legless torso, and a part of his mind shrieked. A hand crashed against wood. The thing screeched, a sound so piercing Ice thought a spike had just been driven through his eardrums. He stumbled toward the dark outline of a closed door. The knob turned, and he bolted through, swinging the door shut as he did.

And in that movement, spinning and slamming on the run, he glimpsed what appeared to be the upper body of a man suspended in the air by a pair of bat wings protruding from his bare back.

The door closed before Ice could entirely process the image, and he stood there, in the darkness, stunned as if he'd downed an entire cauldron of Long Islands. His mind refused to process what he'd just seen beyond the wooden door, but Ice knew. He'd seen an honest-to-God man-bat *thing*.

But that wasn't even the truly freaky part. Isosceles had seen something much worse in the afterflash of fangs and eyes and leathery wings that somehow fit into the whole of the hallway—a sight he knew would be forgotten in the morning, like the nightmare it was. For the image that truly stood out in Ice's mind was the man's jeans.

Standing.

Idly by, like a mannequin missing its torso.

A weight slammed into the door, shaking the entire barrier. Ice flinched and retreated several paces, ready to run, when he realized he hadn't *locked* anything. His hand shot out for the deadbolt and snapped it home just as the knob turned violently. A second heavy force crashed into the door. Another shriek ripped through the entryway, stunning Ice and leaving him blinking. The lower part of the door bulged inward, but the bolt held. Ice fumbled with the main lock and secured it just as the creature hit the door a second time.

Paint chips fluttered to the carpeted floor.

Ice whirled and ran into the apartment, and his feet dropped from underneath him. He fell forward an instant before a solid edge clacked both elbows and shoved them over his head. He plummeted in a haze of black stars, arms sizzling as if absorbing a thousand volts. His feet slapped floor and shot nerve-bursting streaks of agony up his spinal column, ringing his brain like an epileptic kid with a cowbell. Hardwood kissed his forehead with a meaty *thud*, and he lay there on his forearms and knees as if in desperate prayer.

*Oh fuck*, his mind wheezed, hoisting itself above the rising, searing discomfort of having both funny bones whacked, transforming his arms into buzzing meat slabs.

Somewhere above him, a heavy weight slammed into a door a third time, and Ice heard the weakening whine of wood and metal.

With great effort, using more face than arms, he pushed himself off the floor and gazed upward, spying the shadowy, jagged hole in the ceiling.

A loud and final crash from the apartment above prompted him to stumble into a run. He darted into a darkened living room, narrowly avoiding rapping his knees on a low coffee table. Drawn curtains draped the interior in a perpetual pitch black. Ice glanced around and thought he could make out a huge hole in the north wall, right in the corner.

A scream yanked his attention back to the opening he'd fallen through, and even with the distinct absence of light, he could still see a head popping through the ceiling and twisting this way and that with birdlike eagerness. The monster's eyes fixed upon Ice, and it squealed loudly enough to paralyze a lesser person on the spot, to terrify someone into doing nothing but wait.

Not Ice, however.

He shot toward the hole in the wall, threading his way between the furniture, arms swinging like frozen lengths of rubber. Leather and bone thumped and strained somewhere behind him, and an exasperated howl spurred him to greater speeds. The hole was a ragged, shredded thing, waist high and seemingly clawed out of the wall. Ice didn't pause to see where the opening went, not with the man-bat thing on his heels.

He dove through.

And landed on a bed, the springiness so violent that he tumbled off, feet kicking air, and scrubbed his face and shoulder into a rug.

Dazed, Ice saw a void-like cavity underneath the bed, beckoning.

*Oh, Christ.* Ice scurried into it, his breath and limbs disturbing entire planets of dust.

Not a second after he drew himself underneath the age-old protective shelter, the monster hunting him landed on the mattress, bearing down upon Ice's ceiling. He held his breath, grimacing, while a flurry of ticking—becoming a blind man's frantic stick-tapping—perked Ice's ears.

*Oh Jesus, oh Jesus, oh* sweet *Jesus*, ran through Ice's mind. He tried slowing his revved-up breathing and heart while lying still and just *taking* the terrible burning in his arms. He released each breath as slowly and soundlessly as possible, for he knew the thing bouncing overhead most certainly would silence him. Ice refused his lungs more oxygen and forced them to heel, listening over the flood of blood in his temples and ears, hypersensitive to the monster beyond the surrounding falls of bedcovers. The bed's center bulged deep at times, like the skin of a rotten drum about to burst.

The weight left the bed in a squabble of springs. The dreaded tapping lessened as the creature moved away, leaving the room. Wide-eyed and still struggling to stay quiet, Ice waited, not yet ready to stick his head out. The tapping drifted off, circling perhaps, but farther away with every passing second.

Ice waited, refusing to budge, sensing that doing so would invite a certain and very painful death. Something wasn't right. Something was very wrong. Even though he still heard the *tick-tap* of wood on wood, circling, going one way and then the other, his own internal warning system forbade him to move, fully aware that the thing was still inside the room with him, waiting, to better discern where the meat prize had gone.

Ice lay there, his thoughts blazing as bright as spotlights. *Waiting me out. Oh shit. It's waiting me out.* Ice didn't budge, didn't breathe, and didn't blink.

The bat-mutant was out there. He could sense it just like a person stepping inside one's personal space. Distant tapping or not, it was out there, listening. Isosceles remained on his gut, chin on the floor, arms and legs pressed together to create a human log, and waited as if he'd landed in the middle of a very sensitive minefield, where even the sound of a single strand of hair falling into his eyes would get him killed.

Ice closed his eyes, preferring his personal darkness to the bed's. He breathed in, and a floating tumbleweed of dust jammed one nostril. He snorted it away, softly dislodging the particle, but the tickle remained, the damage done.

*Oh, SHIT.*

He squashed that side of his nose against the floor, spidery fibers caressing his forehead, and exhaled softly, the expulsion sounding like a muffled mouse fart in the dark. Ice cringed, the need to sneeze returning, ballooning to critical mass. The tap-tap-tapping continued from beyond the bed, and Ice smeared his nose across the floor one way and then the other, attempting to extinguish the irritant. Water laced his eyes. He winced, teetering on a precipice of disaster.

The tapping ceased.

The sneeze swelled to the brink of discharge. Ice got a hand up and covered his mouth, even jamming a finger up his nose. He sneezed, the sound like a stifled grunt, the report damn near taking off the top of his head. The reflex to take a breath overcame him, and he breathed in deeply, knowing the creature had surely heard.

Ice waited. He waited, cracked open his eyes, and softly blew away the dust mobbing about his face. He didn't wear a watch, but the flip-phone in his coat pocket had a clock—as long as he hadn't broken the device when he fell.

Time dragged, the seconds stubborn in their passing, and Ice took better control of his breathing. The dust wasn't bothering him as badly, either. He waited, wondering where that fucked-up freak of nature was lurking and what the distance to the elevator was. The last ten minutes or so replayed themselves in his mind, and Ice had no clue as to where or what the monster was.

An even greater concern crept into his consciousness.

*Where* is *everyone?*

He wondered if he'd actually fallen through someone's ceiling and then jumped through another person's wall to… there. Damn straight he had, and he had dust mites the size of rice grains crawling over his person to prove it. The notion of getting away returned, and he considered his position, in a bedroom, under a bed, with an elevator somewhere nearby and a creature straight from a horror flick hunting his hairy ass.

Another five minutes passed, and Ice couldn't hear a damn thing. The tapping had stopped entirely, and other than the tiny, nearly soundless breaths he was taking, the building seemed empty. That bothered Ice, so he kept still for minutes longer, taking his time to shift his limbs every now and again. His arms had returned to normal. His shoulder joints creaked when he moved, and Ice held that pose for several seconds before continuing, listening for any reaction beyond the bedcovers.

Nothing pounced or attempted to grab him by the ankles. Nothing screeched or screamed.

At least twenty minutes or more had elapsed, and Ice decided it was time to move. He glanced around cautiously, his eyesight picking up lines and borders in the dark, and turned himself underneath the bed so that he pointed the way he entered. The elevator was out there. It even had a red button to hit in case of an emergency, and as God was his witness, Ice was having a supernova-sized emergency right then.

He wormed his way along the floor, parting the gauze glazing the tiles. Hairs hung off the bottom of the bed, slipping over his head as he pushed himself along. The bedcover hung not a finger's breadth off the floor, marked by a grey line of light. Ice grazed its smooth fabric with his fingertips.

Claws clamped down on the bedframe and heaved the mattress up and away. Ice sputtered and reversed hard just as a hand gripped him by the neck and slung him against a wall. Ice landed on his ass, legs splayed, gasping for breath. His brain shouted for him to run, to haul ass out of there.

He didn't, however.

There, in the shadowy twilight of the room, bat wings blurred with a hummingbird's grace, keeping a charred torso above the ground. Grey-black skin ended at the waist, and there, hanging by strands of madness, was a sinewy medley of wet ribbons and sloughs resembling fleshy knee socks.

The sight paralyzed Ice. His face went slack. He wrenched his eyes away from the dangling visceral horror and locked gazes with the rabid fury contained in the monster's eyes.

The thing hissed at him, but Ice didn't care. He no longer saw a mouth opening to three times its size. The fangs and shards and the thick stew that spilled from the maw didn't faze him. Not much fazed him at all, really, as a warm wave of euphoric bliss enveloped him. The monster came closer, its frightful visage enlarging, and its warm breath reminded Ice of sun-loved roses in the summertime. The lidless eyes quelled his breathing, relaxing him, and the room about him became an unclouded beach.

Ice put his head back against the wall, lifted his chin, and offered his throat.

# 7

The thing loomed closer, the calming *whrrrr* of its wings generating white crackles of light. A whipcord tongue slipped from the cave of its mouth, droplets stretching from its length. It licked Ice's cheek, the contact as pleasant as a dog's kiss, before poising itself directly before his left eye.

The tongue's tip hardened, becoming barbed, and Isosceles smiled just as a heavy weight crashed into the apparition and hurled it to the far side of the room. The dreamy hypnosis dissipated in an instant, leaving Ice blinking and breathless and rubbing a cheek that burned as if lashed by battery acid.

"Get up, you stupid fucker!"

The monster squirmed against a wall and its captor, head whipping about on shoulders in an effort to determine who had pinned it. It was a man, a big man, who had dug his feet in and had the supernatural creature's arm in what appeared to be an old-fashioned armlock. Bat wings fluttered for leverage as the bat-thing hissed hatred.

The guy glanced at Ice while struggling with his hold on the beast. "Get moving! Through the door!"

Ice stood and regarded the hole in the wall.

"Not *that*! Fuck that! The *door*!"

The creature, perhaps realizing that a simple joint lock meant nothing to it, beat its wings more vigorously, thrashing in the man's grip. Its skull cracked backward, attempting to connect with the guy's head buried between its shoulder blades.

"Run!" the guy shouted.

Ice ran through the doorway and nearly clipped a shoulder on the frame. A short hallway led into a living room that might've been overpowered by a tsunami. Another hole dotted the far wall, and Ice stopped beside an upturned coffee table, spinning around and wondering where to go.

His rescuer bolted through the bedroom door, slamming it shut behind him. "Through the hole!"

Behind him, a force slammed into the door. The wood bulged like a huge paint-crackling welt threatening to burst.

Ice stepped aside as the bigger man ran by him and dove headfirst through the jagged hole. Wood splintered behind Ice, prompting him to run and leap headlong after his rescuer. He landed in a heap.

The man, a huge burly type, darted to the right and headed toward another door. Ice followed as the creature shrieked behind him. He cleared the apartment's main door, and the guy pulled it shut behind him.

"This way," the man huffed.

An elevator lay to the right, but the man ignored it. Instead, he opened another apartment door on his left and urged Ice to enter. A scrabbling of claws on floor tiles got Ice moving.

Once they were both inside, the big man slammed the door shut and locked it. "Come on, we're not safe yet," he said and hurried into the darker regions of the condo.

"Where are we?" Ice asked but was ignored. A nerve-wracking force thumped against the door, followed by a caterwauling that put Ice's nerves on edge. The thing knew it was losing the race, and it was pissed off. The two men passed an entire wall of bare windows, and the distant city lights of Halifax gleamed like a table spread with candles. The stranger led Ice through yet another man-sized hole right beside an immense widescreen television.

"Holy shit," Ice whispered when his rescuer had paused over a dark opening in the floor. "What's with all the fucking holes?"

"Hop down, and I'll tell you everything," the guy said, a heavy beard visible on his face. "You got a phone?"

"Yeah."

The monster pursuing them slammed and hammered at the last closed barrier.

"The main doors are all reinforced," the bearded guy reported, and he gripped the hole's edges and lowered himself with a grunt. "But it'll find another way. Come on."

Ice followed and kept his mouth shut. He lowered himself through the floor, his legs cycling in the air for a moment before a set of arms steadied them. Ice landed on a soft sofa and proceeded to shadow the big guy through a veritable maze of apartments, doorways, and connecting holeways, dropping down through the floor again at several points. The big guy got winded, his actions slowing, and Ice realized his own strength waned as they descended level by level.

Perhaps fifteen minutes later, after a confusing network of openings both constructed and unnatural, they stepped through an apartment door and closed it. There were three locks, and Ice's rescuer used every one.

"There," the guy panted, bent over and holding his knees. "Okay. All right, then."

"You okay?" Ice asked.

"Me? Yeah. Just beat is all. I'll be fine. We're safe in here."

Ice glanced around the place, not seeing anything to differentiate that apartment from any of the others.

"In here," the guy said and led Ice across a hardwood surface that crackled as if sprinkled with sand. The man didn't bother with turning on the lights, but once he was in the kitchen, he reached over an electric oven and flicked on a small light, revealing a windowless alcove. "I'm Sweeney," he said, slumping into a stylish chair he'd pulled from a table somewhere. Ice leaned against a counter, waiting for his newfound companion to steady his breath.

"You got that phone?" Sweeney eventually asked. "I lost mine a couple days ago."

Ice hesitated and dug his flip phone out.

"A dumb ass, I see," Sweeney said with a tired smile.

"Pardon?"

"The phone," Sweeney said, taking the device. "Old style. No nonsense. I like."

The larger man opened it and considered the glow. "Listen, we're safe here. For a while, anyway. Now, they probably know we're here, but they won't come in."

"They won't?" Ice's voice squeaked, and he cleared his throat.

"No, they won't. For some reason, they don't like salt. Whoever lived here before doused the floors with salt. Sprinkled that shit all over the floors, across windowsills, any entry point. There was half a box of it in a cupboard."

Ice blinked. "They?"

"Yeah," Sweeney huffed and regarded Ice. "I was near the door when I heard the elevator go up. Knew you were on it. No one else uses it but them."

"What are they?" Ice asked when Sweeney straightened.

"Fuck if I know," the big man said and rattled the phone at Ice. "But I know a guy who does. But if I had to guess? With those wings? And those teeth? I'd say they're vampires."

"Vampires," Ice whispered in horrified awe.

"Vampires," Sweeney repeated and thumbed in a number.

"But they don't have any legs. Or…"

"Yeah." Sweeney nodded. "The lower half, right? Is that shit freaky, or is that freaky? Like an episode of the *Twilight Zone*, man."

Ice readied another question, but Sweeney held up a hand to invoke silence. His face became stern while Ice glanced around the nondescript, modern kitchen with about half of its cherrywood cupboards opened.

"You gotta be fucking kidding me," Sweeney swore after a moment and shook his head. "Holy shit. Lance? You there? Pick up the fucking phone if you are. This is Stu Sweeney. Calling from Halifax. We met on that Barrister couple case over in Seattle seven years ago. The ones who parked their car off a highway and walked off into the bush. Give me a call back on this number. I'll be waiting. Can't believe I'm saying this, but *I have a goddamn vampire problem in Halifax.*"

**8**

The weight of Sweeney's words fell onto Ice's consciousness like a strongman's hammer ringing the bell of an old carnival's Test Your Strength game.

"Vampires," Ice repeated, numbed by the word.

That earned him a look. Sweeney glared and lowered the phone. "This thing set to vibrate or ring?"

"Vibrate."

"You look like a vibrator kinda guy. For phones, I mean."

"Yeah. Yeah, vibrator. Listen"—Ice held out his hands as if holding a head—"vampires? I mean… *vampires?*"

"I mean bloodsucking, undead, cock-swinging, sonsabitches vampires," Sweeney said with narrowed eyes. "This place. This whole building is a fucking nest. There's no one living in any of these apartments from the fifteenth floor down."

"What?" Isosceles whispered.

"Yeah, it's like that."

"What's below the fifteenth floor?"

"I don't know." Sweeney shrugged. "I can't get down there. The stairwell ends on that level. Demolished. I mean, the steps just stop like they were broken off. And it stinks. Like meat caught in a sink trap. I don't mind telling you I don't want to find out what's down there. It's like someone dropped a goddamn bomb down its throat or something. But there's an earthy smell too, as if someone's trying to heap dirt on it, burying God knows what. Anyway, can't get down that way, and the elevator only stops on the nineteenth or the twentieth. There's like twenty-five floors, and the top one is a penthouse. Between that and the fifteenth, this was the only one that had any salt. They avoid it like it was an overflowing shithouse."

"Vampires," Ice muttered, feeling as if he'd slipped through the ass crack of reality.

"Yeah, vampires. Move past that, okay? Keep up with me here. I'm a private investigator. I came here looking for a missing woman. Some cock bait lured her here—or so I'm guessing—and made her disappear. I came up in the elevator, and when the doors opened, one of those fuckers came sailing in. I was standing to one side when it happened. Missed me, but in the scrimmage, I lost my cell phone. I ran through a series of apartments, just like we did now, opening and closing doors behind me, with that godless fuckhead on my tail. Dropped a few floors through them holes and eventually wound up here. They wouldn't come in here for whatever reason, and I later deduced it was because someone had the good sense to throw salt around in here. This place saved my ass, big time. Only reason I'm still alive. Been here for the last two days. Haven't seen anyone except you. Not even the goddamn cops I thought were gonna back me up came here. They left me high and dry."

"Salt," Ice said.

"You're quick," Sweeney said with a sarcastic glare. "I can tell."

"Why didn't you make a break for the elevator?"

Sweeney lowered his head. "They were out there, waiting for me to do just that. I couldn't see them, but I could feel them. Like they were cats cozied up to a baseboard, right by the mouse hole, waiting for me to show my head. Not always, but I could never be sure when. And when I chanced it, I just explored the nearby apartments. The elevator? Whenever I pushed the button, the damn thing started up like a dinner bell. I could feel something closing in, so I never chanced waiting for it to arrive. Like being on a raft and risking a swim in shark-infested waters."

Ice sank to the floor. "Holy shit."

"Yeah."

"Call the cops."

"Already called the cops before I stepped on the elevator. They didn't come. I don't know what's going on there. Hate to say it, but they might be in on this."

"The cops?"

Sweeney nodded solemnly.

"What are we… What are we gonna…"

"Yeah, well, I know a guy," Sweeney said, his tone softening, "a guy I worked with over on the west coast a few years back. I thought he was a weirdo, y'know? Called Lance Chambers. A paranormal investigator of boogeymen and shit like that. A ghost hunter. Fuckin' ghost hunters. I mean, I was smellin' bullshit the whole time, like it was cologne or something. Eau d'bullshit. Anyway, we were called in to find a missing couple—husband and wife who, by all accounts, were out for a Sunday drive and never came back home. Their car was found on a highway, pulled over onto the shoulder, but they were gone without a trace. No sign of a struggle. Never did find them, or at least I didn't, but about halfway through the investigation, when I started to get to know this ghost hunter guy over a few beers, well, he brought up things that made sense to me. Mysterious things."

"Like what?" Ice asked, still reeling from the dropkick revelation of vampires.

"Things," Sweeney said softly, lost in memory. "Like, things ordinary people don't know. Don't *wanna* know.

Monsters and ghosts and demons and shit like that. Anyway, let's just say we parted ways with me being a lot less skeptical. Lo and behold, this happens. Just my goddamn luck."

"I can't think," Ice said, holding his head. "I can't think on this."

"Take your time," Sweeney said. "I ain't doing nothin' until I can get in touch with Chambers. He'll know what to do."

"Where's he live?"

"Stateside, somewhere. Don't worry. If there was anything I got from him, is that *this* is his kinda shit. He'll call back. Guaranteed."

He stopped talking and hefted the phone as he inspected his midsection. Sweeney wore a light fall jacket and a shirt and jeans underneath. The shirt had been shredded, revealing a black padded vest.

Sweeney caught Ice staring. "This saved my life. Always wear it when I'm on the job, and in the dozen or so years of working this shit, I've never had any trouble. No one tried to stab or shoot me. Not even a fist fight. Plenty of hard stares and all, but no bodily harm. You believe I was sorta thinking about tossing it away? It was getting too tight around the gut. Fuck me gently. Gonna get one custom-*made* for me after this episode. Damn vest kept my innards from seeing the light of day."

"Vampires," Ice whispered.

"Yeah," Sweeney agreed and prodded the vest.

They settled in and waited.

*

After a couple of hours, the phone buzzed in the private investigator's hand, startling Ice with its urgency.

Sweeney answered. "Yeah, man, that you? Excellent, excellent. Hold on a sec."

The private investigator sat down beside Ice, angling the phone so they could both hear or speak.

"Yeah, I got another guy here listening," Sweeney reported. "Okay, listen, fuck me for having to call you up, but I'm riding a shit geyser here."

"So you said," Lance Chambers said in a deep-rooted drawl that reminded Ice of old tough-guy actors from the forties and fifties. "You said vampires. You sure of that?"

"Uh… yeah."

"All right, describe the vampire to me, and don't leave anything out."

Sweeney scowled. "Man-sized. Leather wings. Mouth full of teeth. Claws. Real strong. Looks like one of those South African tiger fish."

"And only has half a body," Ice blurted.

"Yeah, and only has half a body," Sweeney agreed. "From the waist up."

No response from the other end.

"Lance?" Sweeney asked.

"Yeah, taking notes here," Chambers replied. "All right, anything else?"

"Yeah, I tracked one of them to an apartment building," Sweeney explained. "A female. Dressed to kill. She picked up some guy at a nightclub and brought him here. When she was in the club, like, everyone noticed her, but no one approached her. It was fucked up."

"Got it. Anything else?"

Sweeney thought about it and glanced at Ice.

"They cut holes in the ceilings and walls of the apartments," Ice supplied.

"Yeah, you hear that, Lance?"

"Heard it. In an apartment building?"

"High-rise condo," Sweeney said. "Right through the concrete floor and ceiling and between the metal trusses. Place is like a goddamn honeycomb right now."

Silence again. "How many are there, do you think?"

"At least two," Sweeney reported. "A woman and a guy."

"Two?" Chambers sounded surprised. "How're you still alive?"

"'Cause for an old guy, I still move faster than shit through a goose," Sweeney remarked.

"Funny. No, I mean you have a crucifix? Garlic?"

"Ah, we're in an apartment with a shitload of salt on the floor."

"All right."

"So, wooden stake through the heart?" Sweeney asked hopefully.

"Wooden stake? No. No wooden stake."

"That's what they do in the movies."

"And that works in the movies, except this ain't the movies and you aren't fighting a traditional vampire."

Sweeney and Ice exchanged incredulous looks.

"I gotta call someone, all right?" Chambers said. "Clarify some shit. But right now, you stay where you are and wait for my call back. Don't leave that apartment. Hear me? And for the record, I don't think you're up against a true vampire."

"What is it, then?" Sweeney asked.

"I'll find out. Hold on and stay put."

"Should I try callin' the cops again?"

"Don't bother. If those critters are set up like you say they are, they probably have the cops and every other department under their influence. Just sit tight."

*Click.*

Sweeney held the phone out at arm's length. "Well, that was informative."

"So we wait here?" Ice asked.

"Yeah." Sweeney checked the phone's time. "It's 6:44."

The private investigator studied Ice. "What's your name?"

"Isosceles."

"Isosceles?" Sweeney smiled, the faint light from the oven rendering his hard face almost friendly. "That's a new one."

"My folks thought so."

"Different name. Noble sounding. But I bet people call you Ice all the time."

"Yeah, they do."

"Better than being named after a piece of furniture. Or some other goddamn inanimate object."

Ice nodded that it was.

"And why are you here?" Sweeney asked.

"Delivering pizza."

That perked Sweeney's eyebrows. "Pizza?"

"Yeah."

"Oh, man. Where is it?"

Ice pointed to the ceiling. "Meat lover's special. Still in the elevator."

"Well, shit. I've been here for two days living on fumes. There's water in those taps and electricity but nothing to eat. And don't open the fridges unless you want a face full of spores."

"How is this place still going?" Ice asked.

"Damned if I know," Sweeney answered. "But I think a

vampire can hypnotize a person. I've seen it in action. Something like that might have happened. Like Chambers said, under their influence."

"But *all* of them?"

Sweeney shrugged. "At least the important ones. Who knows?"

They stopped talking then, and the private investigator studied Ice.

"How you doing?" Sweeney asked after a few heartbeats.

"Me? Okay, I guess."

"Not faint or sick?"

"What? No. No, I feel fine. Just surprised by all this, y'know?"

"That's good."

Ice shrugged. "Never was one for getting scared. Not much. Not like other people. I hold up under stress pretty good. Up till now, the only thing that freaked me out was speaking in front of a crowd."

"You're holding up well," Sweeney acknowledged. "Just stay in that mind-set. We'll get—"

The phone rang.

# 9

"Yeah," Lance Chambers said in a stoic voice. "Okay, you're both there, right? Okay, listen. You might have a problem. That thing you described to me? I was half right. It's not a straight-out vampire."

"It's not?" Sweeney asked.

"It's not. My guy tells me it's a manananggal."

"A many-angle what?"

"A manananggal," Chambers repeated.

"Say it in English."

"I *am* saying it in English. Mana-nang-gal."

"Christ, couldn't you just call it Sally or Bucky or something?"

The line went silent with an irritated vibe.

"All right, all right, a mana fuck me gal," Sweeney whispered, pinching the bridge of his nose.

"Manananggal," Ice repeated, nailing it the first time.

"That's it," Chambers verified.

"Okay, one of us can say it," Sweeney muttered.

"All right," Lance said. "Anyway, this thing isn't a vampire."

"I think it's a vampire," Ice mumbled dubiously.

"Yeah, well, I think you should just wait until I finish, okay? Since it's your ass in the dinner sling."

That shut Ice up.

"Okay." Chambers brought himself under control. "Anyway, it's not a vampire. It's got vampire characteristics, granted, but it's not a true vampire. Some say the thing's a witch. Other sources say it's a demon returned to earth.

Regardless, it's a can of pressurized shitstorm held to your ear if you encounter one, and it'll drain your ass of blood like a thirsty alcoholic at an open bar. And we figure if it's not a manananggal, it's a breed thereof. But even if it's a breed of some kind, there's a chance the one after your asses might have some of its weaknesses."

Sweeney and Ice exchanged a look above the phone.

"Now, listen, okay?" Chambers continued. "I've got good news for you and bad news. The bad news is, if it is a manananggal or some kind of offshoot, it's going to be hard to kill. That's the bad news. The good news is… you *can* kill it."

"Great," Sweeney said, not overly enthused. "How do we do that?"

"It's dark now, right? The sun's gone down?"

"Yeah. Long ago."

"And you're in a room covered in salt?" Chambers asked.

"Ah, yeah. Floor is. And some of the windowsills."

"Okay, more bad news."

Sweeney and Ice winced.

"The only way to kill the thing is when it's split in two, okay? With these things, you have to find the bottom part of the body. The waist down. Find that and—"

"Drive a stake through it?" Sweeney interrupted.

"No, not a stake. Smear salt over the exposed part. The part with the raw guts."

The two men regarded each other with horrified looks.

"You guys still there?"

"Yeah," Sweeney said.

"All right, listen, as nasty as that sounds, it's the only way to kill it. You have to defile the lower half with either salt— which you have—or ash. Either of you smoke?"

Ice shook his head.

"No," Sweeney reported.

"Too bad. Okay, you have the salt. Gather up what you can of it, okay? Find the lower half and smear salt into the raw bits."

"How's that supposed to kill it?" Sweeney asked.

"I'm getting to that," Chambers answered testily. "Just relax and listen. Okay, Sween? You listen, and you concentrate on what you have to do, because from the sound of it, you're in for a long night. Got it?"

"Yeah."

"If you can start a fire somehow and gather up the ashes, you can smear that in there too. Either salt or ash will ruin the bottom half. Just a pinch of it will do the job. The manananggal won't be able to rejoin or take its human form again if the lower half is tainted by either. And once that's done, it can only wait until the sun comes up, at which time it'll die."

"Sunlight will kill it?" Ice blurted.

"Sunlight or the very arrival of dawn. Cool, huh? That's enough to destroy it. Some good news there. But my guy says exposure to sunlight will probably kill it too when it's just a torso. All the vampiric breeds have an aversion to the sun. Oh, garlic will work the same as ash, too."

Sweeney rattled his head as if it were nearly full. "Garlic. That all?"

"Wouldn't happen to have a whip fashioned from a stingray's tail, would you?" Chambers asked.

"You're makin' this shit up."

"Swear to God, I'm not."

"No, I do not have a stingray-tail whip."

"That's too bad." Lance paused. "Be cool to see, though."

"Any other options here?" Sweeney rubbed his face.

"No. Chances are the thing's been around long enough to hypnotize anyone in a position to hide their existence. I'm talking about mesmerizing folks to do their bidding. You're in an apartment building, right?"

"Yeah, fifteenth floor."

"No way down?"

"Stairs are out, and the elevators only seem to work when the pizza guys visit."

"That's convenient," Chambers said. "Well, then, yeah. My guess is you're fucked."

Ice almost shat himself right there.

Chambers continued, "Sorry, that's harsh. Okay, choices. Here you go. You can either stay where you are, and maybe someone will call the cops, or some other miracle will happen so you won't starve to death. But something tells me these things got that covered, somehow. If they've cleared out the upper levels of an apartment building and made it into a nest, they've been around for a while, so I wouldn't hope for anyone besides more pizza guys coming around. Waiting for the sun to come up won't help, as the thing will only retreat to its lower half and take on its human form. It can walk around in the daylight when it's connected. Might even come for you then."

"Been here two days, and it hasn't happened yet," Sweeney said.

"Really? That's interesting," Chambers admitted over the scratchy phone connection. "Well, anyway, night is the most dangerous time, when it breaks away. I mean, you see a torso flying at you with bat wings and guts hanging out, well, most people will freeze long enough for it to kill them."

"Is there an emergency ladder or something?" Ice asked.

Sweeney's head rolled on his shoulders. "Already looked but haven't found anything."

After a solemn pause, Chambers asked, "You need anything else?"

"Ash, salt, and garlic." Sweeney sighed. "I know a chicken place that would drop this thing in a heartbeat."

"Look, if you don't kill it, it'll wait you out," Chambers warned. "Probably already doing it, y'see? Time and eternal hunger are all these things got. The person who dumped that salt on the floor? Who knows what happened to him, but I can tell you, he probably crawled to *them* in the end. Think about that."

Sweeney and Ice regarded each other again.

"All right," Chambers said in a determined voice. "You have another choice. I'll hit the books here real quick and see if I can't find anything else, then I'll grab whatever I can and fly up there. So instead of you going amateur night, just hold tight 'til I get there."

That lifted Ice's spirits. "You're coming here?"

"Oh, hell yeah," Chambers said as the scratching on the line increased. "Not going to leave you two to a pair of degenerate night-bitches from hell. But you're paying for my flight, Sween. A return flight. And any other expenses incurred."

"Anything, anything."

"All right. Thing is, I probably won't get there anytime soon even if I can get on a plane. You hear what I'm saying? You're on your own for the next five or six hours at least, so stay sharp. Don't bother contacting anyone else, okay? They might be under the thing's influence. You guys did good calling me. I'll do what I can here. Stay alive. Call me again if you have any questions or updates. Otherwise, with luck,

I'll meet you at the front door at the crack of dawn, and we'll take turns shoving a salt lick up this thing's ass."

Sweeney quickly gave Lance the address to the building.

"Got it. Okay, guys. So forget what I said about starving there, okay? Just sit tight, stay on the salt, and wait for me. Got it?"

"Got it," both men said in unison.

Lance hung up, and Sweeney flipped the phone shut. He smiled and waved the device at Ice. "Thank Christ you came along when you did."

"Yeah," Ice said weakly.

"Don't worry. Don't worry. This is Lance's specialty. I feel better already. All the while I was crawling around here, I was asking myself what he would do in this situation. That and looking for a phone or a way down."

Ice looked at his knees. "Yeah."

"What's the matter, then? You sick? Nerves finally getting to you?"

"What? No, nothing like that."

"Well, what then? We're going to be here for the next few hours, probably until dawn. Might as well talk about something while we're trying to stay awake."

"Don't think I could sleep anyway."

"I heard that. So what's on your mind?"

Ice took a breath and checked out the kitchen. It was a small affair, a nook placed in the middle of everything else as an afterthought—electric oven, white cupboards, and an ordinary backsplash. "Something your friend said. You've been here for two days."

"Yeah."

"And it hasn't tried to get you? Even though it could join itself and walk around in daylight."

Sweeney's brow furrowed.

"And then it—or someone—ordered pizza, bringing me here."

"Yeah? So?"

Ice looked the bearded man in the eye. "So my question is… what the fuck is it waiting for?"

## 10

The manananggal called Crisanto pulled away from the apartment door and frowned, its demonic grey-black features becoming even more frightening. He'd only just arrived at the apartment, confirming his suspicions that they'd holed up inside the one condo he could not enter. The first man's escape had been an amusing mistake, but without a means of communicating with the outside world, he was a mouse scurrying along the walls of a bear trap. Crisanto had already discussed the trapped man's fate with Calithea, and they both decided that, when the time came, Sweeney—he'd overheard both men's names—would serve as a replacement for the failing Leonard. The entrance guard's time was nearing an end. Crisanto had been surprised when Sweeney found refuge in Leonard's old apartment. The foreshadowing wasn't lost upon Calithea.

But a second man was hiding with Sweeney, and Crisanto knew from hundreds of years of experience that while one man could be controlled, two could be a problem, and both his and Calithea's continuing survival depended upon decisively dealing with problems. If Crisanto had heard correctly, and he knew he had, then a third man was on his way. Three men—a serious problem which demanded attention. Crisanto's massive head bobbed and grunted.

Allowing Sweeney to live had been acceptable. He had no cell phone, as Crisanto had discovered the dropped device and crushed it. The man's creeping around the maze of the upper levels had even amused Crisanto. Sweeney believed his attempts at stealth effective, but in truth, he was a newborn scurrying about on hands and knees. The manananggal had tracked him easily.

Failing to kill the pizza man, however, troubled Crisanto. He knew that was a terrible mistake on his part. Calithea would not be pleased, especially since the one called Isosceles actually possessed a working cell phone. Crisanto was responsible for both failed attempts, and even though he knew Calithea would be angered, she would help in dealing with the situation.

Crisanto rustled his leathery wings, wanting to spread them and fly under the moonlight, but that night's hunt would be inside their roost. With Isosceles's possession of a cell phone and the contacting of a third man, Crisanto wondered if the days ahead would be filled with searching for a new nest. The thought soured his mood even more. For many years, he and Calithea had existed on the fringes of the city, preying on the unsuspecting, "ordering takeout," and easily manipulating men and women in places of authority into doing their bidding and concealing their activities, whether by diverting investigations that led to the building or simply by keeping the electricity and water going.

But with a third human aware of Crisanto's and Calithea's existence, and with him being well away from their grasp, their urban fortress was no longer secure. Sweeney's contact might have already been spreading that knowledge to another set of ears, the leak becoming impossible to contain. Crisanto considered capture and interrogation, if anyone attempted a rescue for Sweeney within the next day or so, to find out who else might know of their presence within the dwelling.

Even then, Crisanto doubted he and Calithea would be able to stay in Halifax.

He retraced his way through the labyrinth of the upper floors, pulling himself along floors and walls with his claws, hopping through holes with the aid of his wings if necessary. At one point, he paused for several minutes, wondering if he should even alert Calithea at all. He decided he would, of course. They'd been together for so long they were practically a single entity. He knew she would sense something troubling him.

He reached an apartment with the picture windows removed and flew up the side of the building, rising to the penthouse. Behind him, the city glowed with candlelight splendor. Crisanto reached an exposed terrace and perched on an ornate table, his trailing entrails smacking the furniture's surface and leaving a stain. The terrace doors were open, and the night breeze rustled a wall of curtains. He flew to them, parted the heavy fabric, and entered into a magnificent cavern befitting a king and queen of the night. Crowns of crystal, their tips lit, hung from an arched ceiling while marble floors and dark wood gleamed underneath the chandelier's majestic glow. Hundreds of unlit candles decorated heavy tables and ledges while a flat television the size of a door hung on a wall, positioned before a plush curve-around living-room set. A huge mural decorated one wall, depicting a hand-painted cityscape beneath a blood moon.

All Calithea's tastes.

Crisanto maneuvered himself over a bare table and plopped down upon it. He leaned forward, ape-like, and gripped the rounded edges while searching the shadows of the room.

There, at the top of a curved staircase, stood Calithea.

Even in his inhuman state, Crisanto allowed himself a moment to savor the unholy perfection that was his mate, the queen of his unlife for centuries. She remained poised at the top of the steps, wearing only the sheerest wisp of fabric that drew the eye to the erotic outline of her breasts. The garment hung off her shoulders with spaghetti strings, the hem stopping just below her pelvic region. Calithea remained very much aware of the styles through the years, discarding most but holding on to the more sensual designs, the more carnal ones.

Crisanto admitted he never understood all the fashions, some of which left very little to the imagination. Not that it bothered him. Calithea was perfection.

"We have another guest," he rasped, tongue writhing between oversized teeth. "A man."

"Did you order pizza again?" she asked, her voice a sultry blend of restless surf and wind-rustled deep woods.

Crisanto looked away. "The man's name is Sweeney. He saved the new meat."

Calithea didn't answer, waiting for more.

Crisanto explained to her how he'd fouled his attempt at killing the pizza man. He described the resulting chase that ended with both men finding refuge in the one place neither he nor Calithea could enter. He told her what he'd heard of their conversation, watching her face when he revealed the men possessed a working phone. Which they used.

"You should've had Leonard clean his apartment," Crisanto accused her at the end.

Calithea didn't respond, and that alone scalded Crisanto. He knew what she was thinking. She'd warned him several times in the past about his increasingly sloppy ways, how his lazy hunting and disregard for caution would cause trouble. And he was presently seeking her aid in clearing up one of his problems.

"We should have killed Sweeney," Crisanto whispered.

"I like him," Calithea said. "He was to replace Leonard."

"There's no time to break him like Leonard. More may be on the way."

The lady of the house lifted her chin by a hair, the barest movement, but the meaning was clear.

"This is your fault," she whispered, the words lancing Crisanto like sunbeams. "Time has made you overconfident. Careless."

Crisanto didn't answer, conceding the point. "No more. Not after this."

Calithea's lips puckered with displeasure, and she descended. Her bare feet were soundless, taking each step with infinite care. "Never again."

He nodded.

"The damage is done," she said, her voice almost a song. Her eyes bored into him. "This place has somehow dulled you. I wish to return to the bigger cities. I wish to return to the hunting ground of New York. Tokyo. São Paulo. We enjoyed ourselves there. You were sharper there."

Crisanto nodded reluctantly.

"We can return to one of our earlier nests." She reached the bottom of the stairs. "Or build another. One to surpass all of this."

The closer she came, the more Crisanto wished to rip that annoying cloth from her body and ravish her. He studied her charms with undisguised lechery.

"Will you help me… lure them out?" he growled. His hand rose as she stopped before him. An intoxicating fragrance invaded his senses, awakening dark urges and igniting animal pleasures. He drew a single claw down the front of her one-piece. The contact tightened the material in places he very much liked.

Despite Crisanto's true, horrific appearance, Calithea placed a palm at the back of his head and pulled him forward, tilting her face. His attention was lost in her cleavage and the open valley of her neck.

Her lips stopped just before his fanged maw.

"My dearest," she whispered, a coy smile hinting at the corners of her mouth. "After all you told me, if I'm not mistaken, you've already… unknowingly lured them out from their bastion."

Crisanto grunted puzzlement, studying her eyes as her fingers massaged his curls.

"You still haven't realized your mistake, have you?" She sighed.

"Stop tormenting me."

"Your legs, dearest." Her smile widened into a cold sliver of moon rock, and her tangled hand became a fist, steadying Crisanto's head.

His eyes widened.

"Where have you left your legs?"

## 11

"You said you're a private investigator, right?" Ice shifted against the counter.

"Yeah. Why?"

"How come you don't have any weapons?"

"Weapons." Sweeney smirked. "Like what?"

"Guns, knives…"

"This ain't TV. A PI can't carry shit like that around here. Not legally."

"So not even a knife?" Ice asked.

"Not even a knife. The best I can do is a baton. One of those extendable jobs. One flick of the wrist, and it comes out, right? Otherwise, that's it. Besides the vest here."

"Just a vest."

"Hey, Ice, look at me. I'm six two—six three and a half if I wear my cowboy boots—three hundred and fifty pounds, and a hundred of that is bullet-stopping lard. The muscle might be under a layer of beer fat, but it's there. I won't list off my black belts, but just know that I can throw down if I have to. Not that I have to. Most guys usually see the size of me and back off pretty quick."

Ice didn't say anything to that but then realized something. "Holy shit."

"What?"

"I know where the fucker's legs are."

Sweeney froze. "You do?"

"I saw them on the floor where that thing tried to get me. Right outside the elevator like it was waiting for a bus or something."

"You sure?"

"Jesus Christ, it wasn't a goddamn fern stuck in a corner! It was a fucking set of *legs*!"

"All right, I believe you." Sweeney said.

"So what do we do?"

"Huh?"

"What do we do? The legs are right there. I bet half the reason Lance wants us to stay here is because searching for the lower bit of this manny-cock gobbler is too dangerous for us. And if being separated from the lower part is a pretty big weakness, I'd say chances are it's still up there."

"Yeah, and since being separated from the lower part is a pretty big weakness, it might have gone back"—Sweeney rubbed his chin—"because it's vulnerable."

"Maybe, but that bastard chased me all over the place. I say there's a good chance it's still there. He doesn't know we know how to kill it. He could very well be out there, just lurking or hunting or even flown over to Barrington for a quick bite."

Sweeney mulled. "It's a risk."

"A big risk, but maybe we should check it out—scratch up a couple of fistfuls of this salt here and go find it."

"Ain't that much here."

"Look, I say we take what we can, put it into little baggies if you got any, and we go back up there and fuck up that free-floating undead half-squat."

Sweeney still wasn't convinced.

"What's the matter?" Ice asked, annoyed. "You saved my ass back there with pure bare balls when you pinned manny nut-dangler against the wall, and thinking more on it, why didn't you have any salt on you then?"

"I didn't know—didn't realize I could use it like that." Sweeney shrugged.

"We know now."

"Yeah, we do."

The silence stretched on between them as Sweeney gave the matter a good long thinking.

"Might never get another chance," Ice said in a low voice, peeking at Sweeney from beneath his brow.

"All right," the bearded private investigator said. "Let's do it."

"You sure?"

"Yeah."

"All right," an eager Ice growled between clenched teeth.

They got to work. Sweeney searched the cupboards, found a stack of paper cups, and pulled out half a box of salt. Sweeney lined up the cups on the counter while Ice poured out a shaky stream, quickly spilling the mineral.

"Give me that." Sweeney held out his hand. "Thought you said you were okay."

"I was okay."

"You're not okay now."

"Just caught up with me is all." Ice rubbed his hands and shrugged. "I'm good. Really."

"Listen, I'm just glad you're not shitting yourself."

The private investigator poured about three teaspoons of salt into each cup, preparing seven shots. Of those, Ice took three and Sweeney took three, keeping one in hand and pocketing the others. They left one half-full cup on the kitchen countertop.

"A reserve," Sweeney said, "Just in case we need it."

"Doesn't look like much," Ice said, pinching the tops of the paper cups together to make seals of a sort.

"Lance said just a pinch will do the job," Sweeney said, "and there's more than a pinch in each of these."

"We have a backup plan?"

"No."

"We should."

Sweeney thought about it. "All right, how about this. There's at least two of them. We're going for the one with the legs in the hall. We get those legs, sprinkle them, and get back here. Wait for the sun and Lance, and hopefully this shit works, and we'll kill one of them fuckers off. Then it's three against one. You can bet Chambers will be bringing some salt, so once he gets here, we can go hunting in the day. Should be safer. How's all that sound?"

Ice nodded. "Sounds good. Let's do it."

"You're pretty keen now," Sweeney observed.

"This is kinda exciting," Ice said. "I mean, to a guy who cleans shit out of apartments all day and delivers pizza at night, this rocks."

"Yeah, well, just keep your head on straight and watch your ass. Watch my back too while you're at it. These things have killed people. Hell, probably have *eaten* people. So don't be getting cocky. I'll jack-slap you if you do."

"Right. I won't," Ice promised and meant it.

"Okay, we'll take the stairs to the eighteenth," Sweeney whispered at the entrance to the apartment.

"The stairs aren't out?"

"They're out at the fifteenth. As far as I know, the rest is good, right up to the top."

"What's at the top?"

"More apartments, I guess." Sweeney said.

"You never got up there?"

"No."

"Okay," Ice said, ready to get moving. "Let's go."

When they opened the apartment's entrance, they

appeared to have opened a portal to a void. Nothing but black empty hallway greeted them. Ice switched on his cellphone light and gave it to Sweeney, who held it out like a torch.

"You charge this thing today?" Sweeney asked.

"It's good."

"For how long?"

Ice shrugged. "I don't know. Never used it like this before."

Sweeney nodded and looked ahead. A pair of doors, one open, one shut, could be seen. The private investigator went forward, leading Ice. The air smelled of fresh, nighttime cold as a subtle breeze moved through, issuing from the open doorway. The radius of light uncovered more doors left ajar.

"Some windows are opened," Sweeney whispered. "Keeps the stink down."

"What stink?"

"Just wait."

The hall's carpeting dampened the sound of their footsteps, but Ice tensed up whenever they approached an open door. They paused at each entrance and chanced a quick peek inside before darting past the threshold. They followed the wall, passing two more open doorways. A third door, a good twenty feet back from the elevators, had the ubiquitous Exit sign just above it. They reached the stairwell without incident, and Sweeney, with his cup-holding hand, turned the knob. The men cringed at the loud click, as ominous as a shotgun being pumped. After a few seconds, Sweeney swung the door open.

Foul air gushed into Ice's face, stunning him with a raw stench of carrion. He turned his head in a vain attempt to escape the blast.

"Oh, shit," he whispered and put a wrist to his nose.

Sweeney didn't say a word. The big PI placed his back against the door, stifling its metallic yawn, and held the cell phone high. The light illuminated white walls and concrete stairs going down and up into oblivion. The smell enveloped them, polluting their airways and tainting their lungs.

"This way," Sweeney gasped, suggesting he didn't want to spare the air to utter the words—air that would be replaced by the crypt gas filling the stairwell.

"What is that?" Ice asked as they climbed, their shoulders sliding against white-painted cement blocks.

"Don't know," Sweeney replied. "Always bad in here. From below. Like someone's been using the stairwell as a garbage disposal. One thing for sure—that's meat."

Ice agreed. He'd opened enough refrigerators and been repulsed by decomposing beef and fish and shit he couldn't bear to identify—cuts of organic matter that made him wish he'd worn biohazard gear instead of flimsy latex cleaning gloves. The dreaded fridge always was an olfactory jack-in-the-box. In that stairwell, however, the smell was borderline overpowering. Ice's eyes watered, and his gullet hitched ominously.

"Oh, shit." He panted, twisting his head left and right in a vain attempt to escape the smell.

"Come on." Sweeney's face scrunched up as if being squeezed for juice in a tightening vise.

They climbed, unable to silence their gasping, the sounds carrying in the stairwell. The cell phone's light brightened the way a step at a time. When they reached the first landing, Ice felt as if he were rising from something's throat, one in dire need of gargling. They stopped at the landing, and Sweeney held up a hand, wanting to listen. Ice tried to be quiet, wondering if being gassed might compare to the weakness he felt in his knees. He peeked miserably at Sweeney, who leaned around the next corner, trying to discern danger. Sound other than what they were making didn't exist around them, and their footfalls lingered long and loud enough to make Ice wince and fidget.

Sweeney held a wrist over the light, cutting the angle so that it wouldn't be so noticeable from overhead. He motioned for Ice to follow, and they rose unchallenged to the next landing.

Ice stopped halfway between the sixteenth and the seventeenth floors.

"What is it?" Sweeney asked, immediately returning to his companion's side when Ice faltered.

"Oh, God," Ice gasped, leaning heavily against the wall. "We gotta get outta here. I can't breathe anymore."

"Yeah," Sweeney rasped, his face a white sheet in the light. "Yeah. Next landing, okay?"

Ice nodded, not knowing if he could make it or not.

To his surprise, he did. They reached the seventeenth floor, and Sweeney grasped the doorknob like an exhausted swimmer latching onto a pier. A distant slam from above caused both men to flinch and look to the stairs continuing above them. Sweeney raised his cup, poised to throw. The edges of the little globe of light trembled as the PI's hand shook, the darkness jiggling with every flicker, and both men wondered what would descend from the stairwell's heights. Ice tried to ignore the snare drum that was his heart, tried to tell himself he wasn't afraid, he hadn't even had to pay to enter that house of horror, and diamonds really did fall from the skies of Saturn and Jupiter.

After seconds of nothing, Sweeney opened the door

before them and pulled Ice inside. The PI shut the door, cutting off the diseased air.

"What was that?" Ice huffed, taking in great purging lungfuls and not complaining in the least about the dust he tasted. Compared to the smell in the stairwell, the filth on the air was as pure as snowflakes.

"No idea."

"That was a door."

"Yeah, agreed."

"Closing. Hard."

"Yeah."

"That shit's spooky," Ice said.

"Damn spooky." Sweeney swung the light around, inspecting the area they stood within and the regal white hallway beyond. Three doors, one closed and two opened, could be seen within the cell phone's range.

"We're on the seventeenth," Sweeney said, nodding at white metal numbering on a sheet of polished nickel. "Only one more level to those legs. We can take the stairs, but we might meet whatever it was that made that noise. And there's not much room to maneuver in the stairwell."

"Same goes for that thing."

"True."

"Maybe even more so since it got wings."

"Okay, take a deep lungful then, and we'll go."

"More than a lungful," Ice said ruefully. "I need air tanks strapped to my back."

"All right," Sweeney said, inspecting his companion. "You ready for this?"

Ice smiled weakly. "No."

"Only one more level."

"That air smells like…" He couldn't finish the thought.

"I know." Sweeney understood. "This is the quickest way. Else we crawl through a maze of ceilings and walls to get up there. And that'll take a lot of energy. Energy I don't have."

Ice nodded, remembering the man had been here for two days—two days with that smell seeping through the cracks. "Okay." He purged his lungs with two quick breaths. "Okay, let's go."

Sweeney opened the door and moved through with Ice on his heels. Holding the light aloft, the private investigator hiked up the steps. His back was against the wall, and he held a cup of salt at the ready. The smell seemed even worse to Ice the second time around, and his innards clenched and knotted with the first breath.

Upward they hurried in a rustling of shoe soles and reluctant breaths. They turned the corner and reached the next landing. The bubble of light lit up the dark outline of a door and the block number 18 stamped into the wall to the right. Ice focused upon the entrance as if it were an airlock.

Sweeney pulled the door opened without pause and shone the light inside. His face slackened. "My God."

They moved inside, the door closing with a hydraulic sigh, and there stood the monster's legs, right where the thing had left them—free standing and waiting to be finally reunited with their upper half, a malevolent abomination to reality as Ice knew it.

"Holy shit," he blurted and immediately checked the rest of the corridor before once again beholding the madness before him. A pair of jeans was filled with a functional set of legs. Brown loafers covered the feet, but the thing that drew both men's attention like a horrific traffic accident was the ragged separation at the waistline. The skin, tissue, and fluids within glistened in the pale light. The sight mesmerized the two men, who stood staring at the lower half with head-shaking numbness.

"The fuck do we do now?" Sweeney muttered.

"Lance said salt," Ice replied, distracted by the graphic cross-section before him. "Remember?"

"Right. I remember."

"Look at it. That thing's even, like, rippling. Like blood's moving."

"Like a pulse."

"Yeah, like—"

A muffled clump came from behind one of the nearby apartment doors, heavy and shocking and jerking the men's attention away from the deserted legs. A substantial force crashed against the walls, causing plaster to pop like sporadic gunfire. It grew louder within seconds. The two men looked to the absolute edge of their bubble of light, where the manananggal yanked open a door and pulled itself through upon claws like a fright freeing itself from the earth. Livid, ravenous hatred filled the monster's luminous eyes.

Sweeney grabbed the legs, sweeping them up in an offensive tackle. "Get the door!"

Ice rushed to do just that.

The manananggal screeched, the chilling sound lashing the men like a prickly storm of needles. The monster freed one wing from the doorway and pulled its torso along the floor claw by claw until the second wing popped free in an evil unfurling of leather and darkness. The manananggal's mouth stretched wide to an impossible size, and teeth flashed, reminding Ice of ivory tusks.

Sweeney ran by, cracking his shoulder into the doorframe while the pursuing apparition attempted to beat its wings.

"Run!" Sweeney barked.

But Ice didn't run.

Ice remembered the salt.

The manananggal rushed him, the hideous eyes about to explode from its shocking face. The creature screamed again as claws the length of hunting knives went for Ice's throat.

He threw the salt into the manananggal's face.

The manananggal stopped in its lunge as if nailed by a sledgehammer and screamed a twisted, mangled note of surprise and pain. In the retreating light of the cell phone, the monster's flesh hissed and crackled and crumpled under the salt's contact before being doused by the darkness. The thing staggered away from Ice, who held his ground, chest heaving, a crumpled paper cup in one fist.

"Get the fuck out of there!" Sweeney screamed from the stairwell.

But Ice didn't.

The darkness enveloped the manananggal, but the monster's inky outline could be seen, reeling and clutching at its face. The talons shielded its elongated skull and wild hair. Its scream morphed into a sputtering hiss like frying bacon grease while the smell of charring skin wafted. The harsh mewling grew into a stream of pained curses spoken in an obscene language.

"*Move!*" Sweeney shrieked, the word ending with a frantic peal of fright.

The manananggal crouched on the floor, yammering hatefully, twisting, wings snapping, and Ice remembered with a jolt the other cups of salt he was carrying. He reached for one, hooking two fingers in his coat pocket. Seams ripped.

At the sound, the manananggal's face rose from its weaponized hands.

And even though it was pitch dark in that high-rise corridor, the wicked light blazing from the monster's one good eye fixed upon Ice. The other eye was a ruined mash of blistering jelly, but the one focusing upon Ice caused his knees to weaken. He unintentionally jammed the cup deeper into his pocket, squishing the paper.

The demon ceased its agonized moaning.

Ice forgot about his buzzing hand, forgot about the cups. Like someone waking from a trance, he bolted through the door, yanking his hand free of his pocket and flipping paper cups into the air as the manananggal dove for him. Claws flashed down his back, splitting fibers, but then Ice was banging off the stairwell's walls in a panicked frenzy. Each connection bounced him a little lower, and he finally leaped to gain more speed. Ice dropped five steps and stumbled upon the landing, fingers grazing rough concrete. He rebounded and fled farther downward, feet blurring over the stairs. He jumped the final five or so and landed in a crouch, the impact zapping his soles and crackling up his legs.

Ice glimpsed Sweeney's retreating bubble of light just around a corner, bobbing madly as he descended, and caught an unreal glimpse of the monster's feet kicking as Sweeney bore them away.

Sweeney was screaming.

Ice was screaming.

The manananggal burst onto the landing above in a black mass of limbs and leather, squealing in a hideous mind-splitting pitch. That gloomy tangle of rage and pain launched its bulk down the stairs in pursuit. It spewed a hateful verse of syllables forbidden for mere mortals to hear, its voice amplified ten times over in that shaft of cement and steel.

Ice grabbed the railing to steady his own rapid descent.

He fled down the steps in punishing jumps, his feet and lower legs shuddering with every impact, the screeches blasting his ears and sanity. Ice caught up to Sweeney on a landing. The PI strained and held the thing's legs in a bear hug, right arm looped through the demon's crotch. Ice grabbed for a leg to help the big man and nearly had his teeth kicked in, the demon's loafer grazing his forehead.

Holding the lower half like an unwilling abductee, the men hurried at best speed down the stairwell, which seemed hellishly longer. The sound of their shoes slapping concrete became an irregular percussion to the death-metal wailing pursuing them.

They reached the fifteenth floor, the number looming out of the cold darkness, and both men struggled with the legs as they opened the door.

"This way," Sweeney gasped.

"It's kicking," Ice spat through clenched teeth, clutching the amputated shins.

They thrashed into the hall as the insane yowling behind them increased. The door didn't close fast enough for Ice.

"Almost there," Sweeney said, his voice breaking from exhaustion, his words becoming a mantra. "Almost there. Almost there."

He pawed clumsily at an apartment's door, the same one they'd taken refuge in earlier. The two men pulled the kicking legs inside and let the door close behind them. Ice released the limbs and fumbled with the various locks, securing every one two seconds before a massive weight slammed into the metal. Fists pummeled the barrier.

Sweeney and Ice exchanged fearful looks.

"Backup's in the kitchen," Sweeney said and dragged the monster's lower half deeper into the apartment. "Go get it."

Ice ran for the kitchen. He grabbed the salt from the counter, checked the load, and returned to the hall. Sweeney had flicked on an overhead light. The cross-section of madness the PI held in his arms flashed at Isosceles like a huge gouged eye.

"Do it!" Sweeney yelled himself hoarse, throwing his weight against the limbs and trapping them against a wall.

The door shivered in its frame, every meaty blow sounding like a frantic gong. A muffled shriek erupted from beyond, sounding as if the monster was trying to chew its way through.

Ice didn't wait.

He doused the raw, fluid-dripping lower half of the manananggal with the salt like a manic chef seasoning a tough steak. Sinews and guts sizzled. Meat stank of rot. And if the legs had been kicking before, they became a feverish blur the instant the salt made contact.

The screeching beyond the door spiked to a terrifying crescendo.

Sweeney's strength failed. The big man released the lower torso, dropping it as if repulsed by its unholy animation. He staggered away and crumpled to the floor while Ice retreated toward the kitchen, watching the legs twist and thrash and at times even attempt to stand. The lower half eventually righted itself against a wall, wobbling weakly, but then, like a driverless car with its gas pedal stuck, the legs ran, trailing angry ribbons of steam.

The abomination charged into the living room, straight for a set of curtains.

In the hallway, Ice and Sweeney gawked as, with one last pain-powered burst of energy, the lower half of the manananggal's body crashed through the covered window.

It toppled into empty space amongst a shower of glass, ripping a length of fabric down with it. A loafer flew off a bare foot as the legs flipped over the edge and disappeared from sight.

# 12

The two men stood speechless, staring at the shattered window, when the distant impact jarred them from their horrified trance.

"Holy shit," Ice whispered, meeting Sweeney's gaze.

The burly PI lay on the floor and took his time fishing out a pair of salt cups from his pocket. He opened the squished containers, casting an eye toward the suddenly quiet apartment entrance.

"I'm knackered," Sweeney breathed.

"Only a set of legs, but…" Ice couldn't finish the thought.

"It was the salt," Sweeney reasoned. "The pain. Gave it a burst of energy. Just like a guy hammering his thumb."

"But that glass. No one should be able to go through that shit. It's stormproof, for God's sake."

"Not worrying about that right now," Sweeney said, focusing on the door.

A violent shiver gripped Ice's person. The main entrance became a focal point for both men then, for the savage beating from beyond had ceased. Sweeney struggled to his feet and, as an afterthought, held out one of his last remaining salt cups to Ice, who took it gladly.

Sweeney quietly went to the door and studied the stalwart hinges and the locks. He leaned in, closing one eye to better see out the peephole. Ice joined him and placed an ear to the door.

Nothing.

But a presence lingered outside, a monstrous presence, hidden by the darkness.

Blood pumping in his temples, Ice held his breath and waited. He moved his ear just a little over the door's surface, straining to hear anything.

A shuffling emerged from beyond the other side, a weight as ponderous as a boulder, followed by the softest gurgle, barely heard through the metal.

Then, "I'll kill you."

The rough words widened Ice's eyes. Sweeney drew back from the door, readying his salt. Ice retreated deeper into the apartment and regarded the portal as if it were about to burst.

"You see anything?" Ice whispered.

"Nothing. Black out there. And yet I thought… I saw something move. Like a darker shadow against night. Just a flicker of something. Enough to make you think. Then it spoke."

"You heard it, too?" Ice looked at Sweeney's tired profile.

"'I'll kill you'? Oh yeah, I heard it."

"Watch the door for a minute," Ice said and left his companion. He went to the window, scanning the upper frame. He hesitated a second before peering over the edge, searching for the legs and ignoring the diamond glitter of far-off Halifax. Nothing was visible at the building's base, so Ice returned to Sweeney.

"Couldn't see a damn thing down there," he reported.

"It is night," the PI muttered. "We'll see it in the morning."

"I wonder what'll happen then?"

"Who knows? If the movies are anything to go by, maybe it'll blow up. Or disintegrate with the dawn."

"Those are vampire movies. It's not a vampire."

"Look, this is all new to me," Sweeney replied testily. "I don't know what's going to happen in the morning. If Lance said the thing will die at dawn, I'm inclined to believe him. Right now, we got bigger problems. You heard the thing. It's going to kill us. Or at least it's going to try and kill us. And according to your phone, dawn is like nine hours and change away."

Ice took a deep, steadying breath. "You said you searched the other apartments. You didn't find any more salt?"

"No."

"What about garlic?"

Sweeney straightened. "Never knew about it. Until now."

"Those apartments could be full of garlic. Bottles of garlic powder. We just have to go out there and get it."

"I don't want to go out there." Ice said.

"I don't want to go out there either." Sweeney said. "All right. This is what we do. Damn well sure we didn't use all the salt in here, so here we stay. In a little high-rise fortress. We each got a shot of salt if we need it. We sit tight, and we wait that undead bastard out. Wait for Lance and then go hunting for the other one."

The plan sounded good to Isosceles except the whispered *I'll kill you*, spoken in that ancient voice, kept playing in his head.

# 13

When Crisanto returned to the penthouse, Calithea knew something was wrong by the way he flew in through the terrace doors and dropped onto the plush curve-around sofa. She turned her back completely on the blood-moon mural and looked upon her mate with concern.

"They have killed me," Crisanto declared in a stoic voice.

The words struck Calithea as a mortal blow. "What?" she whispered, mortified to the core.

"My legs."

Calithea's hands rose to her cheeks.

"They've ruined them with the hated crust of the earth," he said.

*Salt.* Calithea's mouth became a frown of despair. They had poisoned Crisanto. Her unbeating heart ached as if lanced. Despite the sometimes dull progression of time and a few instances across the centuries where the pair had fought hard enough for her to wish his death, she still cherished her Crisanto.

She took two steps toward him and stopped. "You... you have until dawn."

"Dawn." The monster on the sofa seethed, strands of wet intestinal matter strung out on the lavish cushions like jellyfish tentacles. "Dawn."

Their black eyes met, and Calithea wilted with misery.

"You should leave this place," Crisanto told her. "Go to New York. As you've wished."

Her voice failed her, so she took another step toward him.

"Leave here, and I'll make use of my final hours."

"What will you do?" she whispered and stopped, unable to think.

The smell of his musk flared with anger, and Calithea breathed deeply of it, savoring it, committing the scent to memory, as there would be no more after this night.

Crisanto flexed his lengthy claws like crab legs. His detached frame trembled. His face rose, and the gray-black flesh, drawn and taut, festered with a terrible, impending wrath.

"I shall have vengeance," he whispered.

*

The intercom buzzed and jerked Leonard from the torpor of manning the front desk. He pawed at his face, driving the spiders into his ears and down his collar. He paid them no mind and leaned over as if he'd been shot through the back. One finger landed heavily on a console, and he pushed a glowing button.

"Yes?" he croaked.

"Leonard."

He licked his lips. *It was her.* "Yes?"

"I have need of you."

"What?" Leonard asked, suddenly breathless, his limbs slowly energizing with the sound of his mistress's voice.

Lady Calithea whispered instructions over the scratchy connection. Her commands weren't strange, not to Leonard. When she finished and her voice disappeared, a deep and eternal longing made his heart ache. Leonard straightened in his chair and placed a hand on the desk.

Like trained pets, a number of black spiders raced from his sleeve, down his wrist, and onto the desk. Leonard plucked one from a keyboard and brought it to his mouth. He ate the arachnid like a fancy piece of dark chocolate. He ate several others as well until the remaining spiders escaped to safer regions. When they were gone, Leonard sucked on his teeth, sighed, and rose from his desk. The office was nearby, and he sometimes went in there. Not often, but sometimes. Inside the office were various items potentially helpful in certain situations. Like the one he currently had, to which the Lady Calithea had alerted him.

With a mortician's sombre grace, Leonard walked inside the office and flicked on a light. Baseball bats, fire axes, and various knives all lined the shelves and leaned against the walls, all placed with immaculate care. Leonard studied each item with a detached interest. He'd been instructed to bring any deemed necessary for the approaching task.

His eyes fell upon a well-used pickax. That would be of service to him and Lady Calithea.

Ignoring the rest, Leonard wrapped his bony fingers around the shaft of the digging tool and hefted it. He left the office, not closing the door behind him.

Taking the deep, measured breaths of a man whose mind was far away from the present, Leonard walked toward the remaining working elevator. He selected a button, pushed it, and hummed in tune to the great machine lowering itself to the ground. Such a marvelous machine, he realized—simple, yet *marvelous*. Leonard hadn't thought that way back in the time before his lady took him. He barely acknowledged the machine at all then except when it failed to function correctly. More recently, he thought of the device as a way to lift himself into the sky—to get closer to her.

The doors opened. Holding the pickax across his pelvis, Leonard stepped inside without a word. He turned and studied the control panel and its selection of numbers with a wistful expression upon his tired features. With infinite care, he reached out and pushed one button.

And when the elevator lifted him into the night, Leonard hefted the heavy tool and took aim at the control panel.

<h1 style="text-align:center">14</h1>

Ice peeked through the peephole and couldn't see shit. "For all we know, that thing could be right out there with its thumb covering the hole."

"Forget about that," Sweeney said. "You hear anything now?"

Ice put an ear to the door. "No."

"You sure you heard the elevator start up?"

"Yes, I heard the elevator start up," Ice shot back, not liking Sweeney's agitated tone. He pointed at his own ears. "These work, y'know."

However, Sweeney wasn't looking so certain. Since the manananggal had delivered the death threat, the direness of the situation had apparently begun to sink into Sweeney's brain. *"I'll kill you,"* it had said. Ice didn't want to think too much about it, either. The time neared ten o'clock, and the tension in the room only swelled with every passing second. *"I'll kill you."* Said by a regular joe, one might laugh it off. Said by a street punk, one might call the cops. Said by an unholy creature of the night, a person might just run off and take refuge in a church.

Sweeney paced and brooded, growing increasingly curt. Ice didn't know the man very well, but he liked the idea of sitting tight until reinforcements came. He prayed there truly wasn't any more than a pair of manananggals haunting the building.

"I'm worried," Sweeney eventually said.

"Yeah?" Ice replied.

"It's planning something. I can tell."

"You can tell, huh?"

"Yeah."

Ice looked over his shoulder at the man, who was leaning against the kitchen entryway, the wall seemingly dividing half of him right up the middle. Ice thought the PI was bracing himself for a storm.

"While I was in here," Sweeney said, his one eye fixing on Ice, "the thing would come up to the door. Whisper at it, just to let me know it was out there. Never loud, just whispers. Couldn't even tell what it was saying, but it was there."

"That's creepy shit."

"It *was* creepy shit. I should call Lance."

"Save the power," Ice advised. "There's nothing he really needs to know. We'll surprise him when he gets here. Unless someone hypnotises him at the front desk or ambushes him in the elevator."

"Not him," Sweeney shook his head as if the notion was unthinkable. "Not Lance Chambers."

A loud *whump* came from the front door, and both men jumped. Ice realized he'd leaped backward about five steps when a second blow smashed into the door. The frame shivered. The sliding chain trembled. The pointed end of something exploded through the peephole, shattering the glass in a pop of shards. The tapered iron twisted one way then another before getting yanked free.

"What the hell?" Ice muttered and backed away.

"Get back here," Sweeney ordered. "That door's reinforced metal underneath. Gonna take a—"

*Whump.* The upper hinge on the door shook.

"Well, fuck me," Sweeney said, his eyes wide and staring. "It's trying to come through."

"But we have salt in here," Ice protested.

"Maybe it don't care about that anymore."

The blows became a rhythm, and the door shuddered with every strike.

"That ain't fair," Ice said, getting an uneasy squawk of laughter from Sweeney.

"That's a pickax," the PI said. "It just might do the trick."

"What trick?"

"Punch its way through the hinges. Knock the door off the frame. Easier to get in, then."

"We gotta do something." Ice waved his hands. "*Something.*"

The top hinge popped, the screws bulging from their moorings. Sweeney stared on in dismay. He shook his fist containing the salt. The pickax punched through the peephole once again as the wielder changed targets. Metal squealed on metal as the force behind the pick worked it deeper into the hole.

After a few seconds, the tool pulled free… only to crash home once again, widening the hole just a little more.

"Gonna open up that tin can," a raspy voice called out merrily from beyond, sounding as if he was shouting through an old telephone receiver. "Gonna open up that tin can."

The pickax crunched through the door's metallic hide as if it were paper, wreaking a foot-long tear in its wake. Paint chips drizzled the floor. The pointed iron squealed and squawked and was pulled free. Then the attack's tempo of destruction quickened, and the pickax hammered into the upper section of the door, right at the hinges.

Ice gasped when the tip punched through, popping the hinge and leaving it hanging by a screw. He had his tiny cup of salt in hand, planning to toss the entire load in the face of the first critter to enter.

After a few more strikes, the upper part of the door was utterly wrecked.

The pickax targeted the bottom hinge.

"Listen," Ice said, watching the destruction. "If I don't get out of this, I want you to do something for me."

"You're going to get out of this," but Sweeney didn't sound so sure.

"Just listen. My parents live in Dartmouth, okay? Twenty-five Amber Avenue. White house. Bungalow. Tell them what happened to me."

"You're gonna do that yourself."

"And then—" Ice winced as the lower hinge shuddered. "Then, I want you to go over to Larry's Pizza. That's downtown."

"I know the place."

"Good. I want you to go in there and find a guy called David. Find him and tell him that Isosceles says, 'Fuck you.' And stress the *F* on that. Tell him I always thought he was a goddamn artsy-fartsy, square-holed, pansy-ass bastard who put on airs because he knew he'd be forever working at a pizza place, despite his fucking self-proclaimed three-point-five GPA."

Sweeney frowned.

"You tell him all that and then kick him square in the balls. And do it hard. I'm talking *real* hard. Soccer-goal force, okay? Ring those chestnuts hard enough to curdle milk. You do that for me?"

Sweeney shrugged. "Sure. Want me to kick him when he's down, too?"

Ice immediately nodded. "Good idea. Yes. Soccer kick him again. To the face."

"Consider it done." Sweeney smirked and returned his attention to the door.

"Thanks, man."

"Your last request," Sweeney said. "Hope I get a prison cell with a view."

"Guy your size won't have to worry about anything in prison."

That actually made Sweeney chuckle despite the hammering at the door, and he gazed upon Ice with fondness for a fleeting moment.

The lower hinge burst free. The pickax went to work on the other side, targeting the bolt locks. Whoever was swinging that length of iron was doing the job right, ensuring that when the castle's drawbridge was down, it would *stay* down. The bolts lasted mere seconds before breaking apart. The pick stabbed through the dark seam, and the iron tusk pulled and heaved, twisted and pushed, and after several good tries, the metal groaned and gave way.

The door flew outward at the bottom, falling flat as if it'd had its legs yanked from underneath. Silence reigned for a moment, but then an imposing figure appeared, framed in the smoky blackness and falling flakes of the entrance.

He held the pickax across his pelvis. A ski mask and goggles covered his cocked head as he gazed into the apartment.

Sweeney held his salt in his left hand. In his right, he extended his steel baton, flicking the weapon to its full length and making sure the ski-masked door knocker saw it.

The man did, his chin lifting at the action.

Showing no signs of being intimidated, the pickax man stepped back into the hazy gloom of the corridor, retreating like a nightmare respecting the dawn, and disappeared from sight. In the sudden absence of pickax pounding, the silence was strange. The darkness beyond the apartment seemed as alien and threatening as a portal to a forbidden dimension, and neither man intended to venture forth. They stood in the kitchen's doorway, using the wall as partial cover.

"Sweeney," stated a female voice.

The PI's brow knotted into a question as a woman, a stunningly beautiful woman, stepped up to the doorway. Her appearance startled Sweeney, and he drew back, bumping into Ice. The sparse light from the apartment revealed the woman, her skin damn near alabaster in the weakening illumination.

Sweeney held his cup but didn't throw its salt. Ice leaned around him so he could better see the vision standing just outside. The lady was shockingly beautiful, barefoot and clothed in a sheer one-piece top Ice couldn't determine was a nightie or a dress of some sort that barely covered her nether regions. Her sudden appearance stopped them as surely as the destruction of the door.

Her dark eyes considered one man then the other. She lifted her hands to her chin as if frightened by the men, the movement hoisting the hem of her top higher, inadvertently revealing herself. Ice's eyes strayed while Sweeney looked on, paralyzed by the woman's presence.

She lowered her hands and smiled, and when she did, Ice no longer felt anxious. The air no longer choked him, and the coldness of the concrete no longer reminded him of a tomb. She smiled sweetly, and a wonderful sense of wellness blossomed within him. Ice actually smiled back. He wanted to know her name, wanted to know if she was all right, and wanted to know if she was cold dressed in such a thin top hanging off her shoulders. She looked as though she'd just risen from bed, and Ice wanted nothing more than to take her into his arms, run his fingers through her thick hair, and kiss the sleep from her eyes.

And like the sun quickly eclipsing the moon, her sweet smiled morphed into a sensual pout. She arched her back, breasts making themselves known, and blood surged into places Ice hadn't thought about since the morning. She stood no closer than the apartment's threshold and ran a hand up one side of the doorframe before leaning seductively against it.

The vision regarded Ice, and the power of her gaze made him love her—just like that.

"Uh," Sweeney whispered, equally mesmerized. "Uh… Are you…?"

She focused on Sweeney, the full weight of her attention rendering him motionless. Her chest rose and fell with heat. Her perfect lips hinted at a little smile as she locked gazes with the PI, a sultry question clouding her lovely face.

"Love me," she whispered and placed her back to the doorframe, her hands splayed flat against the wall. One knee rose, revealing an ice skater's thigh that damn near made Ice weep.

Sweeney lurched toward her, took three steps, and stopped. He huffed, inhaled sharply, and snorted again as if struggling with his breathing. Ice stood back and stared and longed to be summoned as well.

Sweeney's mouth fell open, and the woman smiled again, a bright beckoning line of white. The PI's resistance seemed to amuse her.

"Love me," she repeated, a hot murmur that made Ice think of cloudless nights and savannahs moistened by flash rains.

Sweeney nodded. He dropped the cell phone, the clatter frightening. He walked the rest of the way to her. His hand touched her hip, and he stroked her, marring the fabric covering her flesh before cupping one ass cheek. She drew him into her arms.

Ice suddenly blinked, emerging from a dream. He saw Sweeney embracing a woman and wondered, *What is up with that?* when they should've been doing something else, but *What is that something else? Leg. Her perfect leg.* Sweeney had hooked her thigh and pulled it up to his own hip. *Leg. Legs.* They'd destroyed the lower part of the mana-thing's legs, and *the legs, the* vampire's *legs, and there were TWO OF THEM—*

Sweeney's head was only a finger's width away from his lover's receiving face, their mouths open, and just before Sweeney could taste her, Ice saw her teeth.

He flung his cup of salt.

Some particles peppered Sweeney, but most struck the woman.

Her little mouth stretched open three times its size as fangs sprouted. She swatted Sweeney away as if he were a flimsy curtain instead of being three hundred pounds plus, bouncing him off the unforgiving concrete. A screech of agony blasted from her, and her fingers clawed at the points where the salt had stuck and burned. The pale LED light caught smoky wisps issuing from her face. She shivered, a frightening dynamo of rage and pain, before a monstrous energy yanked her into the corridor's depths. Her scream became a layered howl that reverberated off the confined walls, a hideous harmony that threatened to rupture Ice's eardrums.

A hand groped for Ice's shoulder, and he looked to see Sweeney's pained face.

"Come on," the PI urged.

Sweeney picked up the dropped cell phone and stuffed it into a pocket. He gripped Ice by a shoulder and hauled him into the kitchen before releasing him against a counter. The PI stood at the kitchen's corner, peering back at the apartment's ruined front door.

"Oh, Jesus," Sweeney panted. "Oh, sweet Jesus. That was… that was close."

"Too close," Ice said.

"Thanks," the PI huffed. "Saved my ass."

"You saved mine first."

"You say that guy's name was David?"

Ice chuckled. "You okay?"

The bearded face split into a weary smile. "Yeah. It was like I had nothing but tunnel vision for her."

"I saw. Sorta." Ice inspected him with greater scrutiny. "You sure you're okay?"

"Just feeble is all. Too much physical shit in one night. And the night ain't even over yet. My heart… my heart feels like it's taken a couple of shots from a defibrillator. You see what that salt did to her? Holy shit."

"I saw, I saw."

"Like acid."

"Wasn't pretty."

Sweeney sobered. "No. No it wasn't. Thanks again. This shit doesn't bother you?"

"It bothers me—bothers me big time. But I'm not bending over for these things."

"Yeah." Sweeney shook his head, and his eyes moistened. "I almost got killed, then. Almost bought it. From a goddamn demon-bitch. That's the other one—the one I followed from the club."

"Pretty hot demon-bitch."

"Yeah." Sweeney peered into the hallway and the corridor beyond. "Don't see shit."

"Nothing?"

"No. Listen, I need some fresh air. You keep watch here, will you?"

Ice nodded and replaced Sweeney at the door while the big man lumbered into the living room, avoiding the outlines of overturned furniture. The curtain remained on the floor, allowing soft night light to flood the interior. Sweeney stopped at the broken window and placed a hand against the metal frame.

Ice glanced over his shoulder and saw Sweeney at the broken window.

The big man stuck his head out into space.

Alarms went off inside Ice's head. "Hey, Sween, stay inside the—"

Claws descended from above and clamped about Sweeney's skull. The PI grunted in surprise before his formidable bulk was pulled through the hole, his hands scrabbling for purchase.

"Sweeney!" Ice bolted into the living room just as the big man's body cleared the window, pulling away into the night.

Sweeney dangled from the extended arms of a torso with bat wings fully extended and pumping for altitude. Ice stopped at the wrecked sill, oblivious to the crackling glass beneath his feet, and stared as the screaming manananggal carried Sweeney's struggling figure up, up until they became shadows against the face of a full moon. *Super moon.* Ice distantly remembered a news report saying that was the night for such an event. All the astronomers would have their telescopes pointed to the heavens.

The pair rose higher and higher.

Ice could only watch as the monster hoisted the man who'd saved his life into the cold night sky, their shapes receding as the distance grew.

Somewhere over a jagged outline of a black forest, far away from the apartment building, the manananggal decided enough was enough.

It let Sweeney drop.

When Sweeney fell, Ice's mouth dropped open as well. He followed the PI's soundless plunge until he lost the figure in the pitch-black background of low hills and trees. Ice didn't hear Sweeney scream. Nor did he hear him hit the ground.

As his shock receded, Ice *did* hear footsteps.

Ice whirled to glimpse the pickax man—security guard Leonard in full war dress—bringing his weapon downward. Ice lunged clear of the strike and rolled, cracking his left shoulder into a sofa's stout corner. The pick clanged into the floor. Ice scrambled to his feet and barely dodged a disemboweling cut. A coffee table tripped Ice, and he landed on his knees. His left hand slapped the table's surface, and Leonard buried a third of the pick's length in the wood, almost removing Ice's little finger.

Ice screamed, kicked out, and slammed a sneaker into Leonard's knee, buckling the man. Leonard staggered, kept in place only by his powerful grip on the tool's shaft. Wood groaned as the security guard wrenched the heavy tool free.

Panic crackled through Ice, and he slapped floor as he ran, bent over, headlong into the hallway, righting himself as he fled.

There, he saw Sweeney's fully extended steel baton discarded on the tiles.

Boots pounded floor behind Ice. He snatched up the baton and whirled, swinging as Leonard geared up for an over-the-shoulder chop.

The baton was faster.

The lethal steel tip of the rod whipped around with all of

the desperate, adrenaline-fueled strength shooting through Ice's person, nailing Leonard in the throat. The pickax dropped as the security guard staggered against a wall, clutching his crushed trachea.

Ice backed into the kitchen, watching and listening to his attacker's chilling gasps. Leonard yanked the jiggling goggles from his face, eyes alternating between slits and saucers. He slowly collapsed, feet kicking at the baseboards with a weakening sprint. He attempted to rise, fingers pinching and clawing at his neck in a useless attempt to open the airways, and fell face first.

Shoulders heaving, Ice divided his attention between the main entrance and the dying man.

In a short time, Leonard's feet and hands shivered and stilled.

Isosceles studied the corpse, the rush of the fight bleeding away and leaving him drained. He leaned over the body and looked left and right, seeing nothing in the doorway or at the window. Seeing both directions were clear, he grabbed the top of the dead man's ski mask and pulled it free.

Leonard's eyes stared ahead, seeing nothing.

Leaning heavily against the walls for support, Ice glanced around and spotted a crumpled paper cup. He picked it up and found it empty, the particles scattered. The thought of the elevator came to him, and he looked around for his cell phone. Sweeney had dropped it in the hall. Then he remembered Sweeney had picked the device up again and tucked it away in a pocket. Another wave of misery swept through Ice as he regarded the living room. A cold night wind blew through the apartment.

*Fuck this.*

Determined, Ice went to the elevator.

He stepped inside and growled upon finding the panel destroyed, the interface a frayed tangle of exposed wiring. The sight demoralized him worse than Sweeney's demise. He placed a shoulder against the elevator's open doorway. The way he saw things, his options were limited. He had no phone, no salt, and no way to descend from the apartment heights. As far as he knew, there were two very pissed off manananggals actively on the prowl for him, and even though it was in self-defense, Ice still felt pretty shitty about striking the security guard from downstairs and standing by while the guy pretty much asphyxiated to death.

*Salt. Or garlic.*

He'd search for garlic and weaponize it, find a place without holes in the walls or ceilings, and wait for Lance to arrive. However, he wouldn't know when Lance arrived. Nor would Lance know if Ice was still alive, and then there was the issue of actually reaching the upper levels when the elevators and stairs were out.

Waves of despair pulsated through Ice's core.

He wished Sweeney were still around.

With the night air nipping at his face and hands, Isosceles rubbed his cheeks and steadied himself, forcing the misery and self-pity from his person. *Garlic.* That was the first step.

Firming his grip on the baton, Ice glanced around before heading for a closed door.

The sun hung on the eastern horizon, its light lessened by the thick morning haze drifting in from the Halifax harbor. Light shone through an apartment window stamped with residue that might have resembled palm prints, and it crept over upturned pieces of furniture, piles of chalky dust, and cement fragments. Nothing stirred in the apartment, but Ice listened, seeing the morning's glow illuminate the wall just outside the open doorway of the apartment where he'd taken refuge just after midnight. He'd found three unopened bottles of garlic powder in his careful rummaging through the eighteenth and nineteenth floors and, having decided not to push his luck, holed up in what he believed was the most structurally sound place inside the last apartment—the bathroom.

Sitting in the bathtub with the shower screen half drawn, Ice spent the last of the night staying quiet, relieving himself in the tub's drain when the urge took him, and wondering if mirrors might have any effect on the monsters haunting the building. They didn't find him to test that theory, and since Ice was fine with his hiding place, he found little reason to move. The three bottles of garlic he'd found barely smelled, and he suspected if he had split the plastic bottles apart, the spice therein would have resembled fat shotgun shells.

Nothing had come for him during the night—or the predawn hours.

As the sun grew stronger in the hallway, Ice relaxed a little more, knowing that somewhere out there, one monster of the night died with the first ray of morning light. He'd heard nothing, certainly no death wail like in the movies, and no real indication anything had perished at all. But he believed the words of Lance Chambers and felt something had changed in the moments before the rising of the sun.

Thoughts of Sweeney drifted through his mind then, but not of the security guard. He'd made peace with that at some point before the dawn.

With the sun growing stronger, Ice's tired mind turned to thoughts of revenge. He extracted himself from the tub and shook out his stiff limbs. He held the baton in one hand while in the other was a bottle of opened and congealed garlic. He peeked around corners and found the place free of winged horrors and their human servants. A person could get a lot of thinking done in the hours after midnight—a lot of thinking, especially when a person was left alone with one's thoughts and the primordial dread of monsters residing in the closet.

Since the advantage lay with Ice, he figured to do a little hunting himself, to pay Sweeney back and to exact a little revenge on the remaining bloodsucker presumably residing somewhere above. If Ice had bat wings, he'd want to roost someplace high. Sunlight would kill the manananggals if they were in halves, so he wondered if they were somehow weakened while whole and during the day.

He intended to find out.

Wary of corners and dark corridors, Isosceles quietly moved through the upper floors by way of the stairwell, avoiding hoisting himself up through ceiling holes. Nothing opposed him. Ice wondered if the manananggals had hypnotized their victims out of their homes first and then started making the extra portals. Obviously, they'd cleared out the whole building without suspicion or reprisal from families, friends, or even authorities—right under the city's nose.

The scope of the operation left him in disbelief.

The final door at the top of the stairwell was ajar, allowing a weak bar of light to guide him. He peeked into the corridor and balked at the sight. A heap of heavy furniture lay before him, congesting the hall like an overstuffed attic. Light blazed in through a wall-length window at the hallway's end, a pane of glass without any curtains. That interested Ice. Most of the apartment windows below had their curtains drawn. He pushed against the door, discovering it would not budge. Ice squirmed through the narrow opening and then wormed his way through the lavish tangle of furniture.

In the middle of the congested corridor, right across from a private elevator, were a set of impressive hardwood doors. Ice reached out and tentatively turned a knob.

The door opened without a squeak.

The penthouse was a refuge of luxury, but Ice didn't bother with identifying the many extravagances of the home. He kept his back to a wall, slipped out of his sneakers, and proceeded in socks. Chandeliers hung at regular intervals, suspended far above cherrywood panels and a floor of stone. A short hall led to a kitchen the size of Ice's own apartment. Granite and quartz countertops shone. Banks of built-in custom appliances and a large island with multiple sinks dominated the center. He wandered through the room in a state of wary dismay, finding no threat yet in awe of the expensive surroundings worthy of royalty. A wall-length series of windows allowed a breathtaking view of distant Halifax in all its foggy splendor, and Ice squinted against the smoky eye of the sun.

The living room, or what he believed was the living room, remained in darkness. Light traced the heavy curtains along the eastern wall, rendering the interior in an imposing gloom. Ice scanned the room's dark crevices and took note of a staircase to another level, planning to search there eventually. Ice entered, socks making soundless contact upon marble flooring and rich rugs, and stopped to gawk in open-mouth marvel at a blood-moon mural covering a wall. The picture mesmerized him for long seconds until he remembered his mission and glanced around.

A wrap-around sofa drew his attention, or rather, the mess of ashes along one corner of the plush upholstery.

*Ashes.*

Ice noted the empty doorways and the stairs before going to the ash. He stood over the mess, puzzling, and even prodded at the residue with the baton. The tumblers of his brain seized up, as he wondered if the remains belonged to the murderous thing that had killed Sweeney.

The answer might rest upstairs, he thought, so he turned and nearly had his face taken off by an open-hand slap that flipped him over the sofa. Ice saw stars and tried to stand, smearing his cheek against the back of the furniture piece. He rose a second time, glimpsing a water-blurred figure threading its way through the living room—toward him.

He stood on guts alone and faced his attacker, the woman with the sheer, clinging top. Her face was oddly placid and heedless of the buckshot scarring on the left curve of her face, a peppering of holes that bored through smooth skin right to the dull gleam of bone.

Ice swayed on his ankles and scowled in horror at the salt's destruction.

The woman closed in and grabbed him by his shirt and

coat to toss him over a dining-room table. Ice skittered along the surface like a puck on a frozen pond until he toppled off the far end, legs kicking before he cracked against the floor.

Ice lay on his back and gasped. He reached inside a pocket and pulled out a small bottle of garlic. His hand hitched in the material of his coat, and he fought to free it.

The woman appeared before him, and Ice winced. She picked him up by the front of his shirt and glared into his face. Seams ripped.

Ice nearly swooned as he realized how close they were. He got the garlic free. She grabbed his hand, and her small fist squeezed hard enough to buckle flesh and bone. Ice screamed in earnest. The crushed garlic fell to the floor. The woman adjusted her grip, lifted him by the throat, and side-pitched him into the mural of the blood moon, leaving an indentation in the wood's surface. Ice collapsed against the baseboard. A bright rush of pain signals lit up his being.

"Mr. Isosceles." The woman's voice floated over him.

Ice opened his eyes and grimaced at the lovely expression of disdain upon his attacker's features.

"My name… is Calithea."

She was hot even when she was pissed off.

"Wait," he slurred. "*Ack.*"

She grabbed him by the throat once again and lifted him off the floor.

"Waaaaaai—" Isosceles gargled.

She threw him the length of the room. Glass exploded, followed by the sensation of diving into a frozen pool. Ice thought he'd gone down a monster's prickly throat. Daylight enveloped him, but he was too punch-drunk to realize he was outside the apartment, on the penthouse terrace. He attempted to rise but couldn't even muster the energy to turn his head.

When the woman's shadow covered him, he groaned.

Calithea frowned at the sun, but it didn't burn her. She slowly curtsied as if bound by a kimono and clasped Ice's right ankle. She dragged him back into the shade of the penthouse. Glass shards ran underneath his jeans and up his back, biting through fabric and skin, biting him very deeply. His head rattled along the floor as she pulled him back into the shadows.

"Wait," he finally managed to plead, barely aware he'd uttered the word.

Calithea still gripped him by the ankle. She whipped him into the hardwood baseboards, flailing limbs and all, as if he were a rolled-up newspaper and she'd spotted a spider. Then she backhanded him, swinging the other way, into the rear of the plush sofa.

Ice heard the connections more than felt them.

The sun rose behind her, tracing her figure in a halo. The deadly angel stepped between his spread legs and inspected him, and Ice was dimly aware it was still her. Her hand rose to her chest, the fingertips sprouting black knives with a nightmarish fluidity. Ice drunkenly frowned at the effect, yet the curved blades emerging from her were oddly beautiful.

She crouched and extended one of those fingers to his swelling right eye. The razor tip caressed the lower bone of his orbital cavity, from his nose to his ear. He wept red at the subtle contact.

"What's your name?" she asked, her words made elegant by an accent he couldn't place.

He blinked. "I… Iso… sosceles."

"Your full name."

"Isosceles… Muh… moon."

That made her smile.

"Mr. Moon," she said in a sympathetic note, "you have walked into my home while I'm at my worst."

"Yuh," Ice managed, very much aware of his breach of etiquette.

Her razor claw drew a crescent moon down the meat of his cheek, turning at the curve of his jawline before stopping at the soft spot under his chin. The bloody art left rivulets that ran from face to neckline.

"Did you know," she asked him softly, "that monsters can grieve?"

The ballooning of his right eye rendered him blind there, so he blinked with his left.

"Yes. They can," she continued. "That might sound strange to you, but it's true. I'd like you to remember that."

Ice thought he could do that—in his few remaining seconds.

"I've been waiting for you," she said, tapping the fat underneath his chin, pricking it and drawing blood each time. "When you killed Crisanto. And dear Leonard. I knew you would be coming for me. I knew. After Crisanto died at dawn. He died very well, I'll have you know. Very noble. He could have spent his final hours tearing this place apart, hunting you down. Make no mistake, he would have found you and ripped you apart. In screaming pieces. But instead, after killing Sweeney, he chose to do otherwise. In his mind, he'd killed the most troublesome of you. In his mind, Sweeney had been his first mistake, one which he felt he corrected."

Ice once again saw Sweeney plummet to his death over a darkened timberland.

"In my beloved's final hours, he decided to stay with me rather than hunt you. You were an afterthought, you see, and not worth the anguish, which is why you live," she said with grandmotherly wisdom. "And as my beloved's time drew closer, he showered me with his attentions. We talked about many things. Years of things. Entire centuries, in fact, from the first time we met to those final, fleeting moments before dawn. And just before the sun took him, he smiled and urged me to leave this place. His thoughts weren't about his approaching death, Isosceles Moon. His thoughts were about me—what I would do... and about how I should continue on after he was gone. Does that sound like a monster to you?"

Her claw dropped from his chin, and she knelt before him, striking a pose that reminded Ice of a Shinto monk pondering existence.

"I never wanted to come here," she muttered, studying the penthouse walls. "I liked our other homes. But he wanted this. He did. And now he's gone. And the pain... is unlike any other I've ever known."

The sun touched her right cheek, and she didn't shy away from the contact. "Do you know what love is, Isosceles Moon? Some of you mortals do. It's simple, really. Energy and devotion squared by time. Remember that, for it's a powerful equation. Remember that, in the time you have remaining."

Ice squirmed weakly.

She gazed upon his broken, unresponsive body before locking eyes with his one.

"You played your part in the death of my Crisanto. For that, I'm inclined to kill you. But death isn't final, you understand. For some, it's a release. I don't wish to release you just yet. I think I'll do something else, instead—something much more... fitting. My Crisanto was different, you see, and I loved him. I sense you're different as well. Somehow. In some unfathomable way. And since you killed my Crisanto, I wish your death to be as painful as my moments after his passing, as my existence would be… if I chose to endure it."

Ice wasn't entirely sure he understood.

She sighed. "I have no wish to continue on, Isosceles Moon. Not without him."

Ice didn't respond, but his consciousness wavered at the absolute fringes, where light became darkness.

"After this episode," she continued, "you might think you possess a talent—for killing monsters—Isosceles Moon. An incorrect conclusion, you understand, but I wish to give you a gift regardless. One which will help you find other monsters. Or rather, help them find you."

Having tired of speaking, she considered her claws. She drew a thumbnail down the middle of her flawless wrist as if undoing a sleeve. Blood erupted, flowed to her elbow, and dripped. She lifted the wound to her lips and closed her eyes.

To Ice's horror, she then pressed her lips to his forehead.

The kiss burned.

"Energy," she whispered upon breaking contact, her breath warmed by blood. "Devotion. Squared by time. You will learn this… in the days you have remaining. Your time won't be as pleasant as mine, however. I don't think you'll have a very pleasant time at all. In the mornings to come, you will see. You will understand… what I've done… to you. And I pray that, in the days that follow, you will experience a sliver of the pain I now have. If that happens, perhaps, one morning, you will do… as I'm about to do. To spare yourself from another torturous second… of this existence."

With that, she smiled at him gently, her black eyes moist.

Her thoughts conveyed, Calithea stood with a dancer's grace and considered the sun just beyond the smashed windows of the penthouse. She ignored Ice and walked toward the glow, glass crinkling beneath her bare feet. The morning light fired across the ruined glass, causing Ice to squint against its harsh brilliance.

And with the sun blazing through the penthouse, the monster called Calithea faced the dawn. She stepped into the day and lifted her arms over her head in a diver's pose. For a few heartbeats, Ice had no idea what she was doing. Then her skin stretched and strained, exposing a tracery of saturated veins. Bat wings split the smooth flesh of her back and shrugged aside her clothing like tissue, spreading wide.

Isosceles gasped, and his good eye widened.

Pops and wet snaps filled the air as Calithea separated from her lower torso like a wet firecracker being pulled apart.

The sun blazed through her body. Her head cracked back. Rays of light punched holes through her wings' membranes and disintegrated them whole. Calithea crashed to the floor as her hair withered into fiery embers. Organic matter blackened like burning paper. Musculature and sinew became wild fuses.

A breeze rose and blew past Isosceles, but he did not look away.

Calithea choked and whimpered, the sounds a fusion of grief and agony as the sun dissolved her whole. She did not cry out for long. Despite her evil, despite everything she might have done and the victims she'd no doubt amassed, the scene still damn near broke Ice's heart.

It became quiet in a very short time.

Fresh ash blew across Ice's face.

17

The phone rang.

Ice sighed and considered not answering, but then he saw the number. He put down a weathered hardcover copy of *Vampires, Goblins, and other Terrors of the Night* and fished the phone off the coffee table.

"Hello?"

"Hey," his father said. "Your mother and I were heading down to the supermarket. You need anything?"

Ice thought about it. "Toilet paper. Fresh fruit. Maybe a forty-ouncer of Jack Daniel's."

"Aren't you still on painkillers?"

"Finished."

"Antibiotics? Them yellow pills?"

"Finished."

"Oh, that's good," his father said, delight in his voice. "That's wonderful. And you're sleeping better?"

Ice thought about it. He never really slept anymore, only catnapped or lightly dozed, and the lightest creak would jolt him awake. It wasn't entirely restful, but it was how he liked it. Sometimes, he did slip into a really fitful sleep, and when he did, his dreams refused to release him—dreams of beautiful women kissing his forehead in the same place Calithea had. Several nights and mornings, he had awakened with a fading, burning sensation at the very point of contact.

"Doing okay... doing okay." Ice rubbed the side of his face.

"Well, that's something, then. The doctors said it would take time," his father said, skittering around the subject like

478

a beach crab fending off a predator.

Time, the doctors had said, would heal him. The PTSD from Ice's horrific experience could have been medicated, and he did refill the prescriptions when he had to, just to keep up appearances, but he deposited the pills into plastic containers.

"Hold on," his father said. "He says he wants toilet paper, some fresh fruit... and a forty-ouncer of Jack Daniel's."

A high-pitched voice sounded in the background.

"He says he's finished the pills," his father said to Ice's mother. "Well, that's what he told me. What? The boy's a man now. If he wants... No, *I* didn't offer it to him."

Ice massaged a temple and looked toward the picture window of his living room.

"Isosceles," his father said, having switched back, "your mom doesn't feel that alcohol is the best thing for you to have right now." Then he lowered his voice. "But I'll see what I can do."

Ice smiled.

"Your mom wants to visit," his father said.

That placed Ice on guard again. "Not really up for it, Dad. And... besides, it's wise for you two to stay away for the next little while. Just until it's safer. Like we talked about."

The truth was, however, the idea of his parents visiting made him nervous.

The past five weeks had been hard for Ice and his family, who lived only a couple doors down from his tiny house. He'd spent that time healing, allowing his broken hip, leg, hand, and ribs the time to mend. It was imperative that he be well in a short time. He inherently knew it. The time hadn't been particularly pleasant for him. Despite visitations by his parents to clean his apartment, Isosceles quickly convinced them it was best to stay away, on Lance Chambers's advice.

Lance Chambers had found Ice's broken carcass in the penthouse suite hours after Calithea had killed herself. An assortment of police officers, elevator techs, and locksmiths had accompanied the man. The police soon discovered that the bottom of the stairwell shaft, from the fifteenth floor down to the ninth, had been a gruesome compost of decomposing people, the most recent being a young male university student and a television-and-Internet salesman. The remains of Sweeney's missing-person case had also been found, but Ice couldn't remember her name. Several hundred older skeletal remains had been uncovered in a mass grave that a serial killer known only as Leonard had kept throwing dirt onto, dirt excavated from the condo's underground parking lot. Local forensics soon began identifying the bodies and checking off names from a backlog of disappearances around the city over the past eight years. The discovery also resulted in the resignation of the local police captain, who had no explanation as to why a merciless killer had managed to go completely undetected in the city for so long or why investigations had been suppressed.

The police had also found old Sweeney in a nearby forest and wondered how he had somehow fallen from a height of perhaps thirty stories to crash to his death in a place where nothing was that high.

Mysteries upon mysteries.

One of the last pieces of advice Lance Chambers gave Ice while he recovered in a hospital was to make himself scarce—to go into hiding for a while and to stay away from family and friends, just to be safe—at least until things calmed down a little and became a little clearer with regards to the manananggal's final words and kiss. Ice thought it sound counsel and not completely difficult to do. The whole episode with the supernatural creatures had left him a little antisocial—with just a touch of paranoia.

"That serial killer might not have been operating alone," Ice said. "Police said it's possible. The guy might've had friends looking for revenge, y'know. Explain it to Mom. It's best to pick up those groceries and use the delivery service again. I feel better with that… for the next little while, anyway."

A metallic click came from the kitchen. Ice knew it was the pipes. The house was old and creaked and groaned. His hand still tightened around the wooden handle of a sharpened broomstick.

"When will that be?"

"Ah, Dad." Ice sighed and leaned forward to better see into the kitchen. He saw nothing. "I can't talk about this, okay? But could you do that for me? The groceries?"

"How about your cleaning?"

"Already got that covered," Ice lied. "Got that home service. Don't worry."

Silence on the other end.

"All right. Well. If you need anything…"

"Thanks, Dad."

They mutually ended the connection, and Ice devoted his full attention to listening. He looked around past the raw cloves of garlic hanging in strategic areas over the windows and around the house, as well as strings with empty cans. Open jars of marbles were on end tables positioned near doorways. Pentagrams of burnt ash covered large areas of floor, and Ice had even drawn one around his bed. Crucifixes also hung prominently inside the house, in the windows, and on the front and back doors. Isosceles wasn't one for church or religion in general, but he'd recently discovered more faith in a higher power than he'd ever had before.

He didn't care about the stained T-shirt he wore or the crusty pajamas that required cleaning in a very bad way. Nor did he care about how he coated himself in places with aloe vera ointment reinforced with salt sprinkles—nor about the interesting aromas wafting through his little house.

All he cared about was being as careful and alert and prepared as possible, twenty-four seven.

Just in case.

Because he'd realized that when someone slipped into the ass crack of reality, well, sometimes, even if one managed to pull oneself out, the smell still clung.

The doorbell rang, a chipper *Why, hello!* jingle that summoned residents to their front doors with bright, merry chimes.

Ice fully intended to take a rock hammer to the device and gouge the bell out of the wall as if it were a deer tick burrowed into a furry ass.

Right after he addressed his unwanted visitor.

He got his crutches under him, momentarily tangling with the lightweight shafts, and pushed off his sofa with a grunt and a lot of help from his left leg. He intended to tell whoever it was to fuck off and then return to the books he'd bought online, books on the occult, urban legends, and monsters of every sort and size.

Ice realized he had another delivery coming his way. The

talk with his dad and the annoying pipes had distracted him. He swung himself along on the crutches. He had a cane as well but was reluctant to fully abandon his two metal supports just yet. That made him shuffle to the door more quickly.

He looked through the peephole. Sure enough, it was a delivery person. The guy wore sunglasses and had bundled himself in a dark company winter coat designed for the worst of Nova Scotian winters. A stocking cap topped off the picture. The package tucked under the man's arm drew Ice's attention. He considered the visitor, remembered the contents of the box, checked again, and saw that the afternoon sun was pretty much overhead.

Ice opened the door. The winter air gave him party darts and hoisted his boys to warmer climes.

The delivery guy perked up and offered a tight-lipped smile. "Mr. Isosceles Moon, please?"

"Yeah," Ice muttered, glancing at the sunglasses before fixating on the package. "That's me."

"Package for you."

Ice's beard twitched as he regarded the face, debating whether or not to make his thought, *No shit,* known to his visitor.

Ice held out his hands instead.

The delivery guy handed the package over and produced an electronic pad with an attached pen used to scratch the recipient's name upon the offered screen. Ice dithered between taking the package or the electronic pen. He finally took the pen, zipped a chicken scrawl across the pad's screen, and exchanged the device for his package.

Isosceles hefted the wrapped box, guessing the contents.

The delivery guy kept his professional, tight-lipped smile

in place. "This place was hard to find. Drove around a lot before I finally found it. You removed your street number. Why'd you do that?"

"Yeah," Ice muttered, distracted with the package and ignoring the question.

The delivery guy waited and then said, "You took a tumble, I see."

"Huh?"

"You're pretty banged up," the guy's smile widened.

"Oh. That. Worse a while back. I'm okay now." Ice studied the return address on the package. He suddenly eyed the delivery dude, uneasy with the man's predatory mirth. Ice blinked rapidly, agitated about what he was seeing and realizing he'd just spoken to the man.

Ice slammed the door.

He dropped the package, fastened the locks, and scooped a handful of salt from the nearby bowl perched on a corner stand. Ice held his breath and looked through the peephole. There, the delivery guy's face ballooned and deflated as he half turned, paused as if remembering something, and then walked off to his van. Snow surrounded the figure and his vehicle, but Ice watched him… watched him walk all the way back to his ride.

The delivery guy got aboard and hunkered over the steering wheel as if lost in thought. The van, a plain-white cargo job, started up after a few long seconds and backed out of the driveway.

Seconds later, it was gone.

Isosceles swung himself into his living room. He took up position at one corner of his picture window, pulled the curtains back just a crack, and watched the direction the van had gone.

Seconds later, the vehicle drove back and zipped past his house with an angry surge of gas and exhaust.

Isosceles scrutinized the van until it disappeared up the street. He supposed the delivery guy could've been the sort with a lead foot. Perhaps he was in a hurry and had other packages to drop off. Maybe he was just an asshole. There were plenty of them around. Several possibilities, Ice knew. Several. All completely plausible. All harmless. No need for alarm.

But the image that remained with him chilled him to the core: the pasty, pallid skin of the delivery man, the sunglasses, the questions, and the tight-lipped smile.

The smile had widened for a fleeting instant, meant to convey sympathy, but had unconsciously revealed teeth— teeth that, as sure as God was Isosceles's witness, appeared filed to very fine tips.

*"So I wish to give you a gift. One which will help you find them. Or rather, help them find you."*

Isosceles watched the roads.

He watched for a very long time.

# About the Author

Keith C. Blackmore is the author of the Mountain Man, 131 Days, and Breeds series, among other horror, heroic fantasy, and crime novels. He lives on the island of Newfoundland in Canada. Visit his website at www.keithcblackmore.com.

Podium

DISCOVER
STORIES UNBOUND

PodiumAudio.com

www.ingramcontent.com/pod-product-compliance
Lightning Source LLC
Chambersburg PA
CBHW030917120726
47906CB00002B/378